MORIARTY

Moriarty

Book 1

GAVIN COLLINSON

MORIARTY

'What you do in this world is a matter of no consequence. The question is, what can you make people believe you have done?'

— Sherlock Holmes, from *A Study in Scarlet*

Preface

To Professor Moriarty, she is always *the* woman. When he broaches the topic of Doctor Beth Spencer, he does so in a carefully cultured off-hand manner, designed to suggest indifference. Ludicrous, I know. Because if anyone pursues the subject of the good doctor, he instantly becomes animated and enthusiastic.

Now, at times I find him difficult to work out. He remains the great deceiver. But in matters relating to Doctor Spencer, he's easier to read than a book. He's an audio book, with the volume raised to the highest possible level.

To me, she endures as a thing of mystery. I can't say I like her, but I marvel at the way she unlocked James Moriarty with such apparent ease.

I mention Beth Spencer at this point because in a sense, the following story is her story. Her name won't appear on every page, but her spirit is within all the words that comprise the majesty and horror you're about to unfold. And I suppose it could be argued she started the chain of events that led us all to Baker Street, Reichenbach and beyond.

After all, she posted the invitations.

John H. Watson, M. D.

PART I
'Oh, Father, I am risen again.'

Chapter One

'WELCOME BACK, JOHNNY.'

John Watson's world glitched for several uncontrollable seconds. As he turned from the bay window overlooking Baker Street, he at last saw Professor James Moriarty sitting in his late friend's huge, battered armchair. He'd obviously been watching him since he'd walked into the room. Or maybe since he'd hesitated on the doorstep below. Or maybe since Reichenbach.

For a moment, John's vision remained fully functional. That's to say, he saw the man before him. Tall, tanned, and good-looking in a rakish kind of way. Trapped somewhere in the hinterland of late youth and early middle-age. Deep blue eyes. But as the professor began to rise, he watched Sherlock Holmes getting up from the familiar old chair, languid and smiling. The next instant he saw James Moriarty as he'd looked years earlier, when he'd fought above the dark, deafening torrents of the Reichenbach Falls. Younger, dishevelled, determined. And then, for a millisecond, he was confronting the devil himself. Long and lean and red and sleek, with short crimson horns protruding from his skull. Evil at its most clear cut. A tableau out of mythology.

During this final vision, John even fancied he smelt a whiff of brimstone.

He took a step back and reality reasserted itself.

Doctor Watson stood face-to-face with Professor Moriarty.

Even to John, this too felt like a tableau out of mythology.

Except Moriarty was regarding him strangely, as if concerned. Concern from one so uncaring was, in itself, another anomaly. Ten seconds passed. Moriarty waited patiently and John finally declared, 'You're dead.'

'Yeah! I get that a lot. I mean, *a lot*. But I'm...' Moriarty beamed. 'Tickety-boo!' He paused for a reply that never felt likely, but eventually added, in a tone so conversational they could have been two old mates chatting in the pub, 'Caught your podcast on the Teardrop Killer. Not sure if that was your best move, Johnny. This guy clearly enjoys murder. Right now, it's without apparent purpose. If he thinks adding purpose would make the process even more fulfilling ... well, you might have put a target on your back. Or that of your loved ones. I'm particularly worried,' he stressed, 'about Mary.'

He paused again, waiting longer this time, so the silence almost swallowed them.

John shook his head as though trying to figure out a particularly tricky visual conundrum. 'You're dead,' he repeated.

Moriarty offered him his hand. 'It's good to see you again.'

John's gaze travelled from the professor's palm to his face. Both were equally repugnant to him. He slid his own hand under the lapel of his suit jacket as if to check his heart was still beating.

'You're not going to tell me I'm dead again, are you?'

John gave a guttural roar and launched himself forward, swinging his right fist in a wild, powerful haymaker.

With an elegance more redolent of ballroom dancing than pugilism, Moriarty took a light step back, avoiding the strike by inches. John lunged forward again. Another roar. Another punch thrown. Another punch avoided. John steadied himself. He was breathing heavily and watching warily. He stooped slightly, raised his fists, and adopted a boxer's stance as he squared up to his opponent.

'Really?' Moriarty gave a deep sigh. 'Can't we have glass of claret and discuss this like gentlemen?'

'I'll tap the claret, all right.'

'Ha!' Moriarty laughed. The pun, a play on an old English expression meaning to give someone a bloody nose, seemed to delight him. 'Oh, very good!'

John bulldozed into the other man, ramming him into the wall and delivering a grunting blow to his lower ribs.

In a rapid show of unexpected strength, Moriarty pushed him back a couple of feet. He held up a finger. 'John … *John!* Calm down! We've got work to do! We *have* to pool our resources to catch the Teardrop Killer. Right now, he's running around causing all kinds of mayhem. And that's my job.'

'I'm going to kill you.'

'First, I'm dead. Then you're going to kill me. Make up your mind, mate. I actually thought I might be welcome here. You know. A face from the past. A past you seem to venerate so—'

'You're as welcome as a mouthful of bleach.' John drew

himself up to his full height and shouted, 'You murdered Sher-lock Holmes!' Another silence, and as if suddenly exhausted, he sagged and muttered, 'You murdered my friend.'

Moriarty raked the fingers of his left hand through his hair. His humour dissipated and in a tone of complete earnestness, he said, 'Did you ever ask yourself one question? The most important question of all?'

If John heard these words, he gave no indication of actually registering them. He turned and strode to the other end of the room. With his back to Moriarty, so his actions were shielded, he opened a drawer. He raised its false bottom and removed an army revolver from the hidden compartment below. With a soldier's speed and precision, he checked the firearm for bullets. Nodded to himself. Yes. Good. Fully loaded.

He spun around and aimed the revolver at Moriarty, whose reaction was almost no reaction. A shrug of disap-pointment. Nothing more.

John walked towards him, the barrel of his weapon never straying from its target.

He stopped about five feet away from Moriarty. John's breathing became regular. He seemed calm.

Moriarty asked, 'Who was he really?'

And John pulled the trigger.

Chapter Two

EARLIER THAT DAY...

'AMEN!'

Father Pat Kirby finished his short prayer and waited for a response, but none came. He sat in the confessional box of his workplace, a vast, neo-Byzantine cathedral in the City district of London.

This silence was uncommon. Most people who came to confession this early — it was still a little before 8 o'clock — were elderly parishioners, usually those starved of contact. They sat in the darkened booth more to converse than to confess, and Kirby understood this and showed them patience. He was used to their methods of turning an admission of sin into a discussion about how they were struggling and whom they missed. How lonely they felt. How old age had brought confusion and abandonment.

He could cope with that, but he was uncertain in the silence. He said gently, 'Is this your first time? Are you new to the Sacrament of Confession?'

7

The figure behind the wicker lattice moved ever so slightly. A tilt of their head, perhaps.

'There's nothing to be afraid of, my child.'

And at last, a response. Did Father Kirby imagine it, or did the penitent give a brief, quiet laugh?

'You would normally begin by saying, "Bless me Father, for I have sinned. It has been — however long — since my last confession. These are my sins." You can speak openly and honestly. In fact, you must.'

He peered through the screen. Perhaps this was someone here to make a real confession. Not a plea to be heard; not a brag wrapped up in terms of contrition. A genuine confession. Kirby's tone remained amiable. 'I appreciate this can feel overwhelming. But as I said, there's nothing to fear. The Lord—'

'There's always something to fear … when you're with a priest.'

A male voice. Confident. Unafraid. Kirby felt a stab of anxiety.

'What are you here for, my child?'

'Confession.'

'Then tell me your sins.'

'Not my confession.' The priest saw the man lean towards the lattice. '*Your* confession, Father Kirby.'

Chapter Three

'Look...' The cleric tried to contain his fear. 'If you're trying to scare me—'

'You said there was nothing to fear.' The same tone of voice. Confident. Reasonable. And now magnanimous. 'I'll give you thirty seconds. To make peace with your god, if he's still listening to you. Which seems unlikely.'

'Good god, man! What's this about? I haven't—'

'I warned you.'

At last, Father Kirby understood why this penitent was in his cathedral, and all he could stammer was a shrill, 'No, no, no—'

But the voice interrupted again. Aggressive, this time. 'I told you to stay away from children.'

The priest moved forward to the screen, desperate to confess and be absolved. 'You've, you've got to understand — there was a ring! I was forced into it! Evil men — do you understand? Evil men!'

'I understand evil. Only too well. And I understand what you do in the darkness, Father.'

'They're to blame! You need to seek them out!' A thought struck the priest. 'I can help you! You need to find them! I can help you with that! We can deal with them together…'

'No. We can let them lie.'

Kirby understood and crossed himself.

Earlier that morning, in four different churches across the south of England, four priests had entered confessionals. And after less than a minute, the sound of a low, swift '*doob*' shot from each booth. Each priest had toppled sideways from their confessional. Each had been dead before their bodies, all wrapped in the rich, red cloaks of their office, hit the hard, stone floor of their churches.

Pat Kirby begged, 'Forgive me!'

'That's not my role, father. After all…' The man removed something from his pocket. 'God knows I'm not a priest.'

In another church, smaller and prettier and less than forty miles outside London, John Watson sat alone in the nave, perched on the rearmost pew. He heard a woman's gait, her heels clacking across the limestone flagging behind him. The newcomer asked, 'Are you looking for forgiveness or divine inspiration?'

'I haven't decided.' John turned to face her. 'Would a bit of both be too greedy?'

Detective Inspector Zenisha Lestrade said, 'Budge up.'

John shifted a couple of feet to his right, and she took the spot he'd vacated.

'So,' he began, 'you, here. What are the chances?'

'I hate churches. I hate anything you're not allowed to question. Yeah, what are the chances? How are you, John?'

'I'm guessing you're here about the Teardrop Killer.'

'I need your help.'

'No, you don't.'

'I'm desperate.'

'Well, then…' He glanced pointedly towards the altar. 'Maybe you've come to the right place.'

Zenisha grimaced. 'I was hoping for slightly more corporeal assistance.'

And despite himself, John laughed. 'I've just got to do my thing.'

'Hey…' She spread her hands. 'You do your thing.'

THE MAN ASKED, 'Have you made your peace, Father?'

Pat Kirby, weeping now, replied, 'How is this happening? Oh God! How is this even happening? You're dead!' He stared at the wicker screen, and in his last moment of life, the crisscross pattern struck him as a map of his own final years.

'You're dead!'

Straight lines intersecting in a perfect pattern, as if completely ordered, but actually just waiting for—

He heard the quick, quiet sound of compressed air releasing, and a bullet's discharge.

It scorched through the neat wicker work of the oblong panel.

The priest's left eye turned scarlet as he fell sideways from the confessional.

The shooter unscrewed his weapon's silencer, slipped it into a side pocket, and placed his pistol in its shoulder holster. He stepped from the box and, standing over the corpse, Professor James Moriarty replied, 'Oh, Father, I am risen again.'

He walked away, and as he reached the narthex, a short woman with fair hair entered the building by a side entrance. He offered her a cheery 'Good morning!'

She smiled. 'And good morning to you!'

Moriarty reached the main exit, and as he left the cathedral, he heard her long, piercingscream.

Chapter Four

John was approaching the end of his allocated time and said, 'If I'd stayed with him … I mean if I hadn't been such an idiot and so completely taken in by the fake medical emergency that dragged me back to our hotel, who knows? I'm convinced he'd still be alive today. Or we'd both be dead.' He shrugged as if the two eventualities were both as the good as each other. No better, no worse. 'It's odd. The bits I remember about that day. I can vaguely picture the moment the penny dropped. At the hotel, I mean. The guy on reception telling me no one was injured or needed my help. That — *right there* — was then moment I knew that *he* had planned the whole thing so he could get my friend alone … so he could…'

John paused again. Took a sip of water from the tumbler that had a thin crack running up its side, like a single strand of hair stuck against its glass surface. 'And I remember, very clearly, running through the forest. Pelting through it. The Reichenbach Falls are in the Bernese Oberland region of Switzerland. So, lots of pine trees. I remember thinking, *I can do this*. Running. Lots of spruce trees, as well. *I can make it.* And rows and rows of larches. *I can save him.* All crammed into the forest so their branches…'

He interlaced his fingers.

'It creates a kind of dappled light as you run through the woods. The light, flickering I mean. Dark. Light. Dark. Light. Like they're chasing each other. Never constant. I really thought I could save him, but most of all I remember the noise. The rushing and the gushing, and I *really* thought I could save him.'

He reached for the tumbler and took another glug of water. 'People never believe me when I tell them, but the sound of that scene … The noise is what sticks with me the most, because it's deafening, believe me. That falling water! I stopped to catch my breath in a clearing by the river and saw the Grand Reichenbach Fall. It is a dreadful sight. The torrent, swollen by the melting snow, plunges into a tremendous abyss, and the spray rolls up like smoke from a burning house. Christ!'

He shook his head, unwilling to continue. But he pressed on, his cadence quickening.

'Near the very top, there's a man-made path, kind of cut into the rockface so you can walk along it and get a complete view of the falls and the water and the pools at the bottom and the black rocks and … And right there on that ledge, from where I was, in the clearing, way below, I could just about make out my friend … and him. Of course. And seeing them, just talking, both avoiding the edge of the path, yeah, that was when I knew I wouldn't make it in time, after all. And that I was too…'

John took another deep breath. 'The noise!' He closed his eyes. 'The inescapable … *cacophony* of it! Absolutely relentless. Bloody deafening. As if hell itself was being emptied out and I knew I was too late…'

A door at the back of the room, directly opposite John, opened halfway, and Zenisha Lestrade entered and edged along the far wall. A few people heard her heels and craned their necks to check out the latecomer. One or two of them recognized her and John paused, allowing them to register her arrival before their attention returned to him.

'Picture this!' His tone became more upbeat. 'My friend, before he became my friend, stood in a makeshift mortuary. He raised his truncheon and then used it tire-lessly for about twenty minutes, beating the dead bodies. Thrashing them! Pounding their cold flesh until his arm ached.' John Watson smiled and nodded. 'Simpler times. *Happier* times.'

He chuckled, oblivious to the feelings his words gener-ated amongst men and women for whom a sustained assault on several cadavers did not constitute a motif of 'happier times.'

'He was acting in the name of science, of course. Club-bing the corpses to see how far bruises can be produced post mortem. That was the very first image I was given of my friend. Pretty much the first thing anyone told me about him. What a day that was! He needed someone to share a flat with him. And he beat up dead people. That was it. That was all I knew about my guy. And that picture of him, so alive in the mortuary … Ha!' He shook his head. Wistful. 'Yet all those years later. Another mortuary.'

John stopped talking, and it was unclear whether that was that. Perhaps he'd reached the end of what he was prepared to say. Or the end of what he *could* say. As if 'another mortuary' was where he'd leave the matter, which after all, held a kind of circular logic to it. But he cleared his throat and resumed his reminiscence.

'This mortuary is tiny. White tiles. Deep Belfast sinks. It feels Victorian. We're just outside a small, Swiss village,

Meiringen, and I'm amazed it's even got a mortuary. It smells like every other mortuary I've been in, though. Not of death. No more than your fridge smells of food. No, it stinks of pharmaceuticals and disinfectant. Bleach! So strong it made my eyes sting. But you know what? I like the smell of chemicals. Not sure why. Anyway … There are two of everything in this mortuary. Two doctors with me. And two policemen. Two slabs.' Another deep inhalation. 'Two corpses.'

He thought back.

John had been ushered towards the room as though he were a blind man. A policewoman gripped his left elbow. Her uniform indicated she was a member of the *Autobahn-polizei*, so she shouldn't even have been there. Her remit would normally cover motoring offences and other road-related incidents. But Meiringen is not an urban area and she was presumably the highest ranking officer available, or, as John wondered afterwards, perhaps she'd just been bored that day and jumped at the chance of being present at such a grimly historic identification.

A young doctor gently held his other elbow. She'd been talking to him constantly as he'd been guided through the dimly lit corridors. But she spoke in German, so John understood nothing of her monologue. And when they reached the door to the mortuary itself, there was a moment of incongruous comedy. The entrance was wide enough for two people to pass through side-by-side, but not three. Approaching the threshold, the police officer and the doctor both clutched John a little tighter. They leaned forward and glared at each other and hissed terse opinions in German.

Deftly and politely, John pulled away from the two offi-cials and entered the room of death alone.

Years later, he continued his account. 'There was a fog

in my head where my thoughts should have been. The doctor in charge — a perfectly nice medico — continued to babble away in a language I didn't understand, and she only stopped talking when she reached for the shroud. She looked at me then, and I said something stupid like, *Thank you, Frau Doktor.* She suddenly didn't want to go on with it. I'm sure of that. But I nodded. She pulled back the shroud…'

The Swiss doctor folded the material so it formed a triangle over the corpse's chest. John gawped at the figure on the slab. Half of the dead man's face had been obliterated by some blunt and brutal force, but as though it was a piece of modern art, the other side of his face was near perfect. Barely injured. A few cuts and some fragments of mud curved around his left eye socket. Nothing more than that.

'There was nothing transformational about the trauma he'd received. By that I mean, there was absolutely no doubt about who it was. I almost collapsed but pulled myself together, took a step forward, and kissed his forehead. The doctor started talking to me again. In German, of course. And I remember the policewoman's impatience and she interrupted her. *Is it him?* she asked. In English. As gently as I could I tugged the shroud upwards, so it covered his face again. I replied, *Yes.* Then I stood back. *Yes. It's my friend…it's Sherlock Holmes.*'

John raised the cracked tumbler and drained its remaining inch of water.

He blinked and looked out across the room, as if seeing it for the first time. It was hardly a vision of encouragement.

He stood in an old church hall, alone on a tiny stage. About half the tables on the floor beneath him were empty. Some of the others were occupied by groups of men and women who clearly hadn't been paying attention to his talk and a handful of people continuing to play cards. Other members of the audience appeared more interested in their phones than what was happening on the stage. And as John's disappointed gaze past over them, he spotted one table where all three people around it were dozing.

Above these sleepers, stuck to a side wall, a sign read: **Rookthorn Ladies' Speakers Club.** Below this, a list of the 'star guests.' Z-listers, mainly. John couldn't miss the words **SOLD OUT** stamped in bold beside each name, except for his own. **DOCTOR JOHN WATSON**. Next to this he saw the handwritten notification, **All welcome!** with a hopeful, smiley-face emoji drawn to the right of the exclamation mark.

Zenisha Lestrade aside, the audience was made up entirely of older people, predominantly women. John could discern that some had been paying attention. In particular, at the table closest to the stage, there were four superfans who'd hung on his every word. In spite of their vaguely reassuring presence, he suddenly couldn't bear to be here anymore. He wanted out. Away. And fast.

He began to wind up his talk. 'You must forgive me,' he said, 'if my account of these … cataclysmic events is a little inward-looking. A little — let's be honest — selfish. The truth is…'

There was no artifice in his words.

'…on that day three years ago, the world lost a beacon of light. A symbol of hope. An engine of justice.'

But there was no emotion either. He'd spoken these sentences a hundred times and recited them on rote, as a history student might trot out dates of battles which although significant, held minimal personal interest.

'But I lost … I lost my comrade-in-arms,' he said. 'I

lost Sherlock Holmes ... whom I shall ever regard as the best and the wisest man I have ever known.'

And relieved it was over, he didn't invite questions or remind people where they could get more information about the events he'd spoken about. He simply added, 'Thank you!' and began to sit.

But before he could, a man at the back of the room shouted out a single question. 'What about Professor Moriarty?'

Chapter Five

Professor Moriarty leaned against the wrought iron balustrade of Westminster Bridge, an ice cream in one hand, an iPhone in the other. He wore a beige linen suit, a light blue, open-necked shirt, and aviator style Ray-Bans. His back was to County Hall, meaning he was facing the northside of the Thames. His phone began to play "William, It Was Really Nothing" by The Smiths and he immediately took the call.

He looked irked by whatever was being said to him in the ensuing conversation, and after taking a lick of his ice cream, he interjected, 'The security is a joke! Actually, it's not even a joke. It's not substantial enough to be a joke. Honestly, an 8-year-old could mastermind an attack on this place.'

He nodded to whatever was being said to him, and then, as casually as if he was ordering a taxi, he said, 'A drone assault. The timing is paramount, of course, but don't skimp on explosives — within the parameters I gave you. In short, I want a lot of boom and a lot of bang.' Another slurp of his ice cream and he gazed across to the building he was discussing — the Royal Palace of Westminster, the grand, gothic complex better known as the Houses of Parliament, and occasionally called 'the heart of democracy'.

'I'm looking at it now and believe me, it'll be a doddle. Bang and boom! Good. Tonight then. Yeah! Let's make history!'

Chapter Six

'GOODBYE, OLD FRIEND.'

John Watson turned away from the body and began to walk to the door.

'Mr. Watson!'

'It's Doctor Watson.'

One of the two police officers gestured to the slab on the other side of the room. 'Could you … look at … him … Mister Doctor?' He spoke slowly, having to reach for every word.

John glanced towards the mortuary table, which held the 'him' in question.

The policeman added, 'Please.'

The German-speaking doctor began talking again and John interrupted her with an impatient nod.

'Danke, John.'

It was the first time she'd used his given name and from school lessons he thought he'd forgotten he replied, 'Bitte, Frau Doktor.'

She pulled back the shroud covering the second corpse and as its face was revealed, she heard John's laughter.

THREE YEARS LATER, John Watson answered the question, 'What about Professor Moriarty?' with complete candour. 'I was brought up to be a Christian,' he revealed. 'But when I saw the thing that had killed my friend, I laughed. Out of pure delight. I said, *That's James Moriarty. Thank god!* My one regret is that I didn't spit on his corpse.'

Murmurs of surprise rippled through the hall.

'I shed no tears for that monster. The creature that murdered Sherlock Holmes should have——'

The audience member who'd posed the original question interrupted with a shout of, 'No! I mean, what was he doing there?'

John didn't bother to conceal his annoyance. Had this old fool not listened to a single moment of his talk? 'As I said, sir, Holmes had painstakingly created a file on Moriarty. A series of documents and proofs that were enough to bring down his whole criminal empire. My friend had delivered the file to Scotland Yard. Moriarty had been aware of it for some time. You see, the Professor followed us to Switzerland with one intention. To kill Sherlock Holmes.'

After all his recollections about Holmes's triumphs, he finally had the room's undivided attention. He looked appalled that it needed this last fact — grotesque to him — to win their interest and he looked towards Zenisha Lestrade. He shook his head, sharing his chagrin with her.

'I'd like to thank you all for coming this afternoon,' he lied, 'and special thanks to the committee for inviting me and being so gracious with their——'

A woman in the middle of the room called out, 'But why?!'

'Excuse me?'

She replied, 'If this Professor Moriarty had known Sherlock Holmes was a threat … had known he'd been putting this killer file together … why didn't he bump him off sooner to actually solve the problem? Why wait 'til it was too late?'

The man at the back of the hall piped up again. 'Aye! And you said this James Moriarty was an intelligent man!'

John sensed he was losing the room and heard a hint of desperation leaking into his voice. 'I said he was shrewd!'

Another audience member called out, 'So what the hell was he doing messing about in Switzerland at the exact time he should have been in Blighty, sorting out the ramifications of Sherlock's file?'

'Well, you must understand that—'

Another woman interrupted in a strident tone. 'Why did he even kill your friend? Holmes had done his worst. Job done! Bit late to worry about him at that point!'

Zenisha raised her eyebrows in an expression of sympathy that seemed to say, *What can you do?*

He held her stare as more questions were hurled at him.

Why didn't Moriarty just forget about him and focus on the people who were about to bring him down?

Don't you think something feels off?

If Moriarty was the vicious head of an organized crime ring, why didn't he just hire someone to shoot Sherlock in the head? Why meet him face-to-face? What had he wanted to say to him?

A buzz shimmied through the audience. Even the three people who'd been snoozing were now calling out their thoughts, but one question silenced them all. The man sat somewhere towards the back of the room who'd started the inquisition yelled, 'What was Professor Moriarty *really* doing in Switzerland?'

Chapter Seven

A MEMBER OF THE COMMITTEE DIDN'T LIKE THE DIRECTION the event was heading and rushed onto the stage. She interrupted the back-and-forth with an unsubtle, 'I'm sure we'd all like to thank Doctor Watson for his very interesting insight into…' She peeped down at her clipboard. 'The Adventures of Sherlock Holmes!'

There was a loose scattering of reluctant applause, but the mumbling and grumbling were unmistakable. The audience's reaction reminded John of a crowd watching a boxing match that was being stopped just as they'd scented blood. He gave the room a nod to acknowledge the desultory clapping and sat down, grateful to be off the ropes.

JAMES MORIARTY FINISHED his ice cream and caught a taxi to Browns, a little brasserie that claimed to be in Covent Garden but always feels more like Leicester Square. He sat in a corner, in the slightly raised area that has broad windows overlooking St. Martin's. A waitress asked if he was ready to order and he requested a glass of the Dom Pérignon. She politely replied it was only sold by the bottle.

'How much?'

'£240, sir.'

'240? My lucky number. Wheel it in!'

As he waited for his Champagne, he surveyed the room. A few tables down, he saw a couple clearly entranced by each other. The larger of the two people, a thuggish-looking man with enormous shoulders and a crooked nose, offered his companion a small box. She took it. Prized it open. Gasped and grinned. It contained an engagement ring, and the tiny wren of a woman receiving it began weeping and nodding enthusiastically.

After his order arrived, Moriarty made a phone call. 'I'll need handcuffs, anaesthesia, and a subscription to *Woman's Own*.' He sipped his Champagne. 'Yes, yes, yes! Fabulous! Oh, and I'll need a boat. With an outboard motor. And it must have a stereo.' Another sip. 'Well, no. It's not essential to the plan, but I insist on music whilst I travel. It can so dull without it, don't you think? I'll What-sApp you a playlist. But Zadok the Priest is a must. Could you? Thank you, darling! You're an absolute gem! Oh! Almost forgot. Memory like a colander! I'll need a double decker bus!'

He finished the call and his flute of Champagne and slipped several notes beneath the glass.

As he walked towards the exit, he placed the nearly full bottle of Dom Pérignon on the table of the recently engaged couple.

'Congratulations! I hope you'll both be very happy.'

He smiled but didn't stop to chat. Moments later, they watched him stride down St Martin's towards Charring Cross, and both commented what a lovely bloke he was.

Chapter Eight

ZENISHA LESTRADE OWNED A MERCEDES-AMG G-CLASS. It's the kind of car that people usually drive too fast. But it offers top-of-the-range luxury, meaning if you're going to have a fatal crash in it, you'll at least die in comfort. This thought occurred to John Watson as the inspector sent them hurtling through country lanes at a speed that made the hedgerows blur.

He peeked at the speedometer's needle. It pointed to 50 mph like a blunt accusation. Zenisha spotted his check and to deflect his attention said, 'Rookthorne Ladies' Speakers Club?'

She eased her foot off the pedal.

John shrugged, a little more at ease as they decelerated. 'If I kill my agent, do you think I could get away with justifiable homicide?'

'Give me a shout when you've done it. I'll have a word with the SIO.'

They both smiled.

John said, 'Tell me about the Teardrop Killer.'

Zenisha hesitated. 'Are you okay?'

'I'm okay.'

'I heard you lost another libel case.'

'What's his MO?'

'Was it libel? Or slander?'

'Both. Okay. Here's what I know from the papers. He's killed five people. Men and women, which is unusual. His victims are all from different walks of life. Different age groups. Different cultural backgrounds. Different socio-economic statuses. The media implies there's no single factor that links them. Is that true?'

Zenisha replied cautiously, 'As far as we can make out, it is. But I personally feel there *must* be some thread that … *binds* them. We just haven't found it yet.' The lane narrowed and Zenisha reduced her speed to 30 mph. 'How's the podcast doing?'

'Good!'

'It's keeping you afloat? Financially, I mean.'

'The audience figures are through the roof! People can't get enough true crime. Talking of which — the Teardrop Killer. Is it just five people? Do you suspect more victims?'

She shook her head. 'Just the five. Here's something we've managed to keep out of the press, though. He uses…' The lane widened again and she put her foot down. '…different methods for killing his victims.'

'How different?'

'The first two were shot. One was strangled. Two died from a lethal injection.'

'What?' John shifted in his seat to face the inspector. 'A serial killer using such *completely* different methodology? That's unheard of!'

'Uh huh. Crazy, right? So, your podcast. It's bringing in enough filthy lucre to pay the rent?'

'It's difficult to monetize. Are we even sure it's the same guy committing the murders?'

'We're not sure of anything. What do you mean — difficult to monetize? You've got advertisers, yeah?'

'My sponsors have dropped out. Don't want to be associated with all these court cases I'm having to fight.'

'You should do a live show. That's how a lot of podcasters rake in the cash.'

'A live show? What, like today's rip-roaring success? Can we get back to the case? Tell me about the tattoos.'

'I don't mean some pokey little village hall. I mean a proper venue. The South Bank. Some theatre. A live version of your show with a Q&A afterwards. You'd sell out.'

'The tattoos?'

'He tattoos a single teardrop onto the face of all his victims.'

John had read this, of course. It was how the killer had earned his *nom de crime*. But he processed the information anew before asking, 'Are the tattoos done post-mortem?'

'It's surprisingly difficult to be certain. We *think* they're done after he killed the victim, yeah. But for the last two we're not so sure. He injected them with what was essentially a barbiturate, paralytic, and potassium solution, so it's a possible he actually applied the tattoo as they died.'

'Christ!' John looked appalled. 'So, it's possible the victims were awake but unable to move as their murderer tattooed a teardrop onto their faces?'

Zenisha nodded. 'Makes you wonder what kind of man would do that.'

'I'm met one or two, to be honest.' He paused. 'Can you trace the ink?'

'It's a vegan mixture. Probably an off-the-shelf

compound that's had an extra pigment added to make it unique.'

'So that's a no?'

'The market is huge, and anyone can walk into a shop or parlour and buy what they like to make up a specific ink.'

'Is it professionally applied?'

Zenisha puffed out her cheeks and exhaled. 'Depends what you mean by *professionally*. It's not a "stick and poke" job. But you don't need a license to pick up a wireless tattoo machine — basically a tattoo pen. Anyone can order one online or buy a kit in store.'

'So the killer could be a bona fide tattooist.'

'Sure,' Zenisha agreed, 'or he could be someone who's anonymously purchased the pen and ink and has never even set foot in a tattoo parlour in his life.'

'Or…'

'What are you thinking, John?'

'We could be dealing with a scenario where one person kills the victim and another individual applies the teardrop. Possible?'

'Possible. We've collected bugger all trace evidence from the crime scenes, so it's a viable hypothesis. Who was it this time?'

'Who was what this time?'

'That sued you?'

John sighed. Not dismayed. Annoyed. 'The family of the late Doctor Grimesby Roylott.'

'Roylott. The Speckled Band guy?'

'Yeah. Lovely chap. May he rest in hell.'

'What damages were awarded?' And off her friend's silence: 'That big?'

'Big enough.'

'You sure you're okay with the court's judgment?'

'I'm appealing.'

Zenisha shot him a despairing look. 'It's not about how likeable you are, John.'

'No, I meant I'm appealing against the original judgment that…' He broke off as he clocked the grin spreading across her face. 'Very funny! Where were they found?'

'All of them were at their homes. When we get to the station, I'll give you the files. They'll have all the specifics you need.'

'Thanks.'

The country lane evolved into a road lined with shops, houses, and a petrol station. Zenisha hung a left and they merged onto a dual carriageway that carried them towards the M25. Traffic was mercifully light. Zenisha took the Mercedes up to 70 mph and hit 'cruise.'

John said, 'You don't have to do this, you know. Bring me in. Like I'm a charity case.'

Zenisha sounded more irritated than concerned. 'Look, you've always generated leads for us in the past. Whenever I've "brought you in." This isn't a favour between friends.'

'Roger that.' A moment passed. 'I know I was just the straight man.' John hesitated for a second. 'Have you noticed, with comedians, it's always the straight man that survives? Or at least, he dies second. Abbott and Costello, Morecombe and Wise, Cannon and Ball, Laurel and Hardy … I don't know. And when the comic one passes away the straight man's wheeled out onto chat shows and so on, and everyone applauds, and the audience remains … *sympathetic* about his loss. But everyone's really thinking… I wish *he'd* died. I wish the good one had lived. The one with sparkle. The one we'd pay good money to see. I wish *he* was the one on that stage. Right now. Not this guy.'

He paused again. Kept his eyes on the empty road ahead.

'Deep down, everyone's thinking it,' he added. 'Even the straight man. Zenisha … What they said in the village hall. The questions about Moriarty. Did you ever think—'

'John! Listen to me! I understand that you're still grieving. That you're looking for … something. I don't know.'

'Yeah.'

'But if you're going to help me, I need you to be present. Sherlock is dead. And I'm sorry about that. Moriarty is dead. Less sorry about that.'

'I hear you.'

'Good! But somewhere out there is a man who's already murdered five people. And he isn't going to stop until we catch him. Because he enjoys it.'

'And because he's bloody good at it.'

'Yeah, never a great combo. These murders are becoming more than murders. They're terrifying everybody because *anybody* could be next. Questions have been asked in parliament, and I'm taking daily calls from the Home Secretary because even Redford, *even the Prime Minister*, has noticed the entire country is in the grip of some primeval fear about the Teardrop Killer.'

'I get that. I'm only—'

'So,' Zenisha continued, as if she'd not heard her friend's interjection, 'my job is on the line. My reputation. Everything I've fought for. And yeah, I know that's not the important point in the grand scheme of things. Kind of important to me, though. What's definitely important, though, what's bloody crucial is this: If you don't give me a hand … if you don't get your head in the game and do everything you possibly can to help me…' She glanced across at John. 'The Teardrop Killer will murder again. And again and again until the streets are ankle deep in blood and people we know and love are dead by his blade or his bullet … or his bare hands.'

Her gaze returned to the road and she concluded, 'Because I know bastards like this. And sooner or later he's going to come after one of our own. Now, are you with me?'

They left the dual carriageway, swerving onto the M25. London lay ahead of them. And although they couldn't know it, right across the capital something remarkable was happening. Thieves, shysters, and other villains were sharing news and expressions of their own incredulity.

'*Have you heard?*'

'*I can't believe it!*'

'*This changes everything!*'

Somewhere in the city a dark secret was finding the light.

And in Zenisha Lestrade's Mercedes G-Class, Doctor John Watson looked towards London, that great cesspool into which all the loungers, scroungers, rogues, and reprobates of the world are irresistibly drained. 'Yes,' he said. 'I'm with you.'

Chapter Nine

JOHN HELD THE DOOR OPEN FOR ZENISHA AND THEY entered the police station. It had been built in the 90s before the notion of government spending on public buildings had become difficult to imagine. Despite being over a quarter of a century old, it looked modern, with a vast reception area that was all glass and space and steel. In a testament to British society of the 2020s, the wide front desk was behind transparent, bullet-proof plastic. It was manned by a solitary sergeant who hummed to herself as she caught up on her never-ending paperwork. Luckily for her, there were barely any visiting members of the public to deal with. The reception was unusually quiet, with just a couple of pensioners stood at a raised table, filling in a 'stolen item' form for a mobility scooter that had gone missing.

It was sometime after twelve but before 1 p.m. The hour that always feels like the last gasp of morning but is technically afternoon's first breath. As they crossed the empty reception area, Zenisha asked, 'How's Mary?'

'She's good,' John replied abruptly. 'Any news on the Valentino twins?'

He was referring to a couple of criminals who'd been apprehended after he'd issued an appeal for information on one of his podcasts.

'They're going to be flown from Scotland to London to stand trial at the Old Bailey.'

'Well, be careful. Double the number of guards you'd normally detail. Those brothers can hack anything. They'll see the journey across England as the perfect time to—'

'Relax. We've got special dispensation.' They reached a set of heavy double doors that led to the main section of the station. Zenisha nodded to the humming desk sergeant who pressed a button. *Click!* John pulled back one of the doors and they sauntered through to a large hallway that housed two elevator stations. 'We've got permission to put them both under general anaesthetic for the flight, thereby minimizing the risk they pose around anything electronic.'

'How the hell did you wangle that?'

'The judge's mother was one of the investors they embezzled.'

'Fancy that.'

'The only problem is, their lawyers have intervened. We actually need them to sign off on their own transportation! God bless the British legal system, right?'

'Where are they now?'

'HMP Tarrack, up in North Lanarkshire. The governor's a good woman. Bailey Hernandez. Know her?'

'No.'

'She said she'll speak to the brothers personally and try to get agreement from them with minimal fuss.'

'Minimal fuss?' John looked dubious. 'Good luck with that.'

They discussed the Valentino twins' case as they made

their way to Zenisha's office. It held all the normal accoutrements of her job, but there were also startlingly homely elements to the room, including a Turkish silk rug and expensive chintz throws slung over the cheap sofa.

She handed John several files. 'Getting back to the Teardrop Killer…'

'Thanks.'

'They're copies, of course, but please be careful with them.'

John looked mildly offended. 'I'll try not to leave them on the Number 47 to Hackney Wick.'

'You know what I mean. And treat everything in them as top secret.'

He nodded. 'Mind if I grab a quick look at them now?'

'Be my guest.'

He took a seat and began to skim through the reports. After a quarter of an hour, he put them to one side. 'The first victim … Lizzie Domingo. I think I should focus on her. Initially, at least.'

'Why?'

'Because when you appealed for information about her, nobody really cared. It was just a one-off murder at that point. Everybody assumed the husband did it and got on with their lives. With the later killings, well, everyone was interested. It could be them next. So they engage.'

'Fair point.'

'There's something else. Ms. Domingo was murdered in her home. Which is on Cherry Road in Maida Vale. I know it. It's wide, leafy. Up-market. Lots of cyclists. We might get lucky. One of them might have been wearing a helmet cam on the morning in question. And it's the kind of neighbourhood where every third vehicle is a delivery van. Which means dash cams. The kind that records in front of the car and behind. I know it's a long shot, a very long shot, but just imagine…'

'Yeah. Worth a punt.'

'Okay.' John got to his feet. 'I'll get a taxi home and read the rest en route. I want to get a podcast out about these—' He brandished the files. 'ASAP.'

'Thanks, John. I'll walk you down.'

A couple of minutes later, alone in their descending elevator, Zenisha said casually, 'Still in the houseboat?'

'I like the houseboat.'

'Right!' She kept looking at her shoes. 'And how's Mary? You said she was good, but are you and her…'

The question suddenly had nowhere worth going.

'I'm seeing her later tonight. Marcini's.'

'Marcini's?' She pulled a face. 'Date night?'

'We divorced for the right reasons, Zenisha. Doesn't mean we can't give it a second shot for the right reasons, as well.'

'Just be on your best behaviour.'

'And I haven't had a *date night* since medical school.'

The elevator doors slid apart and they stepped into the ground floor hallway. 'She deserves the best you, John.'

'Well, unless something truly radical happens, this is the only me there is, so she'll have to…' He trailed off, looking through the double doors that led to the reception area. He narrowed his eyes, as if unwilling to entirely trust his senses, and astonished by the enormity of what he was seeing, he murmured, 'What the hell?'

Chapter Ten

JOHN AND ZENISHA BOTH STOPPED DEAD IN THEIR TRACKS, astonished by the insanity ahead of them.

Through the glass panels in the set of double doors they could see the station's reception area. Minutes earlier it had been quiet. Near empty.

They moved forward. John pushed open the doors and they stepped into a scene of clattering chaos. The large room was completely chock-a-block with people. All jostling. Shouting. Complaining and cajoling. Mostly men. Mostly queuing, bustling to be seen by police officers as soon as possible. John noticed that every individual was carrying at least one item — a games console, items of silverware, a bicycle. He spotted a teen, apparently able-bodied, who was sat astride a mobility scooter.

Some carried suitcases, others plastic bags. As John and Zenisha shouldered their way through the throng, they could see a selection of the items they held. Mobile phones and wallets and glittering clusters of jewellery.

It was a scene of Hogarthian roguery, modernized and brought to life. John knew several of the men who were clamouring to be seen. Dips, housebreakers, and a few opportunistic thieves. He exchanged a puzzled glance with Zenisha.

A handful of policemen, all at the edges of the room, appeared overwhelmed by the sudden bedlam. One shouted out, 'You'll all be seen to!'

And another added, 'Please stand in line … Come on!'

A third bellowed, 'Once you've been given a form, please move to one side to fill it in as best you can!'

'Form an orderly queue! Come on!'

The desk sergeant from earlier, now joined by a couple of colleagues, boomed over the PA system. 'Once you've completed the paperwork, please return the forms and the biros. Do not steal the pens! Repeat — do not steal the pens! Looks like we're going to need them today…'

John and Zenisha made their way towards the side of the room and the Inspector nodded *hello* to one of the harassed coppers who'd been pulled from the offices to keep order in the public areas. 'What's happening, Lee? What's going on here?'

Detective Sergeant Lee Jones looked weary. 'You've not heard, guv?'

'Heard what?'

'Scenes like this are happening in every nick right across London and the south!'

'What?'

John asked, 'But what's triggered it? A crime wave?'

'The opposite!' Before Lee could explain, she was swept away as more desperate visitors surged into the station, meaning she was bundled along in a flurry of shuffling desperation.

Zenisha turned to John 'What's the opposite of a crime wave?'

'I haven't the faintest idea!' He scanned the crowd. 'I

know a few of these villains, but seeing as how me and Holmes put most of them behind bars, I don't think...' He spotted someone. 'There's a friendly face! Joe Cisto. Holmes got him sent down for a robbery. He was very grateful.'

'Grateful?'

'Holmes cleared him of murder by proving to the satisfaction of the police that he was busy at the time, blowing open someone's safe.' He called across to him. 'Joe!'

Cisto was a short, wiry man who was strong enough and brusque enough to haul himself through the crowd. 'Doctor Watson! Good to see, sir! And you must be Inspector Lestrade. Read about you online. You worked with Mr. Holmes, God rest his soul.'

'Yeah, quite a few times.'

John had to raise his voice to be heard. 'What's going on, Joe? What's everybody doing here?'

'You haven't heard?'

'No!'

Joe shook his head and turned to Zenisha. He seized her sleeve, desperate but not aggressive. 'Inspector Lestrade! I want to confess! I *need* to confess!'

'And what's brought about this sudden need to come clean?'

'I done the Mile End job last night. Here's everything I took—'

He was carrying a shoulder bag that he opened to reveal three silver frames and a slick of expensive-looking trinkets. 'Swear down it's everything, Inspector! Could you just—'

'You'll have to fill in a form!'

He opened his mouth to reply, but clearly frustrated by her answer, he chose to move away, shouldering his way back into the coterie of criminals. Before disappearing from sight, he turned to John. 'God save you, Doctor Watson!'

'From what?'

Joe Cisto shook his head and melted into the crowd.

John and Zenisha pushed their way to the corner of the room. Although the commotion showed no signs of abating, the position afforded them a little more space. John held up his phone and the screen showed breaking news. 'Lee Jones was right,' he said. 'Stations right across the capital and beyond — every one is overflowing with people, just like here! It's some kind of biblical plague, except it's a tsunami of thieves. All wanting to confess their crimes!'

Zenisha looked at the swell of visitors. 'What do you think Cisto meant?' She received no reply and added, 'Something's happened…'

But John saw the fear on the criminals' faces. 'No,' he said. 'Something's coming…'

Chapter Eleven

AN HOUR AFTER PRIZING HIMSELF OUT OF THE POLICE station, John stepped from a bus which had stopped yards from the London Planetarium. He hurried to Portman Square, found the apartment he needed, and pressed the call button. Nothing. He tried again and finally heard a familiar voice berate him through the comms grille. 'This had better be important!'

'Is that any way to speak to an old mate?'

'Johnny!'

'How are you?'

'Well, I was having a splendid afternoon until you turned up like a bad penny! Come in, come in! Can't have you loitering on the doorstep. You'll bring the neighbourhood *right* down!'

John heard a click and pushed open the door. He jogged up the stairs to the top floor.

Julian Emery was a little older than John and considerably richer. His apartment, in one of London's most expensive locales, was spacious and beautifully decorated in an art nouveau style. He collected musical boxes and fine wine. The former featured in a display that adorned the center of his living room. The latter seldom saw the light of day.

He opened his apartment's front door even before John had reached it. 'Good to see you again, Johnny!' He wore a navy flannel chalk stripe suit and a white shirt that held tell-tale smudges of dark lipstick on the collar. His hair was thinning and his waistline widening, but he remained a handsome man, blessed with a disarming smile.

'Good to see you, too.'

As the two friends shook hands in the doorway, a tall, striking-looking woman appeared behind Emery. She drawled in an Eastern European accent, 'Just as things were getting interesting…'

John said, 'Please don't go on my account.'

'Oh,' she replied airily, 'he was wracking his little brains for a way to get rid of me…'

'That's a monstrous slur!' Emery complained. He added, 'I'll see you at 7 for cocktails before the party tonight?'

'Maybe, baby.'

She sashayed towards the staircase.

Emery persisted with, 'Our usual table?'

She seemed to consider the request as she began to descend the steps, finally calling back to him. 'If you're a lucky boy … Stinky!'

And then she was gone.

John feigned concern. 'Stinky?'

'She says I wear too much cologne. Come through!' He ushered John inside. 'Can I get you a drink?'

'Just a cup of tea. Thanks.'

'Tea?' Emery's disappointment was obvious. 'I'll see if I've got any in. Tea…'

'I was after a favour actually.'

'You have but to name it.'

'Do you still have your podcasting kit?'

'I do!' In a fit of enthusiasm, Julian Emery had begun an audio series centred on musical boxes. In a fit of laziness, he'd allowed it to stall after the third episode. 'It's through there. In the dining room.'

'Could I borrow it?'

'Is yours in hock? If you're short of money, just say so.'

'It's not in hock!' John protested. 'I'm fine.'

Emery nodded, clearly not believing a word of it. 'All these court cases, Johnny. I know how expensive they can be. They must be crippling you.'

'I'm A-okay and really never been—'

'From what I can see,' Emery pressed on, 'it's all to do with you defending Sherlock Holmes to the *bloody* hilt. And, well, glorifying the old boy. No offence. But he's holding you back, Johnny. He's dead. But he's still holding you back.'

The words took several seconds to sink in. 'What am I supposed to do?'

'Move on.' Emery squeezed his friend's shoulder. 'Find a way to move on.'

JOHN RECORDED and released the latest episode of his podcast within 90 minutes of arriving at Emery's pad. It was, he conceded to himself, a rush job — he regurgitated the public details about the Teardrop Killer and stressed the fact he apparently chose his victims at random. John felt uneasy using such a cheap ploy. The implication — *it could be you next* — was crude. He knew that. But he hoped it would be effective enough to reach people. To make them listen. Because if they didn't listen, they didn't get involved and offer up their consequent insight and feedback.

No matter how many people heard his podcast, John always maintained the figures that mattered were harder to assess, because what was important remained the number of people who paid attention to it. Sherlock Holmes had often told him, 'You see but you do not observe,' and John felt the success or otherwise of his shows depended on the aural equivalent. If people heard but did not listen, he was wasting his time and theirs. But when his words *reached* people, when his audience engaged and reacted to his pleas for information, then — and only then — his podcasts became more than background noise.

They became useful and something more. They became fruitful. And existing alongside the leads they generated, coupled with their value to Zenisha Lestrade, they became his validation.

IN THE EVENT, this latest episode of the podcast inadvertently served as something much more. It became a call to arms — although not in any rousing or positive way. Because across London, moments after the episode dropped, the Teardrop Killer heard John's inelegantly expressed thoughts about him and his work, and he interpreted every last word as an opening salvo.

The killer thought back to their days together. 'Soldier, soldier, solider…' he murmured. 'Why did you leave me?'

Chapter Twelve

When Zenisha Lestrade called him, he was standing at the side of the canal. Detecting something in his voice as he answered, she asked, 'Have I caught you at a bad time?'

'No.'

But he'd been too slow to respond. 'Are you sure?'

'What is it, Zenisha?'

She paused then plunged in. 'Five years ago, we investigated a group of five Catholic priests. We suspected them of … well, children were involved. We didn't have enough evidence to bring charges, which was as frustrating as hell until…'

John pressed his phone closer to his ear. 'Go on.'

'The guy we suspected of being the leader of the ring was found dead before we finished our investigation. A single bullet to the head. His body had been moved from London to Bristol where he was found in the early hours.'

'Go on…'

'His corpse had been positioned below a stone statue.'

'Of what?'

'A cherub that represents justice.'

'Making a fairly obvious message, I'd say.'

'Oh, there was more. This statue is on St. Nicholas Street.'

'St. Nicholas? The patron saint of children.'

'One and the same. Anyway, the remaining priests suddenly become as good as gold. We continued to monitor them, but they didn't put a foot wrong. They even started donating large sums to kids' charities.'

'Great. But you'll forgive me if I don't nominate them for a Pride of Britain Award.'

'About a week ago, I got a tip-off they were slipping back into their old ways. Before I could follow it up…'

'Someone has followed it up for you. Let me guess. A single bullet to the head?'

'Every one of them. All dead. Executed.'

'I'm not going to lie. I won't lose sleep over their deaths.'

'Me neither, but John! We've already got one serial killer to hunt. We really don't need a second. And there's something else.'

'Look, my day couldn't get any worse. Just spit it out, eh?' He'd sounded angrier than he'd intended. 'Sorry, Zenisha. Tough afternoon. You see, right now I'm looking at…' He sensed she needed to speak. And sympathetically this time, he said, 'What is it?'

'Moriarty.'

John registered the ensuing silence. The dread his name could still inspire. 'What about him?'

'Well, I'm pretty certain Professor Moriarty was the one who warned the priests away from the kids and murdered one of them to ram the point home.'

'Yeah. And Hitler was good to his mother. So what?'

'That's not what I mean! I'm looking at the overall picture. The priests being killed. The criminal classes suddenly looking to the law for protection and confessing their crimes … And the feeling you had earlier … that sense of … something returning.'

John didn't respond immediately. He was watching his home being towed away.

At length he replied, 'Moriarty is dead. I stood over his corpse, and I laughed.'

'I know that. It's just…' Her voice faded.

'Holmes was killed. Moriarty was killed.' John saw the houseboat he'd lived in for over a year being hauled down the waterways by a much larger vessel. He stood alone on the towpath, watching it arc around a bend in the canal. 'I was the only one who lived.'

Chapter Thirteen

She'd been in bed, lightly dozing, when the man broke into her home. He'd slipped around the back of her two-floor semi, carrying a cardboard box and wearing a grey jacket with generic insignia on its sleeves. But it could have been a cape of invisibility. He looked like every other bored and busy delivery worker and went unnoticed. He made light work of the back door's Yale but his lockpick created a slight metallic *click* as it sprang open the tumblers.

Inside, the woman stirred.

The man pushed open the door.

She turned over. Her eyes opened.

He paused in her kitchen, taking in the room. Listening for any sound.

A couple of moments passed. She, upstairs and he directly below her. Both attentive. But the woman lived on a busy street and her brain was conditioned to filter out almost every background noise. To classify unidentified sounds as unremarkable.

Not a threat.

Her eyes drooped and she turned over, her body shifting back to the warm side of her bed.

Using his right heel, he closed the kitchen door without turning around. He put down the cardboard box and slipped off his jacket. He hung it on a hook on the back of the door, picked up the box and began to move cautiously through the downstairs rooms.

Empty.

He walked up the staircase, careful to place his soles as close to the wall as possible to prevent the wooden stairs bowing and creaking underfoot.

Her bedroom was the last room he checked. He pushed open the door and saw her lying on her bed, resting on her side with her back to him, her duvet pulled right over her shoulders. She was muttering something and for a couple of seconds he thought she was talking to someone on the phone. Then he became attuned to her voice and caught the random words she was saying. She was talking in her sleep.

He sat down on the edge of her bed and placed his box by her feet. He opened it and removed the syringe. It was already full. He flicked the tip of the needle with his finger-nail and pushed the plunger upwards, only fractionally, to ensure there was no air caught below the bevel.

Very gently, as if he was afraid of what he might find, he tugged back the duvet. She was wearing a sleeveless vest, and as the cooler air hit her shoulders, she stirred again, but the intruder acted quickly and deftly. He grasped her elbow with his left hand and angling her arm slightly, drove the syringe's needle into the soft flesh immediately below her deltoid muscle.

She sat bolt upright and looked into the face of her attacker, too panicked to even scream.

She gasped, 'No!'

'Don't worry about anything.'

Her eyes widened and closed completely. A brief explosion of fear before the anaesthetic took near-immediate effect.

The man, still retaining his grip on her elbow, gave it a reassuring squeeze as she fell backwards onto her mattress.

'Don't worry about anything,' he repeated. 'I'll take care of you.'

Chapter Fourteen

IT WAS BARELY EARLY EVENING, BUT THE LIGHT WAS already beginning to slip away. Darkness always makes the rain feel colder, and John turned up his suit lapels, less for warmth and more for protection from the drizzle.

He'd already called the woman who leased the boat to him. She'd explained he was three months behind on his rent and she was perfectly within her rights to reclaim her property. His belongings had been stored and would be available in a couple of days. And when John — stoic and careful not beg — had requested an extra week after which she could have all money owed to her, the old harpy had cackled and informed him, 'Not every landlady is an angel like Mrs. Hudson, dearie!' before ending the call.

He'd traipsed from Tower Bridge to Waterloo, but every hotel and every B&B had been full.

Finally, feeling tired and beaten he took out his phone and called Mary.

∼

THE INTRUDER HAD SAT on the edge of the bed and scrutinized her face, weighing up the contours of her skull, the light lines between her eyes, the fullness of her pallid lips, the decades-old pock marks in her cheeks, the tiny hole in her left nostril that suggested a nose ring from long ago, the white, inch-long scar beneath her left ear, her thin, inexpertly plucked eyebrows, and her curiously long, natural lashes, so long in fact, that curving and dark that they appeared, as she slumbered, to be vaguely cartoonish. In short, he studied the image which he knew constituted beauty to the one who loved her. The man who had spoken of him in such banal and tawdry terms. The man who looked at this woman's face and saw perfection.

Satisfied with his study, he fully pulled back the duvet, slipped off his shoes, and got into bed with her. He kept his clothes on but looped his arms around her. Felt her warmth. Felt drowsy. And within a minute or two, he drifted off to sleep besides his unconscious victim.

He was awoken by an unexpected sound and felt annoyed that his sleep had been interrupted. But he was awake now, so got to his feet and opened the cardboard box he'd left at the foot of the bed.

He kissed the woman's forehead, his lips lingering on her as if to imprint his own DNA upon her skin, before he turned away and carefully removed his tattoo kit from the box.

Chapter Fifteen

JOHN HUNG UP AND SLIPPED HIS PHONE INTO HIS POCKET.
He spent another couple of hours checking hotels for last-
minute cancelations and trying, in vain, to book a room
online. The rain had cleared up, but the night felt uncom-
monly cold. As he walked head down through an icy
breeze, he remembered part of an exchange shared with
Julian Emery earlier that day. His friend had asked him if
he had somewhere to go and he'd assured him, 'I've always
got somewhere to go.'

He stopped. Looked up. His legs had brought him to
Baker Street. He reached a decision and hurried past the
cafes and estate agents, past the newspaper vendors,
tourists, and denizens of W1.

John looked up at the ancient building.

At its middle story.

221B Baker Street.

He gazed at the property as one might regard an old
friend who knows too many of your secrets. And as he took
in the familiar façade, a thousand memories fell onto him
and into him and he took a deep breath.

He reached into his suit pocket and pulled out a small, square jewellery box. Opened it. It was the kind of container that should have housed an engagement ring. But nestling in this one — a key.

JOHN TRUDGED UP THE STAIRS. Even the way his palm touched the wooden banister felt like a reconnection. He reached the top step and stood by the first door on the landing. Gently, he pushed it open and stepped into his own past. Stepped into…

The room!

His eyes narrowed.

The room where so many adventures had begun!

The curtains were open, allowing artificial light from outside to seep into his once-haven. He immediately saw the room remained pretty much as he'd left it three years ago. Walking across the Egyptian rug, he picked out certain items -

The violin.

A tabletop cluttered with test tubes, a Bunsen burner, and a microscope, all suggesting an abandoned experiment.

A dressing gown draped across the red velvet two-seater sofa.

The back of a tall, battered armchair.

But also, on a walnut coffee table, he spotted a syringe lying by the side of a leather pouch. He moved on from this quickly, half-smiling at the sight of an ornate Persian slipper on the mantelpiece, and besides it, of course, a pipe.

Pausing in the middle of the room, he looked across to the broad bay window, and willing it to happen…

'Is it you?' he murmured.

As if his imagination couldn't quite conjure up the man in his entirety, he saw the back of Sherlock Holmes. The tall figure stood motionless, peering out over Baker Street. Suddenly the figure moved and John heard—

'Hello! Watson! Here, unless I am very much mistaken is our next client. The young lady down there! She obviously left home in a great hurry…'

Recognizing the absurdity of the illusion, yet desperate to cherish and perpetuate it, John whispered, 'How can you tell?' He smiled in anticipation of the response.

But as Sherlock began to turn around and offer his explanation, he ebbed away. A shadow — already a thing of nothingness — fading in the sunlight.

John's smile faded, too.

He walked to the window. Stared at the familiar view of London. Even the scent of this room — the smell of chemicals still lingered — and the sounds from the street below were unaffected and undiminished.

He was home.

As this realization dawned, from behind him he heard a voice.

'Welcome back, Johnny,' said Professor Moriarty.

Chapter Sixteen

JOHN WATSON'S WORLD GLITCHED FOR SEVERAL uncontrollable seconds.

The confrontation that followed hurtled by in a blur of rage, mystification, and fisticuffs. In fact, his emotions only gave way to intent a couple of minutes later when James Moriarty, referring to Sherlock Holmes, asked, 'Who was he really?'

But by this stage the question felt moot, largely because John was pointing his loaded army revolver at the other man's head.

Strangely, the reaction was almost no reaction. Moriarty appeared remarkably unconcerned by the gun, and John pulled the trigger.

MOMENTS EARLIER, Inspector Zenisha Lestrade had checked her phone and noticed she had a call coming through from John. She picked up. 'Hello?'

No answer.

'I caught your podcast. Thanks for getting it out so quickly. You okay?' She'd been enjoying a late dinner, but rose from her chair, no longer interested in food. 'You've not got feedback already, have you?'

Still no answer.

'John?'

She could just about make out distant words being exchanged and raised her phone's volume. Now she recognized John's voice and his firm assertion, 'I'll tap the claret, all right,' came through loud and clear.

The next thing she heard chilled her to the marrow. The sound of laughter. The devil's laughter. 'Oh, very good,' said Professor Moriarty, and Zenisha sat back down as if she'd been physically pushed into her chair.

JOHN'S INDEX finger had begun to retract his revolver's single-action lever, but Moriarty made no attempt to avoid the logical consequence.

Was he blind? Fearless? Both?

John's face hardened, shifting from calmness to a kind of livid refusal to accept. He rasped, 'Say something else!'

'Excuse me?'

'Say something else — not about him! I won't allow your last words to be about him. I won't give you that.'

'Look, John, Sherlock may have—'

'Get my friend's name out of your mouth!'

Moriarty rolled his eyes. 'Don't go all Will Smith on me, man! We haven't got time! Like I said — we've got work to do!'

'You don't fear death.'

'Did you hear me before? I vote we join forces to catch the Teardrop Killer. The kids call it a collab. Short for collaboration, but I don't know. That kind of gives off French traitor vibes circa 1942 for me. Whereas *join forces* sounds like something the Avengers would do.'

'I guess that's because you're so used to it.'

'Avengers as in Marvel Avengers. Not Steed and Mrs. Peel. Although let's be real: they were by the far superior Avengers.'

'You've doled it out enough times. Death, that is.'

'Right… I didn't want to do this but…'

'Well, now it's your turn.'

'I am the Great and Powerful Oz! And I command you to sleep!'

'Are you serious?' John's finger tightened on the trigger again.

'Am I serious?' Moriarty considered the question. 'Yes!' he replied joyfully. 'But I have a tremendous zest for life!' He added softly, 'You should try it sometime, Johnny.'

'*Zest?!*'

'Life!'

John's index finger stiffened. 'Goodbye, Professor Moriarty.'

His expression made it obvious. This time he intended to kill his old enemy, and as he pulled back the trigger of his loaded revolver, he gave no sign of indecision. Mercy would not be a factor cluttering up his thought process.

And yet…

The trigger suddenly felt immoveable.

John clenched his teeth, willing his hand to carry out this one simple task.

Pull the trigger! Kill him! Kill Moriarty!

He fleetingly and ridiculously thought his inability to act could be due to some deep-seated instinct. A doctor's innate refusal to harm another human. He swayed. Put his left hand to the side of his head. No. Whatever this block was, it wasn't psychological. The fatigue drenched his body and his army revolver suddenly felt like an anvil.

Moriarty was studying him with polite interest, as though he was peering at a friend's new haircut after being asked for an opinion on it. John cupped his left hand around his sidearm and tried to move its trigger by using two fingers to retract it. But the weight of the anvil told and it dropped from his grasp.

He was beyond groggy. His need for sleep — a physical overwhelm. He managed to say, 'What have you done?'

'I told you. I am the Great and Powerful Oz. But I wish you'd call me James. We're practically family.'

Mustering his last vestiges of strength, he shook his head and replied, 'I *hate* you.'

'Yeah.' Moriarty nodded. 'That's exactly what I mean.'

John tried to take a step forward, but his legs felt disinclined to cooperate and he felt himself spinning. He was unconscious before his body toppled onto the Egyptian rug.

Chapter Seventeen

Zenisha snapped, 'I want that phone's location, now!'

She slammed her car door shut, and as the headlights of her Mercedes sprang to life and its engine roared, she took another call. 'Those back-ups — have they been mobilized?' She released the handbrake and began edging forward. 'Good! And tell them this one is important ... as important as they come!'

She put her phone down and put her foot down, already speeding towards West London.

John heard Mary say, 'Only boring grown-ups like mints.'

And his own, slightly amused reaction: 'Are you calling me a boring grown-up?'

He knew then that he was sleeping. Not dreaming as such. Remembering. Re-living something comforting to take his subconscious mind off—

Mary took his wrist and gently slapped a handcuff

onto it. *Dammit!* He was coming to. The real and the recollected awkwardly colliding, like a work colleague meeting an embarrassing family member in the office foyer. He heard a brief wooden scraping. The sound of a window being opened, followed by the noise of evening traffic and the feeling of fresh, cold air on his face.

John still didn't feel strong enough to move. But he sensed movement and forced himself to open his eyes.

221B Baker Street flickered into view and he briefly assumed it was another memory asserting itself. His temples throbbed. No, reality this time, he realized. He closed his eyes.

'I'll let you in on a little secret,' someone said to him. 'I'm not really the Wizard of Oz. But I did coat the banister with a fentanyl-based compound, absorbed through your skin and thence your bloodstream.'

John felt his arms being pushed back and heard the quick, deep *clunk* of something locking.

The voice continued, 'Thence. You don't hear *thence* enough these days, do you? No lasting damage and you were only out a couple of minutes. There we go.'

John opened his eyes again. Assessed his situation. He was seated. Handcuffed to the sturdy oak chair Lady Margaret Carstairs had gifted Holmes for retrieving her diamond, the Star of Rhodesia. He took in his surroundings. The familiar room. A couple of standard lights were on and sat across from him, in Holmes's old armchair, he saw James Moriarty.

The professor leant forward. 'Shall we begin?'

Chapter Eighteen

JAMES ADMITTED, 'N-G-L ... I KIND OF ANTICIPATED YOU wouldn't be entirely cock-a-hoop to clap eyes on me again. So I took precautions. Force of habit.' He sniffed. 'Your head should clear in a minute. How are you feeling? Are you ready to—'

'A wise man once told me,' John interrupted, 'that once you have eliminated the impossible, whatever remains, however improbable, must be the truth.'

'Yeah, well, Sherlock was fond of saying things for the way they sounded and not necessarily what they meant. Once you've eliminated the impossible, the remainder does not necessarily *have* to be the truth. Just possible versions of it. But I guess that doesn't sound as snappy. Or as definitive.'

'But this is impossible. You're impossible.'

'Oh, I'm not impossible, Doctor. Only highly improbable.'

'No, I mean ... I saw your corpse and yet you're here. I mean you're definitely here?'

'In the flesh, baby. We can do selfies later.'

'So the body I saw in Switzerland…'

'As I keep on saying — we haven't got time for this! The Teardrop Killer!' James snapped his fingers. 'Come on! Focus!'

'How did you survive?'

Moriarty wiped a palm across his face. 'How does anybody survive?' He sat back in Sherlock Holmes's chair. 'I did what I had to do. Now can we—'

'Can I ask you one more question?'

'One more? Sure. Shoot.'

John said, 'Why did you follow us to Switzerland?'

It was Moriarty's turn for astonishment. He looked caught off-guard, although John guessed he wasn't so much thrown by the question, but the fact it was coming from him. 'Well, aren't you just brim-full of surprises? I genuinely think…'

'What?'

'You wouldn't believe me if I told you. Right! I've got an offer for you, Johnny.'

'You said I could ask a question.'

'Yeah, but I never promised you an answer. Look, I've got to make this quick, because A: I'm a busy man. Evil genius at work and all that. And B…' He gave an apologetic shrug. 'I saw through that pantomime when you faked a cardiac arrest, or whatever it was you were doing. Putting you hand under your suit jacket like you were checking your heart.'

'Am-dram was never my thing.'

'You hit speed dial for the gorgeous Zenisha who is now, I imagine, flanked by a police battalion, racing across London with the express intention of slapping me in handcuffs. And not in a good way.' He leant forward again. His voice became urgent. 'Tick tock, tick tock.'

'So, what's your offer?'

'You're helping Lestrade on the Teardrop Killer case.'

'Yes.'

'It wasn't a question. You won't catch him without me.'

John shook his head. 'You arrogant bastard.'

'I'm many things' Moriarty insisted, 'but I'm not an arrogant man. Arrogance would be turning down help that could lead to the capture of a murderer and prevent more deaths, simply because you don't like where that offer of help is coming from.'

'Go to hell.'

'Very likely. But aren't you going to ask me the question? Come on!' He raised his eyebrows. 'You know you're dying to ask me the question!'

'All right…' John breathed in, then slowly exhaled. 'I'll ask the question.'

Chapter Nineteen

John said, 'What do you want in return?'

'There it is!'

'You don't give a damn about the Teardrop Killer or any of his victims. So, what do I have that's worth so much to you that you'd reappear and risk capture — risk *everything* — just to get it?'

'It's a puzzler, isn't it?' Moriarty glanced at his watch. 'I estimate we've less than two minutes before Zenisha bursts through that door with righteous shrieks of *you're under arrest* and all that malarkey.'

'How are you planning to escape?'

John heard the reply, 'Ask a policeman!'

He said, 'Personally, I can't wait, Moriarty. Seeing you arrested and carted away to stand—'

'John! Sooner or later, you're going to accept my offer.'

'Never gonna happen. But what is it you wanted in return?

'Well, here's one thing,' Moriarty replied. 'I want our working relationship to be fun! I don't want to be a dick about it, like Sherlock was. Constantly putting you down.

Pretending he was God almighty because he knew the difference between a million different types of ash.'

Despite himself, John snapped, 'A hundred and forty.'

'A hundred and forty? Fair dos, that *is* impressive. Well, in a *was-there-really-that-little-on-TV-when-you-were-growing-up?* kind of way. Anyway — that whole master-servant thing he had going on with you is not my bag.'

'I wasn't his servant!'

'Yeah.' Moriarty slowly nodded. 'Let's gloss over that. But on this one occasion, I'm going to pull a bit of a Sherlock and keep you in the dark. Sorry.'

'You want me to make a deal with you. You'll help me catch the Teardrop Killer … but you're not going to tell what I have to do in return?'

'Like I said — little pushed for time. I'm guessing Zenisha will reach your phone…' Another peek at his watch. 'Within a minute.'

'No problem. I can give you an answer without knowing my side of the contract.'

'Fabulous!'

'Professor James Moriarty, I make this vow. Somehow, some way, I will take my revenge for what happened at the Reichenbach Falls.'

'Right…' Moriarty nodded again. 'So, just to clear — that's a "no" then?'

'It's a diamond hard pass, but I do appreciate you wasting time, so Inspector Lestrade can get here to arrest you.'

'Well, yeah. About that. Here's the thing…' Moriarty stood. 'She's tracking your phone. And while you were sleeping — great film, by the way — I popped it in a taxi to buy us a few more minutes.'

'Damn you to hell.'

'Knew you'd be pleased.'

Moriarty took out his own phone, and as he drifted to the side of the room, John, in his peripheral vision, watched him swiftly typing what he assumed to be a message.

'She'll work out where we are sooner rather than later, Moriarty.'

And as if on cue, the wail of police sirens sliced into the room. 'So it would seem.' Moriarty pocketed his phone. 'I better skedaddle. When you've reconsidered, call me.'

'How do I do that?'

Moriarty ignored the question, hurrying to the bay window overlooking Baker Street. He looked down onto the action below and saw police officers were already storming the building.

'Crikey! They're all wearing hard, dull expressions. Always a bad sign. Policemen always look like that when they think they'll be able to kick someone's head in. Impassiveness is like foreplay for them.' He stepped back from the window and added, in total earnestness, 'And remember what I said. Your podcast has brought you to the attention of the Teardrop Killer. Tell everyone you love to be on their guard. *Especially Mary!* And you, my friend — look after yourself!'

Both men heard police officers hurrying up the stairs, their heavy boots pounding the wooden steps. Moriarty moved to the far end of the room, checking his watch.

John craned his neck to face him. 'Why are you so bothered about my welfare?'

The noise of a dozen people galloping up the stairs grew louder and nearer. They were seconds away.

Moriarty replied, 'Doctor Watson. You are the one man on this planet that I can't afford to lose if I want to regain my empire.'

The door behind John crashed open.

Zenisha Lestrade burst in, immediately followed by six armed officers. They fanned out around Moriarty, who remained unfazed by the array of firearms pointing in his direction. 'Inspector Lestrade! God, you're even more beautiful than I remembered!'

He winked at her and—

What???

Was John glitching again?

No! Moriarty was actually running towards the window!

Zenisha and a couple of the officers yelled out for him to stop. 'Don't do this, Professor!'

But moving at full pelt, Moriarty dived through the open window. John saw him arrow through the air, his arms windmilling through the emptiness before he plummeted from sight.

Zenisha jogged to the window and peered downwards. She hesitated. 'Oh my god…'

John shouted, 'What just happened?'

She turned to face him. 'You're not going to believe this.'

Chapter Twenty

THE PRISON OFFICERS WORKING IN 'D' HALL OF HMP Tarrack were fascinated by the Valentino twins. The fact they were hardened criminals for whom extreme violence was an instinct and not an aberration didn't make them remarkable. This maximum-security jail in North Lanarkshire housed a little over 500 convicts, and the vast majority were serving a significant stretch, each of them as hard and cold as Scottish Silver Granite.

No, what intrigued the wardens was how the twins communicated. It wasn't the way they spoke to each other. It was more the way they *didn't* speak to each other. Never. When they were brought face-to-face in the governor's office, there were no greetings or manifestations of acknowledgment on any level. They didn't smile or nod or outwardly express any recognition of the other brother. But everyone in the room felt an unknowable and silent language pass between them.

The governor, a young-looking 43-year-old called Bailey Hernandez, was not a fanciful woman, but she sensed their invisible exchange was the closest she'd come to witnessing some kind of telepathy, and it chilled her for reasons she couldn't quite articulate.

She explained to the twins that the government had granted the police and prison services special dispensation to have them rendered unconscious by means of a general anaesthetic when they were transferred from Tarrack to a holding facility in London, immediately prior to their Old Bailey trial. However, she went on, their lawyers had insisted that all details of the transportation procedure must be made clear to the brothers beforehand, and if they were unhappy with any element, both of them were entitled to lodge an official complaint, even if it meant their journey to England would be delayed.

Bailey asked if they understood, and when neither replied, she said, 'Good!' to imply that she'd discerned some sort of confirmation, then handed them both a document that detailed the proposed process of moving them down South. She anticipated they'd take an age to read it, which would have been fair enough. It ran to 50 pages of dense text in small font. She anticipated argument and abuse, feigned disbelief and genuine scorn.

But she hadn't anticipated what actually happened next.

Both brothers, without even glancing at the other, signed the disclaimer on the document's final page. And that was that. They hadn't read a single sentence, and as simultaneously, the twins pushed their documents over the desk to signify they were done, the governor realized she should be relieved. No arguments, and signed agreements, all achieved without fuss or fury. She found herself thanking the Valentinos, but as they were taken away, marched silently from her room towards 'D' hall, she shuddered. Like the warders she worked with, she wasn't fazed by her prison's criminals or their easy recourse to violence.

But there was something different about the Valentino twins. Something daunting. Something almost supernatural. Something somehow deeply harrowing.

When Bailey was alone in her office, she sat at her desk and perused the two documents the brothers had so readily signed. She compared their cover pages to satisfy herself that they were, like the Valentinos, identical. Yes. Except … She put on her reading glasses. At the top, right-hand side of both cover pages there was a curious marking which could have been—

A knock at the door interrupted her thoughts. She looked up. One of Tarrack's most senior wardens poked his head into the room. 'Sorry to interrupt, guv. Problem in the Segregation Unit.'

'When is there not?' She put the files to one side. 'Tell me the worst.'

And just like that, the mystery of the Valentino twins, their easy compliance and the markings on the documents, were pushed from her thoughts as she focused on an altogether more obvious crisis.

JAMES MORIARTY SAILED through the air above Baker Street. His descent was smooth and fast and would have been fatal, if it hadn't been for the bus he'd arranged.

It was an open-topped double-decker, its upstairs seating ripped out and replaced with crash mats. He landed across a couple of them, sprang to his feet, and gave the policemen outside 221B a cheery wave.

Moriarty bounded down the tight, coiling staircase and opened the inside door that accessed the driver's cabin. He patted the shoulder of the figure behind the wheel. 'Good to see you again, Alfie! How've you been?'

Alfie Butler was a middle-aged man with sallow skin and dark hair that was sleeked back with half a tub of Brylcreem. 'Professor! I didn't really believe you were alive! It's good to see you again, sir!'

Moriarty nodded to the road ahead. 'Lovely evening for a drive!'

His eyes darted to the side mirror and he counted five police cars in pursuit. Three were standard Incident Response Vehicles — 4-door Fords with blocky, yellow and blue Battenburg markings. A single BMW patrol motorcycle stayed a little ahead of this trio, while at the head of the chasing pack, two BMW X5s led the charge. Although similar to the Fords, James saw that both had yellow discs displayed in the top corners of their windshields. The circles indicated this couple of cars were Armed Response Vehicles and the officers they transported would be carrying firearms.

Alfie had spotted them, too. 'We seem to have half the Met following us, sir.'

'Only half?' Moriarty grimaced. 'How disappointing! Don't they know who I am?'

'What happened, Professor? If you don't mind me asking, like? One minute you're dead. Then you're alive…'

'Let's put it down to my terminal indecision. It's always been a fault of mine. Or has it?'

'You haven't changed, sir!'

'Now pull over! You've taken enough risks. Your fee's already in your bank account, but it's time I took over.'

Butler shook his head. 'We've only just got you back, Professor. We can't let the rozzers collar you just yet!'

'You're a good man. But I can handle it. I can do the job, Alfie.'

Butler remained unconvinced. 'Have you ever driven a bus before?'

Moriarty scratched his cheek, giving the matter some thought. 'I don't think I've even *been* in a bus before. But how difficult can it be?'

'Pretty difficult, sir.'

'It'll be fine. I've seen other people driving them.'

'I've seen other people flying a plane! It don't make me a pilot!'

Moriarty laughed. 'I've missed you, mon ami! But when I say *now*, I want you to slam the anchors on! Keep the engine idling but get out as quickly as you can and simply mingle with the pedestrians. The police will have their hands full following me, so you'll be peachy. Is that all clear?'

'Well, it's all clear but I'd prefer it if—'

'Now!'

Butler hit the brakes and Moriarty urged, 'Go, go, go!'

'Good luck, Professor!'

Butler kicked open the side door, leapt to the road, and hurried to the pavement. By the time he shouldered his way into the watching crowds, Moriarty was already in the driver's seat.

He looked frantically around the cabin. 'Where is it, where is it, where is it?'

Butler looked back at the stationary bus and whispered to himself, 'What the hell are you waiting for, sir?'

He glanced to his left. The police cars with their blues and twos now in full force, were speeding towards the double-decker.

In the cabin, Moriarty finally found it. 'Perfect!' he declared. He took the bus driver's peaked cap from the back hook, slipped it onto his head at a jaunty angle, and switched on the stereo.

Blur's 'Song Two' began to play, and putting his foot down, so did Moriarty.

Chapter Twenty-One

'WHAT THE HELL IS HE DOING?'

John sat beside Zenisha at the work desk in his old digs. She'd used a police pass key to unlock one side of the handcuffs Moriarty had used on him, so the open double strand and single strand — the two halves of the steel ringlet — dangled from his wrist like a piece of outlandish jewellery. Her laptop was open, its screen showing the professor's progress as he fled across London. And above them, on the otherwise bare expanse of wall, the letters ER were written in precise bullet holes, a lasting reminder of Sherlock Holmes's unerring aim, fervent patriotism, and questionable attitude towards gun safety in the home.

Zenisha had asked her question with exasperation. She added, 'I mean, he went around Grosvenor Square three times, stopped to collect passengers at Marble Arch, and then took off towards Speaker's Corner.'

'And now he's…' John leant forward and tried to decipher the information being relayed to them. 'Good god! He's actually driving through Hyde Park towards Knightsbridge. This is…'

He trailed off.

'It's like he's playing with us,' Zenisha opined. 'It's so random and...' She searched for the word. 'Whimsical!'

'No, no, no,' John replied sharply. 'This isn't random. Nothing is ever random with Moriarty. But you're right about the whimsicality — except he uses it as camouflage. That's his trick. His modus operandi.'

'What do you mean?'

'Take our meeting just now. He talked ten to the dozen about everything from the *Wizard of Oz* to the Avengers, how I should get more out of life, the usage of the word *thence*. It's all a smoke screen. To disguise the real man. Or rather, his intentions. It's to make us underestimate him. Wrong foot us. Throw us off-guard. And this behaviour...' John pointed to the screen. 'It's just him throwing apparent chaos into the mix. It's randomness that isn't random at all.'

Zenisha sounded unsure. 'But his route *is* all over the place.'

The claim seemed to galvanize John. 'No!' He placed a fingertip on the screen and followed the course the double-decker had taken since careering down Baker Street. 'That's just want he wants us to believe.'

'What are you thinking?'

'This is his comeback. His grand return. He wanted to make the offer of help, the offer to help us catch the Teardrop Killer in person. But he also wanted to announce his return in spectacular fashion. Otherwise, he could have just phoned me.'

'So where does that get us?'

'This,' he gestured again to the screen, 'has all been planned. Planned with military precision. And I know something about that.' He swivelled in his chair, focusing his attention on the bus's progress. 'He must have manipulated the traffic somehow to avoid jams and...' He smiled. 'The route he's taking! I mean it's higgledy-piggledy, sure. But don't be distracted by his stunts, Zenisha. Overall, he's heading south. South! And that means he'll hit the Thames, which means that if he wants to continue, he'll arrive at one of only a few bridges...' He scrolled up to check out the lower portion of the onscreen map. 'Judging by his general direction, I'd bet on it being one of these two.'

He tapped Lambeth Bridge and Westminster Bridge.

'Yeah, you're right!' Zenisha nodded enthusiastically. 'Given where he is now, the more southerly of the two, Lambeth Bridge, looks the most likely.'

'Which is why he's probably heading towards...' John's fingertip circled the area above County Hall. 'Westminster Bridge.'

Zenisha reached for her phone. 'I'm calling it in. I'll have them prepare stingers for when he tries to cross it.'

John's smile widened. 'Roger that, Inspector!'

'This is DI Lestrade...' Zenisha gave the police operator her clearance code and glanced at John as she waited to be put through to command. 'I've not seen you like this for as long time.'

'Like what?'

'Happy. Animated. Engaged.'

His look of mild surprise was tinged with embarrassment. 'Well, I suppose' he replied, 'it's just like old times!'

Chapter Twenty-Two

Zenisha quickly relayed John's deductions to command. 'Get Westminster Bridge and the surrounding area cleared immediately. I want Moriarty to have a clear run to the bridge, but I don't want any members of the public in the vicinity.' She nodded as her instructions were confirmed. 'Good, and I want stingers — but at the southern side of the bridge, so when his tires blow, he's got nowhere to go. Actually...' A thought struck her. 'He's got people on the bus. Can you deploy Talon?'

A controversial asset for many officers, Tire Deflation Devices (TDDs) were generally known within the police service as stingers, stop sticks, or spike strips. They are metal ribbons of jagged teeth, spikes, and thorn-like skewers designed to ensure that any tires passing across their surface will be ripped to shreds, causing them to deflate, rendering their vehicle undrivable. Talon was a development of the standard TDDs, designed to halt a car, van, or lorry in a secure fashion, forcing the vehicle to skid forward to a standstill, but not erratically. Although not perfect, it was generally recognized that Talon allowed more control in a 'forced stop' situation.

The officer on the other end of the line assured Zenisha that it was an available option. 'Excellent!' The conversation continued for another half-minute and concluded with, 'I can't take any of the credit. Doctor Watson was the one who worked it out ... I'd forgotten about his military background.'

This last bit was intended as flattery, of course. A verbal tip of the hat to the old soldier's prescience. But as she finished her call, she saw her words had not engendered the effect she'd intended. To her surprise, John suddenly looked concerned. Concerned to the point of fear.

'You all right?'

He didn't answer.

'I told them we'd meet them at the bridge. I'd assumed you'd want to be there when ... hey, what's up?'

'You said you'd forgotten about my military background.'

'I suppose I think of you more as a doctor and a detective.'

He frowned. 'Moriarty would never forget my background. He wouldn't make a mistake like that.' His mind was racing, now. 'I asked how he intended to escape, and I thought he said, *ask a policeman.*'

'Yeah? So what?'

'Supposing he'd said "Ask a Policeman." As in, the title of an old movie.'

'I don't follow you.'

'*Ask a Policeman* is a black and white film, and at the end of it, the hero escapes across London in a double-decker. Even collects passengers. And then he stops, gets off the bus and confronts the forces of law and order. He tries to reason with the head of the police. But he gets nowhere. He's rejected. So, he escapes again. But just before running away on foot. he punches the authority figure in the face.' John was speaking faster. 'That's what Moriarty is going to do. Metaphorically. He's going to punch us in the face. Tap the claret. Give us a bloody nose.'

'How?'

'I have no idea.' John looked back at the screen and the blue blip that represented Moriarty, moving inexorably southwards. He was at best, a minute away from Westminster Bridge. 'But you've got to call your people off! Tell them to observe only. It's absolutely vital he isn't stopped!'

Zenisha was already making the call. She quickly conveyed her concerns and added, 'Do not engage — repeat, do not engage!'

She listened to the feedback and murmured, 'Christ...'

John snapped, 'Tell them this is what he wants and to pull back immediately!'

Zenisha shook her head.

'What is it?'

'The stingers have already been deployed. It's too late to retract them. If you're right, John...'

'You know I'm right!'

'Then this,' Zenisha peered at the laptop, 'is playing out exactly how Professor Moriarty intended.'

John nodded. 'He's got something big planned. Something no-one will ever forget. The question is, what?'

'He's almost at Westminster Bridge,' Zenisha pointed out. 'So whatever it is, we're about to find out.'

Chapter Twenty-Three

Moriarty drove the bus steadily along the A302, less prosaically known as Birdcage Walk. He passed Parliament Square and decelerated, noting with interest the constables and specials who were hastily ushering Londoners and tourists away from the edge of the roads.

'Good…' he murmured to himself. He'd wanted the area to be cleared. This was perfect.

The police vehicles which had pursued him from Baker Street had fallen away, so as he passed New Palace Yard, he could have veered right and then hung a curving left onto Victoria Embankment, and from there travelled northwards along the Thames-side road.

But instead, he continued straight and drove onto Westminster Bridge, heading directly towards the stingers. He rang the bell a couple of times and cheerfully bellowed, 'All change, please! All change!'

～

A SHORT DISTANCE AWAY, in 221B, John and Zenisha watched the situation develop on the inspector's laptop. They saw the bus draw to a halt meters before the stingers that stretched across the surface of the road, like metallic Rubicons. A moment later, the passengers alighted and tottered towards the edge of the bridge. Zenisha patched herself into the bodycam feed of Clarke Tuson, the commanding officer on the scene. She'd worked with him before and found him reliable and thorough but unimaginative. A reassuring presence, but not an inspiring one.

It was clear the policemen on the south side of the stingers hadn't expected the double-decker to pull up this early, and Tuson, as thrown as his colleagues, snapped on his walkie-talkie. 'What do we do?'

Someone told him to move in.

In Baker Street, Zenisha said, 'He's trying to use the passengers as cover. To escape in the midst of them.'

John shook his head. 'No, it's more than that…'

He was proved right almost immediately. As the passengers continued walking towards Victoria Embankment, Moriarty leapt onto the bridge's balustrade and leant idly against one of the gothic style lampposts. Within seconds, over a dozen armed officers fanned out in front of him, some of them yelling, 'Step down onto the pavement!' whilst others shouted for him not to move.

He showed them his palms in a '*Quieten down!*' gesture and said, 'Please stop barking at me! I can hear you all perfectly well! How are you all? Are we well?'

John said to Zenisha, 'Tell your men to be careful. Moriarty is at his most dangerous at times like this.'

She pressed unmute on her phone and relayed the warning.

On the bridge, Tuson stepped forward, breaking away

from the curving line his colleagues formed around their target. 'James Moriarty, I'm placing you under arrest.'

He looked indignant. 'What for?'

The policeman realized he had no idea.

Zenisha swore under her breath then spoke into her phone. 'Dangerous driving.'

This was relayed to Moriarty, who blurted out, 'I resent that! My driving was completely safe! The only dangerous thing about this whole situation was your use of stingers. Do you have idea how many people are killed or injured by those things on an annual basis?'

'I need you to step off the balustrade and raise your hands.'

'Boring!' Moriarty looked directly into the officer's bodycam. 'I'm speaking to Inspector Lestrade now. Zenisha. I'm about to leave without a scratch. You know the offer I made to John. I can understand his reluctance to consider it, but you know accepting it is the right play. Just remember, the proposal only stands if it's me and Doctor Watson working together and I get the favour I need from him when it's all over. Otherwise, you're on your own. So, you'll have to persuade Johnny to do the right thing.'

Zenisha and John exchanged glances.

Moriarty added, 'Before it's too late.'

Zenisha raised her phone. 'Enough is enough. Get him down and bring him in, Tuson. Use force if necessary, but try to avoid opening fire.'

Clarke Tuson instinctively murmured, 'Copy that!' and hearing this reply, Moriarty raised his palms again, but this time it was a *back off!* warning.

The policemen on the bridge stood stock still but none of them retreated. Tuson said, 'You can't just leave without a scratch, sir. You're surrounded and we've been given permission to use force if it's deemed necessary to bring you in.' He risked a single step forward. 'Just hand yourself over to us, James. You'll be given a fair crack of the whip. I promise you that.'

'You're sweet, but here's what's going to happen. I'm going to turn around and make a daring dive into the Thames. You'll all rush to where I now stand, peer into the dark waters and think, "We've got him!" Because a couple of you *could* jump in after me — I'm guessing the drop is between five and six meters — so that would be doable. You'll also be thinking you can line the riverbank with your people to arrest me as I soggily stagger onto dry land. Oh, and you'll be eager to get the river police here as soon as possible. Except as you look down over the Thames, you'll all be told to abandon the hunt for me because something more important has come up.'

Tuson looked confused. 'What could be more important than you?'

Moriarty smiled. 'Well, that's a question I ask myself *a lot*. And I could tell you, but where's the fun in that?' Serious for a moment, he looked into Tuson's bodycam. 'John, Zenisha — we need to work together to stop the Teardrop Killer. Don't let pride prevent you from making the right decision. We've got lives to save, *mes amis*.' He glanced up and addressed the officers on the bridge. 'It's been lovely meeting you all!'

Moriarty turned and, ignoring Tuson's protests, dived from the balustrade. He disappeared beneath the surface of the river and, as he'd predicted, Tuson and his officers raced to the spot where he'd been standing. They stared down but none of them could spot the professor.

Zenisha spoke into her phone again. 'What's going on there?'

'He said something was going to happen…' Tuson looked up. 'But…'

He never finished his sentence because in that moment, it happened.

Chapter Twenty-Four

IT FELT AND SOUNDED LIKE A SINGLE, GIGANTIC EXPLOSION but later, experts deduced that twenty-two bombs had been detonated simultaneously. The result looked impossible. A second or so earlier, Tuson had been able to clearly make out the familiar, iconic form of the Houses of Parliament. Now, peering in their direction he could only see a vast sheet of flames, so huge that part of his brain dismissed it as an illusion. He'd seen massive fictional explosions in action movies, created by SFX trickery and a framed perspective, and so he instinctively equated the vision that confronted him with Hollywood unreality, as if a film was somehow playing out right in front of him.

But the heat against his face was real. The deafening sounds of air buffeting in the blasts were equally undeniable. He instinctively knew he was witnessing an incident that would become a touchstone for his generation. A real, 'Where were you when…?' moment that would help define the decade.

But Zenisha had been correct about Clarke Tuson being reliable and thorough. He turned away from the immense conflagration and spoke to his colleagues. 'Is everyone okay? Do any of you guys need help?'

Nobody was injured, but he heard Zenisha's voice in his earpiece. 'What about you? How are you doing, Clarke?'

'I'm fine. Just … stunned, to be honest, Inspector Lestrade.'

'Can you confirm what's happened?'

'Sure.' Tuson gazed from Central London's oldest road bridge towards the site of the Palace of Westminster. 'Professor Moriarty just blew up the Houses of Parliament.'

THEY WATCHED the extraordinary scene without comment. There was nothing to say. The flames filled the screen but when Tuson angled his bodycam upwards, they saw black smoke, darker than the night, was curling moonwards in huge billowing clouds.

Zenisha was the first to recover. She handed John her police pass key. 'You might want to take the handcuffs off. They wouldn't be a good look for where I'm taking you.'

'And where's that?'

'After that…' She nodded towards the screen. 'Isn't it obvious? Let's go!'

John had to hurry from the room to keep up with her. As they clattered down the stairs, he asked, 'When you found my phone, how did you know I'd be here?'

Zenisha opened the front door but paused in the threshold. John saw she wore an expression of incredulity. 'This is 221B Baker Street! Sooner or later, it's where Doctor Watson is always going to end up.'

He opened his mouth to reply but she wasn't hanging

around. 'Come on!' she called over her shoulder. 'We don't want to be late!'

Without the vaguest notion of where the evening was taking him, John followed her from the hallway. He closed the door, looked up at the building and despite everything, as he turned away and raced down Baker Street, there was a hint of a smile on his lips.

Chapter Twenty-Five

ZENISHA ENDED HER PHONE CALL AND PUT THE HANDSET ON the dash. Her Mercedes pulled away from the row of liveried police cars and eased into the flow of London traffic. John Watson was buckling up in the passenger seat. He'd heard the intel that had been relayed to her, and as he yanked the belt across his chest, he said, 'So they're saying you guys had him surrounded and yet somehow he escaped?'

'You saw what he did,' Zenisha replied. 'Any attack on the Houses of Parliament is considered to be a—'

He interrupted her. 'Considered to be a Crisis-1 situation and all officers are *obliged* to prioritize that emergency over everything else, no matter how serious. I know. Hey, sorry if I'm a bit snappy. It's just—'

'Forget it.'

'I can't believe … did you see the explosion? He's insane.'

The traffic lights ahead turned amber, and Zenisha put her foot down to beat the red. 'Maybe.'

John eyed her with a degree of scepticism. 'Maybe?' It hadn't been the reply he'd expected or wanted.

'At least we know for certain why our criminal classes were suddenly so keen to hand in their loot and confess. They'd overstepped the mark that Moriarty laid down when he ran London's underworld. They'd heard he'd returned and would rather face our justice than his.'

'And the priests. That's why you knew there'd be no more killings.'

'It was only a hunch,' Zenisha admitted. 'I knew Moriarty had threatened them before he disappeared. He promised them — one more transgression and there'd be no mercy. But I didn't realize until tonight it was Moriarty himself who'd been their judge, jury—'

'And executioner!' John interjected. 'Like I said — insane.'

'Talking of which...' Zenisha had adopted a gentler tone that made John vaguely uneasy. 'Back in 221B...'

'Yeah?'

'Would you have shot Moriarty?'

'You have to understand that he and I have—'

'Would you have killed him, John?'

His silence was not a satisfactory response, but she'd conducted enough interviews in the course of her career to know when another question was the only way forward. She asked, 'What do you think he wants?'

And relieved by the change of topic, John said quickly, 'With Moriarty, you can never tell.' He shrugged. 'World domination. Face on a first-class stamp. Could be anything.'

'I mean from you. What does he want from you?'

'Does it matter?'

'Maybe.'

'Will you stop keep saying "maybe"? I hate it when police officers say "maybe." You should deal in absolutes.'

They drove in silence for a couple of blocks. Eventually Zenisha broke it with, 'Why don't you just spit it out? I can't stand it hanging in the air.'

The bitterness in his tone was unmistakable. 'You want me to work with him, don't you?'

'Maybe.'

John smiled. 'Stop it!' And ditching the bitterness for firmness, he added, 'I can't do it.'

Zenisha hung a right and said, 'I'm getting a lot of heat about the Teardrop Killer. From the highest levels. The Prime Minister contacted me this afternoon.'

'Never trust a politician.'

'Even Redford? He's a good man. Look, he wants this lunatic caught — and fast. Using whatever means necessary. And it's more than that, John. You know it is! Right now, we have no clue who this psychopath is!'

'We've been in worse situations and not needed anyone's help.'

'That's not really true. We needed Sherlock's help. In some desperate times, we needed that guy's genius. And he was always there to give it. To save the day. But he's…' She stopped herself from finishing the sentence.

'So now when we need help … what?' John swivelled in his seat to face Zenisha. 'What are you saying? Professor Moriarty is the new Sherlock Holmes?'

'I'm saying the Teardrop Killer is in the dark. And James Moriarty knows the dark better than any man alive. And let's be honest, we both know, if we don't catch the Teardrop Killer soon, he *will* kill again.'

John faced forward again. 'One more question.'

Zenisha took a peek at her watch and took the Mercedes up to 40. 'Go for it.'

'Where the hell are you taking me?'

Chapter Twenty-Six

THE STRETCH OF THE QUEEN'S WALK THAT RUNS BETWEEN Waterloo Bridge and Blackfriars Bridge is dotted with wharfs and small piers. Most of the latter are simple wooden structures, little more than planked walkways jutting out a few feet over the Thames. The majority aren't even represented on maps, but people visiting the South Bank often stroll down them in the sunshine to enjoy a packed lunch whilst overlooking the river. In the evening, couples invariably saunter to their furthermost points to sink a few drinks, smuggled out of the area's many pubs and bars, whilst taking in the moonlight across water.

The woman waited by one of these piers. She looked to be somewhere in her 40s. Tall and strikingly glamourous, she wore a long, midnight blue velvet coat over a daring designer dress. She stood alone, but a couple of paces back, two more women flanked her. They wore smart uniforms that suggested the military without actually conforming to the design of any official militia. They were vigilant and, without saying a word, like all the most effective bodyguards, they somehow contrived to appear slightly intimidating.

To the trio's left, the night was still alight, thick blazing petals of fire fluttering into the London sky. But the tall woman's attention was caught by something nearer. Something on the Thames. She peered into the darkness. Tutted. She removed a small device from her coat pocket. It resembled a pair of opera glasses, but these binoculars were military grade and equipped with infrared illuminators that allowed her to easily see through the darkness.

Even so, she heard him first. Or rather, she caught the dramatic strains of Handel's Zadok the Priest. It boomed across the Thames. She watched him emerge from the river mist. Professor James Moriarty stood upright at the stern of his small motorboat as it glided towards the shore. The flames over Westminster formed a dramatic backdrop to his arrival, and although she would never admit it, the woman was impressed and realized how much she'd missed this vain and at times ridiculous genius.

He reached the pier and scampered up the rope ladder she'd prepared for him. 'Ahoy there!' he exclaimed.

She smiled but didn't reply.

He walked quickly along the pier to where she waited.

'Why the hell didn't you tell me you were alive?' she demanded to know. 'I may never forgive you, you vile, beautiful man!'

He grinned. He was sopping wet, his suit glistening with river water and stuck to his limbs and torso as if glued to them.

'Good to see you, too, Colonel! Thanks for organizing everything!'

'It was fun!' As Moriarty reached her, she added, 'And I really did miss you, Jamie. Criminal masterminds are so *fucking* dull these days. But you? *Grrrr*! I could hug you!'

He went to embrace her, but she raised a warning finger. 'I said *could*, baby boy. I love you, darling, but this...' She gestured to her dress. 'Is Dior.'

Moriarty beamed. 'Colonel Sébastienne Moran! You are a woman of infinite style and fabulous taste!'

'Well, obviously. How did it go with John Watson?'

'Oh, we got on...' He glanced back at the blaze enveloping the Palace of Westminster. 'Like a House on fire.'

'Any more jokes like that and I'll push you back in the river myself.'

'Let's just say Johnny wasn't terribly thrilled to see me. I'm hoping Zenisha Lestrade can persuade him to see sense.'

'Before we go on...'

'Yes?'

Sébastienne lowered her voice. 'What's this about, Jamie? Your resurrection. Looking for Watson's help. Tonight's stunt. This whole thing with Lestrade. I understand you want to stop the Teardrop Killer, but you're not doing all this to capture one murderer. What's this really about?'

Moriarty paused. 'High stakes, my friend. High stakes.'

'How high?'

'Higher than I've ever fought for.'

The Colonel regarded her old comrade. She knew him to be an explosive character, prone to exaggeration and theatricality. Yet she also knew that at this moment he was in complete earnestness, and she wondered what colossal dangers he was facing.

Chapter Twenty-Seven

THE MERCEDES DEW TO A HALT AS ZENISHA ANNOUNCED, 'Here's where you get out!'

John peered through the darkness. 'Where are we?'

'Marcini's. You've got a date with Mary, remember?'

'Course I remember!' His tone suggested the matter had completely slipped his mind.

'Good.'

'Hey, how's it going with *your* new chap?'

'Don't change the subject! Go! Put today's events to one side and enjoy your meal.'

He nodded, opened his door, and stepped onto the street. The earlier drizzle had cleared, and the cold breezes had blown away. John paused, turned back towards the Mercedes, and tapped on the passenger window.

Zenisha lowered it and he said, 'Whoever your new fella is, he's a lucky man.'

'I know.'

'But does he?'

'I'll be sure to tell him.'

John still hesitated. 'I was an idiot to let you go.'

'What? You want to do this *now*?' She gave a good-natured laugh. 'Timing was never your strong suit.' She pointed to Marcini's. 'Go!'

'Just one more thing. Let me know if Moriarty gets in touch, won't you?'

'I think it's a question of *when* and not *if*, don't you?'

JOHN CROSSED the road and entered Marcini's. It was a labyrinthine establishment, full of dimly lit booths, deft waiters, and a sense that this is a public place offering privacy. Definitely a date destination on the whole, although John recalled many evenings spent here when Sherlock Holmes had been around.

They'd often celebrated the successful conclusion of a case at this discreet little restaurant, the Great Detective treating him to fine food and French wine as they talked over the investigation's merits and peculiarities. Sherlock would dazzle his friend over starters, offering insights into how he'd triumphed against yet another thief, fraud, or killer, and John would constantly marvel at his ingenuity. Many a meal had gone cold as they dissected their latest job.

John recognized the maître d', a man who looked like John le Mesurier reincarnated but with raven black hair and dark eyes this time around. He stood behind an ornate lectern and looked up from the reservations book it held. 'Good evening, sir.'

'Hi!'

The maître d' served up a polite, professional smile. 'Do you have a reservation, sir?'

'Yes, indeed.'

'And is that under your name, Mr...?'

In the old days, this same man had always greeted both John and Sherlock with warmth and open arms. He had never failed to recognize either of them, and there was never any question of checking the book to establish which table they would be seated at. It was always the best table. The best service. It had, after all, been the best of times.

John said, 'I think my partner is already here. The booking is probably under her name.'

'And her name, sir?'

'Mary Watson.' He cleared his throat. 'Or Mary Morstan.' And off the maître d's mild confusion, he added, 'She goes by both names.'

'I understand, sir.' He scanned his list of reservations. 'Ah, yes! Here we are. Mary *Morstan*.' He said this last word with a hint of regret, as if awarding John last place in a race he hadn't known he'd been running.

Feeling a flush of anger he snapped, 'Yeah, like I said—'

'If you'd like to follow me, sir.'

John decided to let it go and trailed the maître d' through the restaurant to a small booth that housed a table for two. It was very dimly lit. Not quite as badly illuminated as Dans le Noir, another of Sherlock's favourite haunts, where diners ate in complete darkness, but not far off. The scent of brazed meat and rich sauces should have made him hungry, but the aroma simply took him back again. Back to the meals when he'd—

'Mary!'

His former wife sat in the chair, her back to the wall. She was talking to a waiter who hovered by her side, but looked up when she heard his voice.

'John! You made it!'

He reckoned her greeting was part admonishment for his tardiness, and part genuine happiness that he'd arrived.

The maître d' pulled back a chair. John felt a peeved annoyance at the fact that the restaurant staff had inadvertently conspired to ensure he couldn't greet Mary with a hug.

John took his seat, quietly thanking the maître d'.

Mary said, 'I've ordered us the Sancerre. Is that okay?'

'Perfect!'

The waiter and the maître d' scuttled away.

John grimaced. 'Sorry I'm late.'

'You're always late.'

She wasn't reproaching him — it had been a simple statement of fact, but John felt stung. Nevertheless, as with his earlier, brief burst of anger, he decided not to pursue it. He remained in good spirits and was determined not to let anything screw up the evening. 'Anyway,' he said, 'it's really good to see you.'

'You, too.' It sounded like she meant it, and John's hopes rose.

'Well, I say it's good to see you. I can barely make you out. Why's it so dark in here?'

Mary smiled. 'I think it's called ambiance. How've you been?'

'Good, yeah. All good! How are things with you? You're looking great, by the way.'

She exhaled in a way that implied disbelief. 'Like you said — it's dark in here! But I'm fine, you know. The usual. Hey — what a night!'

Mary's apparent enthusiasm nudged John's hopes even higher. 'I know, right! I can't remember the last time me and you got together for an evening like this.'

Her pause telegraphed the fact he'd misunderstood her meaning. 'I meant the Houses of Parliament!'

'Oh…'

'I mean, it really looked like someone tried to blow them up!'

Slightly deflated, but hiding it well, John nodded. 'Oh, that! Yeah. That was … a thing.'

'A pretty big thing.'

'I don't think the bombs were intended to damage the Palace itself.'

When the flames had fallen away, it became clear that the buildings were slightly scorched but otherwise unharmed. The bombs had been carefully positioned to create maximum explosion with minimum damage. A lot of boom and a lot of bang, but no devastation.

'It was a warning. A demonstration of ability. Not so much a terrorist attack. More a terrorist display.'

'Oh my god! You're involved in it, aren't you? Has Zenisha Lestrade roped you in?'

Mary's tone suggested she was impressed, and very fleetingly, John wondered if he'd sounded like her when he'd questioned Sherlock Holmes about his remarkable methods in this same establishment.

'What makes you say that?' he asked.

'You're in a good mood!'

'I'm in a good mood because I'm here with you!'

Mary gave him a doubting, albeit playful, 'Hmmm…'

'It's true!'

'Yeah, right. Well, I'm sorry to disappoint you, but—'

To John's annoyance, the wine waiter appeared from the shadows and poured a mouthful of the Sancerre for Mary, who tried it and nodded her approval. Two glasses were third-filled, then the waiter melted back into the darkness.

Mary asked, 'Are we having staters?'

'What were you saying?'

'About what?

'Just before the wine came. You said, *Sorry to disappoint you but* ... and then broke off. Don't leave me hanging!'

'Oh! Yeah! It's no big deal. I was just going to say, sorry to disappoint you, but I'm not at my sparkling best today.'

She lightly scratched her cheek.

'Well, your sparkling *worst* is better than everybody else's sparkling best, so it's fine by me.' John took a sip of the Sancerre. 'But are you okay? Is everything all right?'

'Yeah, it's only that I tried to get a bit of shut-eye this afternoon — just a ten-minute snooze because I had a late one last night.'

'Nothing wrong with a quick power nap!'

'Exactly. Except it didn't turn out that way. I was zonked.' She scratched her cheek again. 'I was out for a good couple of hours. Slept through my alarm, and when I woke up, I had the mother of all headaches. Even my face ached. My head still feels so—'

'Had you been anywhere right before you fell asleep?'

'No. Why?'

'Because it sounds like you might have been drugged. Had your drink spiked or something. Unexpected deep sleep. A dull ache. Waking with a persistent headache — these are all signs of—'

Mary interrupted with a shake of her head. 'I didn't leave the house today! First time I set foot outside the door was after I woke up and I dashed over here to see you.'

'Are you sure?'

'It's nothing sinister. I'm just run down. Maybe I'm getting old.'

'Hey, growing old is something we can do together.' He immediately regretted the suggestion, and an awkward silence magnified his embarrassment. 'Not *together* together. I meant when you start to get old, which is a *long* way off by the way, I'll be getting old, too, so... Shall I shut up?'

'I heard today's podcast,' Mary said diplomatically. 'Liked it. I prefer the ones where you're not just going on about Sherlock.'

Going on about Sherlock? John pondered the phrase. *Is that what people think I do? Is that how I'm perceived? Is all my grief and praise and sharing dismissed so easily?*

'Thank you very much.' *Going on about Sherlock.* 'I think.'

'You know what I mean! So, the Teardrop Killer. Are they going to catch him?'

'Hopefully.'

'I mean before he kills again.'

'Honestly? I don't know. It's hard to say. Being truthful, we just don't know what he's going to do next. There's a fear he'll start escalating. Or he'll start selecting his victims by...'

John Watson paused. He thought about what Mary had told him and Moriarty's warning. A horror was beginning to seize him. Gently at first, like a light squeeze on his forearm.

Caught your podcast on the Teardrop Killer. Not sure if that was your best move, Johnny.

He said, 'What time was your sleep?'

'I woke up just before coming here. Practically flew out of the house.'

'So the podcast had been out a few hours by that point?'

This guy clearly enjoys murder. Right now it's without apparent purpose. If he thinks adding purpose would make the process even more fulfilling... Well, you might have put a target on your back.

Mary scratched her face again. 'Why?'

Or that of your loved ones. I'm particularly worried...

She was leaning back slightly, meaning the booth's shadows hid her face.

'About Mary.'

Sweetheart...' Despite his best efforts to remain sanguine, John could hear panic seeping into his voice. 'Could you lean forward for me?'

Chapter Twenty-Eight

As Colonel Sébastienne Moran's limousine hummed though the back streets of Waterloo, Moriarty said, 'I almost forgot. Could you thank your man William for his help with tonight's escapades? I might have been a little short with him on the phone earlier.'

'Will do. But can you answer my question from earlier? What's this *really* about?'

They were alone in the rear section of her long, low vehicle, but Moriarty still spoke quietly, as if afraid he might be overheard. 'There's a war on the horizon. A war I can't afford to lose.'

'Go on.'

'It's a fight to the death. Not just my death. I mean, I could live with that.'

There was something forced about his joke. He was trying to lighten the mood, which worried Sébastienne. 'What's at stake, Jamie?'

'If I fail,' he said, 'England may fall and right across the free world, precious things like justice and liberty…'

'Yes?'

'They will be lost forever. Ever heard of the Red Circle, Colonel?'

'The Red Circle is a myth. A powerful, criminal organization with operatives everywhere and at every level. Mighty and invisible. And non-existent, Jamie.'

'But what if they—'

'The first known reference to the Red Circle was in a short report in 1911. That was over one hundred years ago, but in all that time, there's been no solid proof to confirm it really exists.'

Moriarty nodded. 'But what if…'

'LEAN FORWARD?' Mary was spooked. 'What for?'

John took a cigarette lighter from his pocket and lit the candle in the middle of their small table. Its tiny flickering flame provided very little illumination, but at least offered a faint orange glow.

'You're scaring me, John.'

'Mary, I just need you to—'

But the horror had enveloped her fast and threatened to smother her now. 'We were talking about the Teardrop Killer… Oh, god… Oh, god!'

'Lean forward very gently.'

Terrified, she inched towards John. She watched his eyes and couldn't miss the anguish in them.

'Oh god, what is it?

'I don't want you to panic.'

She raised her butterknife and in the broad silver blade she saw it.

She saw the tattoo.

A teardrop inked into her face.

Her eyes widened and she stopped breathing. As she

dropped the knife, the reflection of the teardrop seemed to fall.

And at the lectern by the entrance to Marcini's, as he greeted the arrival of a party of four, the maître d' was interrupted by the loudest and most chilling scream he'd ever heard.

'Mary. Mary I need you to look at me.' John clutched the hand of his former wife. He said, 'I won't let him harm you. I will do *anything* to keep you safe.' And off her brave smile, he added, 'I meant what I promised you on the first night we met.'

Chapter Twenty-Nine

BEFORE MEETING SHERLOCK HOLMES, John Watson had seen combat in Afghanistan. He'd been a doctor serving as a soldier, an apparent paradox that had brought him over 3,500 miles to the kind of warzone where those fighting had long forgotten what the war was about.

He'd been in a bar with friends one night, shoulder-to-shoulder with locals. It was that time of the evening where everyone was speaking to everyone else, language no longer a barrier as the booze ushered in that universal dialect of laughter, whiskey shots, and gesturing bonhomie. John stood a little unsteadily and excused himself.

'I'm going for a smoke.' He looked across the table to his army friends. 'Anyone got a gasper? I'm all out.'

David Gunn felt his pockets. He was a big smile of a man. Broad shoulders, messy hair, and a good-natured grin pretty much a permanent fixture on his face. 'Here you go…' He tossed him a fresh packet of Lucky Strikes. 'Don't smoke 'em all at once!'

'Cheers, Tommy!'

Watson always called him Tommy. But army nick-names often derive from unexpected sources, and others in the unit called him 'Crick.' The joke was that talking to him for too long would give you a crick in the neck, and he was such good friends with the doctor that 'Crick and Watson,' a droll allusion to the men who discovered the double helix structure of DNA, was a wryly appropriate name for the twosome.

'Aye, aye, sir!' Watson gave him a lazy salute and began to walk away. The locals he'd been chatting with responded with wide-eyed indications that he could smoke whatever he wanted right here. They laughed and hauled him back, making him feel like Alec Guinness in one of those early Ealing comedies. Too proper for the moment.

But the Englishman in Watson was hardwired to smoke outside. He exchanged some parting banter with his army mates and slapped the shoulders of his new friends from Kabul as he pulled away from them. There was a bowl of mints on the table, and he slipped several into his pocket, then weaved through the crowds, reached the outside, glanced up at the moon, and put a Lucky to his lips. As he lit it, the bomb went off.

JOHN WOKE up in the hospital, drenched in blood, some of it his own. He was in the concourse that months ago had been a reception, but now served as an area for assessment and where necessary, triage application. It was busier than he'd ever seen it, and without even thinking about the matter, he realized the blast he'd been caught up in must have been one of many, coordinated to detonate more or less simultaneously to overload medical responders and inflict maximum chaos and, of course, maximum hurt.

He lay on a bed that was little more than a raised stretcher. A coat had been slung over his torso. He pushed it to the floor, and even as he got to his feet, he was assessing who needed his help most urgently. It was bustling but surprisingly quiet in the building. Never a good sign because somehow, the sounds of anguish always felt more immediate when they were low.

John paused. Glanced at his fingers and thumbs. All ten were intact. Excellent. He had everything he needed to work, and using his sleeve to wipe the grime, sweat, and blood from his eyes, he approached a child who sat with her back to the wall, clutching a patch of red where her left shoulder should have been.

'Hi!' He knelt down. 'Do you speak English?'

She shook her head.

'Good! I don't speak Dari. We should get along just fine.'

He smiled, and as if she'd somehow understood, the kid laughed with him.

'I speak … a *little*,' she said.

'In that case…' John pulled a mint from his pocket and handed it to the girl. 'Here. Take two of these, twice daily.'

She hesitated.

'Go ahead,' he urged her. 'It'll make me feel better.'

John took another mint from his pocket and popped it in his mouth. She mimicked him and gave a thumbs up as she realized it wasn't medicinal.

'What are you doing?'

The words had come from behind John. Without looking around, he replied, 'They've been in my pocket, but don't worry. They're in mint condition. They're mints.

I'm a doctor.' He looked over his shoulder at the woman who'd asked the question. She was dressed in predominantly western-style clothes, and only her light silk scarf, looped around her shoulders, looked local. She had a fresh cut below her left ear, where her jawline met her throat, that she was pretending not to notice.

John had never seen her before, but he knew that robbers, as well as surgeons, operated in these hospitals. They drifted into zones like this and quietly pilfered the personal possessions of disorientated patients. And although John instinctively knew she was no thief, he guessed she might be wondering if he was there to steal, not heal.

But she proved him wrong. 'Look, I saw them unload you from the ambulance. That was only a couple of minutes ago. Are you sure you should be—'

'Well, one man's ambulance is another man's taxi. I work here.' He turned back to the kid to examine her injuries. His tone became less cheery, and he quietly added, 'More to the point, if I don't stem this girl's blood loss, it'll be bad. Can you find me a bandage?'

She was already sliding the scarf from her shoulders. 'Here.' She handed it to him. 'Use this.'

'Thanks.'

As he used the strip of silk to fashion a tourniquet, he said to the child, 'Wearing these around your neck is so last season. Scarves around the upper arm — bang on trend. How's that? That okay?'

She rewarded him with another thumbs up.

'Now I'm gonna find a doctor who can patch you up, princess. I'll be as quick as I can.'

The woman dropped to her haunches, teetering next to him. She pulled a Hershey Bar from her pocket and said,

'Whilst he's gone, we can have chocolate! Only boring grown-ups like mints. Eughh!'

'Are you calling me a boring grown-up?'

'No. But hey, if the tourniquet fits…'

He smiled. 'I'm John.'

She nodded and handed a piece of Hershey to the kid. Gesturing to the improvised bandage on the girl's upper arm, she commented, 'Not a bad job.'

'Does it win me a piece of chocolate?'

'No, but I'll take it into account when putting together your overall assessment.'

'How am I doing so far?'

'The jury's still out.'

John laughed and the woman finally flashed him a smile. 'I'm Mary,' she said.

'Well, Mary, when I get back, I'll take a look at that laceration across your upper neck.'

'What? Can you make it magically vanish?'

'No. But I'll do my best to take care of you.' Their eyes locked and for a moment, in this seething theatre of war, they were alone. 'I promise you.'

Chapter Thirty

THE DAY AFTER MORIARTY ROSE FROM THE DEAD IN A flurry of fire, chaos, and unexpected propositions, Detective Inspector Zenisha Lestrade began the slow process of creating a contract that would legitimize his help in capturing the Teardrop Killer. By mid-afternoon, it had become clear that authorization would be needed from the very top, so arrangements to secure this confirmation were made swiftly.

Even so, Zenisha's appointment with the Prime Minister was for the following day. Moriarty raged at the delay.

'There's nothing we can do about it,' Zenisha told him. 'It's just red tape.'

'If the Teardrop Killer takes another life whilst you lot are faffing over official due process, you can tell the Prime Minister the victim was strangled by his red tape.'

The next day, at five o'clock, Zenisha travelled to Number 10 to formalize the contract drawn up by a size-able team of lawyers, high-ranking police officers, and anxious cabinet ministers. It was her first time in the property that serves as both the Prime Minister's official office and primary residence, and she was astonished at the lightness of security that accompanied her visit. She privately reflected that she'd suffered lengthier checks at Heathrow before taking a flight to JFK. Hell, getting into the Apple Store on Regents Street on the day of a new iPhone release was trickier than this.

The size of the place surprised her as well. She vaguely recalled it had once been three separate houses and contained over 100 rooms. But still, its maze-like quality — narrow staircases, linking a warren of long corridors and endless doorways — plus a clash of everyday home furnishings, fine paintings (she picked out two Turners and a Vernet) next to stark, office-like fittings, was unexpected.

Her guide, a young civil servant who breathlessly introduced himself as Percy Phelps ('At your service'), escorted her to the first floor. 'He's just through here, DI Lestrade.'

He knocked on a door, prompting a friendly, booming response. 'Hi Percy! Come in!'

He smoothed his hair down using the palm of his left hand, then pushed open the door. Zenisha was led into a grand chamber she recognized from news footage. 'Detective Inspector Lestrade,' said Phelps, as the only other man in the room crossed the floor to meet her. 'This is Andrew Redford.'

FOR THE PAST SIX MONTHS, Andrew Redford had been First Lord of the Treasury, Minister for National Security, Minister for the Civil Service, and Minister for the Union, all thanks to a landslide win at the general election which had obliged His Majesty the King to trigger the constitutional process known as 'kissing hands.' In other words,

Charles III summoned him to Buckingham Palace, where he invited him to form a government and become the Prime Minister of the United Kingdom of Great Britain and Northern Ireland.

Or to put it more succinctly, Andrew Redford was the PM.

His rise had been extraordinary. He'd come to politics relatively late in life, joining his party six months shy of his thirtieth birthday. Within three years, his star quality had made him a darling of the left. A Labour man through and through, he nevertheless possessed a Tory's disdain for 'wokery,' social media fads, and 'other elements that distract policy makers from what really matters: the overall good of everyone.' He was for the many, which he pointed out, embraced the few.

'Standing up for what unites us all,' he proclaimed, 'should benefit every individual, regardless of demographic.'

That was his early mantra in a nutshell. Easy to grasp and get onboard with, this credo had been central to his brand, a brand so successful that he'd been given a safe seat by his thirty-fifth birthday and as he turned forty, his party elected him Leader of the Opposition.

There'd been a hardness to him, however, that alienated many voters and for months he'd polled neck-and-neck with the incumbent PM. And then came the tragedy that took Redford from being darling of the left to darling of the nation.

His wife died.

Andrew Redford looked a broken man. Grief added ten years to his features, but also lent him an unexpected nobility. His speeches in the House evolved into pleas for social justice, driven by emotion and heart-felt resolve. His language became more reckless, and voters warmed to his passion, urgency and lack of ambiguity. He achieved a duality that many MPs considered to be the Holy Grail of spin: he managed to be a successful politician (which meant a salary of just under £100,000) as well as an authentic, much-loved 'man of the people.' Redford emerged as the 'normal' guy who'd suffered but fought back, not just for himself, but for all of us.

When the election was called, the bookies stopped taking bets on Redford's success within 12 hours of the first Gallup polls. His victory was inevitable, his landslide a certainty. His obligatory confirmation speech, outside the front door of number 10 Downing Street, accepting the call to lead his nation, held a sense of purpose that transcended politics. Some wily commentators noted it felt less like a governmental shift and more akin to a coronation.

Even in office, Redford still wept when he spoke about his late wife, Tania, and sometimes called being Prime Minister his 'side hustle,' declaring he was first, foremost, and forever 'a full-time dad to my amazing daughter, Millie.'

James Moriarty had watched his meteoric rise from afar. He'd never fallen under the spell of Andrew Redford. Never liked him. Never trusted him. In fact, if he'd remained at the head of the London underworld, he would have quietly and deftly launched an investigation into whether Redford himself was behind Tania's death. As it was, having feigned his own demise and relinquished the immense power he'd once enjoyed, he'd been forced to operate a policy of non-intervention. Redford's ascent could not officially concern Professor Moriarty, because Professor Moriarty had officially died in the loud, dark waters of Reichenbach.

But even in those shadow years when the world believed him to be dead, Moriarty had suspected that somehow, somewhere, their paths would cross, and their meeting would be a collision of two unstoppable forces.

THE PRIME MINISTER signed the contract and put down his pen. 'It just needs Doctor Watson and Moriarty to sign it and then this whole mad scheme is legal.' He pushed the document towards Zenisha. 'Do you think Watson will sign it? Will he want to work with the man responsible for the death of Sherlock Holmes?'

'John made a podcast that made him an enemy of the Teardrop Killer. His ex-wife has already been threatened in a pretty horrific fashion.'

'Yes, I heard. If anyone ever threatened my Millie, I suppose I'd be prepared to go to extremes to ensure her safety. But still ... Watson and Moriarty joining forces? I can't help thinking there's going to be more than one twist in this tale.'

Chapter Thirty-One

'SIGNED WITH REGRET.' JOHN WATSON HANDED THE document to Zenisha, who passed it to Professor Moriarty.

'Once we have your signature, we're good to go.'

They had met at midnight in 221B Baker Street. And now John and Zenisha Lestrade stood over Moriarty as he examined the document Andrew Redford had earlier verified. He occasionally murmured a response to one of its many clauses. 'Good...' or 'You really don't trust me!' or 'Lawyers' jargon should come with a health warning. Their approach seems to be, why use one syllable when half a dozen will do?' He looked up hopefully at this last observation, but neither John nor Zenisha smiled. He turned another page.

'There's really no need for you to read it,' Zenisha told him. 'You can trust me. It covers everything we discussed. Help us catch the Teardrop Killer, and you'll receive a pardon for your past crimes. But I should stress, it offers no indemnity against any misdemeanours or felonies you commit in the future.'

'Fair enough. And it ensures my name will be kept out of the media?'

'Using D notices, as opposed to super injunctions, as you requested.' Zenisha sounded impatient. 'It's all there.'

'Almost finished…' He turned the final page. 'I never trust documents like this.'

'It's signed by the Prime Minister!'

'Well, exactly!' Moriarty pulled a fountain pen from his inside pocket. 'But it seems to be in order. Johnny, I know how much this must pain you. Working with me.'

'What makes you think that?'

The sarcasm in John's voice was unmistakable, but Moriarty replied as though he hadn't discerned it. 'Because when you saw me for the first time in years, when you realized I wasn't dead, the horror in your eyes was quite appalling. It was as though "O Fortuna" from *Carmina Burana* was playing and only you could hear it.'

'However much I loathe you and want you dead, I want the Teardrop Killer caught more, because I want Mary to be safe. The man who murdered all those people was with her today. He placed a tattoo on her face … *because of me*. Do you have any idea how that makes me feel? Have you ever loved anybody?'

Moriarty hesitated. 'It was a warning. The tattoo.'

'Do you think I don't know that?'

'All your friends and family should be given security, but I've a feeling he'll focus solely on Mary. He knows she's your weak spot. Your Achilles heel. So … she remains in very great peril. I did try to warn you, but you—'

Zenisha interrupted him. 'We're not idiots! We recognize the danger she's in! We've already taken her to a top-secret safe house where she'll have 24/7 high-level security.'

Moriarty put down his fountain pen and stood to face

John. 'I can have my people pick her up, and I give you my word I'll keep her safe.'

Zenisha replied, 'The place we're using is run by MI5 and is the most covert, secure, and completely *safe* safe house in Europe. Only the Home Secretary and a handful of officers even know of its existence and it's without doubt—'

It was Moriarty's turn to interrupt as he cut across her, reciting the address of the safe house.

Zenisha swore under her breath and for a moment, nobody spoke.

The rain, which had paused earlier in the evening, was back stronger than ever. It tapped furiously on the windows and the wind was growing in pace and ferocity.

John walked to the mantelpiece and picked up the Persian slipper. 'It seems sacrilegious to be doing this here.'

'You ignored my warnings once, Johnny. I'm promising you, I can keep her safe.'

Zenisha said, 'It's your call, John.'

He lay down the slipper. 'Have your people pick her up. But I swear, if she's hurt, Moriarty, I'll—'

'Yes!'

John frowned. 'Yes, what?'

'Yes, I have. You asked if I've ever loved anybody, and I'm telling you — yes.' He took a breath. 'So I know how you're feeling right now. Full of fear and self-reproach and anger. But worse than all those things — you're feeling powerless. I can help with that. You might hate to admit it, but we're stronger working together. I'll keep her safe for you, Doctor. Because I know the importance of loved ones.'

John's face remained impassive. 'Just sign the bloody document.'

Moriarty took his fountain pen, removed its lid, and

scrawled an elaborate signature on the lower half of the final page. He picked it up and gently blew on the ink to dry it. 'I'm old-fashioned, though. Aside from this "piece of paper," I'll need one more thing to make our deal binding. A handshake.'

He gave the document to Zenisha, who studied his autograph. 'I'll just double-check this, John. Make sure it's legit.'

A low rumble of thunder rolled across West London.

John turned from the mantelpiece and crossed the room to stand immediately in front of Moriarty. 'We begin first thing tomorrow. We find the Teardrop Killer, I grant you some mysterious favour, then whatever arrangement you and I have is off. Finished. When we've got this murdering lunatic in custody, I reserve the right to kill you.'

'Not gonna lie,' Moriarty reflected, 'that's not the most inspiring pep talk I've ever been given.'

Zenisha looked up from the document. 'This is all good, John. Legal, watertight, and binding. So you two just need to do what he said, and then we can all go home.'

'Mary can't go home.'

'I'm sorry.'

Moriarty said quietly, 'I'll make sure she can go home very soon.' More thunder and over it, the loud electric whipcrack of lightening. 'Is no one going to say it?'

Zenisha asked, 'Say what?'

He looked at John. 'There's a storm coming.'

Nobody replied, at least not with words. But as more lightning tore open the skies above Baker Street, Professor Moriarty and Doctor Watson shook hands.

Chapter Thirty-Two

AFTER SHAKING HANDS WITH HIS NEMESIS, JOHN FELT A surge of relief. It came with the self-realization that he'd put his own hatred to one side and was focused on the important variables. Saving Mary. Catching a serial killer. And yes, keeping James Moriarty on-side so when the moment came, he could take down the man whom Sherlock Holmes had called 'the Napoleon of Crime.'

He had agreed to Moriarty's personal terms, which comprised two caveats. When it was all over, John Watson would do him a single 'favour,' as the professor had somewhat quaintly phrased it. The nature of it must remain unspecified presently but would not involve violence or indeed anything illegal. John reluctantly nodded his head to this. The second caveat was more unexpected. There must be no questions regarding Sherlock Holmes or the time before Reichenbach, or indeed anything that touched upon that fatal visit to Switzerland, including how Moriarty had somehow faked his own death.

'Too much anger, John.'

'I accept.'

'Even about Sherlock?'

Another, more reluctant nod.

He thought about Holmes a lot. Too much, Mary had often told him.

'You need to move on, John. Sherlock died in the waters of Reichenbach. But sometimes it feels like you're still drowning.'

He could never explain it to her fully. He remembered the curiously outdated expression Sherlock Holmes would use: 'The game is afoot!' Words which carried the force of a clarion call for adventure and something thrilling and meaningful. It was these small things, close and unshake-able, that kept dragging him under.

After signing the contract, he walked aimlessly towards Soho and eventually found himself in one of those subter-ranean Spanish bars, just off the Fitzrovia-side of Oxford Street. It was hot and packed with people, and a few women tried to talk to him, but he politely declined conversation and drank alone, downing a bottle of Rioja and three, maybe four vodka chasers. He lost count before leaving to retrace his steps through W1.

John spent the night in 221B Baker Street, sleeping in his old apartment for the first time in three years. His bedroom had remained unchanged, but when he stirred at six in the morning, he felt like he'd woken up in a stranger's house, and this dismayed him. He found he missed the familiarity and smallness of the houseboat. Like many people who reside on barges and other crafts, he'd always enjoyed the fact that it offered a chance to move on at any moment. Perhaps romantically, John equated this notion with freedom. Whereas this place, his old digs, were simply too much of a fixed point.

But he remained a military man and carried the routines of his army days into civilian life. He kept them close and wore them like a uniform. They gave him structure and certainty in a world that seemed hellbent on eradicating both qualities. So this morning, as with every morning, he rose, made his bed as though he was preparing it for a show home, drank half a litre of water, and prepped for a run. He dug out a tracksuit and trainers from the back of his wardrobe and quickly changed into them.

It was a cool, sunny day. The rain had cleared and reports indicated the weather would be summery. John jogged along Baker Street, then headed eastwards along the much quieter Dorset Street and Montagu Place. He passed the Swedish Embassy (to his right) and the Swiss Embassy (to his left) and reached Bryanston Square Gardens, that tree-lined oasis that forms a quiet pocket of forestry in the heart of Marylebone. He had access to the gardens and jogged around their inner perimeter thrice before heading back to 221B.

He bounded up the steps and entered the living room to find half a dozen strangers sat around the table enjoying breakfast. They were a mixed group, aged from their mid-twenties to early-sixties. A couple wore suits, three were casually dressed, and one man was clad in blue overalls. They all chirruped a friendly 'Good morning!' to John, who was immediately vexed by their ease in his home.

James Moriarty entered the room, carrying a tray laden with two carafes of orange juice and a plate of toast. He was wearing a black, slim fitting Ted Baker suit and a high, white chef's hat that struck John as a preposterous affectation. 'Morning, Johnny! I'm guessing you're a bacon sandwich guy! Am I right? We've saved you some rashers. Do you want white or brown bread?'

'Who are these people?'

'They're my friends!'

'How did you all get here so quickly?'

'We convened in my apartment, then decided it would be fun to surprise you with a bit of breaky.'

'Get them out of here.'

'They're more than my friends, John. They're part of my service. Every one of 'em as sharp as a needle! They are my eyes and ears and can go anywhere I need them to go.'

John gave a mirthless laugh. 'Bit on the nose, isn't it? You sound like Holmes describing his Baker Street Irregulars.'

Moriarty looked like he was about to reply immediately but changed his mind. He placed the tray on the table and said quietly, 'Sherlock used a bunch of *children* and placed them in situations of great danger. For all my faults, I would never do that. He paid them a pittance and wasn't even keen on them all entering these hallowed rooms at the same time. So please remember, John, my helpers — my friends — are *nothing* like Sherlock's Baker Street Irregulars.' He took a seat. 'Would you like a glass of orange juice? I've got *with bits* and *without*.'

'What are they doing here?'

'I've been bringing them up to date and letting them know what would be useful from this point onwards.'

'In my home.'

'We're supposed to be working together.'

'So?'

'The clue's in the *together* bit.'

Conceding the point without missing a beat, John said, 'You've told me who they aren't but not who they are.'

'They are the invisible workers who keep the engines of government running. The admin assistants, cooks, plumbers, and PAs to PAs. They all toil within Number 10 or thereabouts. Each of my friends helps because they wish to serve their country and the wider world. They are brave and they are good. They are an agency of justice. They are...' Moriarty whipped off his chef's hat as though it was a mark of his respect. 'The Downing Street Irregulars.'

John considered this for a moment. 'I'll have a glass of the *with bits*, please.'

Chapter Thirty-Three

WHEN THE LAST OF THE DOWNING STREET IRREGULARS
had filed out of 221B, Moriarty brewed a fresh pot of tea.
As he stirred the loose-leaf English Breakfast, he asked, 'So
what's the plan for today?'

'Inspector Lestrade arranged for us to interview Lizzie
Domingo's husband just after lunch. At his house in
Surrey.'

'Lizzie Domingo. The first victim, right?'

John nodded. 'Haven't you read the files?'

'I never read police files. They always skew one way or
another. I prefer not to be influenced by their bias.'

'Or their information?'

'We can gather all the information we need.' He
popped the teapot's lid back into place. 'What does this
morning hold?'

'Lestrade suggested we talk with Annie McDee, the
widow of Ethan McDee. Third victim. She believes
Annie was holding out on her. Not necessarily in a sinister
way. Just ... she wasn't telling the police everything she
knows.'

'No one ever tells the police everything they know. Secrecy is hardwired into the best of us, Johnny. Tea?'

'Yeah. Please.' He nudged his cup and saucer across the table. 'I'm not denying that.'

'Did you get any intel from your podcast?'

'Maybe. It generated half a dozen possible leads that I've given to Inspector Lestrade to follow up.'

Moriarty poured their tea.

'Thanks.' John added, 'Plus, I received an *interesting* tip-off a few hours ago.'

'What kind of interesting tip-off?'

'Got a bite from a CHIS who's normally reliable.'

'CHIS?'

'Covert Human Intelligence Source.'

Moriarty added a splash of milk to his English Breakfast. 'Yeah, I know what it stands for. Why don't you say informant or narc or grass? Or associate?'

'Err, because I'm living in the twenty-first century.'

'No one says CHIS except people writing gritty dramas for BBC One. Who is he?'

John hesitated before replying. 'His name these days is Graham Marsh. I know him through Holmes.'

Moriarty gave a vague, 'Oh…' He shifted in his chair. 'Where's Annie based?'

'She lives on her farm. Out in the sticks, not far from Domingo's place in Surrey.'

'And your Covert Human Intelligence Source?'

'Just outside Shere. Also Surrey.'

'Can you trust him? Do you two have Chis-tory?'

'Like I say, he's always been reliable.'

'Good. We don't want to go down any blind alleys thanks to a Covert Human Intelligence Source. We can't afford to make that kind of chis-take.'

'Chis-take. Really?'

'Not my best,' Moriarty conceded. 'Why don't we drive over to Surrey? We can meet with Domingo together. Then I'll interview your guy, Graham. Whilst I chat with him, you catch up with Annie. We'll meet afterwards to compare notes and head back together.'

'Are you saying we should interrogate people of interest *separately*? Maybe I should be the one who touches base with my CH-' He stopped himself. 'Maybe I should talk with my source.'

'Source is even worse! It makes him sound like a bottle of ketchup. I can talk to Graham. Don't worry. I'll be gentle.'

John remained unconvinced. 'In the past—'

'In the past, Sherlock dragged you along so he could show off. You're a good detective. We should utilize that.'

'Holmes wasn't simply showing off.'

Moriarty said nothing but the face he pulled left no doubt as to what he thought about John's reply.

THEY LEFT Baker Street a little after nine o'clock and walked towards Regent's Park. London was already wide awake. The traffic was busy and noisy and office workers barrelled down the pavement as if training for a speed walking marathon.

'That's my ride!' Moriarty was pointing to a metallic grey Volvo 1800S parked on the corner of Clarence Terrace. The coupé was a classic from the late 60s; a car of rare beauty that looked to be in immaculate condition.

'Where d'you steal it?'

'I'm sensing trust issues, Johnny. But that's fine. We can work through those.' Moriarty took the car keys from his pocket and held them aloft. 'Wanna drive?'

'No.'

'Liar!'

Half an hour later they were speeding through the leafy lanes of Surrey. Moriarty had been *pom-pom-pomming* away to a 1954 recording of Bizet's *Carmen* whilst John had remained silent since leaving the city. But he finally initiated a conversation.

'Zenisha told me your people collected Mary last night.'

'Yeah. Well, early hours of this morning. She'll be safe and well-looked after.'

'Where are you holding her?'

'Holding her? You make it sound like I kidnapped the woman!'

'Where is she?'

'That's on a need-to-know basis.'

'I need to know.'

'No. You *want* to know. That's a different thing entirely. I'm sorry, mate. But it's for Mary's own good. Try focusing on the matter in hand. Catching the Teardrop Killer so you two can be together again.'

'Together again.' There was something tragic about the way John repeated the phrase, as if it was an impossible dream that he could barely grasp because the very concept was so far-fetched.

'We've got this,' Moriarty told him. 'Keep the faith.'

John asked, 'So how are we going to play this interview?'

They were nearing the Surrey home of Troy Domingo, the Vice CEO of a global electronics company whose wife, Lizzie, was believed to have been the Teardrop Killer's first victim. He owned several properties in London and the

South East, and judging by the online articles John had read about him, he was a multi-millionaire who enjoyed his wealth, but gave a great deal of his time and money to charity.

Moriarty replied, 'Let's play it by ear. But you've done a thousand of these interviews with Sherlock. It'll just be a standard Q&A.'

Domingo's home proved to be a huge manor house just outside Shamley Green. The estate's gates opened automatically, and as they approached the property's Bath stone façade, the tires of the Volvo 1800 crunched over the gravel that coated the lawn-lined driveway. Moriarty parked up and a moment later, with John by his side, he rang the bell.

Domingo himself opened the door.

'Good morning, gentlemen. May I help you?'

There's something overtly affluent but strangely elusive about the superrich. There was nothing particularly striking about the way he was dressed — black brogues, grey suit trousers, and a crisp, open-necked white shirt. But these simple clothes managed to look tailored and expensive. His haircut was precise, his skin appeared to be perfect, and he wore a cologne that was subtle and sweet without being musky. Yet he looked drawn. John recognized the signs of grief, but inferred something more. Something he struggled to define.

'Mr. Domingo? I'm Doctor John Watson.'

They shook hands. 'Please, call me Troy.'

'I'm James!' The professor's bonhomie was bubbling over. 'Hiya! Love what you've done with the garden!' He shook Domingo's hand enthusiastically. 'I say "you." Probably a gardener. Well. I say "a gardener." Probably a team of them, yeah? Green-fingered artisans. Bet they never say no to a cup of tea, do they? Am I right? Always difficult to know which mug to give them, isn't it? Can't risk your best…' Moriarty paused, as though assessing what kind of crockery Domingo would own. '…porcelain Spode. But you can't make it obvious you're giving them rubbish ones. I mean — awkward! Guessing you never get *your* hands dirty.'

Domingo looked a little stunned. 'I … I quite enjoy gardening, actually.'

'Yeah, but you just snip off a rosebud every now and again. Pop it in your lapel buttonhole.' And off Domingo's surprised expression, he nodded to the lower sleeves of his shirt. 'Your hands. Dead giveaway. So smooth.'

Sensing the need to intervene quickly, John said, 'Mr. Domingo — *Troy* — we're here to ask you a few questions, if that'd be all right? I believe Inspector Lestrade reached out to you.'

'Yes. Yes, she did.' His eyes lingered on Moriarty for a moment before he shifted his attention back to John. 'But I really don't see how you can help. The police have done everything in their power. Although the Inspector did say you both have *remarkable* experience.'

John answered in a low, solemn tone. 'I worked with Sherlock Holmes.'

'And I killed him!' Moriarty said brightly. 'So we've got both ends of the spectrum covered.'

Around about that moment, John realized it would not, after all, be a standard Q&A.

Domingo lowered his eyebrows in confusion. 'Doctor Watson, is your friend serious?'

'Believe me,' John replied, 'he is *not* my friend.'

Chapter Thirty-Four

DOMINGO LED HIS TWO GUESTS THROUGH HIS HOME, heading towards the sitting room.

John said, 'We appreciate you've already spoken at length to the police, but we want to try a different approach.'

Moriarty added, 'Yeah. We want to ask questions that might actually help us find whoever killed your wife.'

Domingo stopped dead in his tracks. 'Are you saying the officers assigned to Lizzie's case are incompetent?'

'Yes.'

'No!' John exclaimed. 'Inspector Lestrade is one of the finest—'

'The word incompetent,' Moriarty interjected, 'literally translated from its Latin derivation means *not able*. Right now, the police are not able to find the person responsible for your wife's murder and so...'

He trailed off.

Moriarty had paused by an antique writing desk that held framed wedding day photographs of Troy and Lizzie Domingo. But above it, the space was dominated by a huge oil on canvas picture. It was in the style of John Everett Millais's *Ophelia*, but more than this, it was an iteration of that work. This painting showed the same river setting and the same natural landscape as the original, and the same figure was at the centre of the piece — a pale, auburn-haired woman who held a kind of hopeless beauty. But in this version of the scene from Shakespeare's *Hamlet*, Ophelia was not about to die. Rather, she was pulling herself from the river before its waters hauled her down to 'muddy death.'

John was struck by the work and momentarily reflected on it. In Millais's masterpiece, we find Ophelia, palms upwards and peaceful. Perhaps welcoming death. Perhaps resigned to it. But here, John noted, she is struggling from the narrow river and although the sense of ease is missing, it is replaced by a sense of purpose and is no less arresting for this triumphant amend.

Ophelia Rising.

John was stood behind Moriarty, who seemed to be dumbstruck while gazing at the extraordinary piece of art.

'She looks beautiful,' the professor murmured.

John wondered if he saw himself in the picture. The character who should be dead, ascending from a watery grave.

'My wife painted it. She was very talented.'

Moriarty turned around and wiped tears from his eyes. 'Clearly.' He smiled wanly. 'Forgive me.'

'Of course … Professor Moriarty — you were saying?'

'What? Yes!' He sniffed. Shook his head as if to clear it. 'I was saying that currently, the police are not able to find the person responsible for your wife's murder. But I am, Mr. Domingo. I am.'

'Can you promise me that?'

John quickly replied. 'No! We can never give an absolute—'

'Yes,' said Moriarty. The other two men looked at him. 'I can. Shall we go through?'

A young woman appeared at the door of the sitting room. She wore a French maid's outfit that should have looked ridiculous but somehow appeared perfectly in keeping within the manor house setting. She greeted Domingo with the slightest movement of her deep brown eyes. Nothing more. But off her presence, he asked, 'Can I get either of you a drink? Tea? Coffee?'

'I could go for an absolutely massive G&T,' Moriarty told him. 'Three parts gin to one part tonic. Two ice cubes. No lemon or lime. Thanks.'

'We're both fine, thank you,' John said, 'My colleague was joking.'

They were ushered into the sitting room. It was, inevitably, large and airy. Large enough to house a Steinway baby grand piano, two sets of cream sofas, and three wide bookshelves without any sense of being over populated. Airy enough to feel cool. French doors at the far end of the room were open, allowing a gentle breeze to sift through the house.

Domingo said, 'So what questions can I help you with?'

John looked at Moriarty, who replied, 'My friend is better with questions than me. I tend to ask them because I'm nosey. In his medical line of work, when he puts a question to you, it's so he can save your life, which must give him some experience of asking the right thing.'

John's surprise only showed for a second. He'd attended countless similar inquiries with Sherlock Holmes, but the famous detective had never once invited him to take the lead. Moriarty sauntered across to the French doors as if suddenly uninterested in the process. It struck

John as a sign of confidence in him. 'What sort of woman was your wife?'

'She was kind and loving. Fiercely intelligent. Funny. She was interested in everything. Science, the arts, history and what have you. A *polymath* is the word, I think. She was wonderful.'

Something about that *wonderful* made it obvious his description was over, but John waited. 'Go on.'

'Well, what else do you want to know?'

'With respect Troy, you've just given me lines from your eulogy. I'm not suggesting they're untrue. But I'll need more if I'm to help you. Who was Lizzie Domingo?'

John expected a biting response. A *how-dare-you-come-into-my-home-and...*

But Domingo seemed to be evaluating the request. When he threw his hands into the air it was a sign of frustration at himself, not his guests. 'Lizzie was Lizzie! A mass of contradictions. She really was kind and loving. And thoughtful. Then she could just leave you. I don't mean literally. But I've spent whole evenings in her company and had the feeling she'd not been with me at all.'

John gently asked, 'Where do you think she was?'

'I wish I knew. I put it down to her being a what's-its-name ... polymath. It's like she saw more than most people and sometimes it sucked her in. People like me can just enjoy the stars on a clear night. Lizzie would name them for you and tell you how far away they are. Don't get me wrong. She enjoyed life. It's just sometimes, it wasn't enough. All this...' He gestured to his surroundings so he wouldn't have to say *my riches*. 'It wasn't enough.'

'Who do you think murdered her?'

This time Domingo's anger was immediate. 'If I knew that, do you think he'd still be out there? She was killed at random, man!'

Moriarty was leaning against the doorframe, over-looking the garden. He didn't bother to turn around when he said, 'Murder is never random, Mr. Domingo. It's like love. There's always a reason for it.'

'I'm sorry to press you on this, Troy. And I've read the police files and know you told the Inspector you couldn't think of anyone who'd want to harm Lizzie. But if your life depended on it, could you tell me anyone who benefitted, either emotionally or financially, from your wife's death?'

Domingo threw his head back. Thought. Exhaled. Looked back at John. 'I can only think of one person. But it won't get you anywhere.'

'Well, it's better than nothing, Troy.'

'Lizzie's ex-husband. She married young. Their split was apparently amicable. But an ex is still an ex for a reason.'

'A former partner seems a pretty good line of inquiry,' John reflected. 'Why do you say it won't get us anywhere?'

'Because he passed away seven years ago. And before you start forming any sinister theories, he died from pancreatic cancer. But honestly, Doctor Watson, he's the only person I can think of whoever fell out with Lizzie.'

Moriarty had wandered over to the baby grand and was poring over the framed photographs that stood on its dark wooden lid. One or maybe a couple of the pictures arrested his attention, and as John looked across, it struck him as the first time he'd seen the professor appear shocked. His guard only slipped for the blink of an eye, then he glanced over to him and wordlessly indicated he needed to see the photographs for himself.

'I met Lizzie after she divorced. She was always … reluctant to talk about her life before me. Not secretive as such. I got the sense that the past was the past for her, and she focused on moving forward.'

As John drifted to the Steinway, Moriarty said, 'Would you mind if I asked you a question out of personal interest?'

Domingo couldn't have sounded more suspicious if he'd practiced. 'Sure…' He managed to stretch the single syllable across a couple of seconds.

'What you've achieved is remarkable. I mean — amazing. It's probably second nature to someone as effective as you, but how did you manage to achieve so much?'

John knew the question was a distraction, giving him time to look over the photographs. Men love chatting about their success, raising it up through explanation. They especially enjoy it when talking to people they feel haven't reached their own level of success. Like whizzes at cryptic crosswords who always seek to amaze anyone who'll listen by deconstructing a particularly baffling clue and serving up the answer like a magician plucking flowers from his sleeve, so business magnates will run with any opportunity to recount their ascension in excruciating detail, covering everything except the sizeable good luck that usually accompanies most of their journeys.

Domingo was no exception and began to waffle on about his early life, set-backs, dreams, et cetera. John reached the piano and studied the photographs. Their owner was banging on about how he never missed a thing, oblivious to the fact that neither of his guests were paying attention to him.

There were two separate clusters of framed photos. On one side of the lid, eight pictures that were all business related. Troy Domingo in a dinner suit shaking hands with Barack Obama. Troy Domingo in a Newcastle United football top, handing over a large charity cheque to former England manager Sir Bobby Robson. Troy Domingo in a hard hat on a building site with Angela Merkel, leaning across her and pointing something out to the German Chancellor, who looked bored to the point of tears.

The other grouping held photos of Domingo and Lizzie. On top of the Rock at sunset. Cutting into their wedding cake. Sitting on a punt on the River Cherwell with Magdalen Bridge in the background. Arms around each other on the bow of a boat, the Northern Lights shimmering behind them. The one photograph *sans* Lizzie was a shot of Domingo with an old woman. His mother, judging by their facial similarity.

'And when it comes to corporate gambles, let me say four words to you, gentlemen. Big risk. Big rewards. Oh yes, many's the time I've...'

John peered at each photograph but couldn't spot anything unusual or out-of-place. James whispered, 'The frames!'

And at last John saw the secret hidden in these clusters of memories.

Chapter Thirty-Five

JOHN CUT ACROSS DOMINGO'S MONOLOGUE. 'YOU LIED TO the police.'

'I've what? Look I've been patient and courteous but—'

'This room is full of photos, Troy. The only ones of your wife are right here on the piano. And judging by the dust around them, compared to the dust around the others, not of Lizzie, they're the only ones that have been added in the last few weeks. But they're still faded by exposure to sunlight.'

'Which tells us,' Moriarty said, 'That the photos of Lizzie and you were displayed at one point, but you chose to put them away.'

John continued, 'The dust tells us you only put those back up *after* she was murdered, probably to suggest a happy and loving relationship. So!' John could see his words had hit home and Domingo looked deflated. 'What happened?'

Moriarty asked, 'Did she find out you're fucking your

maid? Was it more deep-seated? Or did you just get on her nerves so she left you?'

The crudeness pushed Domingo into attack mode. 'I'll be letting Inspector Lestrade know about this, and also contacting several of my friends in Cabinet!'

Moriarty sounded unimpressed. 'Oh, give over!'

Domingo seethed, 'This is *outrageous*!'

'I'll let you know when I'm about to be outrageous,' Moriarty told him. 'You might want to run or put on a stab vest at that point.'

John tried a more placatory approach. He softly said, 'Tell us what happened.'

'I'll have you both thrown off the—'

Moriarty shouted, 'Tell us!'

Domingo folded. He didn't say anything and his shoulders didn't droop, but John could tell he knew he'd been found out. 'All right,' he murmured. 'All right...' He walked to the sideboard and picked up one of the decanters it held. 'But you need to know....' He poured himself a large whiskey. 'You're wrong.'

Moriarty replied, 'Well, that would be a novelty, but—'

'I mean it's not what you think!'

John asked, 'And what do we think?'

'That the husband is usually the killer. That because Lizzie and I grew apart that I must have been mad with rage, or I wanted rid of her without the expensive divorce settlement. None of that is true.'

'What did cause you and your wife to ... drift?'

Domingo half-shrugged. He started to raise the whiskey he'd poured, but before it reached his lips, Moriarty yelled, 'Stop!' He pointed to the glass. 'Do not drink that scotch!'

As he rushed over to him, Domingo blanched and held

the tumbler at arm's length, as if afraid it might explode in his hand. 'My god! Do you think it's been poisoned?'

'No!' Moriarty reached him, took the glass, and downed its content in one gulp. 'I just *really* needed a drink.' He handed the glass back. 'Get me a top up. And don't be stingy, baby. Help yourself to one while you're at it.'

'Troy…' John attempted to get things back on track. 'The break-up. You were saying…'

Domingo gave the tumbler back to Moriarty. 'Help yourself.' And to John, 'I believe my wife loved me. God knows I loved her. She never left me — officially. She just became ever more… *distant*, I suppose the word is. I couldn't bear seeing those photographs every day. Reminders of better times.'

John nodded his understanding. 'Go on.'

'Oh, she was a dream wife in many ways. But our relationship … she never committed. Not 100 percent. That might sound crazy, but there was always something that stopped her from fully—'

'No!' Moriarty snapped. 'Some*one*.'

Domingo said firmly, 'She wasn't having an affair.' And with a little less force. 'Also, if it's any of your business, Bianca and I…' He looked towards the door. The maid was silhouetted in its threshold. '…it's a recent thing. Grief can bond people, you know, and Bianca has been—'

'Oh well, that's all right then!'

Moriarty sounded livid, but so did Domingo as he roared, 'Who the hell are you, anyway?'

Suddenly calm, almost studious, the professor answered, 'I'm the man who promised I could find out who was responsible for your wife's death. Don't forget that. Doctor Watson, are we finished here?'

'I do have more questions for you, Troy. But I can see you're upset, so I'll leave them for now.'

Domingo mouthed, '*Thank you.*'

John walked over to him. 'And hey. You and your wife didn't have a perfect relationship. Welcome to the human race.'

The millionaire had flicked from fury to sadness. 'She was the love of my life.'

In his peripheral vision, John saw the maid rush away. He gestured towards the piano. 'Well judging by those photographs, I think that love was reciprocated. One more thing…' He embraced Domingo and pulled back. 'Don't feel bad about Bianca. From what you've told us about Lizzie, she'd want you to be happy.'

Domingo murmured, 'You're a very kind man.'

'I'm not sure my ex-wife would agree.'

They swapped sympathetic smiles.

'But I give you my word I'll do everything in my power to find the person who took Lizzie from you. And if I do, and it's humanly possible, I will bring him to justice.'

Domingo nodded, a picture of grief and gratitude. 'God bless you.'

John could see Moriarty lingering by the piano, watching the exchange as a young child might watch a wedding ceremony. He was clearly impressed by the spectacle he was witnessing, but looked as if he didn't understand one moment of it.

Chapter Thirty-Six

'YOU DRIVE!'

Moriarty tossed his keys to John, who caught them smartly. 'Sure.' He unlocked the car. 'But only because you've been drinking.'

They left the estate and John guided the Volvo onto the Hog's Back, an ancient road named after the outline of the ridge it follows. Stretching between Guildford and the market town of Farnham, it offered striking views across the North Downs and the Devil's Punchbowl.

Moriarty was uncharacteristically quiet, pensive, almost brooding. John left him to thoughts. He noticed his passenger received a message on his phone. Eventually, after reading it, the professor wiped a palm across his face. 'Why were you so nice to Domingo?' he asked. 'At the end — when we were leaving?'

'What do you mean?'

'The hug. The reassurance. All that stuff.'

'Oh! *All that stuff*. Well, I'm a member of a club. We occasionally try to be kind and empathetic.'

'Sounds intriguing. What's the name of the club?'

'It's called humanity.'

Moriarty gave a short laugh. 'I walked into that one, didn't I?'

'I could propose you for admission, if you like?'

'No, thanks. I know a few of the members and don't think they'd have me.'

'It's not up to them. Permission to speak candidly?'

'Aye.'

'I find you despicable.'

'Even after I made you breakfast?'

'But no one is beyond redemption. No one.'

'You're wrong, John. There can be no redemption for whoever murdered Lizzie. No redemption, no forgiveness. Only justice. I promise you that.'

John was familiar with such bitterness and certainty; the way one sustained the other. He'd seen it a hundred times in combat when friends had been lost, and amongst survivors, grief had taken the form of an immutable hatred. He used Moriarty's vow to bring the conversation back to a more practical angle.

'Well, we need to capture him first. What did we learn from Domingo?'

'I was about to ask you the same question.'

'Let's start with the obvious. Troy Domingo is insanely rich. Do you think money's got something to do with it?'

'Money's always got something to do with it.' Moriarty lowered his window a couple of inches. 'Did you see the security the manor house was packing?'

'No.'

'Exactly! That suggests it's top of the range. Which suggests the house in Maida Vale, where Lizzie was murdered, has equally good security. So what alarm bells does that set ringing?'

'Pun intended?'

'Of course.'

John contemplated the broader issue. 'It's generally assumed the Teardrop Killer is striking at random. But if he's a rookie murderer, why start with such a difficult target? He'd have had to bypass the Maida Vale home's security. That's no easy matter. Why bother, *if* he could have chosen literally anyone else? The world is full of easier hits.'

'And that suggests that Lizzie was not chosen at random. Which in turn begs the question — what marked her for death?'

John said, 'Do you think Domingo could have been lying? His wife wanted a divorce, and he didn't fancy the settlement that would have triggered. So he has her bumped off. The guy doing it gets a taste for murder and starts a killing spree…'

'No. You saw that place and the way he is. Troy Domingo is a neat and tidy man. Murder is always messy. Even the best-planned kill leaves a residue of chaos. He wouldn't have wanted to go down that road.'

'Yeah, I agree. He's the type of guy that would have lawyered up, reached the best settlement possible, then paid it off in one chunk and moved on.'

'I think you're right. So why did the killer choose her, Johnny? And why did he tattoo a tear on her face?'

'To symbolize sadness?'

Moriarty asked, 'What is a teardrop?' as though the thing itself was alien to him.

'An indicator of extreme unhappiness,' John speculated. 'Or extreme happiness. Tears of joy and all that. Was the murderer trying to throw light on something? Lizzie's secret sorrow?' He shrugged. 'Or secret joy. I've no idea. You?'

Moriarty looked out over the Surrey hedgerows, meadows, and ranges. Their greens and browns streaked into one as they sped through the countryside. 'He kills the wife of a multi-millionaire. He takes the time and effort to ink a tear onto her face. Then he kills other victims who are seemingly unrelated. His crimes are so horrific that the Prime Minister gets involved. Could that be something to do with it?'

'Hard to see how. But that doesn't mean we should dismiss it.'

'And why is the PM's daughter continually making jokes about an old family pet?'

John looked sceptical. 'What do you mean?'

'When I made plans to return from the dead, I knew that if I was going to work with you, Andrew Redford would have to sign off on the whole thing to make it workable. So I had him looked into. To see if I could trust him. To see what kind of a bloke I'd be dealing with.'

'And?'

'And one of the PM's tea ladies is a member of my Downing Street Irregulars. Through her, I learnt that Redford FaceTimes his daughter, Millie, every morning at the same time. He likes a cuppa while they chat.'

'Heart-warming but irrelevant — surely?'

'Surely not! Millie is currently in Asia. Traveling through India, to be precise, on an extended break,' said Moriarty, 'And I just read a transcript of some of their recent chinwags. It's still happening, John! On *every single* call, Millie mentions the same old pet and makes some in-joke about it. Doesn't that strike you as weird?'

'No! Like I say, it strikes me as *totally* irrelevant to the Teardrop Killer case.' He took his eyes off the road for a moment, glancing at his passenger. 'Why are you bothered by it?'

'Because it seems inexplicable. I don't mind the unexplained. The unexplained is fun. A bit of a tease. But the inexplicable? No, thanks. The inexplicable is an affront to human learning.' He was interrupted by a song playing loudly from his phone — 'Sound of da Police' by KRS-One. Moriarty joined in for a few bars, then hit 'Answer.'

'Inspector Lestrade! What a pleasant surprise!'

John listened to Moriarty giving a brief recap of their day so far. He closed with, 'And tell the Prime Minister his daughter may be in trouble … No, I don't want to go into why. *Why* always takes far too long.'

Ten minutes later, John pulled up just outside Shere. Moriarty opened the door but lingered in the car for a moment. 'Be careful, John. My sixth sense is telling me that this case is even more dangerous than we thought.'

'Not my first rodeo, Moriarty.'

'Don't be so glib! We're in the dark, John. And our enemy may well strike before we have time to find the light.'

Chapter Thirty-Seven

ETHAN McDEE HAD BEEN, AS FAR AS THE POLICE KNEW, the third victim of the Teardrop Killer. His widow, Annie, waved cheerily to John Watson as he stepped from the Volvo into the big open yard in front of her cottage.

John slammed the car door shut. The sound this made seemed to echo and then die, leaving a conspicuous silence. John raised a palm towards Annie. More respectful than a friendly wave, he thought as he walked towards her.

He took in her property as he crossed the yard. This was no new build with twee rustic touches, touted as 'a much sought after farmhouse' by estate agents hoping to flog the old pile to Londoners wanting somewhere 'authentic' for the school holidays. No. This was a house in the middle of a sprawling arable farm. A mud-spattered Land Rover Defender was parked by the door, and a couple of collies yapped and danced in giddy circles as John reached Annie. He extended his hand.

'Thank you for seeing me, Mrs. McDee.'

'Call me Annie!' She brushed his hand aside and hugged him. 'I appreciate you looking into Ethan's death.'

John was used to the way relatives said *death* when they meant *murder*. She relaxed her embrace. 'Well, I hope I'm able to help,' he told her.

She guided him through to the kitchen and he took a seat at the pine table that dominated the room. It struck John that if he'd written about a place like this in his memoirs, he'd have been accused of falling back on stereotypes. All the farmhouse cliches were present. The huge, cream-colored Aga. Wellington boots in the corner, besides the inevitable Welsh dresser laden with dusty nick-nacks. Overalls hanging up by the backdoor. Two broad wicker dog baskets that the collies lay down in. And Annie herself. Ruddy cheeks and unkempt hair. She even wore a green, battered Barbour.

It looked to John like the set of a show set on a fifties home counties farm, except for two elements. On the dresser's lower shelf, John counted five tiny screens that relayed CCTV feeds of fields surrounding the cottage. And on the table, an open laptop displaying graphs defining — John took a swift glance — 'YoY expected productivity yields.'

'Can I get you a brew, luv? Cuppa tea? Or coffee? We've only got instant but it's not decaf. It's the fully leaded stuff.'

'A tea would be great — thanks.'

As Annie filled the kettle, John said, 'I've worked a lot of cases. A lot of them with Sherlock Holmes.'

'Oh, right.'

The detective's name normally elicited more of a response.

'And I often find that after people have spoken to the police, they sometimes remember things and wish they'd mentioned titbits of information. But they don't pass them on because they feel they might not be important. Does that chime with you?'

Annie lifted one of the Aga's huge lids and placed the kettle on its hot ring. 'Not really, luv.'

She sat across the table from John, and before he'd asked a single specific question, before he'd peeled back any layers or established any hint of a rapport, he knew, without a smudge of doubt, that she would volunteer nothing of use, and he wondered. Not so much what her secrets might be, but more, why she gripped them so tightly. He recalled Moriarty's words and knew them to be true.

'Secrecy is hardwired into the best of us, Johnny.'

But intuition told him there was something more at play here.

JAMES MORIARTY HADN'T LIED about the so-called CHIS, but he hadn't been entirely forthcoming. As they'd driven from London and John had told him about Graham Marsh, he'd listened carefully and asked appropriate questions as though seeking to understand him. He didn't mention that he'd been acquainted with Marsh — or Roddy Fingers, as he knew him — for well over a decade and a half.

'He was a Londoner when I first met him,' John had revealed. 'He moved out to the country about three years ago. Said he'd had enough of the rat race. He works in a little village library now. Seems to keep his nose clean. Not heard from him for the best part of eighteen months.'

Moriarty had asked, 'So what exactly did he say to you about the Teardrop Killer?'

'Left me a voice message. He said there was more in

play. Those were his exact words. *More in play*. And he told me to steer clear of the whole thing.'

Moriarty walked through Shere. It was a pretty and improbable village full of quaint cafes — one specialized in scones, which felt entirely appropriate — and small, artisanal shops. Most of its buildings were centuries old and many were half-timbered. It retained an old-fashioned, quintessentially English air and as such had been utilized in countless films and television productions. Movies as diverse as Powell & Pressburger's *A Matter of Life and Death* and the Cameron Diaz/Kate Winslet romcom *The Holiday* had used the setting to good advantage.

When an Agatha Christie adaptation, set in the prewar years, was filmed in Shere in the early 2020s, location managers joked that they'd need to spend considerable time and money doctoring the village so it wouldn't look too old-fashioned for the 1930s.

Moriarty strolled past The Dabbling Duck, crossed the tiny stone bridge that spanned the River Tillingbourne, and followed the main road past one of the village pubs, The White Horse. The library that Roddy Fingers ran was a ten-minute walk from the centre of Shere, but Moriarty wanted to assess the terrain. Smell the air. Hear the birdsong. See the net curtains twitch and catch random conversations.

He liked the place and felt glad his old friend had settled here after he'd disappeared following events in Reichenbach. He felt guilt as well. Guilt that Roddy had relocated based on a lie that he himself had fabricated.

A vicar was chatting to a postman outside The Bray. They waffled about the weather and the chance of afternoon rain. Both men broke off and said, 'Morning!' to Moriarty.

'Looks like another fine day!' he replied.

James Moriarty wondered if the next time he saw the vicar, he'd be conducting the funeral of Roddy Fingers, because he knew his friend had become lazy in this Edenic village. He'd grown fat and happy on scones and pints of real ale. The Tillingbourne had washed away his shrewder instincts. He'd been stupid enough to leave John Watson a message, and Moriarty knew that this lapse, this stupid, amateurish lapse, meant Roddy was probably already dead.

Chapter Thirty-Eight

ETHAN McDEE'S WIDOW WAS MOVING ON, JOHN THOUGHT to himself. She didn't think anyone can help her and she only agreed to see him today because a refusal would have appeared discourteous or worse, uncaring.

'I know Inspector Lestrade asked if there was anyone Ethan ever clashed with. Any business competitors, family members, former lovers—'

Annie snorted with laughter at this suggestion.

'...or old friends he'd fallen out with. You said you couldn't think of anyone.'

'Aye.'

'Have you revised that opinion?'

'Have I what, luv?'

'Have you changed your mind? Have you thought of anyone who...'

She was already shaking her head.

John diplomatically asked about Ethan's financial situation. Annie said they were in a good fiscal state. 'We're not rolling in it. But we're not going short, you know?' She gave a few examples of their hits and misses with grain deals over the past couple of years. John hoped he made the appropriate noises but was relieved when the kettle started to whistle.

Annie rose and used her left hand to lift the heavy kettle across to the drainer. She removed the teapot's lid, threw in a spoonful of loose PG Tips, and poured the boiling water over the leaves. This process entailed turning her back on John. He looked at the laptop and could see it rested on a thin sheaf of paper. A corner of one piece of A4 jutted out and John angled his head to read the black printed text that ran across it.

So when Annie turned and asked, 'Do you take sugar?' and caught him gawking at the edge of the document, it changed the atmosphere.

He replied, 'No, but a splash of milk would be great. Thanks.'

She didn't move. 'Do you want to know what my confidential paperwork is about? I could tell you. But then I'd have to kill you.'

She spoke the corny old line with such a straight-faced sobriety that John momentarily believed it was some sort of veiled threat. But the next second she was laughing, so John laughed, too, although he noticed that as she added milk to his tea, she kept half an eye on her inquisitive visitor.

She passed him the mug.

'Thanks, Annie.'

And as he blew on his tea he was already wondering how he could find a way to examine the papers below the laptop.

~

MORIARTY SLIPPED on a pair of thin, kid leather gloves and glanced over his shoulder to double check he wasn't being watched.

No one in sight. Perfect.

He didn't bother ringing the bell or calling to Roddy through the letterbox. The front door's Yale was a joke that surrendered almost before his picklock found its tumblers.

'Good for you!' Moriarty thought. It suggested Roddy had refused to live in fear. He pushed the door open and slipped inside the building. It had once been a house, and even now it felt more like a home filled with books than a traditional library.

There was a high counter in the hallway and on top of it, James spotted a mug with the words 'St. Jude's College' in gold lettering on its side. The final 'e' was at an angle to suggest the college itself was falling apart. Moriarty smiled. Glanced into it. Three inches of cold tea suggested an interruption. He touched the side of the mug. It was cool but not completely cold. Recent, then.

Moriarty stood still for a half-minute, listening. Eventually, satisfied he was alone, he moved through the library. The first room contained 'Children's Literature.' The second offered 'Non-fiction.' Roddy's corpse was in the third room, lying face up in the 'Crime' aisle. There was no sign of a struggle. It had been, Moriarty noted with relief, a professional job.

He removed one of his gloves, then stooped over Roddy's lifeless frame and put two fingers across the side of his neck, checking for a pulse that wasn't there. The dead man's flesh was still warm, like it didn't fancy the idea of death and wouldn't be cooperating with rigor mortis any time soon.

Moriarty put his glove back on and scanned the scene. A paperback had been placed on the dead man's chest.

Cover downwards. His watch, an Omega Seamaster worth about five grand, remained on his left wrist. Livid red marks about Roddy's throat indicated he'd been garrotted.

Moriarty murmured, 'I'm sorry, mate.'

He picked up the book and turned it around so he could check out the front cover. The title of the slim tome halted him for a moment. A grim joke made by the killer. A cheery, complicit wink to whoever found the corpse. The book was *The Body in the Library* by Agatha Christie.

Chapter Thirty-Nine

'WHAT SORT OF MAN WAS YOUR HUSBAND?'

Annie answered with words that John discerned she'd used many times before. *Kind. Caring. Eco-conscious.* John recognized the cadence of her voice. It was the same timbre he fell into when he found himself giving the same talk for the tenth time. Not mendacious, as such. But the retelling of facts somehow diminishes them. The narrative becomes just that — a narrative. A story. This wasn't even how Annie wanted to remember her husband. It was how she wanted other people to remember him.

They drank tea and her impromptu eulogy continued. She outlined Ethan McDee's green credentials. No artificial pesticides on the crops. Electric tractors. Biodegradable packaging for all their shipping wraps. He'd hired former prison convicts to help with harvests. 'Not fancy work — but it gave them a foot in the door, you know?'

Annie explained her husband had never employed men put away for 'rape or kiddy fiddling.' She added they both thought that type of criminal 'should be hung from the yard arm, then cut down and used as mulch.' She finished her tea. 'Do you agree?'

It was the first pointed thing she'd said.

John hardly paused. He smiled. 'I'm not sure what *mulch* is.'

She remained amiable but at arm's length. John recalled her welcome — how she'd brushed aside his hand and hugged him. He pondered why that had been.

'I wonder — could I have a photograph of Ethan?'

'Nothing easier. Give me your phone number. I'll send you a recent one.'

'This may sound like a strange request, but could I have one of your husband when he was younger? In his twenties.'

Annie was pointed for the second time. 'What for?'

'It's a technique Sherlock Holmes taught me. It helps us understand the man if we see him at different points in his life.'

Absolute tripe, he thought.

John, who simply wanted to get her out of the room — he had no use whatsoever for an old picture of Ethan — hoped he sounded plausible.

Annie eyed him.

'If it's too much trouble…' he began innocently.

'No.' She rose. 'Wait there.'

'Thanks very much.'

Annie left the door open and John could hear her walking up the flight of stairs.

He lifted the laptop, tugged the papers across the tabletop and began to read them. He became engrossed by the documents' contents, flicking through them quickly but establishing beyond any doubt the story they told, and how it disproved something Annie had said to him.

John was so caught up in the papers he didn't notice the face at the window, starring at him as he continued his illicit work.

Chapter Forty

MORIARTY EXAMINED THE BOOK, *THE BODY IN THE Library*. The cover illustration showed the shadow of a woman, arms raised in self-defence, cowering in front of a bookshelf. Another set of shadows — a pair of arms lunging towards her — indicated she was being attacked.

He riffled through the paperback, but nothing fell from its pages. Moriarty took a glasses case from his pocket. It contained his Ray-Bans and a small, pencil-thin metallic cylinder with the words LENS CLEANER on its side. He sprayed a thin sheen of the liquid it contained across the front of the book, then turned the tube around and pressed an indentation below its aerosol head. An ultraviolet light beamed from the lower end of the cylinder.

The fluid was in actuality a compound of thenoyl europium chelate, essentially a fat binding agent, and an everyday dye. It ensured latent fingerprints would be rendered visible when scrutinized by a UV light source, but the book's cover was totally print free, suggesting it had been wiped clean.

Moriarty turned the paperback over and repeated the

check on its back cover. He found a three-quarters print on the top right-hand side corner.

'Gotcha…'

He took out his phone, applied an inbuilt bespoke yellow filter, much finer than most on the open market, and took a snap of the partial. A moment later, he'd sent it to Colonel Sébastienne Moran, requesting an ID if possible.

He'd not even put his phone away when the reply came through: 'On it.'

Moriarty opened the book. On the inside cover he saw the library loan slip that had been glued in place. Below 'SHERE VILLAGE LIBRARY' was a snaking list of dates indicating when the paperback had been borrowed and the days it had been due for return. Below the last date Moriarty saw a curious marking that—

He froze.

A noise from the hallway, made loud by the surrounding silence.

He relaxed as he realized it was Roddy's post being delivered. He kept the paperback in his hand as he stood up. He wouldn't let the police find this grim joke. Roddy's demise wouldn't be associated with any humour, mordent or otherwise.

And something about the convenient partial print bothered him.

'Whoever did this to you will pay for it, Roddy.' He slipped the book into his inside pocket, and as he walked away from the shelves, he added softly, 'Goodbye, old friend.'

Chapter Forty-One

ANNIE MCDEE RAPPED ON THE WINDOWPANE. JOHN LOOKED up and, as if rifling through papers was the most natural thing in the world, he waved to her. She disappeared, and he estimated he had thirty seconds at most before she reached the back door and appeared back in the kitchen.

He glanced down at the papers. He recognized them well enough. Bills. Every single one a final demand. All of them a last chance before debtors sought recompense through the courts. And all the invoices had a black stamp diagonally across them in a bold, uppercase font: PAID. And below this single word, always the same marking. Always the same—

'What the hell do you think you're doing?'

Annie's reappearance had been swifter than John had anticipated. He resigned himself to styling it out. He offered a pantomime grimace. 'I just couldn't help myself. I was moving the papers because under the laptop they become a fire hazard. The heat from the motor can…' He trailed off. 'Couldn't resist talking a peek. Did you find a photo?'

'No.' She towered over him. 'And I think you'd better leave.'

John thanked her and she showed him to the door. Annie unlocked it using her right hand and said, 'I know you're just doing your job. No hard feelings, eh?'

'Thanks, Annie.'

She stepped forward as if to embrace him again. A farewell hug.

John took a pace back and grasped her right hand, shaking it with what could have passed for a firm politeness. She winced and pulled back sharply.

'Are you okay?'

'I'm fine. Running a farm is hard physical graft, John. I took a tumble from one of the tractors last week. I know I should go to A&E, but I'd be there for hours, and I've got too much to be getting on with.'

'I'm a doctor. I could take a look if you like?'

He knew she would say no. That it was fine.

'You're all right, luv. I'll be okay.'

'Thanks again for seeing me.'

And as he walked across the yard to the Volvo, the collies did their giddy circular dance around him again, but this time, Annie McDee didn't bother with the cheery wave.

MORIARTY WALKED THROUGH SHERE, past the pubs, past the cafes, past the shop selling the local gin, Silent Pool. He hung a right then an immediate left, and waited in the empty playground for John. The carpark was adjacent to the space, meaning he'd be able to spot his Volvo when it arrived. He sat on a swing and pushed himself back. It had been a bruising few hours.

His phone rang.

'Jamie, it's Sébastienne.'

'Any joy with the print?'

'Is this your little joke?'

He stopped swinging. 'No. Why would it be? What have you found?'

'We ran the print and scored a hit. I can tell you exactly who the print belongs to.'

'You got a result? That's great!'

'Not really.'

'Why? Who does the fingerprint identify?'

'You.' Colonel Sébastienne Moran paused. 'The print you sent across belongs to Professor James Moriarty.'

Chapter Forty-Two

JOHN ASKED, 'HOW DID YOU GET ON WITH GRAHAM Marsh?'

Moriarty paused. They were driving along the foot of the Surrey Hills, about four miles northeast of Guildford. 'It was a dead-end,' he replied. 'No answer when I reached the library. There was no way we could talk. Not my most constructive line of inquiry.'

He didn't mention the corpse or the fact whoever murdered his friend had tried to frame him using what must have been an artificially created fingerprint.

'To be honest, I kind of sensed it was a wild goose chase.'

'Kind of sensed?'

'Just a hunch. Why don't you tell Zenisha I'll follow it up. She needn't assign it.' He added, 'How did you get on with Mrs. McDee?'

John recounted his visit to Annie's farm. He concluded with, 'So the here's the question — who paid her bills? And why?'

'What are you thinking?'

'She knew who murdered her husband, and whoever settled those invoices was paying her off. The payments were the carrot. What happened to her wrist — the stick. We can get Lestrade to follow it all up. Find out where the money came from.'

'I can get my people to do that,' Moriarty countered. 'Much quicker.' He clicked his tongue. 'I don't know. If Annie knew who this serial killer is, could her silence be bought so easily? It feels unlikely.'

'Perhaps she was threatened, as well. The *stick* I mentioned.'

'You're thinking about the injury to her wrist? Good work spotting that, by the way. Text me what you recall of the invoices so I can delve a little deeper. And I'll check if it was something as prosaic as Annie getting money from life insurance Ethan had taken out.'

'Will do.'

'Fancy a brew?'

'Tea doesn't solve everything, you know.'

'True,' said Moriarty. 'But it's a bit early for wine.'

JOHN HAD PULLED into a layby and made the call to Zenisha, telling her to leave the Graham Marsh angle for the moment. She agreed and assured him that she hadn't yet passed the lead on. When John told Moriarty the news, he hid his relief well. Now both men leant against the side of the Volvo, facing the road. The traffic gave them a reason not to look at each other, something which always makes delicate conversations flow with greater fluidity.

Moriarty said, 'I like laybys. It always feels like you've pulled over from life and you're watching other people still racing away.' They were drinking tea from polystyrene cups. He held his up. 'I thought these were against the law these days.'

'You're chatting about the legality of synthetic mugs? You've already murdered four men this week.'

'Don't kill-shame me, man!'

'Oh, god. Don't start talking like a millennial.'

'Hey — *I am enough!*'

'You're more than enough.'

Moriarty removed the lid from his cup and watched steam waft from the tea. 'Back in Reichenbach, at the end, I realized I had a chance to start a new life. Sounds seductive, doesn't it?'

'Maybe. Yeah, I suppose so.'

'People always say they want to start a new life. But they *really* mean they want to adapt their old one. They simply want to change jobs, move house. Start wearing different clothes. Maybe get a new partner. For me, though, it had to be everything or nothing. I thought I could do it, but...'

John sipped his tea. 'So you disappeared for three years. What's that got to do with the Teardrop Killer?'

'After I left, a kind of chaos set in. The crime rate went through the roof because I wasn't there to regulate it. Oh, I can see you look sceptical, John, but without me at its centre, controlling and cajoling, what happened? Murder rates, theft, white collar crime — all of it rocketed! I watched it rise from afar. And it gradually struck me that there was a structure to it. A structure to the apparent chaos that took over. But this new influence controlling the underworld was something more malign and brutal than I'd ever felt the need to become.'

'You're saying someone took over from you?'

'Yes.'

'Who?'

'The Red Circle.'

John shook his head. Even gave a small laugh. 'The Red Circle is just a bedtime story to scare coppers and crims.'

'I've no firm idea who's running it. I suspect a woman, but honestly, that's only an intuition.'

'Well, if you're right about the Red Circle's existence, it must be a huge organization. Like the one you ran,' he added pointedly. 'You must know something about a syndicate of that size!'

'You make knowledge sound so bountiful, Johnny. I can't just go on Reddit and ask whoever's running it to do an AMA session so we can—'

'Don't patronize me!' John interjected. 'I was helping to bring down OCRs when you were still running through Switzerland, pretending to be dead.'

'Sorry, mate.'

'And this organization. The Red Circle. You think they're responsible for the Teardrop Killer murders?'

'It's possible.' Moriarty nodded. 'It's very possible.'

'What would be the point?'

'I don't know. And that's what sticks in my craw. Most murders are easy to understand. They're often tawdry and terrible, but they have a simplicity in their origins. These killings are like murder as a mechanism. But for what? To scare people? To reach the Prime Minister? To reach you? Me? Both of us? Lestrade? *What is a teardrop?* And why do these crimes feel connected to so many other things? And then Andrew Redford's daughter keeps making jokes about an old family pet. Why does that bother me so much?'

John looked away from the streaks of traffic tearing along the road in front of him. He read the confusion and discomfort on Moriarty's face. Without knowing why, he asked a question on impulse. 'Was it easier being on the other side? Was criminality easier?'

Moriarty glanced at him as if weighing up whether to reply. He took a breath and said, 'I didn't specialize in criminality. That would have been a doddle. I specialized in imposing order on it. And that's never easy. Even at the best of times, it felt like I was standing in a blizzard trying to conduct the snowflakes falling around me.'

'You make it sound so poetic.'

'That wasn't my intention.'

'How did you become Professor Moriarty?' John didn't take his eyes off the road. 'I mean, you were an academic. Science, wasn't it? Then all of a sudden you're what — the Emperor of Crime. What the hell happened?'

'Believe me, it wasn't a career progression I saw coming.' Moriarty sighed again. 'It all began when I tried to help the world.' He sniffed. Looked at John. 'They say no good deed goes unpunished. But believe me, no great deed arrives peaceably.'

'What was your great deed?'

'My final paper. It should have turned the world of science upside down.'

'What happened?'

He thought back. To a time of Beth Spencer. To a time before Professor Moriarty. 'It turned *my* world upside down,' he replied, and there was no satisfaction in his answer. Only sadness.

Chapter Forty-Three

THEY WERE BACK ON THE ROAD, DRIVING TOWARDS London.

Moriarty lowered his window another couple of inches, as if hoping the air rushing into the car might help clear his head. 'These murders,' he began. 'The victims. The teardrops. The anomalies. Every strand feels like a thread of gossamer. But I can't see the web they're all part of. Dammit, John! Why can't I see it?'

'Don't think about it and it'll come to you. Focus on something else. I was interested by what you were saying in the layby. How you got started.'

He shrugged. 'What's the point in going over it?' He suddenly sounded listless. Not unhelpful or contrary, as such. Just bored by things he could no longer change. 'It's all in the past. Listen, if you're going to propose me for membership of humanity, I better try some of that kind-ness stuff.'

'What did you have in mind? Are you going to start helping old ladies cross the road?'

'I'll begin with you. What do you need help with?'

'What makes you think I need help? Apart from the fact I'm still grieving for my best friend and now I'm having to work with his killer.'

Moriarty ignored the magnesium flash of bitterness. 'I was thinking more financial.'

John's eyes widened. 'Have you accessed my bank statements?'

'I didn't have to! It's all over the internet. You've been losing court cases all over the shop. That's an expensive hobby, mate.'

'The laws of libel in this country are mad. A newspaper can print the foulest lies, yet I'm the one getting sued left, right, and centre for things that actually happened but I can't prove!'

'Such as?'

'Can we drop it?'

'Come on! I might be able to help. Who's suing you at the moment?'

John replied with more than a hint of venom in his voice. 'The estate of Grimesby Roylott.'

'Grimesby Roylott. The Speckled Band guy?'

'The Speckled Band guy.'

'Does his daughter-in-law represent the estate?'

'Helen Stoner. Yup!' John's exasperation was obvious. 'Holmes helped her! We proved her stepfather murdered her own sister for her inheritance, and this is how she repays me! Unbelievable! She's now claiming we had insufficient evidence against Roylott and therefore my crime memoir, *The Speckled Band*, is libellous because he might not have been the killer.'

Moriarty sat up. Interested. Alert. 'Well, to be fair, he wasn't the killer.'

'What the hell do *you* know about the case?'

'I read your account! It was ridiculous! I mean, no offence, but did you ever stop to think about what Sherlock was claiming?'

'There was a reason they called him the Great Detective, you know.'

'Great defective, more like.'

'Defective? Brilliant. That's right up there with CHIS-take.'

Moriarty acknowledged the substandard pun with a bowing of his head. 'But let's examine it .Sherlock genuinely wanted us to believe that Grimesby Roylott trained a snake — *a snake!* — to slide through an air vent, like it was John McClane in *Die Hard*. Then find a certain room, then slither down a bell rope, and *then* bite his intended victim. I mean — come on!'

John remained silent.

Moriarty laughed. Pressed on. 'And then Sherlock claimed that Roylott had trained this magic adder to respond to a whistle and slide back towards it when he gave a toot on it! Oh my god — that's hilarious!' More laughter, although he stopped himself to add, 'And how does he claim Roylott incentivized the snake to return? A saucer of milk! Haha! Reptiles don't even drink milk! Giving milk to a snake would kill it! Sherlock's whole case was ridiculous.' He managed to stem his chuckling. 'Helen Stoner will sue the arse off you unless you let me help.'

They drove along the Hog's Back without exchanging words for another half a mile.

'You really think Holmes's reasoning was flawed? That there's more to the case than I realized?'

'It's not just about the snake — although Sherlock's claims about that were ridiculous enough. I mean, what was all that guff about Julia Stoner's last words to Helen as she was dying? She was supposedly desperate to let her sister know what had happened … So she said, *the Speckled Band!*' Moriarty shook his head. 'Why didn't she just say, *I've been bitten by a fucking big snake!*'

'The account of that came directly from Helen. You think she was lying?'

'Of course she was lying.'

'Even if I did want to revisit Holmes's deductions, we found Grimesby Roylott dead — bitten by the swamp adder. So he's hardly in any position to clarify the situation.'

'Yeah. I remember now. Roylott died before you could question him, right? That was convenient. Look, have you got Helen Stoner's number?'

'I think so. Yeah, from when we originally took her case.'

'Give me your phone.'

'What for?'

'So I can save you a stack of cash.'

'It doesn't feel right.'

'Neither does you getting taken to the cleaners by Stoner the moaner.'

John handed over his phone, uneasily, like opening his mouth for a dentist.

Moriarty accessed the contacts and made a call. 'Hi! Is this Helen Stoner? Great. You knew my brother. Sherlock Holmes. My name's Mycroft.'

John hissed, 'What the hell are you doing?'

Moriarty ignored him. 'Yeah, *Mycroft*. I know, right? My parents and crazy names. It was kind of their thing. We even had a sister called Mephistopheles … No, that was a joke, Miss Stoner!'

John was making frantic gestures, imploring him to end the conversation. But he pressed on.

'I just wanted to say, I support your case against John Watson entirely. He made my brother look like an idiot. So anything I can do to help…' He winked at John. 'Oh, and Miss Stoner, let me phrase this diplomatically in case this call is being bugged. I know who *really* murdered your sister. I went through Sherlock's personal records a couple of years ago, and he knew damn well who was to blame. I'd have contacted you sooner, but I've only just tracked down a key witness. The man who sold the swamp adder, the so-called Speckled Band, to the killer.'

Moriarty broke off to beam at John. It was a smile of mischievous delight.

Returning to the call he said, 'Of course I don't want to go public! Actually, thinking about it, maybe having my brother look like an idiot is the best way out of this. I never did like him, to be honest. When we were kids, he used to practice the violin first thing in the morning — god, that used to get on my nerves! Tell you what — I'll forget all about this whole thing if you drop your suit against John Watson.'

Moriarty listened for a moment.

'Yes? Fabulous! Oh, and send him a cheque for ten grand to cover any legal expenses he's already accrued. Actually, let's be generous. Let's make it twenty thousand pounds. It's still a mere fraction of the inheritance you received, and it always feels good to give a little bit back, doesn't it?'

He gave John a thumbs up.

'Lovely to do business with you, Miss Stoner. And there's no rush with the cheque. Any time in the next 24 hours is fine. Ciao ciao, miaow!' He ended the call and handed John his phone. 'Sorted!'

'What … what did you just do?'

'Johnny! It's blatantly obvious that Helen murdered her

sister and then fixed it for Grimesby to be killed so he'd take the blame and she could claim the whole inheritance!'

'But Roylott sent the snake into Helen's room!'

'Did you actually see it there? No! In your account, you admit you saw nothing! In fact, you only saw the snake for a moment *after* it had apparently killed Roylott. I'm guessing Helen orchestrated that hours earlier. If you take a second and actually stop believing everything Helen told you, the case becomes quite simple. Julia was killed and Roylott was killed. Helen therefore got all the money. Hmmm, I wonder who could have had motive, means, and opportunity…'

'But why on earth would Sherlock tell the world Roylott was the killer? He must have known Helen was behind the whole thing!'

'I'm sure he did.' Moriarty shrugged. 'But Roylott was a prick. He threatened Sherlock. Maybe it was petty revenge. Maybe it was because he liked Helen. Maybe he took a cut of the inheritance.'

'How dare you! Sherlock Holmes was a man of integrity!'

'Who wanted you to believe that someone was training a swamp adder using a saucer of milk. Come off it, John!'

'What are you saying?'

When Moriarty replied, there was no triumph in his voice. 'That not all snakes are Speckled Bands.'

THE ATTACK HAPPENED FAST and without warning.

They'd arrived back in Baker Street an hour and a half after leaving the layby. John had pulled up outside 221B. 'I'll drop you here and park around the corner.'

'Sounds good.'

Moriarty got out of the car. He sensed, rather than heard or saw, a sudden movement. But the first three men jumped him before he had a chance to look over his shoulder. John thought he glimpsed a syringe, but recounting the event afterwards, he realized he couldn't be sure.

Moriarty pivoted to his right, sending a sharp jab into the throat of one attacker, who instantly dropped to the pavement, gurgling and clutching his neck. Another man was now facing Moriarty, holding him at close quarters. He arched his back, as if shaping up to deliver a head but. But the professor was too speedy and too vicious for him; his hand was already in the guy's face, his fingers pushing his eyeballs into his skull.

John was quickly out of the car.

As he darted around the hood, the second man Moriarty had fought off was back-peddling and screaming in blind plain. But more thugs were piling onto Moriarty, and John saw his body go limp. Before he could reach the pavement, the men were carrying their unconscious victim to a van parked meters away.

'Moriarty! Hang on, I'm—'

John felt a blow from behind. It was a simple shove to his shoulders, but it sent him crashing into the gutter. He looked up and glimpsed Moriarty being thrown into the back of the van. It took off as the doors were being pulled shut from inside.

The man who had pushed John now stood over him. He was holding a handgun — something small, like a Kimber Micro 9 or one of the more compact Wilson Combats. John didn't have time to take it in.

Two shots rang out in quick succession, then the gunman was gone.

John groaned but got rapidly to his feet. The Volvo's passenger-side tires had both been blasted, meaning pursuit was impossible. Meanwhile, the van had already accelerated away. John saw it hang a left and disappear.

'Jesus…'

In the space of thirty seconds, Professor Moriarty had been set upon, neutralized, and kidnapped.

Chapter Forty-Four

After a half-hour journey, James Moriarty was brusquely hauled from the back of the van. A dark cowl had been rammed over his head and his wrists were shackled by handcuffs, so he cut a forlorn figure as he was pulled, pushed, and frogmarched on his way by a handful of sneering guards who revelled in treating their prisoner roughly.

'I'd be grateful if you removed these handcuffs,' Moriarty said. His tone was relaxed and reasonable. He could have been ordering off-menu at the Savoy Grill. 'There's at least five of you. Surely I don't represent a threat.'

He was pushed to ground. 'Get up and shut up.'

'You'll regret that.'

Someone booted his shoulder. 'Up!'

Moriarty clambered to his feet. More walking. The pace slowed after twelve paces. He felt himself entering a building. Sensed carpet underfoot and heard the nondescript hum of a fully staffed office in the near distance. Someone grasped his elbow tightly and he was escorted into the heart of a warm complex that smelt of disinfectant. Down a staircase — no more carpet — and made to wait in a cold, quiet room. After 27 seconds — he counted them — Moriarty was on the move again. Only a short stroll this time, then another pause.

He heard a gruff, deep voice. 'Walk forward three paces, then go down a flight of stairs. Get on with it. I've had a bad day.'

'One sympathizes.'

Another voice added, 'And go careful on the first step. I don't wanna have to wipe your blood from the handrail.'

'Don't worry, I won't fall,' Moriarty interrupted. 'I know my way around Q-Whitehall.'

For a moment, nobody responded. Moriarty knew his captors would be exchanging stares of bewilderment. Probably mouthing, *How did he know?* and wondering whether they should inform their superiors that despite their best efforts, he was aware of his location.

One of the guards barked, 'Just do as you're told!'

'Never got round to learning that trick,' Moriarty admitted. 'Let's get on with it, shall we? All this pushing and shoving a man in handcuffs must be great fun for you chaps, but I'm bored to tears.'

Q-Whitehall was the title given to an underground complex beneath Central London. Despite its name, the tunnels, rooms, and storage areas it comprised extended far beyond Whitehall, although it started life there in the 1940s — a subterranean centre carved out of the ground below various Westminster offices.

Some of Q-Whitehall was openly acknowledged. The passages leading to the Admiralty Citadel and the bunker that served as the UK's Defence Crisis Management Centre have been well documented for years. But the vast majority of its network remained a closely guarded secret.

Since 2001, it had invisibly grown into a vast, other

city. Some parts of it didn't officially exist but had become relatively well-known. The so-called 'electro-hive' constructed in the early 2020s, and the much older Osiris Bunker, for instance, were both routinely acknowledged off the record. But the 'Ten Suite', a full-sized replica of rooms within 10 Downing Street, was seldom spoken of. The PM was whisked to this fortified lair in times of absolute crisis (this covert procedure had only been activated three times) and can broadcast to the nation from any of the suite's rooms, giving the reassuring appearance of being ensconced in the familiar official, prime ministerial residence.

Professor James Moriarty knew all of this and more.

As one of the guards typed in a passcode sequence at the bottom of the staircase, thereby unlocking a steel door that led into a distribution passage, he spoke the digits out loud as each number was pressed. 'If I know the code,' he said, 'you might wish to consider how long it'll take me to establish the names of the security detail that have shown me such disrespect.' He paused to give his words time to sink in. 'Good luck sleeping at night, gentlemen. And don't think a posting to the Sudan or Somalia will help you. My reach is broad and my capacity for forgiveness — *thin*.'

The next time he was taken by the elbow, the grasp was gentler, and the guard called him 'Sir'.

After a brisk 15-minute walk, Moriarty was cautiously guided up another staircase. He again felt carpet underfoot and could smell fresh paint.

'Almost there, are we?'

'This is where we hand you over.'

'Well, it's been fun. I won't bother leaving a review on TripAdvisor, but I'll be in touch.'

He heard a door open and someone stepped into the room. The new arrival sounded mortified. 'What? What is this? Take off the gentleman's cowl and uncuff him — at once!'

'He's our prisoner, sir!'

'He's also our guest!' He raised his voice a little. 'Professor Moriarty — has anyone even offered you a cup of tea?'

One of the guards spluttered, 'Tea?'

'Yes! Good god, man! We're English! Kidnapping is perfectly acceptable, but a loss of decorum is not.'

Moriarty said, 'A mug of Earl Grey would be very welcome. Just a splash of milk.'

The handcuffs were removed, but the guards insisted that the cowl remain in place until their prisoner had been delivered to 'the big man.' That had been a stipulation of the job.

'I'm most dreadfully sorry, Professor.'

'It's not your fault.'

'By the way, I read your book. *The Dynamics of an Asteroid*. A remarkable achievement. I loved it.'

'You're very kind. I'd be happy to sign your copy. If I make it out of here alive, that is.'

'Wouldn't that be jolly?'

Unable to read the man's face, Moriarty wasn't sure if he meant getting his autograph or surviving the next couple of hours.

TWO MORE FLIGHTS of stairs and a very short walk later, Moriarty was positioned — he somehow thought it was in front of a desk — and he felt eyes watching him. The man who had offered him tea said, 'This is Professor Moriarty. At the risk of speaking out of place — can we *please* remove his cowl? We're not barbarians.'

Moriarty said, 'You may not be, Mr. Phelps. But the jury is still out on your boss.'

He heard a momentary burst of laughter and short, ironic applause. As it petered out, he added, 'I can't say it's a pleasure to meet you, Mr. Redford.'

Moriarty's cowl was removed, and he found himself face-to-face with the Prime Minister.

Chapter Forty-Five

'WELCOME TO 10 DOWNING STREET, PROFESSOR Moriarty.'

Without being invited to do so, Moriarty took a seat. 'Oh, I've been here many times before.'

Redford didn't conceal his disbelief. 'Really?'

Phelps placed a cup of tea on the desk in front the professor.

'You're very kind — thank you.'

'Biscuits?'

Redford cut in. 'Phelps!'

'Sorry, sir.'

'Where was I? Oh, yes. I've been here on business and for social calls. I helped out quite a few of your predecessors.'

'You?'

'Well, of course!' Moriarty had raised his voice. 'Isn't it obvious? Even for an MP? Who do you think tidied up after the infamous Smith-Mortimer succession case? Or averted war with Canada following the Addleton tragedy? And I still shudder when I recall the fiasco with the politician, the lighthouse, and the trained cormorant that I only just managed to—'

A knock at the door interrupted his flow. John Watson and Zenisha Lestrade were shown into the room. Moriarty turned to watch their arrival. 'Did either of you know Redford intended to kidnap me? No, I see from your faces that you didn't.'

'I didn't kidnap you! I had you detained under covert conditions.'

'Don't play word games with me, Redford.'

The Prime Minister's face hardened and his tone became sharper. Tougher. 'Oh, this isn't some cosy get-together, Moriarty. I despise you. I loathe every murdering ruffian like you. If we didn't need your help to capture the Teardrop Killer, I'd have thrown the book at you.'

'Many have tried. Most of them more powerful than you. All of them more intelligent.'

'Don't fence with me.'

'Don't fuck with me.'

'Gentlemen!' John took a step forward. 'We're supposed to be working together. When this murderer is caught, we can all go back to hating each other. But until then…'

Zenisha said, 'Doctor Watson is right. Prime Minister, sir, there must have been a reason you brought us all here?'

'Oh, there is!' Moriarty replied. 'Redford was peeved by my little display in Westminster the other night. This is *his* show of strength. This is your glorious leader hoping to demonstrate that he has nerve and resources and that I need to watch my step.'

'Are you insane?' Redford looked startled. 'I don't care about your childish little pantomimes. I had you brought here because you threatened my daughter. And that I will not tolerate!'

'I threatened your…' Clearly nonplussed, Moriarty insisted, 'I've never threatened Millie! Why would I?'

'You told Inspector Lestrade she could be in danger. Your implication was clear.'

'In danger — yes. But not from me.'

Zenisha interjected, 'To be fair, sir, the professor's comments about your daughter didn't come across as threatening.'

'Don't be taken in by this man, Inspector. Moriarty remains a dangerous criminal with the blood of countless people on his hands.'

Moriarty stood up. 'That's a bit rich coming from a British Prime Minister.'

John hissed, 'Working. *Together.*'

The PM took a breath. 'Yes, you're quite right, Doctor.'

Moriarty nodded. Wiped his palm across his face. 'I never threatened your daughter. Quite the reverse. I was concerned for her.'

'I hope so. Truly. And in the spirit of our new coopera-tion, I'd *like* to believe you. But can you give me any proof?'

'Is my word not good enough for you?'

'I'm afraid not.'

'Then you force me to be blunt. Is that acceptable?'

'Always.'

Moriarty half-turned. Looked at John. His expression seemed to ask, *'What else can I do?'* He retook his seat. Ran his fingers through his hair. 'I didn't threaten Millie. There would be no point.'

Redford tried to keep his voice steady. 'What do you mean by that?'

'Prime Minister, if I'm right, your daughter is already dead.'

Chapter Forty-Six

Andrew Redford opened his mouth but found his famous powers of oratory were suddenly defunct. He looked from Moriarty to Zenisha and John, and finally gave the slightest, shortest laugh before doing what most would do when confronted with a claim they find too catastrophic to accept. 'That's absolute nonsense!'

'You invited me to be blunt.'

'This is the kind of lowlife we're dealing with!' Redford pointed at Moriarty. 'Trying to scare me with tactics like this. Appalling. You should be ashamed of yourself!'

'Oh, I frequently am. But in this instance, I'm telling you the truth.'

'You're saying Millie is…'

'Dead. Yes. It's not an absolute certainty. But in all probability…'

John eased his way past Zenisha. 'Are you all right, Andrew? Stupid question. Of course you're not. Moriarty, can you give some context to your claim?'

'He doesn't need to!' Redford exclaimed. 'I'm in constant contact with Millie!'

'No.' Moriarty shook his head. 'No, you're really not.'

'I speak to her every day!'

'No!' Moriarty took a deep breath. 'If I'm right, you haven't spoken to your daughter for a long, long time.'

THEY GATHERED around the Prime Minister's laptop. Redford sat at his desk in his personal office, opened the computer, pressed a couple of keys, and its screen sprang to life. Moriarty, Zenisha, John, and Percy Phelps stood behind his chair. There was a charged but dismal atmosphere between them. It was the kind of situation that would often be called a car crash, except this was worse. They were waiting for the crash. For a collision involving one of their loved ones. Because Redford had agreed to FaceTime his daughter.

Moriarty handed him what appeared to be a USB stick. 'Could you put this your laptop, please?'

'Has it been security cleared by IT?'

'No. But it will help us.'

It was a measure of Redford's state of mind that he simply mumbled, 'All right.'

Moriarty made a brief call. 'Colonel? The breaker is almost in place. Can your people trace the call? And this is important — I'd like them to break through the covering interface as quickly as possible. Doesn't matter if it's not pretty. Just bring it down.'

Redford inserted the USB.

'It's in place now. Have you got it? Is it transmitting?' A pause. 'Good! Thanks for your help! Any problems, let me know.' He hung up. 'All right, Prime Minister. Make the call.'

The PM used the sequence he activated every day to

contact his daughter. Moments later, her face appeared on the screen.

'Daddy? What's wrong?' She looked to be in her late teens. She had her mother's deep brown eyes and fair, fine hair lashed back, although strands of her long fringe still fell across her face. Behind her, a small, basic hotel room was visible. 'You don't normally call at this time. I was just going out. Is everything okay?'

Redford beamed. 'Everything is more than all right, darling. I was just worried about you. That's all. You're absolutely sure everything is good with you?'

'More than good! The forecast was for rain, but it's holding off! Result! Why were you suddenly concerned?'

'That's a dad's prerogative. Listen, if you're fine, I've got to dash.'

'Sure! Speak soon?'

'Count on it.'

Moriarty leant forward. He whispered. 'Ask her about her morning.'

Redford paused. 'Before you go — what have you been up to today?'

'Oh, you wouldn't believe it! You know I told you about the taxi driver who…'

And as she spoke, Moriarty placed a piece of paper on the desk. It contained three words. Redford's eyes darted to the message. It read: SHE WON'T GLITCH.

And sure enough, as Millie recounted a run-in with a local driver, the audio and video feed remained perfect. As she neared the end of her story, Moriarty murmured, 'Now ask her about an early family holiday. The first time she swam in the sea … a time she got separated from you and Tania. Anything like that.'

'No!'

John said, 'I'd be inclined to take his advice — on this occasion, Prime Minister.'

He nodded. 'Guess what, Millie. I bumped into Archie and Shell the other day.'

'Oh! How are they?'

'They're well. We got to talking about that holiday we went on. That long weekend on the French coast. Seems a lifetime ago. You got any memories of it?'

'I remember we all had a nice time. We were only there a few days, weren't we?'

Moriarty said quietly. 'You already told her that. Ask her something specific.'

Pen in hand, he reached over Redford's shoulder and crossed out one word of his previous message and wrote in another which he underlined.

Redford said, 'Do you remember breaking your finger? We thought it was just badly bruised, but you insisted it was broken, and you were right! I was arguing with Archie about how you did it. My memory must be going. Remind me how it happened, luv.'

He shot a glance at the amended message. It now read, SHE <u>WILL</u> GLITCH.

'Well, it was a long time ago, Daddy! Hey, I've really got to go. Can I settle the argument later?'

'How did you break your finger, Millie?'

She paused. 'Well, we'd all gone down to the French Coast and—'

The audio became distorted and faded completely as the picture of the young woman became grainy before dropping out. The occasional word could be heard. 'Finger … hurt … holiday…' and glimpses of Millie, hidden by white lines and interference continued to be relayed.

Moriarty said, 'In every call you have with your daughter, whenever you ask her a specific question that's private to you and your family, the feed drops out. I knew that couldn't be coincidence.' He glanced at his phone. 'Message from the Colonel. She's almost broken through. We have to keep her on the line just a few seconds longer.'

'No!' Redford spoke forcefully but without conviction. 'I'm satisfied she's well and nothing is wrong.'

The onscreen image stabilized and the audio crackled back into place. They heard Millie say, '…but it's fine now! Anyway, Dad, I've really got to go.'

'All right…' There were tears forming in Redford's eyes. 'I love you, darling.'

'Love you too.'

Moriarty half pushed the PM to one side and stooped into the line of the laptop's camera. 'My name is James Moriarty. I work with your father. And I don't think you're real.'

The woman's eyes widened. 'Are you serious?'

'I'm afraid so. When Millie Redford was six years old, she stood at the lectern of her dad's party conference. And not knowing the mic was switched on, she recited a nursery rhyme. Do that now and prove to me I'm wrong. Just recite the nursery rhyme.'

Her eyes looked to Redford. 'Daddy?'

He nodded. 'If you could do that, darling. For me.'

She smiled. 'Sure.'

Zenisha whispered, 'That clip went viral! Everyone knows it!'

Moriarty hit the mute button. 'Doesn't matter. We just need to keep comms open for another few seconds longer so the Colonel can get us the real feed.'

Millie began, *'Humpty Dumpty sat on the wall…'*

The image flickered slightly. *'Humpty Dumpty had a great fall…'*

Moriarty said, 'The Colonel's breaking through!'

And now the sound of Millie's words became mangled and stretched. Sinister. Her voice fluctuated between a soft, feminine timbre and a harsher, much more guttural tone. *'All the king's horses…'*

The young woman on the screen glimmered bright, but when the glow quickly faded, someone else could be seen in her place. This figure glitched and Millie returned.

'And all the king's men…'

A final glitch. Millie snapped from the screen completely and the oral fluctuation stopped.

Moriarty said, 'You've been talking to an actor whose lines, image, and voice have all been AI generated.'

The white lines and interference had vanished from the call. But Millie had also vanished. In her place, a large man in his forties was visible. He had swarthy, pock-mocked skin, unkempt black, curly hair, and he wore a khaki jacket. He clearly had no idea his interface had been compromised, and he finished the nursery rhyme.

'Couldn't put Humpty together again.'

Andrew Redford breathed, 'My god…'

And the man on the screen smiled a crooked smile. 'Did you like that, Daddy?'

Chapter Forty-Seven

THE PRIME MINISTER SLAMMED THE OPEN PALM OF HIS right hand onto the desktop. 'What have you done with Millie?'

Moriarty said, 'He's hardly likely to tell us,' then pivoted the laptop so its camera pointed directly at his own face. 'I've told you who I am, so you know I don't make idle threats…'

The man onscreen who'd been masquerading as Millie looked shocked.

'I'm working with Andrew Redford. That makes him my ally. If his daughter is dead, the men responsible will die. Everyone else in your organization has twenty-four hours to disappear. Melt away. Leave its ranks. Let them know. I don't care how you do it. Just do it. I guess you think your boss can protect you, but that isn't the case. No one can protect you, now.'

He moved slightly closer to the laptop.

'I'm declaring war on your syndicate. Tell your colleagues they can leave the field of battle or face the consequences. I don't take excuses. I don't prisoners. But I do take screengrabs. And you're first on my list.'

He closed the lid of the laptop.

Redford said, 'Is Millie dead?'

Moriarty shrugged. 'Probably. I figured the people behind all this were using an AI-generated interface to create what was in effect an avatar of your daughter. She kept mentioning a family joke. Why would she do that? It struck me that the joke had been fed into a set of AI algorithms as something Millie would do. But that's the problem with AI. No nuance. And it didn't have enough information, so it kept re-using the data it did have.'

John said, 'And that's why you were suspicious when you read the transcripts your source provided. The feed would glitch at certain moments.'

'Always when the conversation turned to something that a third party couldn't possibly know.'

Redford was still struggling to take in the tragedy. 'But two agents are with her. They've reported to me on a daily basis.'

'The reports could have been faked. Or the agents coerced into making them.'

Zenisha asked, 'Why would anyone want to harm Millie and then create a kind of replica?'

Moriarty puffed out his cheeks and exhaled. 'My best guess? They took Millie. She tried to escape and was killed. Possibly accidentally. That's when they had to resort to the AI interface.'

Redford could only say, 'But why?'

'I honestly don't know,' Moriarty admitted.

John said, 'But you think it's connected with the Teardrop Killer?'

'Oh, the Teardrop Killer is just the tip of the iceberg.

One that makes the iceberg that sunk the Titanic look like a minor inconvenience.'

'Professor Moriarty…' Redford was keeping his voice low and level, but he sounded like a man on the verge of cracking. 'You must do everything in your power to find my daughter — if she's still alive. You must smash this syndicate of terror. Completely and utterly … using any means at your disposal. Do you understand me? *Any means!*' He clutched Moriarty's forearm. 'Give me your word.'

'I can't promise you anything. But I'll do what I can.'

This reply was a rare slip from James Moriarty. The moment he uttered the words, he realized his error and glanced over at John. He became aware, instantaneously, that the doctor had picked up on his lapse. Neither man said anything, but Moriarty knew John was thinking about the implications for Troy Domingo, the husband of the Teardrop Killer's first victim.

The ensuing silence was broken by Percy Phelps. He'd remained quiet throughout the facetime call and subsequent exchange, but he was first to the obvious question. 'So what do we do now?'

Moriarty was studying his phone and without looking up, replied, 'The Colonel should have traced the origin of the call soon. She says it's close. So, Prime Minister, could you have a car waiting for me and Doctor Watson? I'll drive.'

Redford nodded. 'And I can have a dozen of my best men detailed to help you immediately.'

'No!' Moriarty interrupted. 'Your men would have to follow the rules of engagement. If we find the building where that call was played out, I want to be able to go in and sort it out my way. Having Special Branch or MI5 personnel with me would simply bind my hands with red tape.'

'I understand. Percy — can you organize transport straight away?'

'Of course, sir!' Phelps had that English civil servant's knack of being in the room and then not being in the room, although no one actually saw him leave or even cross the floor.

'Moriarty — what are the chances Millie is still alive?'

Moriarty sounded tetchy. 'As I've already said, I—'

John cut him off. 'The truth is, Prime Minister, none of us knows. Not for certain. Now that's bad. It's hell. But it gives us one thing. Hope. So hold onto that. Don't let yourself crumble. At this moment, that would be selfish. Because Millie might need you. Yeah?'

'Yeah. Thank you. You've got a way with words.' The PM managed a half-smile. 'You should have been in politics.'

Moriarty was suddenly rushing from the room. 'The Colonel came up trumps! We know where the call was coming from!' He paused in the doorway and addressed John directly. 'Let's go!'

MORIARTY GLANCED AT HIS PHONE. 'Target location is less than eight minutes away!'

As they hurtled down Horse Guards Road in one of the PM's Range Rover Sentinels, John said, 'You told Redford that you couldn't make any promises.'

'Yes. I knew you'd pick up on that.'

'What aren't you telling me?'

No reply.

'It's all connected, isn't it?'

'All of it. Yes. That's the terrifying thing. A country farmer suddenly having her debts paid off. The killing of a millionaire's blameless wife. A librarian strangled in his quiet little village. The Prime Minister's child taken and recreated. Even the movement of the Valentino twins and the ongoing horror of the Teardrop murders. All connected.'

He jumped a red light, careering over a crossing whilst blithely ignoring the blare of horns and angry shouts which the move precipitated.

He calmly continued, 'I'm not one for quoting Sherlock, but he once said to you, *There's the scarlet thread of murder running through the colourless skein of life, and our duty is to unravel it, and isolate it, and expose every inch of it.'*

'I remember it well.'

'Well, that scarlet thread of murder is tying together every mystery and crime that's confronting us. And our duty is to sever it, Doctor. Snap it and cast it aside so the sins it bundles together can topple and be seen.'

'Moriarty. Tell me! What connects these crimes?'

'The organization I told you about. There can be no doubt, now.'

'But what is it?'

'It's everywhere and nowhere. I can't answer your question fully because I don't *fully* know. Yet. But its agents are all around us — who knows who might be working for them? And on more than one occasion I've been uncomfortably aware of its stamp. Of its calling card.'

WHEN SHE WAS ALONE AGAIN *in her office, Bailey Hernandez, the governor of HMP Tarrack, sat at her desk and looked at the two documents the Valentino twins had so readily signed. She compared their cover pages to satisfy herself that they were, like the brothers, identical. Yes. Except … She put on her reading glasses. At the top,*

right-hand side of both cover pages, there was a curious marking. A small, red circle.

JOHN HAD GLANCED down at Annie McDee's papers. He recognized them well enough. Bills. Every single one a final demand. All of them a last chance before debtors sought recompense through the courts. And all the invoices had a large stamp diagonally across them in a bold, uppercase font: PAID. And below this single word, always the same marking. Always the same symbol. A red circle.

MORIARTY HAD OPENED the book he found on the chest of Roddy Fingers. On the inside cover, he saw the library loan slip that had been glued in place. Below 'SHERE VILLAGE LIBRARY,' a snaking list of dates indicating when the paperback had been borrowed and the days it had been due for return. Below the last line, James spotted a curious marking. As if in lieu of a date, he saw a red circle.

'OKAY,' said John. 'We're up against some kind of crime ring. Let's accept the Red Circle *is* real. That's terrifying enough. Now let's get back to what you told Redford. You promised him you'd do your best but admitted you couldn't promise anything.'

'Correct.'

'When Troy Domingo asked if you could find out who was responsible for his wife's death, you gave him an unequivocal yes. Now, you see, at the time, I thought that was just something you said. That you always said *yes* when someone questioned your ability to do something. But the way you replied to the Prime Minister proved that wasn't the case. So when you told Domingo you could, at some stage, tell him who was responsible for Lizzie's death, there was only one way you could have made that statement so unambiguously.'

'Go on.'

'You *already* knew.'

Moriarty slipped down a gear and weaved in between two lines of traffic flow.

'Sherlock would have been proud of you.'

'Tell me now. Otherwise Mary or no Mary, this is over.'

'Before I do that, you have to understand, the Teardrop Murders are only one piece of the jigsaw puzzle scattered before us.'

'Who is the Teardrop Killer? Who is behind the murders that we know about?'

'Oh, John. You're so trusting.'

And Doctor John Watson felt sick as he said, 'Who is responsible for the death of Lizzie Domingo?'

'Isn't it obvious?' Moriarty took his eyes off the road to look at John. 'I am.'

PART II
The War and Grief of James Moriarty

Chapter Forty-Eight

LIKE MOST MEN WHO BELONG TO THAT BROAD DIASPORA sometimes called 'the criminal classes,' Martin Grimble did not consider himself to be a bad person. He had embezzled thousands of dollars but didn't think of himself as a criminal. The illegality of his actions was something he chose to ignore. He saw no victims and felt his fraudulent activities were entirely justified, so their criminality was, for him, a technicality. An unfortunate by-product of what was otherwise a wholly wholesome process.

So as he sat alone in the meeting room in Mariposa, California, he felt fear and injustice. Fear, because the CEO of the firm he worked for had finally called in external auditors who would doubtless pinpoint his cash grabs. And injustice, because even now, Martin Grimble felt his theft didn't warrant the shame and retribution that must surely follow.

He'd started small. An admin error had meant he'd missed out on a Christmas bonus. He'd been hurt and incensed. As an IT specialist, he'd been able to make a few minor, hidden amendments to the company accounts and siphon off some money to ensure that he achieved parity with his colleagues. Nothing wrong with that, surely.

He took funds from projects that were due to be shut down in the new year, and if anyone discovered the short-fall, the accountants, FD, vice-FD, and account handlers would be suspected. That's the way it worked. Everyone eyes the prowling suits. No one ever looks twice at the guy who hassles you about system updates and the importance of not using PASSWORD as your password.

The Christmas bonus had been so easy to arrange that he soon began awarding himself more windfalls. Soon the extra money wasn't a bonus. He accounted for it. Expected it. In his eyes, it was a chunk of undeclared wages. Nothing more. And if a manager slighted him, if he worked over-time or saw a colleague get a raise, he pocketed off a little more than usual. After all, *he'd* not had a pay raise for over three years, so his actions seemed appropriate. Maybe that's why they called it *appropriating* funds when there was something covert about the process. He was driven not by greed, he told himself, but the pursuit of even-handedness.

So that morning, when Della on reception excitedly told him the boss had informed her that hundreds of thou-sands of dollars had been stolen, he had to fight the urge to say, 'Not stolen as such, Del. More an off-the-books redistribution. No more *theft* than the sales team using petty cash to pay for a client's drinks after the client has left the bar.'

That was the way he perceived it, but he knew better than to share this view.

'Oh my god,' he'd whispered to Della. 'Who took it? Must have been someone pretty high up! The FD? Freddie from accounts has got two ex-wives and a Maserati. You don't think…'

Her eyes fluttered, enjoying the conjecture. 'Posh

Steven went to Rome three times last year! Who *does* that? Unless you're the Pope or some shit like that? And Mack!'

'Mack?'

'Mack from Sac. Great girl. Oh, yeah! Got nothin' against her. Honest to God. But she didn't get those new tits from a Goodwill bin, you hear me?'

'Oh, I hear you.'

'The auditors have been in all weekend. I bought one of those bitches a coffee and a donut, but she still wouldn't spill. Like she was fuckin' CSI Mariposa or some shit. Still, I guess we'll soon find out who the real criminal is.'

Criminal.

The word fell like a heavy hand on his shoulder. Ten minutes later, he was sent to the upstairs meeting room, where he looked out of its windows, over the quiet highway and across the Sierra Nevada Mountains, waiting for the lead auditor who was apparently insistent on inter-viewing him asap. There, for the first time, as the ancient aircon rattled and his stomach churned, Martin Grimble realized what he was. Not just a criminal. But a criminal about to be caught.

Chapter Forty-Nine

THE LEAD AUDITOR WAS FROM NEW YORK. THEY'RE always from New York.

She breezed into the meeting room and said, 'Thanks so much for coming!' like he'd had any say in the matter.

'No problem.'

She took a seat at the table, adjacent to Martin. Pulled his résumé from her Chanel lambskin handbag. Looked at its two-pages and *uh-huh*ed to herself as her eyes darted down the salient points of his career.

'You're from England?'

'Yes.'

'London?'

'Yeah.'

No. But Americans always asked him that, and he'd stopped correcting the assumption years ago. One of his friends from Omaha said it was the equivalent of some Brits thinking the USA was comprised entirely of New York, LA, and wherever their favourite CSI was set.

'I love London! *Uh-huh … Uh-Huh … Uh-huh …* That's great!' She tossed his résumé onto the table. 'You're great!'

'Errr … thank you.'

'How much have you fucking stolen?'

'I haven't actually taken anything that—'

'Ballpark. 200 thousand? 250?'

'What I'm saying, Ms. … Sorry. I didn't catch your name.'

'This place. Mariposa. It was one of the Gold Rush towns, right?'

'I believe so.'

'That why you came here? Do a little panning in the company accounts?'

'I've no idea what you're talking about.'

'Okay. That was the last time you ever lie to me. I'm here to help you, Martie. Lie to me again and I'll kill you. Understand?'

'No. Not really.' He quickly added. 'You told me not to lie.'

'That I did. *That I did.*' She nodded. 'I figure you weren't prospecting when you arrived here. You started small. Hell, you stayed small. Why was that? Actually, I don't care. You do you. But you're better than you think. You're a fucking genius. You aware of that?'

He shook his head.

She said, 'It took me 48 hours to find your loops, and I'm the best at what I do.'

'Am I under arrest?'

'You know why this place is called Mariposa?'

'It's Spanish for butterfly.'

'That's right. I did not know this until I arrived this morning. This very morning. You have a festival, apparently.'

'We do, yes. The Butterfly Festival. Every May.'

'Yeah. That must be fucking dull. So every year feels like a bit much, but what you gonna do? No. You're not under arrest. I want you to come with me, Martie. I want you to go from being a grubby little caterpillar to a beautiful butterfly. A Red Admiral.' She smiled at a joke that Martin didn't understand. 'Are we aligned?'

'I thought you were here to arrest me.'

'We can pin the whole thing on Steven from accounts. No one likes him. He's posh. I'm offering you a job.'

'As an auditor?'

'Spoiler alert! I'm not really an auditor. Well, I am. But only like Peter Parker is a photographer or Clarke Kent works for *The Daily Bugle*.'

'Planet.'

'Whatever. My real job is with a much bigger, much more powerful, and much more lucrative organization. And right now, my friend, we're hiring.'

Chapter Fifty

Turned out the lead auditor from New York was right. They're always right. When it came to illicit IT, Martin Grimble was indeed, 'a fucking genius.'

He joined the organization she represented and thrived. The blinkers that he'd worn to avoid seeing his culpability in his early days of corporate theft had to be tossed aside to make way for a thicker blindfold he now wore at all times. The company he worked for operated outside the law, but they'd exist without him, so his participation made zero difference. That's how he squared it, closing his eyes to everything but this reassuring illusion. He missed Mariposa County, sweet Della, and the innocence of his old life, but now he had money, status and a four-door sedan he could rely on.

Martin Grimble was able to hack systems as if security wasn't a thing, ghosting in and out without trace. He wrote programs that could gather and analyse mind-twisting amounts of stolen data, and he refined existing protocols to make them unbreachable and unbeatable. His AI program that had transformed his own appearance into that of

Millie Redford had been another triumph. Sure, he'd worried about the lack of data he could feed into the algorithms, but by that point in his career he'd grown a little lazy. His superiors assured him it would be fine. And Martin was used to fine. Fine was fine with him.

He knew the reputation of Professor James Moriarty, of course, and when he'd seen him onscreen and heard his threat, he felt the same way he'd felt all those years ago in the small meeting room with its clanking aircon and striking views of the High Sierra.

Sick to his stomach.

He knew he wouldn't be rescued this time. He had to escape, to vanish, all by himself. It was time for their Red Admiral to flutter away.

HE PACKED LIGHT. Just a few items that held sentimental value, his bank cards, IRS documents and passport. These didn't bulk out the small backpack he habitually wore, so anyone watching him wouldn't have reason to suspect he was about to cut loose. He walked across town to his favourite cake shop, NY Bakery and Desserts, where he bought a slice of the same German cheesecake he'd had a hundred times since arriving in New York. He paid by card and paused when the tip option came up. He wanted to leave the maximum figure as a parting gift but knew that any deviation from his normal habits could draw attention to his routine.

He hit 15%, said goodbye, walked up Broadway, through Times Square and across to Grand Central. He bought a ticket using cash and his train to Philadelphia pulled out just before noon. He had friends there. The trip wouldn't be seen as unusual, and he regretted not using his card to pay for the journey. Cash always looked suspicious in his business.

He made the call on his burner phone, early in the journey. He told his contact he'd need a fake passport and immediate access to a bank account with at least 20 grand available within it. He stressed he must have both before the end of day but could pay handsomely very soon. They struck a deal and arranged a meet.

'The usual place? 5 o'clock?'

'The usual place. 5 is good.'

Martin Grimble put away the phone and pulled out the small box containing his sweet treat from the bakery. He glumly reflected he was about to lose another life which, in time, he would doubtless romanticize and look back on with fondness.

He finished his käsekuchen.

New Yorkers could be supercilious and bizarrely hostile, but they made great cheesecake.

The trail pulled into Philadelphia a little after one-thirty. As he left the station, Martin saw the famous, friendly sign by the exit: WELCOME TO THE CITY OF BROTHERLY LOVE!

Chapter Fifty-One

SONNY'S, IN PHILLY'S OLD CITY, WAS ONE OF THOSE TRAD-style steakhouses that critics drool over, and reviews loaded with superlatives had made it a solid draw for tourists. But the food was exceptional and the atmosphere laid back, so it had remained popular with the locals. When Martin walked in at about 5 o'clock he reckoned there was a 50/50 split, with most of the holidaymakers choosing to eat their meals on the sidewalk in front of the place's smart, black and white façade.

He took his place in the queue. There was only one customer in front of him, a tall guy who was studying the menu on the wall like his next decision would dictate the course of his entire life.

'I can't decide,' he said aloud to no one in particular. Then turning to Martin, he asked in a lower voice, 'Are they really the best cheesesteaks in Philadelphia?'

'I've never had better. But the burgers are also good.'

'Hey! That accent! Where are you from, man?'

'England.'

'London?'

'Yeah.'

'I used to love that show on PBS with the old guy. The cop who used to drive around in an old car, solving crimes. Being kinda cranky and doing crossword puzzles.'

'Morse.'

'Yeah! D'you ever meet him?'

'Morse? No. Never met him.'

'That's a shame. He looked like fun, you know? Like snarky, but fun. Here, you go in front of me. I can't decide what I want.'

They swapped places and Martin noticed none of the servers were behind the counter. He felt a cold panic shoot through his core and immediately turned to leave, but the Morse fan was blocking his way. A woman, who'd been sitting at the table that ran along the far wall, had risen and was striding towards the exit. As she passed Martin, she pivoted and stabbed him with what looked to be a ceremonial dagger.

She said something — just four words — and stabbed him again. Four more words. Then she stabbed him another three times without pausing.

Martin began to fall. The man who'd asked him about Sonny's cheesesteaks caught him and hauled him along the tiled floor, then out onto the street. A GMC Vandura was idling beside a water hydrant. The woman slid its side door open while her partner thrust the body into the back.

The van took off within moments.

Later, most onlookers agreed — the attacker seemed to drive the blade into the guy's chest and guts with an almost religious conviction, and the blood was suddenly everywhere, although nobody screamed or shouted or even stood up. One of the cops asked why and a regular explained the onslaught lasted way less than ten seconds, and besides, no one wanted to get involved.

Patrons disagreed about which one of the two attackers had driven the van, but most were pretty sure it screeched off along Market Street towards the river.

The next day, police used traffic cam footage to track the Vandura to the docks, where a couple of longshoremen vaguely recalled seeing two people carrying something from a black van to a small boat moored on the east side. Could the *something* have been a body? Both dock workers found their memories grew fuzzier when the cops sounded like their questions were part of a larger official investigation.

'Body? Like a human body? I don't know, man…'

The boat sailed to the middle of the Delaware, then returned to its original location. Again, eyewitnesses spotted two individuals — a man and a woman — leaving the vessel. They were empty-handed, and a thorough search of the boat revealed nothing. The GMC Vandura was never found, and the couple who attacked the guy at Sonny's, and the victim of the attack himself, were never identified, although a couple of customers were adamant that one of them spoke with an English accent. The only thing the diners agreed on was yes, they were all certain about the words the woman had used as she stabbed the Brit to death — 'God help him.'

It had been just two short sentences. No doubt about it. And the words had been, 'Professor Moriarty says hello. This is for Millie.'

Chapter Fifty-Two

FLASHBACK

TROY DOMINGO LED James Moriarty and John Watson through his home, heading towards the sitting room.

John said, 'We appreciate you've already spoken at length to the police, but we want to try a different approach.'

Moriarty added, 'Yeah. We want to ask questions that might actually help us find whoever killed your wife.'

Domingo stopped dead in his tracks. 'Are you saying the officers assigned to Lizzie's case are incompetent?'

'Yes.'

'No!' John exclaimed. 'Inspector Lestrade is one of the finest—'

'The word incompetent,' Moriarty interjected, 'literally translated from its Latin derivation means *not able*. Right now, the police are not able to find the person responsible for your wife's murder and so…'

James Moriarty trailed off as his world fell apart.

John, who was stood behind him, assumed the professor had been struck dumb by the extraordinary piece of art that hung on the wall.

Ophelia Rising.

Troy Domingo, well-used to the admiration and awe the painting generated, made a similar assumption.

But Moriarty wasn't studying the astonishing reinterpretation of Millais's work. He was looking at the framed photographs that were on the desk below it. They were pictures from the wedding day of Troy Domingo and his wife, Lizzie Domingo.

Or, as Moriarty had known her, Doctor Beth Spencer.

The moment could have been called heartbreak, but it was in a very real way, much worse than that. Moriarty didn't feel as if his heart was broken; he felt as though he would never need it again. Never use it again. The colour and warmth had been drained from his life in that single second when he realized Beth had been murdered.

From that point onwards, there was no longer any necessity for his blood to pump through his isolated body. No reason for oxygen to keep alive his lonely limbs. Both physically and metaphorically, his heart was unneeded.

Unneeded and yet unbroken.

He gaped at the images of *the* woman on her wedding day, knowing he should be the one by her side in the photographs. The embarrassing first dance that really wasn't worth the rehearsals. The corny cutting of the cake. And that last, candid moment, caught unbidden, of two people looking at each other with something instinctively obvious as love.

That should have been me!

He wept, not just for his loss or even hers. But for the

awful chasm that *is* loss. Unfillable, unmendable and, of course, heartless.

And now, more alone than ever, he stared and swayed and could only say the words he had always said in his head when she walked into the room.

'She looks beautiful.'

Chapter Fifty-Three

JAMES MORIARTY AND JOHN WATSON REACHED THE building in a street off Charing Cross which, according to Colonel Moran, housed the server used to communicate with the Prime Minister. She'd surmised the people fooling the PM with the enhanced FaceTime calls, ostensibly with his daughter, Millie, were operating from this location. But the two men were to be disappointed.

When they entered the address, they found a deserted office. The dilapidated state of the place indicated no one had worked from here in weeks, maybe months, although the one computer on the premises, found by Watson on the second floor, was recently burnt out.

Moriarty contacted Moran and described the scene. She suspected the messages had simply been routed through the now useless computer and they'd tripped a destruct protocol when they'd approached it. She was impressed. Whoever had made it look as though the messages originated from Charing Cross had done an exceptional job in camouflaging the real initiation point.

She was full of enthusiasm for the skills required to pull off such a deception. Moriarty and John were less thrilled.

'We need to talk,' John said.

THEY LEANT on the stone balustrade and looked out across the Thames. Moriarty tried to tell John the story of his time with Beth Spencer. He was able to articulate the pedestrian elements of their relationship. Where they'd met. How he teased her about the way she kept pens lodged in her hair and would sometimes forget they were there. Her genius for pretty much anything she turned her hand to. The way her eyes seemed to change colour when she frowned.

When he neared genuine emotion, he stammered and made do with, 'You know.'

And of course, John knew. So with everything that was unsaid, he glimpsed a picture of love and complete adoration.

Moriarty told him what had happened when he delivered the paper that earned him his professorship. Of the bloodshed that flowed immediately — an assassin called Adam had been sent to end his life, and had done so in every sense excepting the literal one — and how the course of his relationship with Beth had been changed by that single, brutal attempt to kill him.

He also talked more about Beth Spencer, the woman known as Lizzie Domingo in later life. Yes, they *had* tried to carry on.

Suddenly, halfway through a reminiscence about a café she used to visit, he simply gave up and fell silent.

John said gently, 'Go on.'

Moriarty simply replied, 'For me, she will always be *the* woman.'

A minute passed. They watched the waters and from nowhere Moriarty looped back to the start of his revelations. 'I wasn't weeping for Hamlet's Ophelia. I was weeping for mine.'

Chapter Fifty-Four

THEY SAT IN THE LIVING ROOM OF 221B BAKER STREET. IT was not a cold night, but John Watson lit the fire out of habit, and he and James Moriarty sat around the cosy blaze. Minutes past in silence. The rococo ormolu clock behind them chimed 7 o'clock.

As if this was interpreted as a kind of signal, Moriarty said, 'Beth was killed because of me. Because I loved her.'

'That doesn't make it your fault.'

'But it makes it my burden.'

'Did you ever see her again? After what happened with Adam? That first attempt on your life? You briefly mentioned…'

'We lived together for a while. Stupid, I know. Selfish. But the danger that put her in…' Moriarty took hold of the poker and needlessly prodded the fire. 'I told her we couldn't even be friends. It would be too perilous for her. But…' He put the poker back in the copper coal scuttle.

'But what?'

'I sometimes watched her from afar.' Moriarty stared at the fire harder than ever. The flames were useful. Like the traffic when they'd conversed in the layby, they gave both men something to look at so they wouldn't have to regard each other. 'I'm not proud of that. But I couldn't stand to be completely separated from her. There was a café she went to every Sunday morning. On her own. It was a kind of ritual for her. I rented a room across from it, so I could look down and see her, sat at her table by the window. Once a week, she was my world.'

'Did it help?'

Moriarty hesitated, disconcerted by the prospect of his truth. 'I found her grief comforting,' he finally confessed. 'And I'm not proud of that, either. But it *was* a kind of grief, you know? For both of us. She looked dreadful. Sunken eyes. Not bothered to do her hair. She looked ill. You'll laugh at me, but I used to talk to her. Me in my room. Her down below, oblivious to me. I'd say stuff like, *You look like I feel.* And, *You really need to eat, sweetheart!* Stuff like that. Daft, I know.'

'No. Not at all.' John looked about the room. At the Persian slipper over the mantelpiece. The violin on the bookcase. The battered armchair and behind it, the initials E:R shot into the broad, white wall. 'Losing someone you love is difficult. I couldn't have stood it.' He leant back in his chair. 'Weren't you ever tempted to go down and see her? Just once?'

'Yeah, just once. A few months had passed. She still looked glum. Defeated. And she had this lost look in her eyes. When she sipped her coffee, I know this sounds egotistical, but I knew she was thinking about me. So she arrives at the café one day. Takes her normal seat. And I couldn't stand it. Something snapped and I grabbed my jacket … I remember, I'd just had my hair cut, which I regretted because she always liked it longer, so as I left my room, I looked in the mirror and ruffled it up a bit. I practically ran down the stairs and across the street and raced to the café and opened the door and…'

For a moment John heard nothing but the crackling fire. 'And?'

'And there she was. With another guy. He'd just joined her.'

John said 'Ouch!' and instantly regretted it.

'It was as though she'd placed the barrel of a rocket launcher on my stomach and pulled the trigger. It's your heart that's supposed to hurt, isn't it? But I just felt empty. Like part of me was missing. I'm not sure how I made it back up to my room.'

'Were they dating?'

'Not at first. But … Well. I couldn't blame him. I mean, I *did* blame him, of course…'

'Of course.'

'You know, I'd never felt guilty about watching her before then, but after that — I did. This guy would turn up every Sunday and join her at her table. Before he arrived, I'd still see a look in her eyes. Like a secret. And she'd hide it the moment he walked through that door. Put it away like a tube of lipstick popped into her handbag. *But that secret was me!* A look of sadness. Resignation. Guilt. Dunno. But that was me. That secret. *Our* secret.' He sighed. 'But do you know the one immutable thing about secrets?'

'Tell me.'

'They never last. They are emblems of transience. Those looks in her eyes became fewer. Then Doctor Beth Spencer and this guy … they started turning up together. And as she heeled before my prying eyes, I realized what grief was. Without knowing it, she told me.'

'Then please,' John said. 'Tell me.'

'Grief is learning to live without. That's all. It's a never-ending process because we're always learning — and this bit's the killer — whether we like it or not! It's not about feeling sad or happy or suppressing the anger or accepting the loss, or any of that garbage. It's about figuring out how we can continue to function *without*. To move forward *without*. To still belong in this world — without. She worked it faster than me. She showed me it was possible. That hurt me the most, I suppose. Another direct hit with the rocket launcher.'

'Why?'

'Not having her was the one thing I had left. Suddenly she was taking that, as well.'

'Do you think you went mad?'

'It was a kind of madness. Yeah.'

The fire spat and sizzled. And Moriarty, sensing John needed to talk, fell silent. He eventually rose, fixed two large glasses of Glenlivet's, and placed both tumblers on the hearth.

'Thanks.' John sipped his whiskey. 'I went mad. After Sherlock. The grief. That learning to live without thing…' He shook his head. 'Just couldn't. Didn't want to. Didn't feel…'

Moriarty saw the other man's face crumple. Saw him purse his trembling lips.

'Weep if you want to, John.'

'Christ…' He downed his Glenlivet's. Wiped his eyes with the butt of his right hand. 'If every tear took me closer to getting over it, I swear to God I'd have been over it years ago.'

Out of relief, John gave a short laugh.

Moriarty watched a single tear crawl down the doctor's cheek and fall from his face to the floor. This brief sight unlocked something and he opened his mouth to speak, then thought better of it, stashing the revelation away for later. But in that moment, he felt he had glimpsed a little more of the Teardrop Killer's reasoning.

And with the case now in his mind, he reached for the police files that detailed the Yard's investigations into the murders. John sensed his reluctance to open them.

'You're afraid of what you might find in there.'

'I'm pretty certain Beth won't be the only victim of the Teardrop Killer that's known to me. But we both know it's time. If we don't catch him, he *will* murder again.'

Moriarty opened the files and, with a sense of dread, began to read and to understand.

Chapter Fifty-Five

THE GOVERNOR OF HMP TARRACK, BAILEY HERNANDEZ, was, like most successful people, pragmatically curious about the world around her. She thought about the Valentino twins and their ease in accepting the proposal to render them unconscious for their journey to London. Their laissez-faire attitude bothered her, not because she felt it was problematic on a practical level. Quite the reverse, their compliance made her job simpler. It bothered her because she simply didn't understand it.

They could have negotiated for additional privileges during their final days in Tarrack. That's the way it usually ran. It's the way everything usually ran in this place. Bartering was a way of life in prisons. It formed the spine of a private, cashless economy that ran on everything from bars of chocolate and cigarettes to smart phones and amphetamines.

But they'd simply signed on the dotted line, literally, and walked from her office. No hustle, no hassle. Bailey considered the documents themselves. She recalled the red circles. One on each set of papers. Two identical markings which for some reason lodged in her memory.

She convinced herself that any prison governor worth their salt should be aware of everything that was happening in their jail. It was their domain, one where secrets could lead to trouble. In reality, the mystery of the two brothers was bugging her, and she wanted answers.

But whatever propelled her to do it, Bailey had reached a decision. She would confront the Valentino twins and ask them, face-to-face, what the hell was going on.

'ALL FIVE OF them died because of me,' James Moriarty announced, tossing the police files to the floor. He ran his palm across his face.

'You knew them all?'

'Every last one.'

'Even Annie McDee's husband? His name didn't ring a bell with you when I interviewed his widow.'

'Ethan used to work for me. I knew him by a different name, of course, and his appearance had changed considerably since we ran together but … He was a good man, John. And a good friend. When he wanted out, I gave him my blessing. I really hoped he'd escape the lunacy of our profession. Do you think we ever can?'

'Let's save the philosophizing for another time.'

'Fair enough.' Moriarty took a tumbler from a trolley and loaded it with White Horse. 'The second victim was a friend of my father's. I always knew her as Auntie Sall.'

'Sally Grainger?'

'Yeah. I've not seen her since I was a kid. Never knew her full name, so it didn't hit me at first. She used to babysit me. I liked her. That's why she was killed, of course. The kindness she showed me. The Red Circle may not be showing us their hand, but their heart is there to be seen and reviled. I've met monsters before, but I've never encountered such forensic sadism. Whoever is behind this, John, is in love with cruelty for its own sake.'

Chapter Fifty-Six

Léa signed the words, 'Are you crazy?'

Bailey's wife, Léa Hernandez, was profoundly deaf. She'd spent two years with a cochlea implant but hated it, and the day she'd had the device removed was the first time she'd experienced peace since the embedding surgery. She recognized the pros and cons and respected how people reacted differently to the ever-evolving aural technology. But it wasn't for her, and Bailey had fully supported her decision to move forward without the technology.

She'd learnt BSL for her wife and replied, 'I must be. I married you!'

Léa pursed her lips, unwilling to let Bailey's humour distract her. 'The twins are bad people. Just let it go!'

'I can't do that. Why would I?'

'This whole thing…' Léa looked distraught but continued. Anyone unversed in sign language might have thought she was saluting her wife. But the open-palmed movement meant 'dangerous' and reluctant to lie, Bailey could only shrug in a half-hearted admission that the action she intended to take could be risky — for both of them.

THE ORMOLU CLOCK behind them chimed 10 o'clock.

'I only met the fourth victim, Dev Khan, on one occasion. I'd forgotten him and had to rack my brains, but...'

'But what?'

'I was in my early twenties. Taking a flight to the US. The seat I'd been allocated was away from my mates. I was the one who'd drawn the short straw.'

'Let me guess. Middle chair in a central row of five?'

'The flier's hell. Exactly. Anyway, Mr. Dev Khan spotted I was a nervous flier, so he came over to me and offered to swap seats with me, so I could sit with my group. He swapped his aisle seat for my middle-of-the-row seat. For that one act of goodheartedness, so many years ago, he was killed.'

'And the fifth victim? Jane Rossi.'

'Again, I only met her once. At her mother's funeral. I'd been a good friend of her mum's and knew Jane disapproved of her relationship with me.'

'Were you two...'

'Oh, it was purely platonic. But she meant a lot to me. One the day of her funeral, I entered the church late. Snuck in and took a pew at the very back. She saw me, walked down the aisle, took my hand, and insisted I sit at the front with her and her brother. She said it was what her mother would have wanted. That she'd considered me to be family.'

'That was thoughtful.'

'A quality she got from her mum. Pity none of it never rubbed off on me. It's odd, John, how many lives we touch. How many touch our own. Maybe *touch* is the wrong word. Collide with? Caress? It depends, I suppose, but it's all so random.' He walked to the window and leant against its frame, looking out over Baker Street. 'We fall through our lives. Bouncing off each other's kindnesses, apathy, and enmity on our way down. The good people, they ensure we're not too bruised by the time we hit the bottom. All five people — they saved this world a little bit of bruising. As I get older, I recognize the nobility in that.'

The sound of the traffic from below filtered into the room.

John said at last, 'And I thought Holmes was off his rocker. At least he could blame it on the cocaine.' He finished his drink. 'I thought we agreed to shelve the philosophizing?'

DOCTOR JOHN WATSON left London early the next morning, traveling from Victoria to Arundel in just under 90 minutes. A couple of cabs were idling at the train station, but he chose to walk into the town itself, following a riverside path along the Arun and then striding up the High Street towards the castle. He was presenting a talk — arranged months ago — in a large Georgian hall just across from the cathedral, and two members of the society's committee met him in the building's musty-smelling foyer.

'There's a good turn-out!' the younger of the two women told him.

John smiled. 'That's reassuring to hear.'

'They're all here to see Mary Berry,' the older committee member explained with a sigh. 'She's on after you. So keep it as short as you like.'

John's talk proved to be a barn-storming success. He spoke with passion, wit, and energy, drawing the audience in with his tales of true crime. He regaled them with tales about his current case, enjoying their rapt attention. 'You must have heard of the Teardrop Killer? Well, I can tell you this…'

His stories were verbally redacted in places, but he made the omissions clear and thereby added to the notion that he was giving everyone the inside story. He spoke of Downing Street and Andrew Redford and amused his audience when he crafted an anecdote about interviewing a person of interest and how to act naturally when you're caught snooping through their personal papers. He was deadly serious when appropriate. Humorous when covering the lighter side of his work. He shone and he dazzled.

Poor Mary Berry was kept waiting for a quarter of an hour as John kept taking 'just one more question' during the lively Q&A that followed his talk.

As he left the hall, the two committee members he'd met before the event caught him up.

'That was marvellous, Doctor Watson. Marvellous!'

'Thank you.'

'I saw you at the Rookthorn Ladies Club,' the elder lady informed him. 'But today, well…' She beamed. 'You seemed like a new man!'

As he walked back along the river, John realized that although, of course, he had spoken about Sherlock Holmes with fondness and respect, he hadn't once mentioned Reichenbach.

Chapter Fifty-Seven

THERE IS NO NEUTRAL GROUND IN PRISON, BUT HMP Tarrack's long, narrow garden was as close as it got. Karl Valentino had put in to work there when he'd first arrived, but Bailey had denied the request. She considered him too much of a threat to be outside and unguarded, no matter how brief his stints would have been. Watching him now, she wondered if she'd been wrong.

He was replanting a delicate, pink flowering plant with a sensitivity that surprised her. He placed its roots in a hole he'd prepared, scattered feed around it, then gently added soil, careful not to damage the roots. Then again, Bailey thought, maybe she should have expected this. It was what he did on the outside. Work patiently and assiduously to embed something and then let it grow. In the world beyond the prison gates, it had been viruses and bugs. Here it was something a little more innocent.

She approached him and in the most genial tone she could muster, asked, 'What are you up?'

He was patting down the ground above the roots. 'Bleeding heart.'

They were the first words he'd ever spoken to her. 'Excuse me?'

He gestured to the flower. 'Bleeding heart. A member of the poppy family.'

'It looks very fragile.'

'It is. They had it over there.' He pointed to a wall. 'Madness. The gardening books will tell you they can grow in the shade. And maybe they can. But they need the sunshine to flourish.'

'Are you going to move anything else?'

'Not got time.'

His comment was accusatory, of course. A loaded reminder that he hadn't forgotten Bailey had originally nixed his request.

'You've got a few more days.'

'Your warder said it was too delicate to be moved. He said the roots would shred or the flowers get damaged if we tried to replant it.'

'Well, you've proved otherwise.'

It had been intended as a compliment, but as he looked up from the plant, Bailey could read his expression. The fact he'd been proven correct had been the whole point. That's why he'd told her about the warder. He viewed her words as obvious and clumsy.

'I came to ask you something, Karl.'

'I know. Why did you come to me first? Why didn't you go to my brother?'

'How do you know I didn't?'

He gave her that look again and got to his feet.

'Why were you both so ready to sign the waiver?'

Karl circled the plant, checking his handiwork.

'There's no reason you can't tell me, is there?'

His inspection complete, Karl nodded, satisfied. 'I could have done good work here.'

'You could have requested this as a special privilege when the documents came in. But you didn't. Tell me why not. Why did you just go along with the whole idea? Please, I'd like to know.'

Karl stepped closer to the plant, raised his right boot, and brought it down heavily. The stems, flowers and buds broke and flattened. He continued to stamp on the bleeding heart, quickly and forcefully, stamping on it like it was a small fire he was determined to extinguish completely.

One of the warders called across, 'What's going on?'

Karl Valentino stepped back. The pink and white petals were crushed into confetti and the thin, fleshy stems lay, two dimensional, across the soil. He looked at Bailey and gave her a single thumbs up with his left hand.

The warder had arrived. 'What the hell d'you think you're playing at? I'll make sure—'

Bailey shushed him and he fell silent.

Karl dabbed his forehead with his right thumb, then lowered it so the tips of his left and right thumb touched. He finally broke eye contact from Bailey and strode away.

The warder swore under his breath and added, 'What was all that about?'

'It was British Sign Language,' she told him. Bailey watched Karl Valentino marching across the garden towards the main prison building. 'It means, *'Remember!'*.'

THEY MET at The Ivy Club. Zenisha was a member ('Of course she is!' Moriarty exclaimed) and was already waiting for her two guests in the Piano Room when they arrived at 9 p.m. John reflected that the place looked comfortable and the ambiance was just fine, but it didn't have the 'wow' factor he'd been expecting from such a high-end brand.

They ordered a bottle of Kiwi Sauvignon Blanc and he had to check twice that the menu had the decimal place in the right place on the price line. Still, it wasn't a bad little plonk.

He announced, 'We have a lead.'

'Great, because right now,' Zenisha conceded, 'I've got about ten million suspects.'

'We think the killer is someone who has a personal hatred of Moriarty.'

Zenisha shrugged. 'That doesn't really narrow down my suspect pool.'

Moriarty laughed. 'You're developing a certain, unexpected vein of gawky humour, Lestrade, against which I must learn to guard myself.'

'So this lead — give me details.'

John updated her about the fact Moriarty had known all five of the victims.

The DI listened carefully, then frowned. 'Well, that takes us somewhere. Not sure where. But somewhere. It still doesn't explain the tattoos.'

'They're what make the murders stand out, and they ensure they can all be linked.' John lowered his voice. 'And maybe the killer wanted to be sure his murders gained some sort of media traction. A dramatic element like tattoo would guarantee that for him.'

Moriarty thoughtfully repeated the words, 'Media traction…'

'It's a horrible phrase but—'

'No … No it's not that, John. It's just — I hadn't thought of it like that. *Media traction*.' He looked at his companions. 'It's another strand to take into account.

Along with the Prime Minister's involvement. But let's not get lost in the details. We don't need them. Because knowing what we now know, I believe we have enough data to capture the Teardrop Killer.'

Chapter Fifty-Eight

'HERE'S WHAT I PROPOSE,' MORIARTY CONTINUED. 'I DRAW up a list of people that are important to me, or folks who've made a positive contribution to my life. These are all potential victims. We then sift through their lives.'

'Sift?' Zenisha said, 'How?'

'We get as much footage of their everyday comings and goings as possible. The stores where they shop. Their route to the gym. The streets where they live. Footage from the cameras outside the playgrounds where they drop their kids off to school. We assemble a visual record of their lives.'

John raised an eyebrow. 'Then what?'

'Well, we do the same for the first five victims. It seems inevitable that the killer had to have been watching them to assess the best time and place to strike. This guy left zero trace evidence. I still find that remarkable, by the way.'

'It's unheard of,' Zenisha agreed.

'Which indicates he's a pro. He's cautious.'

John picked up on the drift. 'So he carries out extensive reconnaissance missions before executing his attack.'

'Exactly! Spoken like a true miliary man! Actually — the phrase *military precision* applies to all these murders, does it not? I wouldn't be surprised if the Teardrop Killer serves or has previously served in the forces. Like yourself, John.'

'This idea of soldiers leaving the army and then going on some rampage due to PTSD is utter bollocks. PTSD is still woefully misunderstood, Moriarty. It tends to lead to sorrow and depression, and not—'

Moriarty interjected, 'I'm sorry. I didn't mean to imply any disrespect to your comrades.'

'I hope not.'

Zenisha asked, 'So what do we do with all the assembled footage when we have it?'

'We search for people who appear in multiple sets of footage. Find the face that's watching, watching, watching…'

'Look, scrutinizing video material is something we do a lot in the police. *A lot*. And I can tell you — it's bloody arduous. Jumping through all the legal and practical hoops of actually obtaining one single piece of footage to begin with — that's time-consuming and difficult enough as it is.'

'I'm sure it is,' John agreed.

But Zenisha was far from finished. 'Then analysing it in real time is another slog. Don't get me started on the problems of grainy footage and gaps in surveillance because of faulty equipment. Then matching up faces that might only appear for a moment — nigh on impossible. And after all that, it's incredibly tough trying to positively identify people that might be wearing hoodies or hats or wigs or face masks. Add to that the problem of—'

'I get your drift,' Moriarty interrupted without rancour. 'Have you got any better ideas?'

'I'm just saying it will be a long, hard pig of a job.'

'Welcome to my life,' John said with a half grin. 'To be fair, Moriarty has got a point. And a line of attack.'

They agreed to push forward with the plan. Zenisha would collate the video footage already held by the police that related to the first five victims. Moriarty intended to draw up a list of potential victims and work with John to secure recordings that might shine a light into their lives and thereby prove useful in their hunt for the killer.

As they talked through the scheme, a collective recognition emerged that the process would be lengthy and fraught with complexities. But equally, the trio seemed to bond as they ironed out the details of their arrangement. This was a joint plan — something they were all investing in, and the shared nature of their actions and intentions tethered them. But above all, they were united by hope. Of course, their way forward held no promises. But John intuited that they all felt it was exactly that: a way forward.

Action points decided, they agreed to catch up the following afternoon. Moriarty excused himself to take a phone call.

Zenisha said, 'I better start prepping for this video trawl. See if I can assign a few Specials. It'll mean extra paperwork tonight, but it will get the job done faster.'

'Paperwork? Your life is just one long Mardi Gras.'

'It's a mardy something. There's another evening's plans up in smoke.'

'What do you mean?'

'I was supposed to have a date tonight.'

'With your new boyfriend?'

'Don't ever use the word *boyfriend* again or I might have to stab you in the face. I'd better be going.'

She stood and put on her coat.

'All of the prep will wait!' John rose from his chair. 'Go out! Have fun! The last thing you need is to burn out.'

'Maybe. But right now, the last thing I *want* is to spend time with someone who doesn't understand any of this.'

'The escape might do you good.'

Zenisha hesitated. 'Did Mary get it?'

'Honestly? Not really. It can still be … problematic. What's this guy like, then? Your date. Is he a keeper?'

'I don't know. He seems like a good man. He's a plumber. I ask him about his day, and he tells me about old ladies with leaky pipes.'

John's eyes twinkled with mischief. 'Is that a euphemism?'

'I never thought to check. He asks me about my day and what do I tell him? I'm trying to catch someone who's already slaughtered five innocent people and I haven't got a clue how I'm going to manage it, because the perp is — to all intents and purposes — a ghost.' She reached down for her glass and took a final sip of wine. 'I'd just like to have someone in my life I could talk to about it.'

'I'm always here for you. You know that.'

She gave that off-hand nod that people always give when they really mean *no*. 'Mary's a lucky woman.'

'I'm not sure she'd agree with you right now.'

'You know what I mean.'

'I know what you mean.'

'We should have gone for it when we had the chance, shouldn't we, John?'

Before he could reply, Zenisha Lestrade placed a light kiss on his cheek, then turned and pattered across the floor towards the exit.

Somehow — he never found out how, precisely — Moriarty had materialized immediately behind him. 'You and Zenisha, eh? Give me the goss, mate!'

'There is no goss, *mate*.'

Both men sat down again. 'You're only making it

worse, Johnny. Saying there's no goss indicates it's *good* goss.'

'You know, and this is from the heart, Moriarty, I never in a *million years* thought you'd be this childish.'

'What can I say? I'm eternally young.' He picked up the book that contained the bill, opened it, and glanced at the invoice. 'Now spill the beans!'

'I have zero beans.'

'You have beans.'

'I'm beanless.'

'Tell me everything.' Moriarty slid the bill across the table. 'Or you're paying.'

'I'm not telling you anything!' John picked up the bill and blanched when he read the bottom line. 'What do you want to know?'

Chapter Fifty-Nine

Léa was awake at 1 a.m. She normally turned in early with Bailey, drifting off to sleep with the ease of an innocent. Not this morning. She lay in bed, trying not to think about the Valentino twins, but there was something malevolent about them that imposed their faces into her thoughts. She looked forward to them being taken to England and away from—

She looked sharply to her right towards the bedroom window. Léa had always been sensitive to light, even before she lost her hearing. But now that sensitivity was acute. She checked Bailey was asleep, got out of bed, and slipped into her dressing gown.

The outside light, on the side of their house, shone on the side path leading to the back garden, and she felt sure that, momentarily, it had flickered. Not completely on and off, but just enough of a double-dip in brightness to suggest that something had passed in front of it. Or, as it had been a *double*-dip, two things. She opened the thin curtains and peered downwards.

Nothing.

Léa tightened the cord of her dressing gown, left the bedroom, and began walking downstairs. She checked the locks of her front and back doors. They were untouched. Apparently.

Next, she went into every room. All clear.

But she was awake now and knew sleep would be improbable, at least for a while. She fixed herself a decaf Darjeeling, finished her marking, and when she went to take a sip of her tea, found it was only lukewarm. A quick peek at the watch. Huh — she'd been downstairs half an hour. Feeling pleasantly sleepy again, she traipsed upstairs and into her bedroom. As she slipped off her dressing gown, she detected something was wrong, but couldn't quite put her finger on what it was. She was too tired. It would come to her in the morning, probably. But as he sidled into bed besides Bailey, as she drifted off, she realized what it was. The roses weren't in the vase where she'd left them.

Bailey must have moved them.

The Teardrop Killer took a pace to his left. He'd been behind the door when Léa had re-entered the room. His eyes had become accustomed to the darkness, and he watched Léa with interest as she coiled her limbs around her dead wife before drifting off to sleep.

Chapter Sixty

In the early hours of the drunken morning, Moriarty and John hurtled back to Baker Street in a black cab.

The professor remembered his earlier questions and re-opened the question of John and Zenisha Lestrade.

'You met through Sherlock, right? I'm guessing you two got on well, and your friendship was bolstered by the things you had in common relating to '*the Great Detective*'.' He spoke the sobriquet with a hint of rancour. 'You both licked him.'

'We both licked him?'

'Liked him. I said, *liked* him. You were both in awe of him. Don't deny it! But you both saw his flaws. You felt you could talk to each other about him with ... an *honesty* that was reserved solely for your conversations.'

'Moriarty — what ineffable twaddle!'

'No one says *ineffable twaddle* anymore. So why didn't you get together?' He considered the matter as the cab hurtled along The Strand. 'You saw a lot of each other

243

through work. So, you both thought there was no reason to rush it. Probably enjoyed the frisson of UST.'

'UST?'

'It's what screenwriters call unresolved sexual tension when they need to stretch out a story arc.'

'Got you.'

'Then something happened. Best guess — she got together with an ex.'

'If this whole criminal empire thing doesn't work out for you, you know you've got a solid career path writing for Mills & Boon.'

'But am I right?'

'How did you know?'

'Intuition. Observation. Genius. Why did it finish with her ex?'

'He was an addict. A gambler. Lost a hell of a lot of cash and relied on her. Incessantly. She's rich, you know. Rich!' He frowned with the effort of getting his facts right. 'Or rather,' he added, raising a finger, 'her family is.'

Moriarty half-shrugged. 'I guessed she's from aristocracy. She wears poverty and wealth as if they're a pair of matching gloves.'

'Aristocracy? Yeah, near enough. Her parents live in one of those Downton Abbey-style piles in the country. Her mum's dead, but her dad's still going strong. Her ex always expected her *people* to bail him out. She took him back once, but only because she felt sorry for him.'

'So getting back to you and Zenisha. She gets back with her ex, and you've missed your OMR.'

'OMR?'

'Optimum Moment for Romance. She breaks up with her ex, but by that point you're a smitten kitten with Mary Morstan. Am I right or am I right?'

He was right. 'You're wrong.'

'You're a *terrible* liar! Honestly. You're abysmal. After you and Mary broke up, you thought that getting together with Zenisha would have been inappropriate. You were wrong about that, by the way. You missed your OMR but that doesn't preclude an SMR.'

'You're all about the acronyms tonight. You couldn't STF up, could you?'

'SMR. Satisfactory Moment for Romance. Not as strong as an OMR, but not to be sniffed at.'

'I'm not sniffing.'

'I think you'd make a very bonny couple.'

'I'm with Mary!'

Moriarty gave a non-committal 'Hmmm…' Their cab pulled up at a red light and he clapped his hands together. 'Anyway, Johnny, we can't sit around yapping about your love life all day! We need to start putting our plan into action! We've got a killer to catch!'

John glanced at his watch. 'What? Tonight?'

'Oh yes … Absolutely! I've got a surprise for you!'

Chapter Sixty-One

When Léa awoke, she was still enveloping Bailey and knew immediately that something was wrong. Her wife felt warm, which reassured her a little, but it was somehow a different *kind* of warmth and there was a stiffness and slight clamminess to her body that immediately panicked her.

She was later told it can take 12 hours for a corpse to cool, whereas rigor mortis is a rapid, greedy process and begins to spread through a lifeless body not long — around three hours — after a final breath has been taken. So when Léa pulled her forearm from under Bailey's arm, the rigor made it feel much heavier than usual.

She nudged her lover's shoulder. Gripped it. Tugged her towards her.

Bailey fell from her side onto her back. Her eyes were open and seemed to find Léa, who saw the tattoo of a teardrop and knew immediately what had happened.

Death tends to repel, and Léa's automatic reaction was to spring from the bed. She looked on the scene, praying she'd remained asleep and all this was some horrific, photo-realistic dream. But she knew, of course, with the certainty that death always brings with it. And without thinking or reasoning, Léa Hernandez could sense her wife had already left her.

Her breathing became shallow and she repeatedly murmured, 'Oh no, oh no, oh no…'

Later, the first two policemen arrived before the ambulance. One was fluent in BSL. He asked Léa, 'What's this? Did you make this?'

He pointed to the floor by Bailey's side of the bed.

Léa walked across her the room. Paused. Her breathing dipped again, because she saw the flowers Bailey had bought her.

Her eyes widened.

The roses were arranged on the carpet to form a small, floral ring. A red circle.

Chapter Sixty-Two

WHEN THEY REACHED 221B BAKER STREET, JOHN FINALLY gave Moriarty the satisfaction of asking, 'What kind of surprise?'

'A good one! Come on, we need to go to my apartment. My Central London apartment.'

John, who had just taken a seat, shrugged and stood up. 'I never thought of you as having an apartment.'

'Really? What did you think I lived in? A dark castle with a portcullis and drawbridge?'

'No … Just … I don't know.'

'I thought you knew.'

John picked up his coat. 'Why would I?'

'What are you doing?'

'What does it look like? I'm putting a jacket on. Looks like rain later.'

'Oh my god, you really *don't* know. You must cultivate a sense of curiosity, mate. I thought Sherlock would have told you.'

'Told me what?'

'Come on!' Moriarty led Watson into the hallway. 'For all these years you've lived in 221B Baker Street.'

'So?'

'And you never once thought to find out who lived in 221C Baker Street? Follow me!' He padded up the stairs and reaching the door which stood opposite the flight of steps, he paused and boomed, 'Welcome to my apartment!'

'You…' It was as though Watson's world had unaccountably shifted. '*You live in 221C?*'

'Yes! Well, off and on.'

'How?'

'Sherlock and I shared digs in 221A — that's the ground floor apartment — back in the old days. That was when he had office rooms on Montague Street. No one worked from home in those days. Seems weird that now, doesn't it? So, it came to pass that Mrs. Hudson needed the ground floor space because her niece is a wheelchair user, and she couldn't afford to install lifts, and so—'

'Wait!' If John's world had shifted moments earlier, now his voice suggested it hadn't simply shifted on its axis. It had fallen from its position in the heavens, tumbled to Earth and was being used in a game of volleyball on Huntington Beach. 'You lived with Holmes?'

'Yes! Of course! We were good friends, once. Anyway, when we got booted out of 221A, we drew straws to see who'd get which of the two remaining apartments.'

'And Holmes won?'

'I won. Sherlock was livid! Ha! Threatened to leave London entirely. Talked some rubbish about moving to Sussex to keep bees. He was a terrible loser! In the end he moved into 221B but needed someone to share with.'

'What? I'm not understanding any of this! Why didn't *you* continue to live with him?'

'Are you kidding me? That bloody fiddle!' Moriarty shuddered at the mere mention of Holmes' violin. 'His coke habit, moodiness, ridiculous disguises, singing, and smart arse observations I could deal with. Just about. But his—'

Watson rose to his old friend's defence. 'What smart arse observations? The man was a genius!'

'All that — *I see you have visited Eel Pie Island today because your cuff is frayed and there's an 'R' in the month.*' Moriarty drooped at the memory. 'I know you loved all that business, but it just got on my nerves.'

'And singing?'

'Well, to be fair, he was a very good singer. We performed together from time to time. The duet from Bizet's *The Pearl Fisher* was our best, ironically enough. But as he got older, he lost the heart for it. That was sad.'

'*Why* did he lose the heart for it?'

Moriarty delved in his pocket as if buying time to think of a suitable reply. But as he pulled out a key, he simply said, 'Anyway! I couldn't put up with his violin playing any longer. I lived in 221C for a few years. Finally got an apartment on the South Bank, although I always retained this place.' He unlocked the door. 'I lived here whilst you and Sherlock were in your pomp. Your early days together. He only shot "E:R" into the wall to annoy me. He knew I had friends over that night.'

'This is all new to me.'

Moriarty pushed open the door but paused. Without looking 'round, he said, 'I remember when you moved out to be with Mary. He popped upstairs for a drink and a moan. He was upset. No, it was more than upset. He was empty. He missed you for months, very badly, you know?'

This latter revelation seemed to hit John the hardest. 'No,' he said. 'I never knew that.'

THE FIRST THING that struck Watson about the living area of Moriarty's apartment was its similarity to 221B in terms of architectural layout. It bore the exact same floor size, and the angles of the walls — the way they created an obtuse angle by the far wall, for example — were identical. The windows, fireplace, and doorways were also all in corresponding locations.

But the comparisons ended there. This space blended modernity with classical. There were two huge channel back sofas in the middle of the room, around a low, travertine table. A massive television hung on one wall, and two computers, side by side to the left, sat besides a sleek looking B&O sound system. Watson was surprised by the absence of books. The shelves instead held an eclectic range of objet d'art and items of interest, including a matte black statuette of a bird of prey, most probably a falcon, a bust of Napoleon, and a little jarringly, a small stuffed elephant.

The building had no loft or garret rooms, meaning its wooden eaves were exposed. The ceiling was, in effect, the underside of the roof ,allowing for two vast, oblong skylights that ensured the stars over London were piercingly visible.

Watson was also struck by the difference in views given by the main windows. 221B offered a fascinating, constantly changing view of Baker Street. But as this room was higher, and higher than the buildings opposite, it afforded a vista across the city itself. To the right of the casements, an astronomer's telescope stood angled to attention.

'What do you think?' Moriarty was holding a remote

control, pressed a button on it, and Franz Waxman's score for *Rebecca* began to play.

Watson remained stood in the doorway. 'This is a lot for me to take in. Not just this place. You and Holmes were friends. I mean…'

'I shouldn't have told you. That was thoughtless of me. I'm sorry, John.'

'No, not at all.' He took a couple of paces into the room. 'I want to know more! I want to know everything!'

'We agreed we'd save all that until this case is finished. Like I said, I know the truth will conjure up certain feelings in you, and I can't deal with that hatred right now.'

'I won't hate you for telling me.'

'John…' Moriarty's tone was that of a doctor delivering a delicate, potentially devastating diagnosis. 'The hatred wouldn't be for me. It would be for Sherlock.'

The music continued to softly play in the background.

Watson shook his head. 'Never!'

'Ha! Good for you!' Moriarty seemed delighted by the other man's intransigence. 'And now for that surprise I promised you!'

'What the hell?' Watson closed the door and gawped around the living area. 'I thought *this* was the surprise.'

'Oh, I'm full of surprises.'

'You're full of something.'

'And the old Johnny is back in the room! Glorious!'

'So what else have you got up your sleave, Moriarty?'

'We have a mystery guest to help us with our hunt! Exciting, eh?'

'Who is it?'

'Let's bring him on!' He raised his voice. 'You can come through, now!'

Watson heard one of the bedroom doors open,

followed by footsteps across the parquet floor. He spared the new arrival a glance, then looked back at Moriarty, who cheerfully said, 'Doctor John Watson, I'd like you to meet the newest member of the team. Mr. Martin Grimble.'

Chapter Sixty-Three

Moriarty waited for a response from John, but when none came, he said with exasperation, 'It's the man Lestrade told us had been killed!'

'I can see that!'

'Well, aren't you surprised? Oh, come on! If Sherlock had pulled a trick like this, you'd be open-jawed in astonishment and begging him to reveal how he pulled it off!'

'Let me guess…' John wandered around the room as he spoke, taking in the ornaments and technology on display. 'You and a colleague staged the attack on Grimble in Philadelphia. Inspector Lestrade mentioned it was a knife attack, so … You used theatre knives that retract on impact. They can store blood in the handle, which spurts out when the blade is pushed back. You used one of those. And as Grimble was being stabbed' — he put the word in air quotes — 'the other attacker used a concealed syringe to inject him with a compound that rendered him unconscious.'

He paused by the bust of Napoleon. Cracks were visible in the plasterwork, suggesting it had been broken and glued back together. 'Therefore, to onlookers, and on any recording of the incident, it looks like Grimble was murdered in a brutal attack. How am I doing so far?'

'Spot on. Although some applause, however muted, would have been appreciated. But do go on.'

'So you throw the unconscious Grimble into the boot of your car and … What is it?'

'They call it a trunk in the States.'

'Pedant. You put him in the *trunk*, then drive to the docks. But you actually take out a dummy when you reach there. And you're careful to make sure any security footage won't pick up on its head. You put the dummy in the boat. Wrap it in black plastic and then—'

'Gonna have to interrupt you, again. It wasn't plastic. It was entirely biodegradable.'

'James Moriarty — the green gangster.'

'Not a bad campaign slogan.'

'You return to the docks and drive off, with Grimble still in the boot. AKA trunk. Once clear of prying eyes, you get him out, and the rest is obvious. You smuggle him back to the UK, and here he is.'

'Bravo, doctor!'

'Elementary, my dear Moriarty.'

Martin Grimble cleared his throat. 'I can hear all this, you know? I mean, I'm still in the room, fellas.'

'Indeed you are!' Moriarty patted his shoulder. 'John, our friend here was forced to work for the Red Circle, and they made him rig up those communications with Andrew Redford.'

'Mind you,' he said, 'I'm not claiming I was blameless … Helping you with this is my penitence, if you like.'

'I murdered Martin for pretend so the Red Circle wouldn't murder him for real.'

At Moriarty's insistence, John and Grimble took a seat

on the sofas. He disappeared into the kitchen, and when he re-joined them, he was carrying a tray laden with three tumblers and a bottle of wine. 'It's a white Burgundy,' he explained. 'Sturdy and uncomplicated. Perfect for what we need.'

He poured three glasses, then their discussion began in earnest.

Chapter Sixty-Four

Martin Grimble revealed that despite working for the Red Circle for years, he knew very little about the organization. He'd received his orders remotely, seldom met fellow agents, and with the exception of the woman that recruited him, he never encountered the same one twice. His jobs were all related to IT and covered hacking, data acquisition, sorting, and internal security. Standing in for Millie Redford had been the first deviation from these duties, and he was honest enough to admit he bitterly regretted branching out.

Moriarty, who had evidently heard Grimble talk about this before, did not ask for any more details on the nature of his work, but he repeatedly interrupted with questions about the methodology involved. How was he paid? Did he ever feel threatened? 'Tell me more about the corporate ethos of the Red Circle,' he insisted.

A picture emerged of a well-run business that seemed to care for the welfare of its employees. Grimble was paid primarily in cash and received a bonus for any job that his employers felt he'd delivered in a way that could be described as 'above and beyond.' Six weeks paid holiday a year ('Although even then, I had to be on call at all times') and a kind of health package that involved private doctors visiting him if he felt the slightest bit unwell.

John tried to take this all in without registering surprise, but even he expressed his astonishment when Grimble revealed his unseen bosses sent him generous birthday presents and Christmas gifts. 'And when my late mother was ill, they made sure she got the best of everything. The best medical supervision. The best care home. Even a trip to Rome. She'd always wanted to visit the Eternal City, bless her.'

'I'm surprised they didn't arrange for an audience with His Holiness the Pope while she was there,' Watson muttered.

'Oh, believe me,' Moriarty said, 'if she'd wanted it, they'd have made it happen. They obviously do everything possible to keep their employees happy and stress-free.'

'Are you saying Grimble's superiors genuinely cared for his well-being?'

'No. I'm saying they made sure their asset operated at peak efficiency. That's not necessarily *caring* on their part. It's good, old-fashioned logic, intended to maximize the effectiveness of their workforce.'

'I suppose so, yes.'

'The attention they gave our friend, here — no more than a farmer dutifully caring for his flock, before sending it to the abattoir when there's a sudden demand for lamb.'

They'd finished the Burgundy and Moriarty broke off to fetch another bottle from the fridge. He called through from the kitchen, 'Oh, there was one other thing I wanted to ask you, Martin…'

He sounded so casual that John felt sure his next question was the most important of all.

'Did you ever receive messages from someone you thought might be at the top of the Red Circle's hierarchy? Their *numero uno*, so to speak?'

'Yes — a few times. The more personal messages around Christmas and a couple when I first started working for them.'

'Oh, right.' Moriarty sounded bored with the subject that he himself had raised.

He returned, and as he replenished their glasses, he said, 'Were they from a man or a woman?'

'Dunno. They were never signed.'

'But when you read the good wishes, or whatever they were, what did your instinct tell you? Did you read the message and think, *that was kind of him* or *that was kind of her?* Don't think about it — give me an answer without processing it!'

'They were from a woman.' The words seemed to surprise Grimble. 'You know, I've never really thought about it, but something told me they were from, yes, a woman.'

'It's probably not important,' Moriarty opined as he retook his seat, and conversation turned to the future. Grimble was told he'd be given a list of people to focus on, including the first five victims. There was no question of permission being sought for the material he was to gather. He would hack systems and covertly extract any relevant footage. He was also tasked with creating and running programs that would isolate and compare all faces appearing in the videos, automatically compiling a data-base of possible matches which would then be double-checked.

John said, 'I'll let the police know we're on it.'

'No!' Moriarty was emphatic. 'The Red Circle's many tenacles stretch far and wide.'

'You think it has agents in Scotland Yard?'

'I'd be amazed if it hasn't. Either the Yard or some associated party in Whitehall. They may not even know they're working for the Red Circle. Or they may be trusted operatives passing on information and insight on a weekly basis. The point is — the world must believe Martin Grimble died in Philly and his corpse lies somewhere in the depths of the Delaware. For his own safety, we must protect that lie.'

'So we can't pass on the intel I've supplied about operational matters?'

'That's right, Martin. At least, not until the Teardrop Killer is found.'

John topped up his own glass. 'Can we tell Inspector Lestrade?'

'I'm tempted to say yes, but there's always the threat she'd do it by the book and others would learn of our deception. So for the time being, our plan should remain between the three of us and Sébastienne Moran. One other thing — I'm creating a new identity for you, Martin. Passport, driver's license, insurance number, bank account. The full package. From this night onwards, you are to go by that new identity. Understood?'

The other man nodded. 'What name will I be given?'

'When we first met, you were open about your skills in bypassing online security. I asked you about PINs, passwords, entry codes and the like, and you assured me that with your abilities, every lock was a poor lock. I rather liked the expression. So, Porlock it is.' He paused. 'Romano Porlock. I think that's rather a fine name.'

'Porlock is fine. But I hate Romano. It's just not me, Professor.'

'It's Romano or Fred,' Moriarty shot back, a little peeved at the interruption.

'I'd prefer Fred, if it's all the same to you?'

'What's in a name? Quite a lot, it seems.' Moriarty gave a deep sigh and took a sip of wine. 'There's no accounting for taste. So be it. Have it your way. Martin Grimble is dead.'

He raised his tumbler and all three men clinked glasses, proclaiming in unison, 'Long live Fred Porlock!'

Chapter Sixty-Five

JOHN SAW VERY LITTLE OF MORIARTY DURING THE following two days. He pursued leads generated from his podcast, but none panned out. Still, he felt a sense of purpose as he toiled away in his Baker Street apartment, interviewing potential witnesses over Zoom and trawling through the feedback listeners had sent him.

On the third day, he realized his relationship with 221B had changed. He had not exorcized the ghost of Sherlock Holmes, but his friend's spirit had at least faded. He would always remain in these rooms, whether peering over Baker Street on foggy evenings or standing deep in thought by the unlit fireplace on summer afternoons. His personality and the impact he'd had on John Watson meant he could never fully leave.

But when John had first returned, Holmes had been waiting in every corner. He saw him brooding in his old armchair. He had heard the strains of Mendelssohn's 'Song Without Words' being softly played on his Stradivarius. He had smelt his tobacco from the hallway. Now Holmes's presence was a remembered thing. John could conjure him up if he chose, but he was a guest, not a flat mate. The violin was back in its case. The Persian slipper and calibash were souvenirs in the literal sense of the word. Reminders, but no longer shackles.

And when John Watson decided to move back into 221B Baker Street, he realized he could only do so because finally, he had broken free of it.

THE TEXT READ: *John! Come upstairs if you're free!*

As he read it, a follow-up landed: *If you're not free, come up anyway!*

John padded up the steps to 221C and knocked on the door.

'Come in! Come in!' Moriarty looked pleased to see him. 'Good news! Porlock has worked miracles!'

'Where is he?'

'Taking a well-earned kip after working for over 24 hours straight.'

'What sort of miracles?'

'Can I get you a drink?'

'No, thanks.'

'He's already amassed a considerable amount of footage and has run a programme that sifts out faces that look more or less identical.'

'So if someone turns up in footage showing Ethan McDee going shopping, and a same or very similar face is spotted in videos taken from another victim's gym, or from footage from the life of a person on your list, then the programme alerts us. That about it?'

'In a nutshell.' Moriarty sprawled across one of his sofas and turned on the huge television. 'There are more faces to get through than I'd anticipated. The definition of a lot of the footage is rubbish, meaning we've got a lot of sketchy hits. I thought we could go through them now. Discount any that appear to be different people and prioritize any hits that look like an individual is obviously spying on the subject.'

John took a seat on the opposite sofa. 'Sounds good.'

'I also printed out some of the faces that have got apparent matches. Here…' He tossed his guest a wad of A4 sheets. 'Then I realized it would be easier to just study them on the screen. Larger images, and we can sharpen them up if necessary.'

John was already leafing through the pages, his eyes skimming over screenshots taken from various sources. Every sheet of paper held two photos, each of a face that the programme flagged as a potential match. 'We might as well make a start.'

'Exactly. I'm just trying to patch the programme through.' As he worked on the connection he asked, 'How's Mary?'

John had spoken to her three of four times a day, meaning they'd had more conversations in one week than their previous few months combined. She always called him on an untraceable phone, and whatever the time, whatever he was doing, he'd always picked up and been present.

'She's fine.'

John had experienced her going through a cycle of stages which he felt must be common in her uncommon situation. First there was fear. A dread of the man who had killed so many others — the monster who had touched her skin and quite literally marked her for death. Anger followed. A fury that someone should do this to her. Curiosity came soon after. Who was he? Why had he spared her life? How long would her time spent incommunicado drag on for?

The penultimate stage was manifest as boredom and fatigue. The necessity of living in secret, unable to go out, return home, or see friends was tedious and surprisingly draining. The final and most inevitable phase — a peppering of all of those shades that had come before. Rage and fear, inquisitiveness, boredom, and tiredness all competing for her attention.

He'd seen similar cycles before, in war, and always marvelled at survivors' ability to normalize even the most abnormal situation.

'I'm glad,' Moriarty replied. 'Sébastienne tells me she's doing well. Perhaps, if we use extreme caution, we could arrange for you both to meet up.'

He paused, expecting a positive reaction. But the silence stretched. John was studying one of the pages hard. Moriarty shrugged. 'I'll start running the faces.'

'Don't bother.'

'Why not?'

John got to his feet, but his eyes didn't leave the photos that had seized his attention.

'Doctor! I said why not?'

'Because I've found him. I've found the Teardrop Killer.'

Moriarty stood up, too. 'How can you be so sure?'

John handed him the sheet of paper. 'Because I know him.'

Chapter Sixty-Six

AFGHANISTAN — MUCH EARLIER.

SOMEONE IN THE BAR SAID, 'Anyone got a gasper? I'm all out.'

David Gunn saw it was his best friend, John Watson. 'Hang on…' He felt his pockets and pulled out a fresh packet of Lucky Strikes. 'Here you go…' He tossed him the cigarettes. 'Don't smoke 'em all at once!'

'Cheers, Tommy!'

He never minded Tommy. Made a change from Crick or Gattling.

Watson said, 'Aye, aye, sir!' and gave him a lazy salute.

'Hang on!' Gunn drained his drink, momentarily wondering what the hell it was. 'I'll come with you! Could do with one myself.'

But he saw his friend was being loudly teased by some of the locals. He'd not heard him.

One of the army lads plonked a bottle of Bells onto the table. 'Help yourselves, boys!'

Another of the younger guys said, 'It's not even a single malt — peasant!' which triggered a round of good-natured jeering. Gunn knocked back a mouthful of the scotch, got to his feet, and followed John Watson from the bar. He paused in the exit, scanning the milling crowds for his friend. He spotted him, standing side-on to the bar, just across the narrow road.

'Johnny!'

But again, he didn't hear him.

Gunn saw his friend put a Lucky to his lips. As he lit it, the bomb went off.

AFTER HE LEFT THE ARMY, David Gunn started buying lottery tickets and lotto scratch cards. He felt lucky, so why not? People said he'd been unfortunate to get hit by the explosion, but no, he disagreed. The young men inside drinking Bells and trading jokes, they'd been the — and he had to pause and swallow before saying the word — *unfortunate* ones.

A stone pillar had shielded him from the brunt of the blast force and flying debris. An inch to his left or to his right and he'd have spent the night in the same morgue as his army pals. He felt lucky.

For a period, he genuinely believed he *was* lucky, as if it was something cellular. As much a part of his physical composition as bone marrow, enzymes, or calcium. Yet the lottery tickets never understood this and refused to make him a millionaire. So in time, he came to suppose he'd used up the last of his good fortunate in that loud, shattered bar in Kabul.

Years later, so-called experts speculated that David Gunn had been suffering from PTSD when he left the army, but that wasn't the case. Not even close. His 'issues' had begun long before he joined up and weren't as clear cut as most observers claimed. It should be noted that actually, when he moved on from the armed services, he'd been scrupulous about looking after his mental health. He rented digs in Kettlewell, North Yorkshire, so he could be near his family and spend plenty of time outdoors, walking, hiking, and enjoying the stunning scenery offered by the Dales. He was, he often told acquaintances, 'happy enough,' which is what people usually say when they're unhappy.

He recognized this. Furthermore, he knew that in truth, he missed the army. Or rather, he missed the regimentation it demanded and enforced. The order. The camaraderie. The buzz. But most of all, he missed the luxury and the bliss and the stone-cold certainty of knowing where he stood.

Mondays were the hardest. Maybe that's why he did it. People who later chronicled his life admitted it was unclear. Perhaps it was simply on a whim, a whim that on one Monday morning he caught the bus into Sheffield. The weather was good. Cold, but bright and dry. Crisp. He walked to the train station and asked how much a ticket to London would cost. The woman behind the desk didn't bother to check her database. 'You're looking at a hundred quid, luv, give or take.'

'Thanks, pet.'

'Daylight robbery, isn't it?'

'Aye. Someone somewhere is getting rich.'

He drifted into the WHSmith's, just across from the ticket booths, for a bottle of water, but out of habit ended up buying a lotto card instead, which he carried in his hand to The Sheffield Tap. It was a station pub, a glorious, Edwardian-style freehouse — all glazed tiles, copper-topped tables, red leather seats, high arches, and low prices for the beer that was brewed onsite.

'Pint of the Sheaf Street, please, mate.'

'Coming right up, boss.'

As he waited for his pale ale, David Gunn placed his lotto card on the dark wooden bar top and using the key to his front door, began to scratch off its grey coating. He uncovered a golden cauldron and inwardly groaned. He had to find three matching icons to win, but a trio of cauldrons would mean he'd scoop a cool million, so the likelihood was remote. He scratched a smiley face next. Two more of those and he'd be a hundred pounds richer.

The barman placed his beer on the counter. 'There you go.'

'Cheers.'

Gunn scratched away another patch of grey to reveal a second golden cauldron.

The barman peered over. 'What'll you do if you get one more?' he asked.

Chapter Sixty-Seven

John said, 'His name is David Gunn.'

'Who is he?'

'He was my best friend.'

'Was?'

'In the army. We were inseparable. He's a good guy. I've got to be wrong. He can't…'

Moriarty ran a programme searching for Gunn's face throughout all the assembled footage. It delivered eleven hits across five different subjects.

'John, that's pretty conclusive. He's our man.'

'I don't understand…' John stared at the photo of him. 'You were right. A military man, you said. Like me.'

'Are you still in touch?'

'No. We left the army around about the same time. But he went up north. We kind of drifted apart after that. There was no falling out. In fact, I don't think we ever had an argument in all the years we knew each other. We…'

John pursed his lips.

'What?'

'Loved each other. We loved each other.'

'Were you just friends?'

John's eyes flicked from the photo of Gunn to Moriarty. 'Why do people say that? *Just friends*. As if platonic friendship is somehow lesser than any other form. It's more, you know. It's much more. There's nothing *just* about friendship.'

And picking up on the unintended ambiguity of this comment, Moriarty murmured, 'Never were truer words spoken.'

'Yes. We were *just* friends. We'd do anything for each other.' His gaze returned to the photos. 'Oh, Tommy. What have you done, mate?' Watson threw his head back. 'Christ!'

'Take it easy, John.'

'Take it easy? We thought these murders were all about you. They're about me!'

Moriarty ran his palm across his face. 'You think he did this for you?'

'I had gotten … down. Life got on top of me. I felt the loss of Holmes, of Mary, of everything I perceived myself to be. Felt it very keenly.'

'And you think that Gunn found about this somehow?'

John nodded. 'Remember what I said? *We'd do anything for each other*. Tommy took revenge for me. He exacted revenge on the person he thought caused all the pain in my world.'

'Me.'

'Professor James Moriarty. And because he believed you were dead, he avenged himself — on my behalf — on all the people who'd been important to you.'

'What about Bailey Hernandez?'

'Best guess? Well, she gave an interview when her prison took in the Valentino twins. My podcast led to their arrest, but she ignored my contribution completely. She made out the forces of officialdom were the only ones who'd achieved their capture and confinement. He must have felt she stole my thunder and … Oh, god…'

His voice trailed off.

'What is it, John?'

'Mary. That's why he didn't kill her. He just warned her. Christ, that's what it was! He saw the heartache she'd caused me, but he couldn't kill her because I love her. So he just threatened her. Tried to somehow reconcile us.'

Moriarty slowly nodded. 'And it kind of worked, to be fair…'

'What?'

'I imagine you've spoken more to Mary this week than you have done for ages. What befell her has brought you both closer. Whatever happens, please remember that, John.'

'I can't hate David Gunn, if that's what you mean. He's still my friend. He needs me more than ever right now.'

'John — he's killed six people!'

'You don't get how friendship works, do you Moriarty?'

'I *get* how murder works. I *get* how—'

'I wasn't having a pop at you,' John interjected. 'If anything, I feel sorry for you.'

It wasn't said unkindly or as an insult, but the weight of the observation pushed the two men apart for several seconds.

After a moment, Moriarty said firmly, 'I still have a job to do. I'm going to bring Gunn in.'

'Alive.'

'If possible. But I can understand that this just got even more personal for you. If you want to take a back seat from this point onwards, I'd—'

'Moriarty!'

'Yeah?'

'We need to bring him in *now*.'

'It'll be dangerous.'

'What else is new?' John slipped the photo of Gunn into his pocket. 'What's our next move?'

Chapter Sixty-Eight

WHEN TALKING TO OTHER PEOPLE, THEY ALREADY USED THE phrase 'partner' for each other, a descriptor which held all sorts of unwelcome connotations for Zenisha, but it felt marginally better than all the other options which a language comprising 250,000 words could offer.

Her 'partner' had swung by her house that morning. He was still impressed by the size of it and the affluence that emanated from its every square foot. She could tell that by the way he remained cautious with it and never fully relaxed when visiting her. He was like a parent herding toddlers through an aisle containing open displays of delicate, expensive porcelain. Not worried, as such, but forever on his guard, no matter how informal he tried to appear. He was a man suddenly concerned that his surroundings were worth more than he was.

She was used to that, of course. She'd had a lifetime of it with friends and suitors and colleagues. They began by being impressed, and the best she could hope for was the feeling would evolve into apathy regarding her familial wealth, although it normally transmuted into a much denied jealousy and spluttering hatred.

Whatever. Right now, her 'partner' was good-hearted and eager, which went a long way.

He had a big smile that Zenisha knew was intended to say, 'I'm happy, I'm happy, I'm happy!' but she read it as 'I need you!' which worried her. Relationships built on necessity never endured, because necessities never lasted.

She wasn't a romantic woman, yet she recognized the value of love in any pairing. Since her mid-teens, she'd held that like the giant marlin in 'The Old Man and the Sea,' love never made it back intact. Any relationship ate away at love, and below the surface, eroded it.

But she knew that to an extent, it could survive and bind, and make two people happy to see each other on the blandest of occasions.

Did he need her? For her money, her connections, her kindness, and the world she gave him access to. Possibly. Or did he love her for the same reasons? She doubted love and needing could co-exist. One was an implied condition, the other a suggested purpose.

When she opened the front door to him, he'd immediately said, 'Are you free today?'

'I've got work. I've aways got work.'

'Can you take a long lunch?'

She started to say it was out of the question, but he interrupted her.

'Please!'

'Is it important?'

'Tell you what — why don't you send your emails and put your out-of-office on, and I'll pick you up in an hour?'

'*Is it important?*'

'Very!'

'Let me think about it.'

'Hey, you're the boss!'

He'd driven off in his van and Zenisha had stood in the doorway watching it go. The 'Very!' had convinced her. She believed she knew what he would ask her when they next met.

Zenisha Lestrade closed the door, returned to her orangery, and vaguely weighed up her answer as she finished her morning coffee and completed the cryptic crossword on the back page of *The Daily Telegraph*.

MORIARTY's metallic grey Volvo sped through the back streets of London, zipping down allies, and twice mounting the pavement to bypass slow-moving traffic. John sat in the passenger seat and apologized to pedestrians forced to scatter and flee. But he never urged Moriarty to slow down. On the contrary, he occasionally snapped, 'Can't you go any faster?' and approaching a red light on one stretch of B road, he shouted, 'Just jump it!'

Moriarty had earlier reflected that given they knew their prime suspect's name and had his description ('and pretty much his whole life story'), that for once, Scotland Yard might be best placed to find him. 'It will also placate Lestrade,' he said. 'Give her something to do. She'll know we had help with the footage, but hopefully this'll distract her from prying into what it was.'

But Lestrade hadn't picked up any of their calls or messages, so they'd left Baker Street, careering across town towards her office.

They reached her station, parked on double yellows, and raced into the building. As they hurried through the wide, open space of its reception, John realized the last time he'd been here, the place had been heaving with penitent thieves, eager to square their misdeeds with the 'proper' authorities before the authority of James Moriarty found them. Joe Cisto had been worried, Zenisha baffled, and John had sensed something cyclonic was whirling towards his life. It had been a recent event, but felt months, *years* earlier. On that day he'd stood in front of people who had come to hear him talk, despite being uninterested by what he had to say. He had felt lost. Without purpose. And remembering those feelings was what made that time seem so long ago.

John flashed an identity pass to the woman on the reception desk. She said, 'Right-oh! Morning, Doctor! How are you?'

'I'm good, thanks!'

'I was sorry to hear about Mary. Sounds dreadful.'

'I'm in a bit of a hurry! Sorry!'

'Don't mind me!' she said and clicked open the side door.

John and Moriarty rode the elevator to Lestrade's floor. Their ascent seemed slower than ever. Moriarty moaned, 'Every minute David Gunn is at large, there's a risk of more killings.'

'I know that.'

'When was the last time you spoke to him?'

'Years ago. He was coming to London. On a whim, so we'd not planned anything properly. But I was supposed to be meeting him, then something came up, so I had to cancel.'

'What was it? What came up?'

'Funnily enough, I think it was—'

Ping!

The elevator slid to a halt and as its doors parted. Moriarty murmured, 'At last!'

The two men jogged down the corridor and without knocking, burst into her office where the two men's worst fears were confirmed: Inspector Lestrade's office was empty.

Chapter Sixty-Nine

He'd called for Zenisha in his van, and as he opened the passenger door for her, he commented, 'You look surprised.'

'I've never seen you in a suit before.'

'I save it for special occasions. What do you think? Do I scrub up well?'

But Zenisha had sat down, so didn't have to continue the conversation. He closed her door and walked around the front of the vehicle. Once behind the wheel he whispered, 'Off we go!' as if they were embarking on an illicit adventure.

They both stood in the middle of the empty office, a sense of deflation and mild anger kicking in.

'Doctor Watson — can I help?'

Detective Sergeant Lee Jones appeared in the doorway. It was hard to tell if her question was an offer of help or a starched rebuke.

'Lee! How are you?'

'I'm fine.' She glanced at his companion. 'You brought *him* in *here*?'

'I know,' Moriarty replied warmly. 'They let anyone in these days. No standards.' He offered his hand. 'I'm James.'

She ignored him and addressed Watson. 'You after Zenisha?'

'Yeah. Any idea where she is? It's urgent.'

'She was supposed to be in but pulled a sickie. She told me — in confidence, so don't go spreading it about — that she was going to see that fella of hers.'

'She's in the middle of a murder investigation and she's wagging it to see her boyfriend?' John's voice conveyed equal measures of astonishment and disapproval. 'Why?'

As they left London, Zenisha got as far as, 'I like to think that our...' before floundering slightly. '...*arrangement* is a good one. It's working.' And with a little more emphasis than she'd intended, she added, 'As it is.'

'Are you asking me what I think?'

'Sure. Communication is key.'

'Communication *is* key. Well, for starters, to be honest, I wouldn't put it that way. You make it sound very cold. *Arrangement*. We've already done great things.'

'Great things?' The expression caught her off-guard. 'Look, I like you, but—'

'I like you, too. But it's about more than that, isn't it? You must see that! It has to be about more.'

MORIARTY GENTLY BRUSHED past Detective Sergeant Jones, rounded Zenisha's desk, and sat in her chair. 'So Inspector Lestrade — a woman governed by duty — takes a day off to see her beau? He must be a keeper.' He drummed his fingers on her desk. 'I wonder where he's taken her.'

'They might be at her place,' Lee ventured.

Moriarty looked wearied by the suggestion.

Catching his expression, John said to the DS, 'Whatever they're doing has to be special enough to warrant her taking time away from the investigation. Anything they're doing at her house could be done another time. And as Zenisha is so focused on the case, well, it stands to reason that the impetus to do whatever it is they're doing, came from him.'

'Hence — I wonder where he's taken her...' Moriarty lightly kicked the edge of the desk, and his chair span around 360 degrees. 'What's he like? This persuasive paramour? Detective Sergeant Jones — have you met him?'

'Yeah. Just the once. He seems okay.'

'He seems okay?' Moriarty gave the smile of a school-teacher wanting more from a gifted student who's resting on their laurels. 'Fabulous! But I'm sure you can summon up all your powers of creativity and description to give us a more useful picture than is presented by *he seems okay*.'

She turned to John. 'Can I arrest him?'

'Not yet,' he replied. 'But if you could tell us more. It could be important, Lee.'

'He's a plumber. They met him on some dating app. Not like Tinder or any of the sex ones. This one puts you in touch with people you wouldn't normally spend time with. So it's not like teachers hooking up with teachers or accountants being paired with FDs. It's mixing and matching. A Detective Inspector being matched with a plumber is a typical outcome.'

'Sounds modern. Sounds vile.' Moriarty looked at Watson. 'They were brought together by algorithms, as opposed to Eros.'

'What's wrong with that?' Lee sounded indignant. 'Lots of people hook up online these days.'

'There's nothing wrong with it, when there's nothing wrong with it,' Moriarty countered.

John finished his drift. 'But anything that exists online can be hacked.'

'Are you saying someone manipulated their getting together?'

ZENISHA LOOKED through her window at the countryside as the urban sprawl of outer London faded into something prettier. Hedgerows, wooden gates, small meadows. It also brought with it a greater quietude and desolation.

'This isn't the way to the village.'

He said, 'I thought you liked surprises.'

She gestured to the dashboard. 'We're almost out of petrol. There's a station up here on the left. Maybe we should put half a tank in.'

'I've got a Jerry can in the back. Full of unleaded.'

'I want an answer, now.' Zenisha turned to him. 'Where are you taking me?'

MORIARTY GOT TO HIS FEET. 'Tell us what he was like. Your impressions of him.'

Lee thought for a moment. 'Broad shoulders, messy hair and cheerful looking. Kind of guy that's always smiling.'

John asked, 'Did he smoke?'

'Yeah.'

'What brand of cigarettes?'

'Lucky Strikes.'

'His name,' said Moriarty. 'What's his name?'

'It's a slightly weird one. That's why it's stuck in my head.'

'Tell us!' John urged.

'David,' the Detective Sergeant told them. 'His name is David Crick.'

Chapter Seventy

DAVID GUNN PULLED INTO WHAT LOOKED TO BE A deserted dairy. After a half-minute hunt in the back of his van, he found the fuel can, double-checked it was full, and started pouring the petrol into the vehicle's tank. Zenisha didn't have to turn around to spy on him. As he'd been rummaging for the Jerry can, she'd quickly wound down her window and surreptitiously re-angled the left side mirror, and now she could see him in it, oblivious to the fact he was being watched. She cautiously removed her phone from her pocket. Saw Detective Sergeant Jones had left her a message. Still keeping an eye on David she pressed 'play'.

'Zenisha, it's Lee. Look, don't freak out. It's about David. We think his real name is David Gunn and he employed criminal tactics to instigate his first meeting with you. Here's where I really need you to keep calm. We think he could be the Teardrop Killer. Call me as soon as you get this.'

Zenisha swivelled in her seat. She knew David to be a tidy, methodical man, but he'd had to rummage for the

Jerry can. She looked over the items in the back of van. Most of it comprised the tools of his plumbing trade. A tool box. Coils of wire. Some copper piping. But immediately behind the driver's seat — a blanket.

She reached across to it. Began to tug it to one side to check out whatever it was covering and—

'Hey!'

Her head whipped to her left.

David was leaning against her door, peering in at her through her open window.

'Don't do that, David! You scared the life out of me!'

He looked at her strangely, as if her face was somehow moving in ways only he could understand. 'They know, don't they?'

'What do you mean?'

'And they've told you. Never mind.'

As he walked around the front of the van to retake his seat, Zenisha glanced in the back to see what the blanket had been covering. It was a small, metal case with a distinctive logo in one corner. During her investigation to find the Teardrop Killer, she'd come across several similar containers, and she was fully aware what they held and what this meant.

David Gunn was secretly storing and carrying a portable tattoo kit.

~

MORIARTY SAID TO LEE JONES, 'I need you to ping Lestrade's phone right now. We need to get a fix on her immediately.'

Together with John Watson, they were riding the elevator down to the station's ground floor.

'I can put the wheels in motion. But the process isn't immediate.'

'Are you kidding me?'

'There are privacy issues, Professor.'

'There are life and death issues, Detective Sergeant.'

'I'm going to work as fast as I can to ensure—'

'Not good enough!'

'Well, luckily, your opinion means less than nothing to me!' Lee glowered. 'I wouldn't expect you — a murderer, a thief, a fraudster — to understand something called due process. The law's just a joke to you.' She looked away. 'Christ…'

'Oh, I understand you hold your petty rules to be sacrosanct. Whereas I hold innocent human life to sacrosanct.'

'You're so noble,' Lee returned with heavy sarcasm.

'Whatever else she may be, Zenisha is a friend of John's. So I'm going to make sure she's all right, with or without your help.'

'Look, you don't seem to get it! Even if I *wanted* to help you trace her phone, I'd have to make an application.'

'Applications are for painting your nails!' Moriarty had balled his fists, but trying to calm down, he took a couple of breaths. 'The whole *having to apply* thing? Never really applied to me.'

He pulled out his phone and made a call. 'Colonel! I need you to trace a handset for me. When do I need it? About half an hour ago.'

John moved fractionally closer to Lee Jones. 'On this one occasion, could we bend the rules?'

Her face indicated she wasn't convinced.

'Or at least turn a blind eye to their contravention? Please, Jonesy … I feel a burden with this one. If it comes to it, we both know Moriarty will run to the hills. But I'll stay to face the fire. And I'll take the wrap for any laws that are broken whilst trying to apprehend David Gunn.'

Lee was wavering.

'*Please…*'

'You win.' She nodded. 'But we do it together.'

'Understood. Thank you.'

'I don't need your gratitude. Zenisha is my friend, too.'

'Yeah. I know. Still, thanks, mate.'

The elevator doors slid open. Moriarty finished his call, pocketed his phone, and as they hurried across the reception area, he declared, 'I've got Zenisha's location, but she's outside London. Traffic is against us. Jones — can you whistle us up a police escort? At least as far as the city limits? I know you're loathe to help me but—'

Lee stopped dead in her tracks, forcing Moriarty and John to pause. 'Shut up, Professor!'

'I just need a couple of liveried cars with blues and twos blaring so we can—'

'Not gonna happen!'

'Not gonna happen?'

Even Moriarty appeared taken aback.

'Not gonna happen,' Lee Jones confirmed, 'because I can organize something much better than that. You know your problem, Moriarty?'

'Well,' he said, instantly genial and spreading his palms. 'Where do I start?'

Lee began walking to the exit and called over her shoulder, 'You've no imagination.'

The two men left in her wake exchanged glances.

'Hot take,' said Moriarty, 'I like her.'

≈

Less than twenty minutes later, the police helicopter banked starboard and followed the Thames southwards at a speed of just over 150 mph. Moriarty and Lee Jones sat in the back of the aircraft, with John perched between them. A pilot and two coes were up front, manning the controls.

Although technically an Airbus Helicopter H145, most old hands in the National Police Air Service still referred to the vehicle as an EC145, which had been the original model's earlier designation. Whatever it was called, it wasn't the fastest or sexiest looking chopper in the skies, but it was a sturdy and reliable craft and offered a surprisingly comfortable and quiet ride.

Lee said to her companions, 'If I'd had more time, I could have drafted in a police marksman.'

'Yeah...' Moriarty surreptitiously patted the Beretta in his concealed shoulder holster. 'Don't worry about that.'

'Wait a second!' John pulled out his phone. 'I've got a call coming through...'

Lee asked, 'Who is it?'

'It's Zenisha,' he replied and pressed *answer call*.

Chapter Seventy-One

JOHN LISTENED FOR SEVERAL LONG SECONDS. EVEN BEFORE one had elapsed, Moriarty was squirming with impatience. 'What's she saying?'

'I'm pretty sure she's with David.'

'What's happening?'

John batted away his inquiry, frowning, trying to hear what was being said on the line. Eventually he revealed, 'She's doing what I did when you first visited me in Baker Street.'

Lee asked, 'What's that?'

'Well, she's called me without David knowing so we can listen in to what they're saying. I've muted our side of the conversation, just in case. I'm going to put the call on speaker…'

Moriarty and Lee leant into John to better catch the conversation. They heard a male voice first: '- in a million years.'

Followed by Zenisha's reply. 'But here we are. I mean, what's happening?'

'I knew they'd find out eventually. They always do, these days.'

Moriarty said, 'Is it him?'

'It's David Gunn.' John nodded. 'My friend. Yes.'

They heard Zenisha say, 'I can still help you. You went through a lot in the army.'

'They were the best days of my life! Don't go pinning any of this on the forces! Best days of my whole life, they were! Good times. Good chaps.' His voice cracked a little. 'Good friends.'

'It's not about pinning it on anyone. Really. It's about the why, David. What brought you here?'

The ensuing silence lasted so long that Watson wondered if the call had ended, but as this concern set in, Zenisha's voice returned. 'This morning I thought you were going to propose to me. This afternoon I think you're going to kill me. That's a hell of a relationship roadblock. Right now, I think if any couple needs therapy, it's us! So let's talk.'

'Relationship? Couple? This morning you described us an arrangement.'

'Clumsy wording! Don't hold that against me.'

'Clumsy?'

'Thoughtless, then.'

'People are always thoughtless to men like me. We don't matter.'

Another long pause, but this time Gunn restarted the conversation. 'I thought I was fortunate when I survived the blast. Thought good luck was in my bloodstream, being pumped round my body. Ridiculous to think like that, I know. That's not how it works! I survived by chance. After everything that happened, I finally twigged. Tah-dah! Nobody cares. Nobody. Fucking. Cares.'

John murmured, 'Oh, sweet Jesus, forgive me.'

'Came as a bit of a blow to realize,' Gunn continued, 'God doesn't care for men like me, no more than the other people he made care for me. I suppose that's what they mean when they say God made man in his own image. Uncaring. Venal. Immune to consequences. That's God. That's man.' In the helicopter, they could almost hear his shrug. 'Both as bad as each other.'

'David…'

'Yes, darling?'

'Are you the Teardrop Killer?

'Yep!'

For Watson, there was something heart-breaking about the implied glibness of the reply. There had been no tortured hesitation. No tinge of remorse. He could have been answering a telephone survey about the price of groceries.

Do you feel you're paying too much for your daily bread?

Yep!

He felt Moriarty grip his forearm. 'Keep the faith, Doctor.'

Zenisha's tone was desperate. 'I need to know why! I just don't understand!'

'I needed to make people realize.'

As the police helicopter banked port, it left the silvery grey ribbon of the Thames. London was already behind them and now they flew over fields, a zig-zag mesh of country lanes and sporadic villages.

The three passengers heard Gunn continue. 'Maybe that's why I survived,' he said. 'This was my mission. Our mission. I'm not talking about some divine quest. This was something that came from within me. I'm talking about tears for the dead. Maybe I can get people to realize — the living need them, too, you know. Who knows, eh? Perhaps

I'll end up being viewed as a force for good. What would you have said, by the way?'

'When?'

'If I'd asked you to marry me.'

'You answer my question and I'll answer yours. That's only fair.'

'Roger that.'

'Why did you do it? And don't give me any *this it was my mission* stuff, or talk about people needing to realize. What turned David the nice guy, the bloke with a smile on his face and a drink in his hand, into a force that's slaughtered six people. Who's to blame?'

A pause.

'Tell me!'

Gunn's words were quiet and regretful: 'You are.'

Zenisha's surprise felt palpable. 'Me?'

'No.' David Gunn's voice was firm and even in the chopper cabin, clearly audible. 'You.'

No one spoke. After a moment, John whispered, 'Who's he talking to?'

And Moriarty, looking at him with sadness clouding his clear blue eyes replied, 'You, Johnny.' He pressed the unmute button on his phone and mouthed the instruction, 'Talk to him.'

Chapter Seventy-Two

John Watson opened his mouth to speak. Closed it again, then blurted out, 'What have you got yourself mixed up in this time, mate?'

David Gunn sounded genuinely delighted. 'Johnny! Ha! How are you?'

'I'm good. How are you, doing?'

'Yeah, I'm fine, thanks.'

'Fine?'

'Okay, I've had better days, to be honest. I figured she'd call you. Who am I talking to, apart from you, soldier?'

John looked quickly from his left to his right, a finger over his lips making the universal plea for silence. But Moriarty bent his upper body, moving his lips closer to the handset. 'This is Professor James Moriarty. And I'm accompanied by Detective Sergeant Lee Jones. That's all. Just the three of us. Doctor Watson told me you loved one another.'

'Are you sneering at us?'

'Not at all. I'm envious.'

'Then why mention it?'

'Because I know the pain of losing someone you love, and I don't want our friend to go through that again. Believe me, I would do a lot to prevent that, soldier.'

'Roger that, Professor. What are you thinking?'

'I'd like this to all end with no one being killed. Zenisha walking away. You and John having a drink and applying some sort of triage to this whole mess. What do you think?'

When David Gunn didn't reply, John said, 'A second ago you told Zenisha I was to blame for all this. I don't get it. Please — explain why this is on me. *And what can I do to fix this?*'

But when his old friend spoke again, he was clearly addressing Moriarty. 'Not going to happen, Professor. It ends soon — with a lot of death. Johnny…'

'Yes, mate?'

'I forgive you.'

The line went dead.

~

'What'll you do if you get one more?'

Years earlier, hunched over the dark wooden bar in the railway station pub, The Sheffield Tap, David Gunn had scratched away the last remnants of the lotto card's grey coating. 'I don't believe it!'

He'd held the card aloft. Charlie Bucket with the final golden ticket in his hand. 'I've won!'

'A million?'

Gunn had laughed.

The barman had persisted. 'Did you get the third cauldron?'

'That's not for the likes of me! I've won a hundred quid! Very happy with that.'

'Ah, well. Better luck next time.'

'It's never about luck, man. It's about signs.'

'What are you going to do with the ton? Big night out?'

Gunn looked through the barroom, through its open doors and across the station concourse to the ticket kiosk. 'Not exactly.'

Minutes later, he was on the train heading to London. As the glass, stone and steel of Sheffield fell away to the green of North Yorkshire countryside, he phoned his friend. 'Johnny, it's me! Yeah! Yeah … Typical you! Guess where I'm heading? Dead right! The train … Just a couple of hours! Yeah, we should definitely meet up! What time?'

THE HELICOPTER TOUCHED down in the cramped carpark of a small Norman church. Lee Jones opened the door and leapt from the vehicle. John and Moriarty followed and they jogged away from the blast of the twin-engines and still-whirling blades.

One of the chopper's co-pilots yelled, 'Wait up!'

She unbuckled her belt and joined the party of three across the road from the church, where they stood beside a war memorial. A soldier made of Portland stone watched over them as the co said, 'We used the location the Professor gave us. But the triangulation points for Inspector Lestrade's phone aren't precise.'

Lee Jones gave her a thumbs up. 'But we know they're near!'

'Exactly, but we can't get a better fix.'

John took in his surroundings. They'd landed in a tiny village, and several residents were already ambling down its main road, eager to investigate the cause of the commotion.

'Don't worry,' he said. 'I know exactly where they'll be.'

'How?'

'Long story. Just — everyone follow me.'

As he turned to leave, Moriarty said, 'John!'

'What is it?'

'Can I leave this next bit to you and DS Jones?'

A half-shrug. 'As you like.'

'Thanks.'

John broke into a gentle run, pursued by Lee and the co-pilot.

Moriarty remained at the memorial for less than a minute. He checked his watch, and after making sure Watson and the two police officers were out of sight, he began to walk briskly through the wave of advancing villagers, heading in the opposite direction from the route the others had taken.

Chapter Seventy-Three

JOHN MOVED AS QUICKLY AS HE COULD, ALONG A LANE leading from the village, past a low, thatched pub and a couple of ivy-fronted cottages. He clambered over a cross beam wooden gate leading to a field. Hurried over it and began trudging up a gentle, grass-covered hill. As he made his way to the top, he finally slowed a little. He was breathing heavily but dismissed the co-pilot's suggestion of taking a break. She'd introduced herself as Jill Longfield, a police sergeant who'd been apprised of the situation regarding David Gunn as they'd soared over London.

'Got to keep going,' John had told her.

Lee asked, 'What makes you think they're over here?'

'Until fairly recently, I lived on a houseboat.'

'What? Like a barge?'

'Yeah. Highly recommended. Anyway, when I was feeling low, I used to take her out of London. Got away from it all. There was a spot near here I used to hole up in.'

'And you think David Gunn has done the same?'

'It would feel appropriate, don't you think?' As he

replied, they reached the crest of the hill. 'There she is.' John pointed downwards. 'I don't believe it. That's my old houseboat. And ... oh, no!'

Lee followed the direction of his gesture and saw it immediately. A footpath ran along the bottom of the hillside and beyond it, a river, perhaps 80 feet wide. Immediately in front of them — a barge.

'Well, there they are! And this is *not* good!'

On top of the vessel, clearly visible, even from the top the hill, Zenisha was strapped to a chair that had been placed on its roof. David Gunn was holding a Jerry can, pouring its contents over her. When she was saturated, he doused himself in the clear liquid before scattering the last of it over the barge.

John narrowed his eyes. 'What the hell is he doing?'

'Isn't it obvious?' Jill replied.

'Come on!' Lee started picking up the pace. 'We've not got long!'

JOHN HADN'T BEEN out of the armed forces long, and at the time was still feeling the strange burden of liberty. He was as free as air — or as free as his income of army remuneration and meagre interest on his savings permitted any man to be. He had stayed for a while at a hotel in the Strand, leading a comfortless, meaningless existence and spending more of his money than was prudent. He'd soon recognized this must change and even contemplated moving out of London and settling in the sticks. Not ideal, but it wasn't an ideal world.

On that particular Monday, he'd stood alone in the Criterion Bar, a pleasant little drinking hole near Piccadilly Circus, weighing up his various alternatives, both in terms of life choices, and more immediately, what he'd have to drink. The wine menu was proving to be a deadly combination. Appealing but expensive.

The phone call had interrupted his deliberations. He'd picked up and been delighted to hear a familiar voice.

'Johnny, it's me!'

'Tommy! Are you okay? I'm just in a bar … Ha! It'd better London — I'm still here, mate!'

They quickly arranged to meet up later that day. John put down the menu, casting aside the expensive temptations.

Maybe David Gunn was going to save him, after all.

THEY REACHED the bottom of the hill and clustered on the footpath overlooking the river. John, Lee Jones, and Jill Longfield looked across its waters to the barge. They could see Zenisha more clearly now. She was tied to a chair which itself was lashed to one of the metal guide loops on the vessel's roof.

'He's covered us both in petrol!' she shrieked.

John shouted, 'We're going to get you out of this!'

Gunn stood a few paces to the side of Zenisha. 'I knew you'd find us!'

'This is crazy, mate! I'm begging you — stop this!'

'Too late for that, soldier!'

'Look, I know why you're doing this. Or at least, I know why you killed the people you did. I know you did it for me. And I'm now the one asking you to stop, so please…'

'Doing it for you? It's the exact opposite!' Gunn took a cigarette lighter from his pocket. 'I'm doing it *because* of you!'

Chapter Seventy-Four

JOHN SAW ZENISHA'S EYES WIDEN AT THE SIGHT OF THE Zippo. He tried to come across as calm, for her sake, and called across to Gunn, 'What do you mean?'

'Oh, Johnny. I love you, man. But you were always slow on the uptake.'

Lee cut in, pleading, 'Let Zenisha go — please!'

'Doctor Watson and me have got business to settle first. So, Johnny. How've you been?'

'I've been all right.'

'But you've had some dark days?'

'One or two. Who hasn't?'

'Aye! It's hard to stay in the light, sometimes.'

'It's impossible.'

'Know why it's so tricky?'

'Tell me!'

Gunn smiled, pleased with his knowledge. 'The speed of light isn't constant.'

'Let's talk about this on dry land.'

'It wavers. Goodness isn't a constant! It ebbs and flows. Like this river. Understand that, and it's less painful. That's why I was able to forgive you.'

'What's less painful?'

'You abandoned me, John!' He was suddenly shouting. 'After everything we'd done together! After all those vows! I'd have done anything for you! Anything! And you abandoned me!' He held up his lighter.

Zenisha screamed, 'God, no!'

'I just wandered around in London when you didn't show. That city can be a cold wilderness, you know.'

'Why didn't you just call me?'

'Why didn't you just respect me? Or our friendship? After everything that happened … That was my lowest point, though. You see, after that, I had a plan. That's what led to the murders. What was it, Johnny? What happened on that Monday that made you miss our catch-up? That caused all this? What was it that made you never call me again? What became so important?'

As HE'D TURNED to leave the Criterion Bar, someone had tapped his shoulder.

'John! My god, it is you!'

'Stamford!'

'You look as thin as a rake!'

'How are you, Stam? You're looking good!'

'Liar! Christ, we need to catch up! Why don't I get the drinks in?'

'I'm meeting a friend, so I've not got long.'

'Well, let's exchange numbers so we can get together for a few — sometime soon.'

'Sounds good!'

They chatted for a minute. John admitted he was

spending more than he should and needed cheap accommodation, preferably in the capital.

'I think I can help you out there, old son. A mate of mine is looking for someone to share new digs with. Central London, but dirt cheap.'

'That would be ideal! Thanks, man.'

'Well, I'm not sure *ideal* is the word. The bloke you'd be sharing with…'

'Yeah?'

'Well, maybe I should tell you about him over a drink.'

John had picked up the menu. 'I'm not sure I've got time…' He hesitated. 'But I'm intrigued. Go on, then! Tell me more…'

He handed the menu to Stamford.

'Whatever I did, surely it doesn't justify you killing six people!'

Gunn's shoulders drooped in disappointment. 'It was many more than six! Christ! Don't you see? I had to show that *everyone* is worthwhile! I need society to see that we all deserve attention. People wept for the victims of the so-called Teardrop Killer. Why? Because they were all nice, middle-class people who helped with charities and cared about the eco-system. And their deaths were so dramatic! The tattoos. The different MOs. I made them stars! Who cared about the other victims?'

John spoke very slowly. 'What other victims?'

'The ones no one cared about. It's all on my hard drive. Everything you and the world needs to know. And to unleash all the information, you'll just need to remember it for once. After all these years.'

'Remember what?'

'I'm sorry about all this, Johnny.' He took a step towards Zenisha. 'I did try to point you on the right path now and again. I was at the talk you gave at the Rookthorn Speakers' Club. I shouted to you from the back of the room. *What about Moriarty?* I shouted.'

'That was you?'

'We're soldiers. We need to normalize things. I was just trying to get you to see things in a different perspective. I wanted you to look at things differently, with more honesty. But we normalize things. With you, it's betrayal. With me...'

He lit the Zippo and lifted his hand so the single flame flickered over his shoulder.

'Don't do it, Tommy!'

'It's murder.'

David Gunn unfurled his fingers.

The lighter dropped.

The flame hit the pool of petrol—

Whoosh!

The heat hit John, Lee, and Jill. The vessel was 40 feet away, but they felt the searing warmth on their faces, full and sharp, as the barge became a blaze. David Gunn was instantly engulfed in flames. He shrieked and span, wind-milling to his knees. The top of the boat was one bright, raging wall of fire.

But the worst, most sickening sight in this vison of hell was a single person. Because in the middle of the blaze, still tied to the chair fastened to the roof, Inspector Zenisha Lestrade was consumed by the flames that were suddenly everywhere.

Chapter Seventy-Five

JAMES MORIARTY EMERGED FROM THE RIVER AND smoothly hauled himself onto the stern of the barge. He had swam to the boat from the opposite side of the bank to where John, Lee and Jill stood and had approached it, quite literally, behind Gunn's back. He'd reached the aft-side of the vessel a moment before the Zippo had been dropped.

Now, without pausing, he leapt onto the roof of the houseboat and ran into the thick, curling flames.

'Hold on!' he yelled to Zenisha and moving at a phenomenal speed, launched himself at her. As he flew through the air, he grabbed her shoulders. The momentum took them both over. The ties binding the chair to the roof snapped and they smashed into the top of the barge. Moriarty seized her and half-dived, half flung himself back into the river whilst keeping his tight hold on Zenisha.

Locked together by his grip, they plunged into the water.

∼

WATCHING FROM THE FOOTPATH, the river in front of John became eerily calm.

He tore off his jacket. 'I'm going in.'

Jill Longfield said simply, 'You'd never reach them in time.'

Lee pointed to a spot between them and the blazing vessel. 'Look!'

Moriarty surfaced, carrying Zenisha in his arms. She looked towards her friends and called out, 'I'm all right … I'm all right!'

STAMFORD HAD LED him up a bleak stone staircase. They made their way down a low arched passage and into chemical laboratory reeking of sulphur. John could see only one other person in the room, bending over a table and seemingly absorbed in his work. Stamford cleared his throat and the man turned around. He looked straight at John.

'I see you've recently been in … *Afghanistan*.'

'How on Earth did you know that?'

'Never mind,' he replied, chuckling to himself. 'Stamford! Aren't you going to introduce us?'

'Funnily enough,' Stamford replied drily, an intrigued look in his eyes as he stood back from his two friends. 'I think I already have.'

LEE AND JILL tended to Zenisha on the riverbank. The water had ensured the flames hadn't been able to take hold or injure her in any significant way, but she seemed in shock, babbling about 'the lighter … the lighter … don't let him drop the lighter…' and she repeatedly patted her scorched sleeves as if trying to extinguish unseen flames.

'You're gonna be fine,' Lee told her. 'The medics are on their way.'

John had dived into the river and dragged David Gunn to dry land. But he didn't need his doctor's certificates to see his friend was in a bad way.

'Johnny?'

'You're gonna pull through. Just stay with me.'

John made him as comfortable as possible. He sat on the grass verge and positioned Gunn so his head rested on his thighs.

'The medics will be here in minutes.'

But he knew this old soldier didn't have minutes.

Gunn looked up at him. 'Sorry, mate. Feel a bit of an idiot now. Not sure it was worth it. Any of it.'

'Why didn't you reach out to me?'

'I did. On that Monday.' He attempted a smile. 'Hey, you still up for a drink?'

'Only if you're buying.'

Gunn clutched John's hand. 'I'm going, Johnny. It really hurts, and — god! — I can feel myself slipping away. I didn't think it'd be like this. Hold onto me, won't you? Don't let me go!'

'I've got you, mate. You'll be fine. You'll be fine!'

'Don't lie to me…' He was weeping. 'Oh god, I'm so sorry! Just this one time. Don't lie to me.'

'I give you my word, you're gonna get that peace and quiet you always wanted.'

'Really?'

'I promise you. And I'll be along soon enough. We can catch up then, yeah?'

Gunn reached up with his left hand and placed his palm around the back of John's neck, then pulled him downwards. He whispered something. John nodded. Exhausted by the effort, Gunn's arm dropped to his side and his eyelids closed.

'Stay with me, man! I'm not having this!' His desperation began leaking into his every syllable. 'I've only just found you again!'

'It's all right, Johnny. It's all right. It doesn't hurt anymore.'

'Really?'

'Of course it still bloody hurts! I was just saying that to make you feel better!' Gunn gave a short, croaking laugh. 'Oh, Johnny. I love you, man.'

'I love you, too, Tommy.'

Watson used his sleeves to quickly wipe away his tears, but when he looked down again, David Gunn was dead.

Chapter Seventy-Six

By the time the NHS ambulance arrived for Zenisha, she was back to her old self, complaining at length about having to go to hospital. Lee Jones listened to her protestations, then ignored them and guided her into the back of the vehicle.

'I'll be with you in a sec.'

She strode over to John and the two of them nodded to each other. Neither spoke but there was nothing awkward in the trade. Lee pursed her lips and turned, almost bumping into Moriarty, who was walking away from the river's edge.

The two faced each other. Again, there was no verbal exchange but this felt more like a confrontation. Breaking away, Moriarty said softly, 'Excuse me.'

'Hey! My duty to ask…' Lee called after him, 'Are you all right?'

'I'll live,' he replied, without looking around. 'Sorry to disappoint you.'

Lee smiled. A minute later she was in the ambulance

with Zenisha Lestrade as it edged cautiously along the foot-path and verge, heading towards the country lanes.

Straight after it departed, a private ambulance arrived for the corpse. John insisted on traveling with Gunn, and Moriarty didn't try to stop him. 'Can I get you anything, Johnny?'

'No. I'll head straight back to London after delivering Tommy. Just wait for me there, would you?'

'Sure.'

'At least we'll be able to rest a little. Now the murders have been cleared up.' Off the other man's silence, John added, 'Yeah?'

'I'm not so sure that…'

Moriarty broke off as they both took a step back, clearing the way for the stretcher bearing the body of David Gunn. It was carried between them and they watched in silence as it was carefully placed into the back of the ambulance.

'It was Sherlock, wasn't it?' Moriarty said. 'On that long ago Monday.'

'I was entranced by him.'

The admission hung in the air, Banquo's ghost gate-crashing another dead man's wake.

'I'll see you back at Baker Street.' Moriarty turned and began walking back towards the village.

IN THE BACK of the ambulance, Zenisha was sleeping. Lee checked her wrists for burn marks, but she seemed okay. Her hair had been singed, though, and bizarrely, even after the immersion in water and being caried through the river, the smell still lingered. There's something acrid about the scent of burnt hair.

Lee brushed her boss's fringe out of her eyes.

'Why did you call John Watson?' she asked the sleeping woman. 'And not me?'

ONCE HE WAS over crest of the hill, Moriarty veered eastwards and followed a mud path that skirted the village. He made a couple of phone calls. The second was to arrange a pick-up. He signed off with, 'There's a war memorial opposite the church. Tell the driver to meet me there.'

He reached a B road and checked with an online map to confirm he'd been heading in the right direction. He was looking for something, and although he didn't know exactly where it was, if his earlier intel had been correct, he should be very close to it.

JOHN HAD BEEN LEFT in no doubt that the matter was far from closed and he wondered what challenges waited for him. But he had a job to do. Best focus on that. He dismissed the speculation from his mind, reached the ambulance and, for one last time, took in the sight of the barge. His former home, burnt away now. A period of his life he could no longer go back to, even if he'd wanted to return.

Grey plumes of smoke twisted into the blue sky and flames still blazed on the port side.

He climbed into the back of the ambulance, closed the door, and it slowly pulled away.

MORIARTY HAD WALKED LESS than a quarter of a mile before he saw it in the meadow. David Gunn's van, driven off the road and parked behind a tall, long hawthorn that almost obscured it entirely. Moriarty circled the vehicle and tried the driver's door.

Locked.

He glanced about the field. No one. Good. He slammed his elbow through the side window, poked his hand through the gap he'd made, and unlocked the door. The van's alarm was shrill and loud. Moriarty popped the hood, opened it, and tugged a wire away from the battery. The siren died instantly. He found the release clasp for the rear doors, pulled it, then rummaged around in the back of the vehicle. He found what he was after in moments.

Next, he opened the fuel cap and stuffed a newspaper he'd found on the front seat into it. He lit its edges using a cigarette lighter before strolling away. The explosion hit just as he reached the roadside, but he didn't bother to look back. He'd already seen enough fireballs for one day.

MORIARTY ARRIVED at the war memorial and studied it. Beneath the life-sized statue of the soldier, a stone plaque, not dissimilar to a gravestone. It contained a list of the village's dead; those killed in the carnage of the World Wars. Under the names, two lines: THEIR DEEDS LIVE AFTER THEM and below this, FAITHFUL UNTO DEATH.

Moriarty wondered what this last declaration even meant. He read the roll call of the fallen. Felt their age in every archaic name. Saw a mother's pain when any surname was repeated. And finally, he read aloud the promise that was etched along the top of the plaque.

'We shall remember them.' He took a step back. 'Some hope.'

A dark blue Jaguar F-Pace SUV zoomed past the church opposite, slowed a little, and completed a tight U-turn. It pulled up beside the war memorial and the driver's window hummed halfway down. 'Good to see you again, Professor, sir!' Alfie Butler beamed up at Moriarty. 'Heard about this job and told 'em I was the man for it!'

He looked as chipper as he had been during their last meeting, in the bus that had served in Moriarty's escape from 221B.

'I appreciate you getting here so quickly, mon ami.'

Alfie ran a palm over his immaculately brylled back hair. 'Well, some people call them red lights. I call them *suggestions*.'

Moriarty got into the back of the car. Even before they'd left the village, he'd opened up David Gunn's laptop and had set to work cracking its security protocols.

Chapter Seventy-Seven

'WHAT THE HELL IS IT?'

John Watson stood in the doorway of 221C Baker Street. The base of the travertine table had risen, converting it into a kind of stand-at work surface. A laptop was open on its top, but it was the surrounding paraphernalia that had arrested John's attention. Four silver pyramids, each about a foot high, stood on the floor, near to the table. One rested close to each corner. Overhead he could see a sheet of what looked like fairly lights, connected by spaghetti-thin strands of emerald green tubing. The illumination was red, blue, purple, and pink. Twinkling, flickering, and pulsing with low but differing intensities, the lights gave the scene an ethereal feel.

It was a little before 6 a.m. The early morning sunlight, shining through the broad windows overlooking London, held a golden quality. Moriarty and Porlock — the online artist formerly known as Martin Grimble — stood by the table. The latter replied, 'I call it a Porlock Cage.'

'A cage? Oh good. That's exactly what we need.' He

nodded vaguely to Moriarty. 'You couldn't lock him up in it could you?'

'Good morning, John!' Moriarty grinned. 'It's not a literal cage.'

'It's like a Faraday Cage,' Porlock proudly announced. 'Except Faraday Cages block out electromagnet fields — things like RF interference, for instance. Whereas this baby…' He gestured to the equipment surrounding the table, 'keeps our stuff *in*, whilst blocking *out* other forms of interference.'

'Amazing. And for those of us not fluent in technobabble?'

Moriarty explained. 'This is Gunn's laptop. When we open it, I want to make sure it doesn't automatically send anything out. We don't want it broadcasting any pre-recorded messages or anything like that. Also, I want to be certain no one outside of this room can access anything that it contains. This Moriarty Cage ensures both of those things.'

'It's a Porlock Cage,' said Porlock. 'You can't call it a Moriarty Cage.'

'It was my idea!'

'Yeah, but I invented it. And besides, a Porlock Cage sounds like a cutting-edge piece of scientific equipment. A Moriarty Cage sounds like something you'd find in an S&M dungeon.'

John tried not to smile. 'He's got a point.'

'Whatever!' Moriarty scowled. 'John, you told me that Gunn said everything we need to know was on his hard drive, yeah?'

'Yeah.'

'Well then…' Moriarty positioned himself in front of the laptop. 'Let's crack on, shall we?'

IN THE HOURS following the death of David Gunn, there was concern *for* Zenisha Lestrade, but also concern *about* her. How had she allowed herself to be drawn into a relationship with a man whose propensity to slaughter marked him out as one of England's most prolific murderers? Had she compromised the Teardrop Killer investigation? (Many argued it was hard to see how this *couldn't* be the case.) Did her catastrophic lack of judgment mean her career was finished? And most pressingly for everyone linked to the matter — how would her connection with the culprit play with the media and the public at large?

Committees were hastily assembled. Late night meetings stretched into the early hours. The initial sympathy for Zenisha dwindled as her own blame was perceived to be toxic.

Moriarty phoned Lee Jones at 3:35 a.m. 'Don't let them burn Zenisha at the stake.'

'Why would they? And what the hell time is it?'

'Redford's instinct will be to give the press all the information at once. But tell him to play his cards close to his chest.'

'You seriously think I have any sway over the Prime Minister?'

'Do your best. And meet me at Baker Street, 10 a.m. tomorrow.'

To the relief of pretty much everyone brought in to unfasten the Gordian Knot that Zenisha's predicament had tied around police and politicians alike, she tendered her resignation in the early hours of the morning. Her immediate superior used phrases like 'reluctantly accept your request,' 'you must be given time to recover,' and 'regretfully move on,' but Zenisha could hear the relief propping up every his every platitude.

The Prime Minister was immediately informed. Although the police service of England and Wales should primarily remain operationally independent of Whitehall, they were intrinsically bound to the Home Office, and it was therefore deemed that in a case of this import, seeking the PM's input was a legitimate way forward. Or, as one Deputy Chief Constable put it, 'Let the buck stop with him! That's what he's paid 250 grand a year for!'

Redford didn't pause when delivering his orders, although he had the nous to package them as 'mere suggestions and personal opinions.' Every scrap of information relating to the Teardrop Killer investigation and David Gunn should be released immediately. Let the media feast on it all. Zenisha's relationship would make big, salacious news, inevitably, but if it came to light weeks down the line, it would become the main headline and not just one amongst many.

Nobody had any reservations about this.

His next 'mere suggestion' proved more problematic. He proposed (very vigorously) that Moriarty's involvement in the case's resolution should remain classified. As this was a thorny issue which the high-ups didn't want to prick their thumbs on, they hastily passed it to a low-down.

And so at 6:05 a.m., as Lee Jones sat on her loo in her modest London apartment, she took a call from the Prime Minister, asking for her help.

USING PORLOCK'S KNOW-HOW, Moriarty had quickly gained access to the laptop, and everything on its hard drive seemed to be available.

'Where do we start?' John wondered out loud.

The three men were arced around the computer.

Porlock took the mouse and investigated various folders and files. 'Most of it's just workaday stuff. Invoices, plumbing certificates. Docs relating to his work … But here we are! This is the important folder. It's labelled 'The Valley'.'

Moriarty peered at the screen. 'How do you know it's the important one?'

'It's the only one that's protected. Watch…' He double-clicked on the folder's icon and a pop-up box appeared. The instruction, 'PLEASE ENTER ACCESS SEQUENCE' flashed in a bold font above four dashes.

'Tommy told me something…' John closed his eyes as he tried to get his recollection dead on. 'To unleash all the information, you'll just need to remember it for once. After all these years.'

'Remember what?' Porlock demanded. 'What's *it*?'

'That's exactly what I asked him.' John shrugged. 'I have *no* clue.'

'Oh, we have more than a clue,' Moriarty pointed out. 'His whole concept of abandonment crystallized when you let him down and you weren't there for him. When you put Sherlock Holmes above him. When you left him alone in London.'

'I'm not proud of what I did.'

'And I'm not judging you for it. But that event was pivotal to David Gunn, and he more or less told you that it holds the key to this.' He nodded to the folder's onscreen icon.

'Oh god…' John took a breath. 'I think I understand. We were supposed to meet at 3 o'clock.' He reached across to the keyboard and was about to press the '3' button when

Moriarty said gently, 'Gunn remained — first and foremost — an army man.'

John paused. Nodded. Understood. He typed in 1500, the numerical designation for 3 p.m. in the 24-hour clock system.

The lights above them suddenly shone much brighter and flickered violently with a kind of snapping ferocity. The silver pyramids began to glow like silver fires, and after a moment, the folder marked 'The Valley' opened.

Chapter Seventy-Eight

JOHN ASKED, 'WHAT'S HAPPENING?'

Porlock glanced at the overhead lights. 'The Porlock Cage is shakin' its bootie, people. The laptop is *trying* to do something — link with an outside server, send a message, broadcast something … Not sure what.'

'But your lash-up means it can't?'

'It's not a lash-up! But yes, it's confining whatever's on the hard drive to the hard drive.'

'Let's hope it holds,' Moriarty said ominously.

The three of them returned their attention to the folder labelled 'The Valley.' They could now see it contained a single file, labelled RISING.

'Judging by its icon,' Porlock mused, 'it's a video.'

'I'm guessing it's not his summer holidays.'

John asked, 'Do you think we should play it?'

Without warning, the laptop's screen went black. The overhead lights stopped flickering and changed colour to provide an intense, white illumination over the three men.

'I don't think we've got any choice,' Moriarty replied.

The screen sprang back to life and they saw a velvet

blackness under a storm of interference. Over this image — a man's laughter. It began low. A giggle. It became a chuckle. Louder. Laced with more merriment. Seconds later it became a deafening, shouting form of laughter which suddenly stopped. Silence. No, each of them picked up the sound of a low breeze and gentle raindrops. As this noise finally faded, the screen cleared and the video began to play.

It began with shots of two women mooching through a garden centre, pointing at plants and idly chatting to each other. The video had clearly been filmed vertically on a phone, shot at an angle, and it was immediately apparent it had been recorded covertly. The couple being followed by the person capturing the footage evidently had no idea they were being observed in any way.

The women stopped and seemed to be weighing up the merits of a line of hanging baskets. They conversed through sign language and now, seeing them side on, it became clear who they were. The individual closest to the covert camera was the most recent victim of the Teardrop Killer, Bailey Hernandez, and she was with her wife, Léa.

John had already read files on the prison governor's murder, passed to him by Zenisha, and going by the photos he'd seen, he realized this video must have been shot recently.

As the couple were about to move on, the phone dropped a little and neared them. The lens angle changed and the video showed Bailey and Léa turning to face whoever was shooting the footage. This person then pointed to a shelf containing a row of plant pots. Bailey gave a friendly smile. Nodded. Reached up, grabbed one of the plant pots, and handed it to the individual secretly filming them. It then looked as if Bailey was responding to the person thanking them as she held up her hand in a 'no problem' type gesture.

Bailey and Léa gave short, friendly waves of goodbye, then turned and walked away, still trading views on the plants on offer.

What struck John was the normality of the exchange. Two people, pottering around in a garden centre. One had been asked for a spot of help to get something from a high up shelf. No problem! Except the person asking for help was surreptitiously filming them. That moment, so insignificant to Bailey, was part of a process that culminated in her murder.

The video showed Bailey and Léa turning a corner. At the bottom of the screen, John, Moriarty, and Porlock all saw the cameraperson tossing something to one side. It was the plant pot that Bailey had taken from the shelf and helpfully handed over.

And then the person turned their phone around to reveal their identity.

All three men in 221C saw the face of the individual recording the video. She looked to be in her mid-70s. She had a pale, wrinkled face, kind eyes, and short white-grey hair. If any of them had seen her on a television advert, her role would have been obvious. The loveable grandma. The sweet old lady who spoilt her grandkids and baked the best apple pie in the neighbourhood.

She raised her shoulders as she smiled into the lens. A knowing gesture suggesting good fun and mischief. If John didn't know that Bailey had been killed shortly afterwards, he'd have assumed the elderly woman was in on some sort of harmless prank, but as it was, he found the footage grotesque.

A freeze frame on the old, lined face and the video

segued into a second section. A woman in a wine bar, stood alone, idly looking at her phone.

Moriarty said, 'That's Jane Rossi, the Teardrop Killer's fifth victim.'

Again, the footage was shot vertically at an angle, and the content suggested it had been captured covertly on a phone. But there was more movement in this clip. The phone neared Rossi quickly. She looked up as the cameraperson placed a glass of wine on a high table next to her. Rossi thanked the waiter — who was evidently the person taking shooting the footage — and they even exchanged a few words. The last clear shot of the murder victim showed her laughing at something that the waiter was saying to her.

'This was shot recently,' Moriarty observed. 'I'd guess not long before she was killed.'

The waiter left Rossi as she sipped her wine. As he walked away, he turned the phone on himself to reveal a guy in his twenties. Short hair, smooth skin and attractive hazel eyes. He winked at the camera. The second section ended.

The remaining footage was all shot in a similar style, but the following section was shorter. It opened on a man strolling down a high street. He looked to be in his 40s, but he had closely cropped, white hair. He occasionally paused to glance in a shop window.

'Say hello to the fourth victim.' Moriarty said grimly. 'Mr. Dev Khan. Killed for a random act of kindness.'

As Khan approached the phone that was secretly filming the situation, the cameraperson stopped him. He or she seemed to have asked him the time because he glanced at his watch, said something, smiled, and moved on. Again, the lens was then pointed at the individual who had been behind it. John felt shock and revulsion as the identity of the culprit was revealed.

It was a young girl. She was about eight years old and wore a blue and white, cotton gingham dress. The child gave a merry 'thumbs up' to the camera and the next section began.

It started with a shot of an open-topped Land Rover Defender. John recognized Annie McDee in the passenger seat. Her husband, Ethan, was driving. Their car was idling by a set of temporary traffic lights, and they appeared to be in the countryside. Again, the cameraperson approached them, seemed to talk to them both, and pointed at something up ahead. The McDees appeared grateful. Proffered their thanks. The lights turned green and the Defender moved away.

The man capturing this moment on his phone reversed the handset. He looked to be in his early thirties. Black tie. White shirt. A dark, lightweight bomber jacket with official insignia running horizontally across the area immediately below the breast pockets. The unform was instantly recognizable. If his garb was to be believed, he was a policeman. He also wore a tall, badged, custodian hat — an iconic piece of headwear associated with the British 'bobby on the beat' since the late 1800s.

This officer — John fervently hoped he was a bogus constable — grinned down the lens and finished with a salute, given with mock solemnity.

'It's very good, isn't it?' Moriarty cooed. 'It leads one to question the smallest interaction we have with anyone. No matter how small. And however much we would normally trust the person we were interacting with, well, this footage invites us to suspect everyone of being part of an illicit plan which, in a worst-case scenario, could end in your murder. I'm not mad about the cinematography, but the film itself deserves an Oscar. Sally Grainger should be next up. Victim number two…'

This section had been shot in a bright supermarket. 'That's her,' Moriarty confirmed, nodding to a woman pushing her trolley along a food aisle. She reached the end of her shop and paid a check-out worker for her groceries. The last moments of this section revealed the store employee — the check-out person who'd rung through Sally's shopping — had been the one shooting the video.

'Nice twist,' said Porlock.

John shot him a disapproving look and said to Moriarty, 'Do you want me to stop the video?'

'Thanks, John. But this is the one I feel like I have to see, above all others.'

The final section began, immediately showing Lizzie Domingo, the person whom Moriarty had known as Beth Simmonds. '*The* woman,' he murmured, then fell silent as the footage played out, proving to be very different to the clips that had come before.

Chapter Seventy-Nine

REDFORD SAID, 'SORRY FOR CONTACTING YOU SO EARLY IN the morning, Detective Sergeant.'

'Not at all, Prime Minister. I'm happy to … serve.' Lee Jones pulled a face, cringing at her own turn of phrase. She looked around her bathroom as if there might be something hidden within it that could help her.

'Appreciate that. I'll get straight to it. We want to be as open and as transparent with the press, and by extension the public, as humanly possible. Over the David Gunn business, I mean.'

'Yes, sir.'

'I'm also keen to protect former Inspector Lestrade.'

The *former* didn't blindside her. Moriarty had updated her via WhatsApp minutes earlier.

'Of course. That's good to hear. She was a good copper. I mean this case was a bit of shit show but … Excuse my language, sir.'

'I welcome your candour, believe me, Lee. May I call you Lee?'

'Of course, sir.'

'It's Andrew. But we've got a problem. How do we give the full narrative whilst keeping Moriarty's name out of it?'

'It's tricky, sir. The Professor and John Watson identified Gunn as the killer and they located him. Then Moriarty was the one who saved Zenisha's life.'

'But you were there at the scene? You and Doctor Watson?'

'Yes, sir.'

'So we could say Doctor Watson — the esteemed and much-loved colleague of the great Sherlock Holmes — worked in conjunction with the police. Full stop. When David Gunn was jointly identified as a person of interest, a joint initiative, again involving the police service and John Watson, was put into play.'

He had delivered this opening thoughtfully and precisely, but now he became more fluid and confident. 'As a result of the NAP's fast and efficient assistance, Gunn was found in the nick of time. He obviously intended to kill the Detective Inspector but...' He stopped. 'Strike that! He obviously intended to kill *the young woman*, but thanks to the actions of Detective Sergeant Jones, John Watson, and others, her life was saved. She sustained injuries, but once again our nation's marvellous National Health Service was there to make sure she pulled through. David Gunn took his own life, and it's understood he had mental health issues which led to this whole tragedy. It's been suggested he was suffering from PTSD, but at this stage we can neither confirm nor categorically deny this diagnosis.'

Had he been on stage, he would have paused at this point, giving the audience an opportunity to applaud his mental and verbal dexterity. As it was, he simply asked, 'What do you think?'

'Well, I guess it's not a lie.'

'So is it the truth?'

'It's part of the truth, sir. I don't want to be difficult but—'

'Lee, Lee! It's quite all right. S'all good! I want you to be happy with the narrative we release.'

When any man told Lee Jones that they wanted her to be happy with something they were about to do, she instinctively knew they meant they wanted her to sign an invisible waiver, indemnifying them from any future comeback.

'What you just described did happen. But there was more to it.'

'Good point. Great point! Okay, so at the end of that release we add that for legal and operational reasons, certain facts about the case must remain classified in the immediate near future, but we look forward to a more detailed account being released as soon as possible. Strike that. As soon as is *legally* possible.'

Again, had he been on stage, he would have paused after delivering these lines and even winked at the audience this time. An acknowledgement of their complicity, as well as his own skilful audacity.

'Does that deal with your lingering concerns, Lee? We have spoken the truth and nothing but the truth, but we're openly acknowledge there is, *as there always is and must be*, a more detailed story which we intend to share at some point in the future.'

Lee felt that despite the Prime Minister's informal tone and attempted kindness, there was a definite 'Checkmate!' vibe to the moment. And something more. As the PR surrounding the investigation was finalized, it seemed as though the case was made final, as well. Over. Done with. And yet, DS Lee Jones instinctively felt that more was to come and that another bloody twist would catch everyone off-guard before this nightmare was finally concluded.

Chapter Eighty

'I TOLD YOU SHE WAS BEAUTIFUL.'

Moriarty's voice held fondness and pride as he, John, and Porlock watched the woman on the screen. She was sat a table in a small, airy café, and she was talking to whoever was secretly filming her with a phone camera.

But this was no brief random encounter. Doctor Beth Spencer was *with* the person responsible for capturing this footage. She was chatting, and although she seemed distracted, she clearly knew the person she was conversing with.

Beth was older than John had anticipated. She had cascades of auburn hair and eyes that looked almost amber. There was a delicacy to her. A fragility. She looked as if she was recovering from some great loss.

'Oh, they've excelled themselves,' Moriarty commented. 'This is cruel and clever. How on earth could they have known?'

In 221C Baker Street, they watched Beth Spencer nattering to her friend, then they saw the door to the café open behind her. Someone moved forward and they witnessed—

James Moriarty stood in the doorway.

The Moriarty they watched onscreen instantly spotted that Beth was with another man. The look on his face was a summation of sudden grief. In an instant, he knew beyond any doubt that his flickering hopes had been extinguished. He swayed for a moment as if he'd been physically struck, then he took a single step back.

'They must have been planning this for years!' Porlock exclaimed. 'I mean, that is *crazy*! I am, like, *made* of questions right now.'

What happened next on the video struck John as remarkable. Beth seemed to sense her former lover's presence and began to turn towards the door, but the man she was with rested his palm on her hand. This rattled her a little. She faced the person sat opposite from her and he slowly withdrew his hand.

Moriarty took another step back from the doorway, then turned and walked away.

Beth gave a half-smile and turned again to look towards the entrance a moment too late. The man she'd sensed had left a second earlier. Shortly afterwards, she rose from her chair and walked towards the counter. At that point, the man filming the whole thing turned the lens on himself. He made a fist of his left hand and pretended to wipe tears away from his own eyes.

All three men watching the video knew he was mocking Moriarty's sadness.

John said quietly, 'You all right?'

'I'm always all right. I'm the Napoleon of All Right. Thanks, though.'

'Hey look,' Porlock said. 'I'm gonna give you fellas five.'

He paused the video and left the room. The screen now showed a mid-shot of Beth Spencer, a cup of tea frozen on its way to her lips. Moriarty said what both of them were thinking. 'If I'd gone into the café that day, as I'd intended ... if I hadn't let the sight of that man repel me ... Beth might still be alive.'

Chapter Eighty-One

THE FOLLOWING MONTH PROVED TO BE AN UNUSUAL ONE, even by John's standards. After spending so much time with Moriarty, he barely saw the professor for the week that followed the death of Gunn. There were glimpses, of course. As John arrived home in the early hours, he might pass Moriarty on the stairs as the latter headed out.

'Morning, Doctor!'

'Good morning. How is work on the…'

But Moriarty was gone, lost to the London darkness.

On one occasion, however, they spent a little time together in the South of France. A taxi collected John and took him to a small airstrip in Royal Berkshire, where he was escorted aboard an unliveried Learjet 75. He found Moriarty waiting for him in the central cabin, which felt narrower than he'd expected.

'Thanks for coming, John.'

'My pleasure. What are we…'

'A quick trip to Nice to interview a friend of yours. Violet Morton.'

'Violet Morton?'

'Née Smith.'

'Violet Smith! Of course! The young lady Holmes and I assisted in the investigation I recorded as *The Solitary Cyclist*.'

Moriarty frowned. 'I always wondered why you called it that, when the whole point was, there was *no* solitary cyclist.'

'Dunno.' Watson cleared his throat. 'Alliteration, I suppose.'

'You should have called it *The Second Cyclist*. That would have made more sense.'

'Violet is hardly a friend of mine.'

'She's even less a friend of mine.'

John took a seat opposite Moriarty. 'What do we want to talk to her about?'

'Her husband — Cyril Morton — is a very wealthy man. I wish to talk to him about his secrets.'

'How do you know he has secrets?'

'Very wealthy men always have secrets. Well,' he reflected, 'all men have secrets. But wealthy men can afford to have more.'

'I've not seen Violet for years. I heard she got married. Two children, I think.'

Moriarty nodded. 'Daughters.'

'Is this connected with the Teardrop Killer case?'

'Of course.'

'How? I mean, we know who committed the murders. He's dead. Isn't the matter similarly…'

'Dead? Sadly not. Although I am in the process of administering the coup de grace.'

A woman in a pilot's outfit bobbed her head into the cabin. 'Ready for take-off, Professor. Are you happy for us to taxi out?'

'Let's fly!'

As the plane scorched over the English Channel at a cruising speed of about 850 km/ph, Moriarty finally replied. 'You're quite right. Gunn did carry out those murders. He applied the tattoos, and every death was by his hand. But in a sense, he wasn't responsible. It was a very modern sequence of crimes.'

'Explain.'

'I suppose you could say he'd been radicalized. He was found by a member of the Red Circle. They took his disappointment, anger, and confusion and used them to her own ends. I don't condone what Gunn did, but he'll have been brainwashed — hypnotized, almost — into committing the murders. Someone else selected the victims. Suggested the teardrop motif. Helped him with the mechanics of it all.'

The plane banked a little starboard.

'But why? If the Red Circle are so powerful, why didn't they simply kill their targets themselves. Why use Tommy?'

Moriarty smiled. 'Oh, that was genius. It meant these crimes are intrinsically bound to us. To you, through your connection to Gunn. And to me through my connection with the victims. Conclusion?'

John shrugged. Pondered. 'The obvious one. That we are central to these murders.'

'Precisely! That is *exactly* the way it appears! But it's all camouflage, John. We are *nothing* to do with these murders. Everyone will be looking for a connection. For a *why*. But the *why* is the same old *why*.'

'Which is what?'

'Like I told you at the very start of our investigation — money! I should have kept that in mind! Some people say cherchez la femme. I say, cherchez la finance. Money, money, *money*, John! Organizations like the Red Circle run operations that are predicated on two things. Money and power. Gaining the latter to generate the former. And vice versa.'

'But how on earth could the Teardrop Murders be monetized?'

'It's the 2020s. *Everything* can be monetized. What was it you said? You made the point these crimes had a high media impact. That can't have been a mistake. The Teardrop Killer was known throughout the world and acquired a reputation for invisibility and unstoppability. If he wanted to end someone's life — he could. Anybody's! I think that's why Millie was targeted. Think of the headlines her murder, at the right juncture, would have generated. It's not hard to see how such a reputation could be exploited for financial gain.'

'Not hard to see? It's pretty opaque to me.'

'Really?' Moriarty took out his laptop. 'I have a little work to do before we touch down. But everything will be explained very soon. I promise.'

Chapter Eighty-Two

THE MEETING TOOK PLACE IN CAGNES-SUR-MER IN THE Mortons' 19th-century chateau overlooking the Riviera's languid sprawl. The face-to-face with Violet puzzled Watson initially. He introduced Moriarty and they chatted about her experiences with Woodley, Williamson, and the others connected with the case investigated by Holmes several years earlier.

They were joined by her husband for a late lunch in their home's rear garden, a reassuringly tatty little space surrounded on three sides by olive treas. The fourth side was open and offered views across the Med towards Italy. Watson soon realized this meeting was the reason for Moriarty's interest in Violet — she allowed him access to multi-millionaire Cyril Morton. The conversation became more serious. Moriarty talked about the pressures of affluence. How people never saw the pressure, only the pleasures. 'And the pressure from those who wish to take away what you have ... that must be immense, I'd imagine.'

Cyril Morton gawped at Moriarty. 'What do you know?'

'I know enough to know I can help you. There's a way out of this nightmare. You're looking at it!'

The other man nodded slowly. 'All right…'

The day before each murder, Morton had received what appeared to be a random video. 'Someone just going about their everyday lives…'

'Could you describe a couple of these videos, Cyril?' John had asked. It quickly became clear that the footage he'd viewed inside the Porlock Cage had also been sent to the Mortons in shorter, bite-sized edits focusing on one victim at a time.

'Please go on with your story,' Moriarty urged.

Morton said the videos came with a warning. Do not contact the police. 'But why should I? I couldn't make heads nor tails of the footage!'

But eventually the horrible truth had dawned on him. He was being sent videos of the victims shortly before they were dispatched. 'The monster behind the Teardrop Murders was letting me know that he had me in his sights.' He shuddered. 'Me, or my family. Violet knew something was wrong. I told her everything.'

John said gently, 'Now tell us everything.'

'I was too craven to go to the police because—'

And here Violet interrupted him. 'I begged him not to contact the authorities. I was terrified the killer would harm our girls. I suppose you think I'm a terrible person for that. For being a coward.'

'Love makes us do terrible things.' To John's surprise, Moriarty leant across the table and squeezed her hand. 'That doesn't make you a coward. It makes you a human being.'

She offered him a teary smile and he withdrew. 'What happened next?'

'We were contacted by a security firm. A high-level

security firm,' Morton explained. 'I can't tell you why, but when they spoke to us, it was as though they knew we'd been targeted. The representative of this firm was...'

Violet interrupted for a second time. 'She was charismatic. Beautiful. But there was something...'

Moriarty told her, 'You can say the word, Mrs Morton.'

Violet shuddered. 'She was evil.'

Chapter Eighty-Three

As the Learjet flew across the majestic Massif Central, John eventually turned from the tableside window and admitted, 'It's genius. I mean, it's extortion without actually having to extort.'

'Quite so.' Moriarty didn't look up from his laptop. 'How can the authorities investigate the woman or her company? They've made no threats. Done nothing wrong. But the Mortons, and many others, pay the security firm substantial sums of money and the videos stop arriving. It's simple.'

'It's ingeniously simple. Almost like a kidnapping where no one is actually kidnapped and the would-be abductors can't be shown to have done anything wrong.'

'And if the police do choose to investigate the security firm, they'll finds it's a shell, within a shell, within a shell.'

'But this takes us further, yes? What's our next move?'

It transpired there was no 'our next move.' Moriarty once again became elusive, but John sensed a dark mood enveloping him. For an entire week he neither saw nor heard from the professor. On the seventh day of this absence, John climbed the stairs to 221C and gently knocked on the door.

'Come in, Doctor.'

The room had changed dramatically. There were standing screens that held huge maps of Europe, the Americas, and Asia. Detailed notes were scrawled across whole nations. Certain cities were ringed in a vivid green. The wall behind Watson was now a gallery of portraits — photographs of dozens of individuals with red threads linking various faces to multiple other faces.

Moriarty sat quite still in a chair positioned in the centre of the room, but he was far from alone. At least a dozen people buzzed around desks, monitoring laptops and making notes. John recognized three of the Downing Street Irregulars, an ex-cabinet minister, and two former criminals he'd encountered during his days with Holmes. The other individuals were strangers. None spared him a glance.

The room offered a snapshot of intense, all-consuming work. Covert, vast and relentless. A web of information that connected Washington DC to — Watson squinted at the screen — to a coastal village in Dorset. The skyscrapers of Tokyo to the pyramids of Machu Picchu. Businessmen in Monte Carlo to schoolteachers in Delhi.

And for the first time in a long while, John remembered the words of Sherlock Holmes as he'd described his nemesis. 'He sits motionless, like a spider in the centre of its web, but that web has a thousand radiations, and he knows well every quiver of each of them…'

The Professor had become that figure once more. He

was fighting a secret war with all the considerable resources at his disposal. But this time, this time John Watson felt they were on the same side.

Moriarty said, 'How can I help you, John?'

'I wondered…' He thought desperately of something he could pretend he needed. 'If you have any more information about the Prime Minister's daughter, Millie. I know you said she's probably dead, but … Redford must be going through hell.'

Moriarty had already leapt from his chair and he half-bundled, half-ushered Watson into the hallway.

'Millie?' he said. 'Yes, she's quite well.'

'What?'

'I followed up intel from Porlock. When she was seized, she wasn't killed as I thought. But she was hurt and fell into a coma. She's recently come out of it and should make a full recovery.'

'That's wonderful news! Have you told Redford?'

'Of course not!'

'Why the hell not?'

'Are you serious?'

'Why can't you tell her father?'

Moriarty took a step back. 'Have you heard of the Coventry Dilemma?'

'Of course. Yeah. Churchill knew Hitler planned to bomb Coventry. But he only knew this because we'd cracked the German's Enigma code. So, if he implemented plans to defend the city, the Germans would realize he'd cracked their code and they'd pivot accordingly. Whereas being able to *secretly* read the messages would swing the war in our favour.'

'Right! So the dilemma was essentially, let the Luftwaffe bomb the fuck out of one city, or save it but prolong the war at the costs of hundreds of thousands of lives. This is my Coventry dilemma, John. Redford's feelings are the city. That's all. Nothing more. So right now I don't give a damn about it. Come, friendly bombs, and rain on Coventry! *I need to win this war.*'

'But we can surely take some sort of action to—'

'How do you think a war like this works, John? It's Ravel's *Bolero*! Not the *Ride of the Fucking Valkyries*!' He hastily checked himself. 'I'm sorry.' A pause. 'As soon as I've secured the services of the people holding Millie and I can guarantee her safety, I'll let Redford know she's alive. Fair?'

'Thank you.' John turned to leave. 'It's vital nobody knows that, right?'

'Until five minutes ago — aside from the people holding Millie Redford — only me, Colonel Moran, and Porlock knew she's alive.'

'Then why trust me with the information?'

Moriarty's impatience and testiness didn't vanish, but it was as though they'd been placed on hold for a moment. 'Because I think you'd rather die than a let an innocent person suffer for a second.' He returned to his rooms.

John Watson descended the stairs to 221B Baker Street.

Two days later, he heard a knock at his door. He opened it to find Moriarty in the hallway, putting on a jacket. 'Millie Redford touches down in less than two hours' time. I'd like you to come with me to collect her. I was hoping you'd give her a quick medical to see if she's healthy. And, to be honest, I'd like you by my side in case anything goes wrong. What do you say?'

Chapter Eighty-Four

MORIARTY AND JOHN ARRIVED AT ROYAL AIR FORCE BRIZE Norton less than two hours after leaving Baker Street. They met Andrew Redford in the 'common room,' which proved to be little more than a bar complete with neon signage, 80s lighting, and a variety of seating. High chairs by the bar itself. Low sofas around the edges of the room. The PM was standing, studying his wristwatch every ten seconds and biting his thumbnails in between time checks. He was surrounded by his usual security detail — two men stood either side of him, with more bodyguards dotted about the room.

Looking around the place, John reflected that they could have been in any provincial town in England. Nothing about this bar suggested it was in the heart of an RAF base. And seeing the Prime Minister in these surroundings, looking so meek and scared, jarred with his notion of Redford being a confident, unshakeable high-flier.

'Something's wrong!' the PM stammered to Moriarty. 'She should have been here by now.'

'She'll be here.'

'We heard from the plane crew,' John told him. 'Bad weather conditions right across northern Europe. Slowed them down, but please, sir — have faith.'

Redford remained nervous. 'And is she all right? I mean healthy. I mean—'

'Yes!' Moriarty snapped. 'Like I told you this morning, she's fine. Stop worrying. I think you should…' He trailed off as he noticed something over the PM's shoulder. 'Excuse me.'

John saw her too. Detective Inspector Zenisha Lestrade had walked into the common room via a side entrance. She had been quickly and quietly reinstated after the initial tranche of press releases regarding the Teardrop Killer had been sent out. Now it felt as if she'd never been away. Moriarty met her at the door. 'Good to see you back in the saddle, Detective Inspector! But what brings you here? Redford?'

'No — I didn't know anything about the Prime Minister being at Brize. The Valentino twins touch down here later today. I'm in charge of getting them to London.'

'Lucky you!' John shook her hand. 'Welcome back! Good to see you.'

'And you, John.' She nodded towards the PM and his guards. 'What's happening here?'

'Millie Redford is coming home,' John told her. He briefly outlined how Moriarty had discovered she was alive and negotiated her safe return. He made no mention of Porlock.

Zenisha looked at Moriarty and smiled. 'Well, aren't you the hero?'

'I try not to be,' he replied truthfully.

THE COLOSSAL AIRBUS A400M Atlas touched down half an hour later. Only one person emerged: Colonel Sébastienne Moran. She crossed the tarmac, called Moriarty over, and the two of them talked intensely whilst the whine of the aircraft's four engines died away. John watched them by the edge of the low buildings on the edge of the airstrip's perimeter. He saw Moriarty finally nod and Colonel Moran spoke into a walkie talkie.

Almost immediately, Millie Redford emerged from the plane, flanked by four women, each carrying a Heckler & Koch submachine gun. One of the Prime Minister's bodyguards said, 'You should wait here, sir.'

John turned and called across. 'He's right!'

He saw the bodyguard was gently holding Redford's upper sleeve.

'That's my daughter! I've waited for her long enough!' The PM snatched his arm away and began jogging across the tarmac. Millie saw him and quickened her pace. 'Dad!'

'Millie!'

They were about ten paces from each other when the gunshot rang out, and then another, and finally two more in quick succession.

Chapter Eighty-Five

THE FOUR WOMEN SURROUNDING MILLIE INSTANTLY MOVED in closer to her, effectively providing a human shield around the teenager. One took a slight step forward and returned fire, aiming towards one of the two-story buildings within the common room's complex.

'Are you all right!' Redford's jog turned into a sprint. 'Millie!'

One of her guards shouted, 'She's fine!' and angrily bundled him to the back of their cluster of six.

Men in combat gear were already charging from the Airbus. The individual leading them peered into the middle distance as he raced forward. 'Up there! Shooter spotted! Up there!' He pointed to the building that one of Millie's protectors had already fired on moments earlier.

Moriarty glanced up at the window that the man had gestured to and began running toward the entrance below it.

John yelled to Redford, 'Are you hit, Prime Minister?'

'No, I'm good! Get the bastard!'

Three of the four women who'd surrounded Millie now hurried her back towards, and then into the Airbus. Redford stayed with them. The fourth woman was haring across the runway, away from the plane. John turned and sprinted after Moriarty.

The two of them reached the complex at the same time, tore up the stairs, and burst into the room where the shots had reportedly been fired from. Moriarty immediately recognized the chunky handgun that was pointing at him. A matte black Glock 21.

Luckily the man holding it was lying lifeless on the floor. Zenisha Lestrade stood over him, trembling and staring at his corpse. 'I saw him…' she whispered. 'But I got to him too late. We fought and…' She looked up at John. 'But I didn't get to him in time! He shot the Prime Minister! He shot the—'

John reached her. Slipped his arms around her shoulders. 'He missed. You must have disturbed him in the nick of time — *he missed.*'

The expression of relief on Zenisha's face was unmissable and, to John's mind, a joyous release of anguish. 'What?' she said, as though unwilling to believe the good news.

'Redford and Millie are both safe. We're all good.' He glanced down at the figure on the floor. 'You got here in time.'

'Now who's the hero?' said Moriarty wryly.

Later, the man holding the Glock was identified as Terry Scarafia, a career criminal who'd escaped from Louisiana State Penitentiary the previous year. When he had his clothes cut away in preparation for his post-mortem, his tattoo was one of the first things the pathologist noticed. It was a red circle, directly over his heart. But before a single fact about his corpse could be recorded, a fire alarm meant the examination was put on hold. And, when the pathologist returned to the lab a few minutes later, the body of Tony Scarafia was gone.

It was suggested that the Redfords should be properly reunited in the base's visitor waiting room. 'Too exposed,' Moriarty argued. 'Too much window space. Can you arrange to clear one of the welfare houses?'

'Can we…' The Commander had appeared mildly surprised. 'His Majesty's Royal Air Force can arrange anything, sir.'

And so the Prime Minister and his daughter were taken to one of the smart, cream-colored pre-fabs, where they laughed and hugged and spoke over each other. Moriarty and John were escorted across the accommodation's neat lawns and shown into a hallway. They heard Redford's voice booming to them, 'Come through! Come through.'

John was the first to receive Redford's thanks. He asked, 'What are you going to do now?'

'I'm going to resign as Prime Minister.'

'What?'

'This whole nightmare has made me realise what's important. I've spent years serving my country. Now I want to serve my daughter.'

Soon after it was Moriarty's turn, and he clearly loathed every second of the experience. He shook hands with Millie, who thanked him incessantly. He shook hands with the Prime Minister, who also thanked him, clutched his palm, and wouldn't let go for what felt like weeks.

'I've heard about the war you're fighting, Moriarty.

With the Red Circle. And I can't, in all good conscience, condone the brutal tactics I've been told you're using. But I thank you for finding the will to fight in the most effective way you can. I'll never know what makes you tick. But I thank God for you. And I thank God my daughter is safe.'

'We had a lucky escape with that gunman,' Moriarty replied. 'So don't thank God. Thank Inspector Lestrade.'

As the father and daughter were driven from the base in a bulletproof Bentley, John said, 'Do you think they'll be safe?'

'I'm working on it,' Moriarty admitted. 'I'm working on it. But I've still—'

He was interrupted by the twin-turboprop roar of a Skyvan. Watson spotted the aircraft. Pointed to it. 'One of the old flying shoeboxes! Made some hairy flights in those beasts back in the day!'

'That'll be the Valentino brothers.' Moriarty watched as the plane began its descent. 'Why don't we pop over and welcome them to England?'

THEY MET Zenisha in one of the base's eateries, Strikers Café, appropriately named as it was adjacent to a bowling alley. Scotland Yard had effectively taken over the place, establishing a comms centre that had charted the Skyvan's progress and the status of transport for the remainder of the twins' journey. Moriarty and John were stopped at the door. 'Sorry, gents. No admittance. Caf's closed.'

Zenisha called over, 'They're with me! They're good!'

The guy on the door stepped aside. 'Sorry lads. Didn't realize you were one of us.'

'Neither did I,' muttered Moriarty.

'How are you feeling, Zenisha?'

'Much better, thanks, John. It just gave me a shock. It was all so sudden.'

Moriarty glanced across the computer screens. 'What's the plan with the Valentino boys?'

'They're still under. They'll be taken to the on-base surgery. When they wake up and they've been checked by a doctor, we'll load them into a sweat box, then drive them down to London.'

'Escorts?'

'Three liveried vehicles. And two unmarked cars. One ahead, one bringing up the rear.'

'Any armed officers coming with?'

'Yeah. Got it okayed last week. We're not taking any chances with these guys.'

'Good to hear. Do you mind if John and I accompany you to the handover?'

MORIARTY AND JOHN followed Zenisha across the tarmac. Two stretchers were being carried from the Skyvan, a short squat craft that John always felt looked like a longer, slimmer plane that had somehow been concatenated into this shoebox of a vehicle that now rested on the runway.

Zenisha showed her ID and approached the man who seemed to be in charge. He beamed at the sight of her. 'Good to see you, Inspector Lestrade!'

'Good to see you. Any problems?'

The man looked to be in his 50s. He was stocky with short, neat hair, and he spoke with a Scottish accent. 'None so far, but I don't mind telling you, I'll be glad to hand these lads over.'

Zenisha gestured to John. 'Jimmy Gale, this is John Watson. John, meet Jimmy. My opposite number, north of the border.'

The two men shook hands. 'I've heard a lot about you, Doctor. Meeting you is a pleasure!'

'Thanks, man.'

The medics carrying the two stretchers paused by Zenisha. The figures they carried were covered in a light gauze, lending them the eerie appearance of a couple of corpses.

Zenisha said to Jimmy, 'And this is Professor Moriarty.'

The Scotsman narrowed his eyes, and his thoughts were easily read. *Are you serious?* He said, '*The* Professor Moriarty?'

'He's assisting us. And he's been a massive help, believe it or not.'

'Oh aye?' Jimmy stepped forward. Extended his hand. 'I've heard a lot about you, too, Professor. Meeting you is...'

He struggled to find the appropriate word, but Moriarty cut in. 'I feel the same way.' They shook hands. 'Any chance we could take a look at the twins?'

Jimmy threw Zenisha a look. She shrugged. 'Knock yourself out,' he replied.

Moriarty walked to the stretchers and tugged back the thin sheets covering the men who lay on them. He looked down on the twins. They were clearly breathing, and both the brothers looked as though they were sleeping soundly and peacefully.

'Did you have any more prisoners on the flight, Jimmy?'

'Absolutely not, Prof. To be frank, these two customers were quite enough for me.'

'I see.' Moriarty turned around and smiled. 'Then you have a problem.'

Zenisha looked at the twins and whispered, 'Oh my god!'

Jimmy said, 'What kind of problem?'

'Quite a serious one.' Moriarty gestured to the stretchers. 'These aren't the Valentino twins.'

Chapter Eighty-Six

THE DRIVE BACK TO BAKER STREET WAS A GRIM ONE. Zenisha accompanied John and Moriarty in the latter's metallic grey Volvo 1800S, and the atmosphere between the three soon became tense. Whilst Brize Norton was still in his rear-view mirror, Moriarty said, 'You've got to get onto Redford immediately! Tell him to convene a COBRA meeting as soon as possible.'

Zenisha sounded edgy. 'COBRA meetings are only sanctioned when there's a national emergency. They're a ministerial level group, led by the PM, to deal with—'

'Listen! I've triggered a few COBRA meetings in my time. I know what they exist to combat. Zenisha — listen to me! The Valentino twins pose the deadliest and most far-reaching threat that the UK, the US, and the rest of the world has faced since COVID was unleashed.'

Even John seemed surprised. 'We know these guys are dangerous, but you're exaggerating, surely?'

'John, immediately before their capture, the brothers developed technology and processes that border on *omnipotence*. And I use that word with precision. Their ability to hack any system on the planet and control it gives them a godlike power.' He let his words sink in. 'I'm not exaggerating the threat they pose. If anything, I'm underplaying it. And it's a power they will be eager to use very, *very* soon.'

By the time John and Moriarty returned to Baker Street, Redford had already quit his post, citing ill-health as a reason for his resignation. Later that evening he gave a short, dignified speech on a lectern in front of Number 10. They watched it together. John expressed mixed feelings. He was glad Redford would be able to spend more time with his daughter, but he felt he'd been a good man and an effective leader during his time in Downing Street.

'Given another term, I think he could have done much more.'

'He couldn't have done much less.' Moriarty was in a belligerent mood. 'Did you hear they didn't even call a COBRA meeting? Bloody fools! The world will hear from the Valentino twins, and it will react in wide-eyed terror. Remember — I warned our so-called leaders and advised them, John. History will condemn their apathy as murderous! Honestly, I'm labelled a criminal for my transgressions. But the crimes of those elected to guide and govern us, they are viler and more deep-cutting than any of my paltry efforts. How did W.S. Gilbert put it? *I don't think much of my profession, but contrasted with respectability, it is comparatively honest.*'

Moriarty watched the rest of Redford's speech with open resentment, heckling the cliches and calling out the tropes. '*Proud to have served my country* ... Do people still believe that tosh?'

Tired of his stream of put downs, John countered, 'Well, what do *you* believe?'

'I believe I have work to do.'

He walked from the room and headed up to 221C, and John didn't see him again for another four days.

THE VALENTINOS' escape made the headlines, and facts emerged in a tumble. The switch with another pair of similar looking twins had been made whilst they'd still be in their Scottish prison. Their files had been hacked, so the faces seen by the new governor corresponded to those he believed belonged to the brothers. New guards specifically brought into assist with the handover were similarly fooled.

Questions were raised about the wardens who had previously interacted with the brothers. Why hadn't they noticed the switch?

Some of their answers felt plausible.

'You see the faces you expect to see — and they're hella similar.'

And:

'I never looked them in the eye. They had this way about them … I looked at them, sure. But not at their faces. I accept I messed up in a big way.'

But still, questions lingered. Unspoken allegations are always the hardest to deny, yet they remain impossible to prove. In the end, it was accepted that the twins had escaped through an ingenious, audacious scheme, and nothing more could be determined with any degree of certainty. Even the murder of Bailey Hernandez, which Moriarty insisted had been central to the plan, was dismissed as a tragic turn of fate which had played into the brothers' hands.

'They are either blind, conniving, or stupid!' Moriarty

had roared. 'I begin to think they are all three! And that all are prerequisites for the offices they hold!'

Zenisha confided to John that she even suspected Jimmy Gale of being part of the escape process. He was one of the very few people who knew all the details regarding the brothers' transportation. The Scot was due to retire in the next few years, and who wouldn't want a few thousand extra to help those long and lean post-career years? She murmured the accusation to one of her bosses and was tactfully advised that at this stage, the crisis was big enough. Finger pointing and tongues wagging in any blue-on-blue context would help no one.

JOHN SENSED Moriarty's war was drawing to a close. The number of people visiting him in his top-floor rooms dwindled. But he'd not seen him for over 100 hours and so couldn't be absolutely sure. After a few drinks late one evening, he found himself knocking on the door of 221C.

'Come in, John.'

He pushed open the door.

Moriarty was wearing grey suit trousers with black braces. No shirt or jacket. He sported a tight, white sleeveless vest, but his torso was otherwise naked, showing off toned muscles. He was alone, leaning against the wall besides the windows that offered such broad and impressive views across the capital. It was late, and the golden light flooded over him.

'Sorry to disturb you.'

'Don't be. Can I get you a drink?'

'Sure.'

'Spirits? Wine? Both?'

'Whiskey.'

Moriarty mixed him a scotch and water and slung together a G&T for himself. He handed his guest his drink and drifted back to the window.

John said, 'It's almost over, isn't it?'

'The battle? Yes. But not the war.'

'I'm a man of my word. Tell me when you're happy you can't make any more progress on the fallout from the Teardrop Killer case.

'And then?'

'And then, Professor, then I'll do whatever it is you wanted me to do. The mysterious favour.'

'I appreciate that.'

John looked at Moriarty, silhouetted against a golden London. 'I think it's a dreadful, heart-breaking shame.'

'What?'

'You and Holmes. Together you could have been … magnificent.'

Moriarty raised his glass. 'Here's to Sherlock.'

'Why did you kill him?'

'We said no questions.'

'We did.' John took a sip of whiskey. 'Why did you follow us to Switzerland? Give me that. Give me that one answer.'

Moriarty drained his drink and poured himself a larger, stiffer chaser. 'All right. This one time — this one time — I'll let you ask any question you want. And I'll answer you truthfully.'

He leant back lightly against the window itself this time. The light was ebbing away from the evening sky, but it still enveloped him, transformed him into a strong, sleek, battered angel.

'I won't try to take advantage of the situation,' John replied carefully. 'So I'll stick to the question I just put to you. Why did you follow us to Switzerland?'

'Because I knew Sherlock was in trouble, and I wanted to help him.'

'But ended up killing him?'

'Crazy the way things turn out, right?'

Moriarty's phone began to play "Trapped" by Colonel Abrams and he answered with a terse, 'Yes, Sébastienne?'

As he listened to the news being relayed to him, he wiped his hand across his face. When the call was finished, he threw his drink down his throat and poured himself a large scotch.

'What is it?'

Moriarty sat opposite across from John. 'It's Ethan McDee's wife, Annie, and Beth's husband, Troy Domingo.'

'What about them?'

But John needn't have asked. Moriarty's reply merely confirmed the inevitable facts.

'They've both been found dead. My people say it'll be treated as suicide, but I think we both know the truth, don't we?'

'Why the hell were they murdered?'

'Domingo had wealth and influence. It's possible that kept him alive this long, but it's also possible he hired people to look into Beth's death. I don't know. Maybe the Red Circle simply thought his death couldn't harm them, so why not?'

'Christ!'

'You same Annie seemed like an indomitable woman, so it's likely the same thinking was used with her. We're entering the endgame, John. One thing is certain.' He downed his whiskey in one. 'Blood will flow.'

Before John could reply, a low, shrill alarm sounded on Moriarty's laptop open on the travertine table. He rushed across to it and scanning its screen whispered, 'No, no, no…'

'What is it?'

Moriarty stood back as if he couldn't bear to stand so close to the information pouring in. 'Right across the UK and US ... banks are being hit ... airplanes being grounded ... broadcasters being forced off-air...'

John was already by his side. 'What's happening?'

'It's already global!' Moriarty gestured to the auto-scrolling text on his laptop. 'Stock markets are in chaos ... all major payment services have been taken out ... 911 lines are down right across the States...'

'Moriarty! *What's happening?*'

'The Valentino twins, John. They are showing the world that they can control anything and everything.' He looked up from the screen. 'And this is just the beginning.'

Chapter Eighty-Seven

Twelve hours after the Valentino twins began to demonstrate their power, IT system across the planet began to return to something approaching normality. As Moriarty predicted, the massive outage, which wiped hundreds of billions from the global economy, was blamed on a security update implemented by a well-known operating system. Most people accepted the lie.

But those in positions of powers knew the truth, and behind the scenes, they scrambled to take action. Moriarty privately warned this relatively short attack had been a mere prelude. 'It was a conductor tapping his baton to gain the orchestra's attention. The symphony of terror has yet to begin.'

Even the British government hastily convened a COBRA meeting.

'Pathetic!' Moriarty observed. 'They're shutting the stable doors whilst the stables are burning to the ground.'

THREE DAYS LATER, John answered a late-night knock at his door. He found Moriarty looking dishevelled and dressed in the same clothes he'd been wearing when they'd last spoken. He now sported a light beard, and his hair was unkempt.

'Hi, Johnny.'

'Are you all right?'

'Uh huh.'

'Is there anything I can do?'

Moriarty shook his head. ''Tis done.'

And John instinctively knew the battle was over and that neither side had won. 'Then rest,' he said. 'Downing Street in the morning? We'll report to the new PM, and then all of this will be over.'

'I wanted to say, John … To tell you … To confess … *I have done terrible things.*'

'I know.'

'And when you hear of them, I want you to remember Churchill looking out over London as the bombers flew across the Channel to pulverize Coventry.'

'I think I understand you a little better these days.'

'Understanding is always easier when you can reason without hate.' Moriarty gave a tired smile. 'But I fear the hatred will return. Greater than ever before.'

'Let's cross that bridge when we reach the Rubicon. Here, take this.' He handed Moriarty an old-fashioned looking piece of kit. It was a cream and black, oblong device designed to be hand-held. It contained a screen, a tiny keyboard, and a fixed antenna. 'This deck can be connected to your phone, then we can keep in touch safely, because I've got its little brother.'

'Attach it when I need to reach out? Sure.' Moriarty weighed the tech in his hand. 'Similar to Meshtastic comms, right?'

John nodded. 'Except longer range. But it's still off-grid and totally unhackable. Send me a message using this, and MI5, the FBI and even the Red Circle wouldn't be able to read it.'

'I've heard about these but never tried them. Do they work?'

'Absolutely. It's how Graham Marsh and I communicated.'

MORIARTY THOUGHT back to Graham Marsh, the man he'd known as Roddy Fingers. He remembered finding him dead, garrotted, in Shere and *The Body in the Library*, doctored with one of his own fingerprints, resting on his corpse. 'I assumed when he contacted you, he just used the online forms on your podcast's website.'

'Not a chance,' John told him. 'He may have become a village librarian, but he remained scrupulous when it came to transfer of intel.'

Moriarty smiled. 'So he remained a pro to the end…'

But his smile faded as he realized the implication of the device he now held in his hand.

THE CONCEPT of change is often thrilling. The reality of change is usually painful. And arriving at 10 Downing Street, John sensed the trauma of change was affecting everyone in the heart of government.

The UK's new Prime Minister was Lourdes Bellinger, a career politician in her late thirties who had a popularity which, in terms of scale, easily rivalled her predecessor's. But the people's love for Lourdes Bellinger was markedly different, both in its roots and its manifestation. She was a sharp, shrewd operator who recognized that voters had endured many years of financial hardship. She also understood that people who suffer have a lust for ascribing blame. To be truly satisfying, it must be placed at the door of 'others.' That's to say, for blame to work, for it to have traction and force, it must be assigned to people who do not look like us, sound like us or — ostensibly, at least — behave as we do.

This simple truth guided Bellinger's every move, thought, and impulse. It was so ingrained in her psyche that she no longer had to think about it when applying its dictates. Her rejection of consideration and empathy had become second nature, as natural as wiping sleep from her eyes upon waking.

The nation's new PM had already pointed the finger at immigrants, asylum seekers, and workers from overseas, amongst others, and the public nodded and grinned and clapped their hands together and adored her for it. Yes, her tactic was an old one, as disingenuous as it is disgraceful. It was also tragic, not simply in its outcome, but as a testimony to society's collective dearth of compassion. And yet Bellinger, and not her principled detractors, now occupied number 10.

She had stood at the same lectern in the same spot as Andrew Redford, and she too gave a politician's smile as she set out her grubby stall. By the end of her speech, no one was in any doubt. The sense of fairness and care that had characterized Redford's time in office was already consigned to history. A memory, difficult to articulate and therefore best forgotten. A new era was dawning. One of harshness, cruelty, and intolerance. The time of Lourdes Bellinger had begun.

Chapter Eighty-Eight

ZENISHA, MORIARTY, AND JOHN WERE SHOWN INTO Bellinger's office. She didn't look up from a set of documents she was signing for a full twenty seconds. Moriarty had sat down, stretched back, and placed the heels of his shoes on her desk, and when the PM finally spared her guests some attention, she shot the professor her most withering look.

'Does that normally work?' he asked. 'Does it make people nervous and compliant? The whole, one-eyebrow up thing. The slight sneer. The coolness in your eyes. You probably think it looks formidable. To me, it just looks like you're having a stroke. How are you settling in? Do the household staff universally hate you yet? Or are one or two still holding onto a hope you may not be quite as gruesome as you appear?'

Bellinger moved her documents to one side. 'They don't *all* loathe me yet. But that will come.'

Moriarty laughed. 'Yes, I imagine so. Look, I'll make this quick because I'm a busy man and I find you repugnant.' He sprang to his feet. 'Your predecessor, Redford, tasked the three of us with stopping the Teardrop Killer.'

'Yes?' Bellinger nodded. 'That was done some time ago. Gunn's guilt was proven. He was killed. Perfect. Everybody happy.'

'You know, there's something transfixing about your *complete* lack of humanity.'

Zenisha cleared her throat. 'Although Gunn *was* the killer, we now have proof that a criminal organization known as the Red Circle was heavily involved in the murders. We further believe they're linked to the Valentino twins.'

'The Red Circle?' Bellinger's disbelief was clear. 'That's a myth. A legend.'

Moriarty rattled through the facts of the matter. The Red Circle's involvement. The tragedy of how Gunn had been used. He spoke of his war with the organization and revealed how people like Cyril Morton had helped him to identify key players. He finally said, 'The Red Circle is a hydra. I've only sliced off a few of its heads.'

'Hydra? Heads?' The Prime Minister didn't hide her annoyance. 'Speak plainly, man! And for pity's sake, let's focus on one thing at a time. You're claiming the crimes of David Gunn were actually part of an extortion scheme?'

Moriarty groaned at the prospect of repeating himself.

Zanisha quickly intervened, simplifying his explanation. 'Many factors relating to the Teardrop Killer case were intended as red herrings. They were implemented to make it look as though the murders were acts of vengeance, either for or against Doctor Watson and/or Professor Moriarty. The choice of victims. The man tasked with carrying out the slaughter. Those elements were there to mislead us. They were a blind.'

Belinger looked at Moriarty. 'Is that true?'

He hesitated before replying. 'Those elements were not the *primary* drivers. The murders were committed for one key reason. Money. The Red Circle blackmailed a number of very wealthy people by persuading them that they, or their loved ones, would be the Teardrop Killer's next victims if certain financial conditions weren't met.'

John added, 'The killer's almost mythic status and his reputation of near-omnipotence were enough to convince the targets that they should pay up.'

The Prime Minister kept her eyes on Moriarty. 'How did you work it all out?'

He shrugged. 'Natural genius.'

'I'm going to need more than that.'

'Certain videos that we took from Gunn's laptop were clues. But it was simpler than that. Like I said a moment ago, once you accept the Red Circle was behind it, you have to ask why. How could they profit from these crimes? It had to be extortion. I asked myself a question. Who would I target if I was running this scheme?'

'And how,' Bellinger demanded to know, 'did you figure out Cyril Morton was one of the targets?'

'He's that rare thing,' Moriarty replied. 'Insanely rich and completely straight. He had no criminal contacts he could turn to for help. He has a pair of young kids whom the Red Circle could clearly threaten. Everything about Morton made him a perfect target. That's why Doctor Watson and I questioned him.'

John took up the story. 'Using the information Morton gave us, the Professor was ultimately able to get a clearer picture of the Red Circle.'

'I was able to identify some of their foot soldiers and a couple of their more important lieutenants.'

'Well?' The Prime Minister's impatience was obvious. 'And then what, Professor?'

'And then I waged war on the Red Circle. I targeted their lower ranks. Picked away at them. Some I bought off. Others I scared off. A few were blackmailed. And there were many more who had to be removed by other means.'

Bellinger held up her hands. 'I don't want to know!' She ignored Moriarty's snort of contempt and asked, 'So did you destroy the Red Circle?'

'I've seriously weakened the organisation's UK and European wings. Damaged its US operations. But I couldn't reach their upper echelons. They remain hidden in the shadows, Prime Minister.' He seemed to study Bellinger's face, then continued. 'So the Valentino twins remain a major concern. I couldn't find out the identity of whoever's running them. Their continued liberty represents a threat of unthinkable potency.' He spoke slowly, now. 'Apprehending the Valentinos and destroying the Red Circle must take precedence over every other governmental imperative, Prime Minister.'

'I'm still not conceding the Red Circle even exists! Let's focus on what we know, not what we fear!' She seemed to reach a decision. 'The Teardrop Killings are definitely over?'

John and Zenisha replied in unison, 'Yes.'

Moriarty confirmed, 'They're over.'

Bellinger at last gave a smile. 'It's over! I *like* those words. They're the only two I needed to hear.'

Moriarty thumped her desk. 'Were you listening me? Did you hear one word? The Valentinos are working with the Red Circle! Together they represent a flame. A flame that could set the whole world alight.'

'They're bound to extort governments across the globe,' John stressed, 'and their demands will be beyond *anything* you can imagine. Even if you comply, they are likely to flex their muscles and set civilization on Planet

Earth back *decades* with a loss of life comparable to any world war.'

Bellinger raised her eyebrows. 'Did my predecessor fall for your hyperbole?'

'No,' Moriarty snapped. 'Which is why we're in the mess we're currently in.'

John tilted his head. 'Prime Minister, the Red Circle is — to put it very mildly — an ongoing concern! Yes, we've defeated one of its schemes, but its reach and power are—'

'Doctor Watson!'

'Yes, ma'am?'

'Sherlock Holmes was your friend?'

'Yes, ma'am.'

'And yet you're now a comrade-in-arms of the man who murdered him.'

Zenisha stepped in. 'The situation is as little more complex than the way you—'

'Doctor Watson!'

'Yes, ma'am?'

'What do you think he would have said if he could see you now? Cavorting with his killer.'

'I've no idea.'

'I'm told your adventures with Professor Moriarty have quite rejuvenated you. Good for you! But I have many duties to fulfil. The Teardrop Killer case is closed. The public know everything they need to know. Inspector Lestrade!'

'Yes, ma'am?'

'I want you to destroy any files pertaining to the Red Circle. It does not exist! I won't have my employees distracted by a fabrication. The Red Circle an invention of this criminal here.'

Moriarty looked offended. 'That's arch criminal, if you don't mind.'

'Watson, Lestrade — what we've discussed today stays within these four walls. You'll sign an NDA before leaving the building. You breathe a word of this to anybody — you even say the words *Red Circle* in your sleep — and you'll be in Belmarsh so fast, you'll think you were teleported there.'

'Got to admit,' Moriarty piped up, 'I was not expecting a teleportation reference. But I think it worked.'

'And you. Professor James Moriarty. One of the most appalling criminals our nation has ever produced.'

'Oh, don't do yourself down, Prime Minister.'

'You have 24 hours to leave the country. To disappear. After that point in time, you will be the UK's most wanted. I will order every law enforcement agency at my disposal, both here and abroad, to make your capture their number one priority. And *when* you are apprehended, you will be tried for crimes dating back years, covering theft, kidnapping, fraud, and, of course, multiple murders. Including the *slaughter* of Sherlock Holmes. You will be imprisoned for life. The closest you will ever get to liberty will be your freedom to breathe.'

'Your government gave me immunity.'

'No! My predecessor, Mr. Redford, gave you immunity. I do not recognize or acknowledge the legality of his shady little deal with you. Start running, Professor Moriarty. In less than 24 hours' time, you will be the most hunted human on the planet.'

Chapter Eighty-Nine

MORIARTY AND JOHN WERE SAT IN THE BACK OF A BLACK cab, which took them through Westminster towards Marylebone.

'It can't end like this,' John reflected forlornly.

'Why not?'

'Because ... because it's not *neat* enough!'

Moriarty laughed. 'It's real life, Johnny. It's a mad, messy bugger at the best of times. And these are not the best of times.'

'We know Tommy Gunn was the puppet. But who was the puppet master, pulling his strings? What the hell happened to Terry Scarafia — the man who tried to assassinate Redford? Why did he want the PM dead? And why the hell was his corpse stolen? Will still don't know why Tommy targeted Mary! Christ, we know next to nothing!'

'It's over, Johnny.'

But he wasn't listening. 'Tommy left no trace evidence at the crime scenes. For him to become that professional would have taken months if not years of training. Who provided that training? Moriarty — we still have no idea why teardrops were tattooed onto the faces of his victims! And there's the big one! The Valentino brothers are still out there. The horror they wreak could be cataclysmic!'

'*It's over, Johnny.*'

JOHN AND MORIARTY RETURNED HOME, where the professor activated pre-arranged plans that ensured his staff, in his words, 'would be well taken care of.' 221C had a steady stream of visitors. Members of his Downing Street Irregulars shuffled across the floor to tearfully embrace him and wish him the best of luck. Other friends and associates hurried across London to make their mournful farewells, and John marvelled at the number of people drawn to Baker Street, when news of his impending exile had only just broken.

Lee Jones proved to be his final visitor. She shared her news — a promotion to the rank of Inspector. 'I might start using my full first name, now. How do you think it would sound? Inspector Athelney Jones?'

John noted that of everyone who had called to see him, Moriarty only had a private conversation with one of them — Inspector Jones. He wondered what they'd discussed but put the matter from his mind as the afternoon wore on.

After he'd concluded his business, Moriarty slapped Watson on the shoulder. 'A farewell drink? You, me, and Zenisha? Not for old time's sake. I hate that expression. For new time's sake! What do you say? Yes?'

The three of them met on the South Bank, on the area in front of the Royal Festival Hall overlooking the Thames. Moriarty ordered Champagne and they drank a couple of bottles, at first toasting the dead. The victims of the

Teardrop Killer, those they had met, and the strangers who fell in the scheme's bloody course.

'I shan't blame either of you if you don't wish to join me in this, but what happened to my friend was abhorrent and he deserved better. Not least from me. So wherever you are, mate…' He raised his glass. 'Here's to Tommy.'

'To Tommy.'

'To Tommy.'

They all drank more Champagne.

Zenisha asked, 'So what are your plans, Professor?'

'I've bought a plane ticket to the States. I'll make it easy for Bellinger's people to follow me to New York. Once I'm there, I'll visit Time Square. A friend of mine recommended a rather good cake shop there. Terrific cheesecake, apparently.'

'And after that?'

'I'll steal a car. Disappear. Slip across the border.'

'Which border?'

He shrugged. 'One border is pretty like any other border. I mean, there's a slight difference, but it's borderline. Borderline! Get it?'

'If you don't want to tell us,' John informed him, 'you can at least spare us the puns.'

'A little gift for you!' Moriarty tossed him a pair of keys. 'My car. I've transferred it to your name. The wheels are repaired and it's ready to go!'

'Thank you, Professor. I'll think of you every time I've got to get the bloody thing MOT'ed.'

'I'd appreciate that. And Zenisha!' He handed her a Mont Blanc fountain pen. 'I saw you casting envious glances at mine when I signed the contract that bound us all on the fateful, stormy night. If ever you have enough of Bellinger's Britain, write your letter of resignation with that pen, and then find me.'

She accepted the gift and thanked him, adding, 'I just might.'

They left soon after. Moriarty hugged Zenisha and said, 'I'll never find the words.'

'You be good,' Zenisha told him, and then she was gone.

'Right,' said John. 'Time for me to fulfil my side of that contract. The favour.'

Moriarty nodded. 'The favour.'

Chapter Ninety

THEY WALKED ACROSS THE GOLDEN JUBILEE BRIDGE AND strode up Villiers Street to Charing Cross. 'What you're after is near here,' John announced and led them to a small bookshop. Cox & Co turned out to be a dusty, disordered place. Shelves were crammed with paperbacks and hardbacks, with recent imprints standing spine-to-spine with antique first editions. A man who always reminded John of Charles Dickens's Pickwick emerged from a rear antechamber.

'Ah, it's the good doctor!' he declared and the two men shook hands. 'How can I help you, today? Or are you just browsing?'

'Good to see you, Mr. Cox! I was after something specific.' John lowered his voice. 'Do you have a copy of the 1887 Beaton's Christmas Annual?'

'1887?'

'Yes, Mr. Cox.'

'Are you sure?'

'Absolutely.'

'Follow me.'

John and Moriarty were led though the shop and down a flight of stairs. They found themselves in a warren of rooms. Most were dimly lit. All were cramped. The corridors that connected them were narrow and seemed to form a maze below the streets of Charing Cross. Eventually Mr. Cox stopped and pulled a shelf of books to one side. It slid smoothly into a concealed alcove to reveal a steel door. The shopkeeper placed his hand on a palm-reader and it slid open. He gave a stiff bow. 'Mr. Cox will assist you from here.'

'Thank you, Mr. Cox.'

John and Moriarty walked down a flight of stairs beyond the door and along a wide, steel-walled corridor decorated with oil painting in the classical style. At the end of the passage, they were greeted by a man who bore a startling resemblance to the earlier Mr. Cox.

'I understand we have an 1887 scenario, Doctor Watson.'

'That's quite correct, Mr. Cox.'

'The box is waiting for you.'

'Thank you, Mr. Cox.'

The second shopkeeper opened a huge teak door, and the two visitors entered a vault lined with lockers. A tin box waited for them, on top of an oak table that stood in the middle of the chamber. The two of them were alone.

'Can I ask *why* you want to see Holmes's notes?'

'Whilst I was gone, someone stole my empire. It looks like it was the Red Circle, but I have no idea of the individuals involved. Sherlock knew the London underworld better than any man who ever lived. The fact he kept notes is well-known. The fact he entrusted them to you for safe keeping is equally well-known. And I know that within his notes, there will be clues to the identities of whoever is running the Red Circle.'

'So you only helped us for this? So you could reclaim your empire? Is this what it all boils down to? You were just getting me onside so I'd reveal the location of that box and bring you here?'

'You can believe that if you like. Ultimately, I did what I did for many reasons. Some, I think would win your approval. Others your contempt.'

John shook his head. 'Then get it over with. Open the bloody box if it means that much to you.'

'There's one more thing I need to tell you before I do.'

'All right…'

'It's about Mary. I've told my people to let her go. She's in no danger.'

John eyed Moriarty with suspicion. 'How can you know that? They got to her once. Even with Tommy out of the picture they could get to her again.'

'No.'

'No, what?'

'Mary is safe. In fact, she was never in any danger.' Moriarty's voice was low and steady. A doctor revealing a life-threatening prognosis to a patient who had thought they were completely healthy. 'You see, Gunn never visited her.'

'What are you talking about? The tear was tattooed on her face. The warning couldn't have been more obvious!'

'No. I just let you think that,' Moriarty admitted. 'You see, the Teardrop Killer didn't break into her house and ink that tattoo onto her face. I did.'

Chapter Ninety-One

JOHN TRIED TO TAKE IN THE RAMIFICATIONS. 'ARE YOU saying that Tommy was never anywhere near Mary? That you … that *you* put her through these weeks of terror and trauma? That *you* made us all think her life was threatened?'

'I stayed close to her to make sure she was okay. I never put her in harm's way.'

'You never … do you have any idea of the hell we've both been through, thinking she was a target?'

'It brought you back together. You said so yourself.'

'Don't you dare!'

'She was my Coventry, John. I had to do it.'

'Why did you have to do it? For god's sake, *why*, man?'

'When I first returned, I knew you'd loathe me and that you'd never willingly work with me. I also knew the only thing that would change your mind would be to think that us joining forces would save Mary. And I needed to do that, so ultimately I could end up here. This box holds the key for me. The key to destroying the Red Circle. And the key to regaining my old empire.'

'I was almost starting to think of you as a friend.'

'I am your friend, John.'

John shook his head. 'When we leave this place, you are exactly what you were when I saw you in Holmes's old chair in 221B Baker Street. I'll ask Bellinger if I can help track you down to bring you to justice. I'll make it my life's work to see you rot in jail.'

'I'm sorry.'

'Now open the bloody box. I hope what's in there was worth it.'

Moriarty nodded. Took a deep breath and finally looked away from John Watson. He approached the box, grasped its lid, and titled it back. The box creaked open, and he peered inside. Unable to resist, John stepped forward to see what treasures had been revealed.

'Is this some kind of joke, John?'

'This isn't my doing. I've no idea what's going on.'

Moriarty nodded and closed the empty box.

Colonel Sébastienne Moran and Professor James Moriarty sat in the VIP departure lounge of Heathrow Airport's Terminal 3. They were drinking cocktails and looking across the runway as the sun set.

'You told him what?'

'That I'd inked the tear on Mary's face.'

Colonel Moran looked flabbergasted. 'Why in god's name would you do that?'

'Because I've seen the way John reacts to grief. I didn't want him to slide into it again when he lost me. I needed him to hate me again.'

'Well, job done, Jamie lad. Job done.' She sipped her cosmopolitan. 'And the box was empty?'

'Yep. Today has been the day that just keeps on giving.'

'So what happened to Sherlock's notes?'

'Your guess is as bad as mine.'

'Don't give me that! You've already formed a hypothesis.'

'Maybe. But it doesn't matter. My flight leaves in less than hour.'

'And you're really going?'

'The alternative is a lifetime of prison food. My dietician advised against it. I share her concerns.'

'If you leave now, Jamie, John Watson will still be in danger. Mary will still be in danger. Christ, *everyone* will still be in danger. The person responsible for the Teardrop Killings is still out there, and if you're not around, who will they look to for revenge? There are so many unanswered questions that I've a feeling only *you* can resolve.' Her tone grew more urgent. 'And the Valentino twins are in the wind! Do you have any concept of the colossal threat they represent? While they're free, no one in the world is safe! *No one in the world!* Jamie, you need to finish this business.'

Moriarty slammed his tumbler onto the tabletop. 'John Watson hates me! The government I pledged to help disavowed me and has sworn to hunt me down like a dog. Zenisha wasn't able to help, and Redford has brought zero leverage to bear in any kind of attempt to change Bellinger's mind. Are these the people you want me to help? Are these the people you want me to risk my life for?'

But she only watched him.

'I tried being a good man. I don't know if you noticed, but it wasn't a great success.'

The Colonel called the waiter over, ordered two more drinks, and finally replied, 'It's up to you. But just remember what your old man said.'

'That's not fair!'

'Life never is.'

~

'TIL THE NEXT TIME, JAMIE.' The Colonel saluted him and he winked at her. She looked about to turn away but paused.

'What is it, Sébastienne?'

'Did you do it? Did you really do that to Mary? The tattoo?'

'What do you want me to say?'

'The truth.'

He shrugged. 'As the bombers flew over the Channel, I did what I thought was right.'

'You know what, Jamie? I think you did. That's why I love you.'

Moriarty watched his friend walk away and he sighed.

'Damn you.'

He was still damning her as he strolled towards the plane. He paused before boarding. Looked back to Britain.

'Damn you, too.'

Finally, he made up his mind. A last glance over his shoulder and he walked onto the Boeing.

Chapter Ninety-Two

JOHN GOT BACK TO BAKER STREET AND PHONED MARY. She picked up after a couple of rings.

'It feels good being able to call you again on your number. How are you doing?'

'Not too bad, considering. It's good to be free. That sounds corny, but you know what I mean.'

'Do you fancy meeting up tonight?'

'I don't know.'

'That's a pity.' John tried to keep the hurt from his voice. 'Let me know when you're up for—'

'Hey! I'm just self-conscious about this bloody tattoo. I'm not about to start daubing make-up on my face to hide it.'

'Fair play.'

'It's part of me now. Whether I like it or not.'

'Yeah. Just like me.'

Mary laughed. 'Where shall we go? Marcini's?'

'No.' John looked through the windows and across the throng of Baker Street. 'Let's try somewhere new.'

MORIARTY TURNED LEFT after stepping onto the plane. An attendant showed him to his seat, where he ordered a glass of Laurent-Perrier. He thought about the Colonel and her words. And about Doctor John Watson. The kindness he'd shown Troy Domingo, which had felt so inexplicable. The empathy he'd shared with Redford during the former PM's darkest hour. And his faith in him, that he could somehow be redeemed.

'Damn you!'

But most of all he thought about Beth and what she'd have wanted.

Moriarty threw his head back like an exasperated teen, but he only saw his father, Harry, drinking Glenlivet in The Rat and Raven. *Never lose your humanity. Never lose that, Jamie lad.*

'Damn you all!'

When the attendant returned with his Champagne, Moriarty's seat was empty.

Chapter Ninety-Three

IT HAD BEEN A LONG AND ARDUOUS DAY FOR DETECTIVE Inspector Zenisha Lestrade. After finishing all her most pressing work, she left London and drove to her home in Surrey. It had been in her mother's side of the family for generations, a huge gothic manor house set within five-and-a-half acres of woodland grounds.

She parked her Mercedes-AMG G-Class on the sweeping gravel drive in front of the building's main entrance. She felt tired and looked forward to having the house to herself. As she unlocked the front door, she considered taking the next day off. She could say she was ill. No — stressed. After everything she'd been through recently, no one would dispute the claim and it would mean she could—

She froze. Zenisha could hear something. Something indistinct and quiet, but this was supposed to be an empty house.

'Is anybody there? Hello!'

She crept down the main hallway and paused at the doorway to one of the smaller reception rooms. The sound was coming from within and now she recognized it. The noise of a roaring log fire. She stepped into the room. 'Hello?'

She saw him only a few paces in. James Moriarty sat in one of the two armchairs which stood either side of the hearth. He had a glass of brandy in his hand. Raised it in her direction.

'What took you so long?'

'What the hell are you doing in my house?'

'I thought you'd be glad to see me! I can help with the capture of the Valentino twins and…' He trailed off. 'Are you all right, Zenisha?'

'What? Yes.' She shrugged off her coat and slung it across a chaise longue. 'You just surprised me. That's all. Especially as we were all given intel that you boarded your plane to the States and it left hours ago. How did the hell did you sneak off a Boeing 787? Were you ever on it?'

'They have their entrances,' he replied. 'And their exits.'

'So what are you doing here?'

'Take a seat.'

She poured herself a brandy. 'Can I get you a top up?'

'I'm good, thanks. I need to keep a clear head. We've a lot to discuss.'

Zenisha took the chair opposite his.

'Okay, Professor, is this about the Red Circle?'

'Yes.' He took a mouthful of brandy. 'How long have you been working for them?'

'Is this a joke?'

'How long have you been a traitor?'

Zenisha's jaw had dropped and her eyes widened. A cartoonish image of disbelief. 'Look, Moriarty. It's been a hell of a few weeks, so I can understand your brain being scrambled, but please don't—'

'You made too many mistakes. So don't tell me you're innocent. Because it insults my intelligence and makes me very angry.'

'Mistakes?' She sounded non-committal. 'What mistakes?'

'There was the curious incident of the trace evidence left by the Teardrop Killer.'

'He left no trace evidence.'

'That was the curious incident.' Moriarty shook his head. 'That was lazy of you, Zenisha. I imagine your superiors said they wanted no evidence, to protect Gunn until he'd finished his work for them. You took them literally. You doctored the files so there was literally *nothing* to go off. If someone enters a house, they leave trace evidence. Simple as that. Even if the perp's wearing gloves, those gloves leave a trace, for instance. To suggest there was nothing whatsoever was madness. And sloppy — very unlike you.'

'I'm not the only one who could have altered reports.'

'Then there was Brize Norton.'

'I saved the Prime Minister's life!'

'No. You made an attempt on his daughter's life.'

'This is crazy! We got the shooter! Terry Scarafia! He had a red circle tattooed on his heart, for god's sake! What else do you want?'

'Hardly anybody — certainly not you — knew Millie Redford would be landing at that airstrip that day. I bet you couldn't believe it when John told you. So, what did you do? You immediately went to one of the Red Circle's men who was working undercover at Brize Norton. Scarafia. I'm guessing he'd been stationed there ages ago in case the Valentino twins hadn't escaped earlier and they needed springing at the airport.'

'This is insane.'

'Yes, it is. You saw an opportunity to win back some brownie points with your boss. Kill Millie and say hey, Moriarty may have negotiated her return, but that doesn't mean she's safe! No one is safe from the Red Circle. Nice propaganda.'

'How do you know Scarafia wasn't there to take out Millie and her father?'

'The gun he was using. A Glock 21. That's not a sniper's weapon. Not even close. If Scarafia was there to take out a target as he or she crossed the runway, he'd have used something like an AR-15.'

'Maybe it was a spur of the moment thing and—'

Moriarty raised his voice for the first time. 'Scarafia didn't fire that Glock!'

'How do you know?'

'I had his corpse stolen from the path lab so my people could run a Gunpowder Residue Test on him. I had a feeling that if you were overseeing it, it would come back positive. But guess what — it came back negative. No GSR. Scarafia *couldn't* have fired those shots.'

'He could have worn—'

'Don't make this worse by suggesting he wore gloves. None were found at the scene. No. You borrowed his Glock, took the shots, missed, then made it look like Scarafia was the would-be assassin. That was cold, Zenisha. I almost admire your audacity. You must have been frantic, though. I'm guessing the way it played out with Gunn meant your people were desperate for a win, and that desperation made you take a chance that was the epitome of a long shot.'

Zenisha finished her brandy. 'Any other evidence?'

'The one *conclusive* proof that I only just learnt. Everything else could be explained away ... I mean, collectively, it's all damning. Then John told me he kept in touch with

Roddy Fingers using off-grid tech. I'd assumed the Red Circle had hacked the message Roddy sent John. But, no. Good old Roddy Fingers! He'd probably picked up some intel from a friend who was still in the game, and his first thought was to warn Doctor Watson. For that, he was garrotted. That's not a painless way to go. It hurts like hell. Believe me, I know.'

'All of this sounds fascinating. But Professor, I haven't the faintest idea what you're talking about.'

'Roddy Fingers, AKA Graham Marsh, the librarian in Shere who just wanted to live a quiet life. He warned John Watson and was killed within hours of that warning. But at the point he was murdered, only three people knew Fingers had sent the message. Me, John ... and you. Just us three, Zenisha. John told you. He couldn't have known he was condemning a man to death by sharing information with someone he trusted.'

'There has been some terrible misunderstanding!' She sounded increasingly desperate. 'Perhaps Watson himself has—'

'John Watson is one of the few good people I know. There were lots more little things that nagged away and pointed at you. The Red Circle were always a step ahead. They *had* to have someone on the inside, someone high up, passing them intel.'

A thought struck the Detective Inspector. 'But Gunn tried to kill me!'

'You know, I couldn't figure that one out for the longest time. When I heard you two had gotten together online, there was an assumption he'd hacked the app because he'd wanted to get close to you. But actually, you'd hacked it. You and him getting together was the first step of his grooming. I'm sure he considered you two had a relation-ship. That it was going well. He honestly thought you bought into his mission. But you'd ceded the idea in the first place. It was just business to you. He was merely an implement to make sure business was taken care of.'

'Moriarty! You heard the way he talked to me when I called John!'

'That was another mistake. You see, you should have called Detective Sergeant Lee Jones so she could have recorded the call. She wondered about that. But you didn't want to call a DS. You and Gunn were riffing to make you look innocent, but you were worried he'd make a mistake. If it was in the moment and unrecorded, you guessed you'd get away with it. If it had been recorded, which Lee would have done on her phone — not so much. And he did mess up, didn't he?'

A long pause.

'Yes.'

It was her first acknowledgment of culpability, but Moriarty saw her relax slightly. Her body language expanded. It struck the professor that her confession was intended to be an admission of guile, not guilt. He'd not anticipated this, but pressed on, saying, 'Yes. At one point he said *our mission*. Not *my* mission. Our mission.'

Zenisha stood and crossed the room. 'You have to hand it to me. The bit on the boat was good.'

'It wasn't bad. I mean the fact he did all that to make you look innocent is extraordinary. But I saw the knots tying you to that chair were loose. You could have escaped at the last moment without my intervention. Of course, I didn't *absolutely* know that before I made that diving leap through fire, but hey…'

As she poured herself another brandy, Zenisha asked, 'So you really risked your life to save mine?'

'Yes.'

'Why?'

'Why do you think?'

'John Watson.'

'He cares for you. I seem to have made a new career for myself — ensuring Johnny doesn't have to endure any more grief.'

She retook her seat by the fire. Smiled at him. Asked, 'What happened to that cold, calculating killer I used to secretly look up to?'

'The way you played John Watson was unforgivable. You made him think he was helpful with his little podcast.'

'Oh, come on! That was inspired! When the Valentino twins wanted to leave the Red Circle, I had John do a podcast on them so we could hand the police information about their location and crimes. It meant nobody within the organization suspected us of snitching. And it meant John looked like a valuable asset.'

'That was useful for your ongoing plans, right?'

'Right!' Zenisha seemed to uncoil before Moriarty's eyes. 'I could anonymously feed John all sorts of useless intel through his podcast channels! That was then passed onto the Yard and kept them looking in the wrong direction. And there was more!' She was beginning to enjoy herself. To relish the reveal. 'When we had a case like the Teardrop Killer, it meant I could tell my superiors I'd enlisted the help of Doctor Watson, and it looked like I was pulling out all the stops, when actually I was making sure the police were tied up with false leads and dead end lines of inquiry! It's hilarious how useful John's efforts became…'

Her demeanour had further changed. For a movie buff like Moriarty, it was like watching an old, pre-code film where the villain's mask is pulled away to reveal a hitherto hidden horror. Her pride in her own work and what she perceived to be her cleverness somehow distorted her features, shifting her face until Moriarty barely recognized it. When she smiled, as she did now, it exacerbated the effect and she appeared almost supernatural.

'Oh my god,' she breathed. '*That's* why you never said anything! *That's* why you didn't expose me! You didn't want to crush John! You knew he cared for me! And you knew he believed my apparent reliance on him offered that poor wreck of a man … validation! You say you didn't know for certain I was the traitor, but there was something else. *You weren't prepared to hurt John Watson!*'

'Don't be so sure I won't change my mind.'

'Oh, James. James! It's too late. In your desire to protect the good doctor, you've given me time. The Valentino twins are the most dangerous asset the Red Circle have ever possessed. That *I've* ever possessed. Their ability to hack into any system is legendary but entirely justified. I spoke with them earlier tonight. Our needs and ambitions are aligned. And here's the thing — if you tell anybody that I'm a double agent for the Red Circle, I will order them to do the unthinkable. They will close down emergency service lines. They will bring this country's traffic infrastructure to a grinding halt. They will switch off intensive care units in every UK hospital, and they will plunge children's wards into darkness.'

Moriarty considered this.

'You really have no choice, my dear professor. Take that flight to the States. Walk away for good and remain hidden. Stay silent. Otherwise, I shall unleash hell.'

Chapter Ninety-Four

JOHN WATSON SHOWERED AND CHANGED INTO A SMART NEW suit he'd bought using some of the money Helen Stoner had provided after Moriarty's intervention. He finger-combed his hair, then dabbed his wrists and throat with Wood Sage and Sea Salt cologne. Slipped into a pair of tan leather brogues and put on a pair of discreet silver cufflinks. He looked at himself in the mirror and liked what he saw.

His phone rang as he was about the leave 221B.

He picked up. 'Yeah? How can I help?'

It was the police.

~

'IT LOOKS like you've won this battle,' Moriarty conceded.

'No. You have lost the war.'

'When did it all start? How did it all start?'

'I needed money to bail out my former husband. I loved him. Before I came to my senses. But back then the family finances were controlled by my mother, and *Mummy* and I did not get on. The Red Circle offered me cash for certain favours. I reluctantly complied. But then I took to it. I soon realized how well placed I was to help them and how powerful they were — which could help me. I shared that power. Basked in it! Now I'm integral to their operations. I like to think I'm irreplaceable.'

'Yes. I imagine you are. Here, at least. I have one more question, if I may? Who runs the Red Circle? Who is your leader?'

Zenisha's face twisted again. It seemed to stretch beyond its natural perimeters in a kind of silent shriek.

'I don't know,' she whispered.

'You don't know? After all this time, after all this power you've ingested ... you still don't know?'

'We are to meet. Soon.'

'Lord, I needn't have bothered with that whole *you've won the battle* schtick.' It was Moriarty's turn to rise. He sauntered over to the tantalus. He discreetly checked his text messages, then refilled his glass. 'That's a real shame. If you'd known names, I might have let you live.'

Zenisha's smile reappeared. 'You can only bluff when the player across the table doesn't know what cards you're holding. And you have a bad hand. If I don't check in with the Valentinos at a certain point, they'll take out a hospital in Greater London. Every hour we fail to make contact, another one will have its power supply cut off. So, scamper away, Professor Moriarty. Please don't think I wouldn't tell the twins to murder thousands if I feel it's necessary. Or maybe, *maybe* if I simply think that it might be fun.'

Moriarty retook his seat. 'Did I ever know you, Zenisha?'

'Yes. Once. When I was who I was. But everything changes.'

'Nothing is constant. Not even the speed of light. But if there is anything left of the old Zenisha…'

'Yes?'

'I'd like her to know, I told John that the elements linking the Teardrop Murders to him and I were attempts at camouflage. There was an element of truth in that, of course, but the connections were primarily intended as torture. Whose idea was it to use David Gunn?'

'Not mine!' She answered quickly, and Moriarty thought that for a moment, in her eyes, he could discern the woman he'd known for so many years. 'He was deemed to be the best person for the job. The boss made that call.'

'And the teardrop tattoos?'

'My idea!' The vain, sly Zenisha was back. 'The boss thought you might still be alive. The tattoos were a nod to your supposed fate. Gentle mockery, if you like. I knew you'd be aware of what a tear is.'

Moriarty remembered John's vast, gulping sadness. The tear crawling down his face and dropping to the floor.

'At its most basic and most literal, a tear is a waterfall.'

'It was us letting you know that you were in our thoughts as those poor people were slaughtered.'

'How tawdry.' Moriarty placed his glass on a small table by his chair. 'I think it's time I brought this evening to a close. As I said, if you don't know the names of those above you, you're of no use to me.'

'Watch your tone, young man! It would only take one phone call and I could—'

'What? Call the terrible twosome? Do you know how pathetic that sounds? The Valentino brothers can't hurt anyone. And they can't do your bidding. No matter what you say or don't say to them.'

Despite everything, she believed him. 'Why?'

'Because I figured you'd make contact with the twins the moment you believed me to be out of the equation. With me gone, who could stop the triple threat of you, the V brothers, and the Red Circle?'

'No one.'

'No one. So when you heard I'd taken off, you met the twins to plan and initiate.'

'I took a clean car and used three teams of four people to ensure I wasn't followed!'

'You met them at a grim little hotel close to Gatwick Airport. Less than twenty minutes after you left the rendezvous, a team of police officers led by Inspector Jones swooped. She reported back to me a couple of minutes ago. The twins are both in custody. They won't be harming anybody. Ever again.'

'What?' Zenisha's whole body seemed to shrink. 'How could you know where we met?'

'The pen I gave you as a farewell present. It's fitted with a micro-tracker. But it's not all bad news. It does write *beautifully*.'

'Let me go!' Zenisha snapped, so suddenly and forcefully that Moriarty almost registered surprise. 'I'll give you anything you want. Money? You can have millions! Power? Join the Red Circle with me and, oh, Professor Moriarty, you can become the *Alexander* of Crime.'

'I'm quite content to be the Napoleon of Crime.' He reached into his suit jacket and pulled a Beretta 92FS from his shoulder holster. 'And I'm only just back from Elba. I'm not quite ready for St. Helena yet.'

'Put the gun away. We both know you won't use it.'

'I think I could have forgiven you everything. Even your treatment of John Watson. I can see your tactics — your justification — for those awful, *awful* deeds. But I'm going to kill you, Lestrade. For the one thing I can never forgive.'

'Why? If you can understand my justification, why can't—'

'She was….' Moriarty's voice cracked. 'She was *the* woman.'

'James, I'm begging you! Please don't shoot! Don't shoot! Don't shoot! Don't shoot…' Her tone had changed as she made her demands, gradually becoming more childish. Her words had become a joke and Moriarty was the intended punchline. She laughed, and he waited patiently.

'You know,' she said at last, 'years ago — no, weeks ago — I'd have trembled at this. At you pointing a gun at my pretty little head. But not now. You know why?'

'Because you're a delusional fool.'

'Because you've changed!' She nodded. 'John Watson has changed you! Just as you saved him, he saved you. Or rather, saved your humanity. I've seen you caring for people. Fighting wars you need never have fought. You turn down alliances and wealth for … what? Your newly acquired morality? To be a good man?'

She took a sip of her brandy and growing in confidence declared, 'The old Professor Moriarty could have murdered me in cold blood. But now? Now I know you're—'

He interrupted her. 'Zenisha.'

'Yes?'

'Her name was Beth.'

Professor Moriarty shot Inspector Lestrade between her eyes. The look of surprise and horror on her face became her death mask. She toppled forward and lay sprawled on the carpet in front of the fire. But long ago, in a college where he found love, her killer also found the need for certainty.

Moriarty fired three more bullets into Lestrade's head before lazily finishing his brandy, stepping over her corpse, and walking from the room.

Chapter Ninety-Five

JOHN WATSON WATCHED THE TWO LIVERIED POLICE CARS pull out of the hotel carpark. Lee Jones walked over to him. 'Thanks for helping out, Doctor.'

'I'm not sure I did a great deal.'

'You were the one who insisted we take them straight away. I was in favour of waiting for back-up.'

'You can't wait with criminals like the Valentino brothers. We had a rare advantage over them, and we had to exploit it or lose it.'

Lee nodded. 'I can see you'll be a valuable man to have around.'

'Always a pleasure to be of use to Scotland Yard, Inspector.'

'Funny you should say that. Karl mentioned an associate in Bethnal Green they were supposed to be meeting tonight.'

'Got an address? You should get there immediately!'

'My thoughts exactly! Wanna come with?'

John's phone rang and he picked up. 'Mary!'

She explained she'd had second thoughts about meeting up. 'I'm just not sure I'm ready to—'

'That's fine. No problem. Let me know when you feel like a coffee. But there's no rush.'

Lee Jones was indicating that they had to leave immediately. John raised his index finger in a *'Give me one second!'* gesture.

Mary said, 'You don't seem too bothered about me crying off. I thought you'd be shattered!'

'No, it's fine. Really. Something important has come up.' From the carpark, he could see the seductive lights of London glimmering like jewels across dark velvet. 'You see…' He began walking towards Inspector Jones, and recognizing he'd made up his mind to join her, she smiled. Doctor John Watson nodded to her as he told Mary, 'The game is afoot!'

ALFIE BUTLER WAS DRIVING an old Hillman Avenger that night. It was parked in front of the manor house, next to the late Zenisha Lestrade's Mercedes. As Moriarty crunched over the gravel, he wound down his window.

'How did it go, Professor?'

'Mixed.' He paused to admire the full moon and the stars that seemed exceptionally bright, free from the light pollution that dims the diamonds over London. 'Good brandy. Bad company.'

He got into the car, and Alfie turned the engine. 'But did you do the job, sir? If you don't mind me asking, like…'

'I did the job. I always do the job.'

'So you've wrapped it up nicely, sir? It's all done and dusted? You've finished?'

'Not at all, mon ami.' The Avenger disappeared into the night. 'I'm just getting warmed up.'

THE END

Although...

PROFESSOR MORIARTY

**DOCTOR WATSON
and
THE RED CIRCLE
WILL RETURN**

About the author

Before becoming a full-time writer, Collinson's career lurched from campsite management to journalism and marketing within the movie industry. He later enjoyed stints on the UK's most-watched soap operas, Coronation Street and Emmerdale, before working on Doctor Who for almost a decade. Since leaving the TARDIS, he's written extensively for the stage, radio, computer games, and Virtual Reality experiences. He scripted The Edge of Reality (starring David Tennant and Bridgerton's Adjoa Andoh) and The Lonely Assassins (starring Jodie Whittaker), hailed by Engadget as 'the best Doctor Who game ever made'. He currently writes for Hammer Films and is the author of several thrillers, including Moriarty, the first in a new series that reimagines the Sherlock Holmes mythos, putting the world's greatest villain centre stage.

A fan of classic film/TV he's delivered talks and events on topics ranging from James Bond, Sherlock Holmes and Ghostwatch, to Leni Riefenstahl, Charles Dickens, and Alfred Hitchcock.

Raised in Blackpool, he currently lives in Guildford, near London.